DARK VARIATIONS

MAKING MONSTERS 2

DARK VARIATIONS

AJ PARNELL

4 Horsemen
Publications, Inc.

Dark Variations
Copyright © 2024 AJ Parnell. All rights reserved.

4 Horsemen
Publications, Inc.

Published By: 4 Horsemen Publications, Inc.

4 Horsemen Publications, Inc.
PO Box 417
Sylva, NC 28779
4horsemenpublications.com
info@4horsemenpublications.com

Cover by AGAZAR and Autumn Skye
Cover Photography by Joe Keum at Studio JK
Typesetting by Autumn Skye
Edited by Kris Cotter

All rights to the work within are reserved to the author and publisher. No part of this publication may be reproduced, stored in a retrieval system, or transmitted in any form or by any means, electronic, mechanical, photocopying, recording, scanning, or otherwise, except as permitted under Section 107 or 108 of the 1976 International Copyright Act, without prior written permission except in brief quotations embodied in critical articles and reviews. Please contact either the Publisher or Author to gain permission.

All characters, organizations, and events portrayed in this novel are either products of the author's imagination or are used fictitiously.

All brands, quotes, and cited work respectfully belongs to the original rights holders and bear no affiliation to the authors or publisher.

Library of Congress Control Number: 2024940264

Paperback ISBN-13: 979-8-8232-0587-0
Hardcover ISBN-13: 979-8-8232-0588-7
Audiobook ISBN-13: 979-8-8232-0590-0
Ebook ISBN-13: 979-8-8232-0589-4

This book is dedicated to Kim Hill, aka "Kimbo" my bestie, who never says NO to an adventure. No matter how insane, spontaneous, or unpredictable our journey may be, you are always willing to go along for the ride. Thank you for being my light in the many turbulent storms of life. I could not have found my way back to shore without you.

Table of Contents

Prologue ix
Chapter 1 1
Chapter 2 8
Chapter 3 11
Chapter 4 14
Chapter 5 18
Chapter 6 24
Chapter 7 29
Chapter 8 34
Chapter 9 39
Chapter 10 42
Chapter 11 45
Chapter 12 49
Chapter 13 53
Chapter 14 57
Chapter 15 61
Chapter 16 65
Chapter 17 70
Chapter 18 73
Chapter 19 80
Chapter 20 88
Chapter 21 94
Chapter 22 97
Chapter 23 106
Chapter 24 110
Chapter 25 118
Chapter 26 124
Chapter 27 127
Chapter 28 131

Chapter 29	138
Chapter 30	142
Chapter 31	147
Chapter 32	151
Chapter 33	156
Chapter 34	160
Chapter 35	163
Chapter 36	168
Chapter 37	173
Chapter 38	178
Chapter 39	181
Chapter 40	185
Chapter 41	189
Chapter 42	193
Chapter 43	195
Chapter 44	198
Chapter 45	203
Chapter 46	206
Chapter 47	210
Chapter 48	214
Chapter 49	221
Chapter 50	230
Chapter 51	235
Chapter 52	238
Chapter 53	242
Chapter 54	245
Chapter 55	247
Chapter 56	251
Chapter 57	255
Chapter 58	260
Chapter 59	265
Chapter 60	269

Chapter 61.. 272
Chapter 62 275
Chapter 63 277
Chapter 64 280
Chapter 65 284
Chapter 66 288
Chapter 67.. 291
Chapter 68 295
Chapter 69 298
Chapter 70 302
Chapter 71..306
Book Club Questions...................................315
Author Bio 317

PROLOGUE

CAN'T GO BACK

VANDER

The Mist

NIGHTSHADE, VANDER'S PIED CROW, EMERGED AS A HARbinger in Vander's path, veiled by the dense, silver mist. His black wings glistened as they cut through the fog like a sharp blade through silk.

The crow's resonant caws echoed in the hushed world and added a layer to the symphony of silence. Despite his ominous surroundings, nine-year-old Vander found an inexplicable solace as he tracked the pied crow and watched as it carved out a corridor through the eerie mist.

Eyes set on Nightshade and the path before him, Vander ignored the hissing clamor of the spirits that swirled to either side of him. There was only one ghost in this dismal abyss that he wanted to talk to, and he was not going to be distracted. "Jack? Jack?! ... Where are you?"

Like a receding tide, the quarrelsome apparitions parted to reveal his quarry. Even though he had called his name, Jack did not turn or acknowledge him. Instead, he sat, body relaxed, attention focused, before a flickering scene that played out on a wall of thick fog. Vander wanted to rail at Jack for ignoring him when he spotted a mirror image of himself. No, not a mirror image. More accurately, he looked at the past version of himself as he stood in the foundation's construction zone back in Cape Town.

In the images, Vander approached a young woman bound in a lone wooden chair. Pain knotted his stomach as he realized this was not just any woman. It was Erin Reese, the kind detective whom he had abandoned to Alexander just a few days earlier.

Erin's eyes pleaded with his former self. Her arms were tied behind her body; her blonde, sun-streaked hair disheveled as she struggled against her restraints. Frozen, save for the single tear that escaped his eye, Vander watched the horrific scene unfold.

"Please, Vander, you've got to go for help," Erin pleaded. Mute, Vander watched as the other Vander backed away from the detective, then fled through a far door. A soft click sounded as Alexander opened the opposite door, stuck his head inside, gave the room a quick once-over, then stepped inside and offered Erin a disappointed smile. "Pity, I had hoped the boy would stay and survey my work."

Alexander brightened. "Nevertheless, I think it best we proceed with haste." He took out his precious scalpel and looked at Erin. "Just in case our young friend has gone to alert the authorities."

Unable to watch, Vander turned away as Alexander sliced through the detective's neck with the surgical steel. Vander clamped his hands over his ears, not wanting to relive Erin's last moments. A shudder coursed through Vander as Erin's disembodied screams echoed throughout the ether and surrounded them.

Jack clapped with glee. "Well done lad... well done!"

I had not wanted Erin to die and most certainly had not wanted to be praised for my part in her death. Hands balled into fists at his side, Vander stomped toward Jack. "Shut up!"

"Come now... You're not the least bit proud?"

"Proud? Detective Reese is dead! She didn't deserve that!" Vander pointed up at the swirling mist that had gone blank behind Jack.

Jack shrugged. "Really? If you'd ask me, I'd say she had it coming."

Vander spat out an angry burst. "She didn't! She was a good person, she..."

Sobering, Jack sighed. "Fine, all right then, maybe the copper didn't deserve such a gruesome fate as she got... But, you have to admit..." Jack hopped off his imaginary bench and stretched. "It must've felt pretty good sticking it to Mbalula and your old man, eh?" Jack gave Vander a mischievous wink.

Teeth clenched, Vander shoved Jack back and away from him. "I didn't enjoy any of it... It's just... it's just that... I didn't want to die." Vander felt ashamed that he had chosen to save his own life rather than allow others to take his.

Sarcastically, Jack held out his open palms to Vander. "Yeah, yeah, of course, lad." Jack returned to his invisible bench. "Anyone with eyes could tell that you had no choice, no choice at all."

Vander's gaze lowered to the ground. "That's right. I didn't."

"You knew how your story would end if you'd have saved Miss Reese." Jack took a deep breath, leaned back, and smiled down at Vander. "Life's about survival, my friend. You got to look out for yourself, 'cause no one else is gonna."

Guiltily, Vander nodded in agreement. Then cast a weary look around. "Is she here?"

Puzzled, Jack asked, "She?"

"Detective Reese?" Vander already knew the answer but wanted to ask, just in case.

Jack rubbed his chin. "Oh, heaven's no. The detective's spirit passed through here like a bolt of lightning. Straight on to those pearly gates I'd imagine."

Jack offered him a sad smile. "Face it, lad. The woman could have helped you at any point, but she didn't. Miss Erin Reese was more concerned with her case, with one-upping the coppers who worked with her and catching the Sculptor." Jack leaned in toward Vander. "I would wager ... if Kgotso had killed you right in front of her, she wouldn't have batted an eye."

Anger rose up within his spirit. Vander did not want to believe ill of Erin. She had been kind to him when she found him in her room, offered him shelter for the night, and seemed like a nice person. Still, Jack was right regarding her being driven to take the Sculptor down. It was as if she was driven mad in her pursuit, just as mad as Alexander seemed to be in creating his wicked art. With a little less steam, Vander argued, "That's not entirely true."

"There's no denying it, lad. Your visions were clear. Had you stopped Alexander, Detective Reese would have sent your would-be savior to jail, celebrated her victory, then gone on her merry way, without a thought or care in the world about you and your grim fate." Jack took a deep breath and fixed him with those dark blackish-brown eyes.

Though part of him knew what Jack said was right, there was another part of him that wanted to believe someone, anyone, might be out there who had enough compassion and kindness to do the right thing. Because, if someone like Alexander, a cold-blooded serial killer, could show him mercy, then there had to be other, kinder souls out there who would as well.

"I guess, but..." Vander started. Sadly, Vander looked past Jack and peered into the mist. He wished he would have had the chance to tell Erin how sorry he was for not doing more to save her. It did not matter what Jack said. Vander knew Erin had been a good person. She had not deserved the fate she had been given.

Torn, Vander felt both relieved and guilty as he pondered his new future. Now, after all the bloodshed, he was free of his old life, he had been delivered from the threats that would have ended his young life back in Cape Town. Sadder still, Vander knew that deep down, if given the chance to do things over, he would more than likely have chosen to do the same things. He would have sought to save himself over Detective Reese, his father, and Mbalula.

Sporting a smug expression, Jack said, "Come now, don't look so forlorn. Things worked out, didn't they?"

"I suppose." Vander bit his lip.

Mood bright, Jack clapped his hands together. "Enough of this foolish talk." Jack smiled at him as he motioned toward an opening tunnel in the fog. "I've got a surprise for ya."

Bristling, Vander remained rooted in place. "I'm not in the mood for your games."

Hurt, Jack frowned. "Oh, come now, you'll like this one... I promise."

"No," Vander growled.

"Fine, fine... I'll tell you." Gleefully, Jack bowed as he once again motioned to the corridor behind him. "It's your mum. She wants to see you."

TWO YEARS LATER

London, England—Day

Eyes fixed on the tall panes of glass, Vander glared up at the two men who nervously stared at him from the safety of the principal's office. Looking back at his actions, Vander realized now that breaking his teacher's fingers on the first day of school might have been a mistake. Still, the man had laid a hand on him, and Vander wanted to make it clear from the start, that no matter how nice he dressed or how educated he was, he was not allowed to touch him, ever!

Like two gazelles who had just spotted a lion, the men behind the large windows froze, their eyes fixed on the doorway next to where Vander sat. Vander did not have to look up to know Alexander had just stepped into the room. His mentor not only moved like a predator but also carried the same threatening air about him, putting everyone on high alert.

"Did we not have an agreement?" Alexander's rich, English timber scolded Vander.

Angry, Vander folded his arms across his chest and slumped farther into his seat. "Not that I recall."

"Vander..."

Cutting Alexander off, Vander growled, "You said I had to go to school... I told you that I didn't want to. And you made me go anyway."

With the teacher nipping at his heels, the principal yanked his door open and barged into the waiting room. "Mr. Dayton, we need to—"

Vander watched as Alexander held up a hand, silencing the man before he went off on his tirade and offered him a smile that did not reach his eyes. "A moment, please."

Taken aback, the principal stammered, "I... we... but..."

"I will join you shortly." Alexander nodded to the principal, dismissing him outright.

Vander fought the urge to laugh as the two men retreated, stumbling over each other in their attempt to scamper back to the safety of the office, then shut the door behind them.

Alexander took a seat next to Vander and removed his hat. "Before I'm forced to listen to your principal and teacher's bothersome rants. I would greatly appreciate an explanation from you?"

Defensively, Vander bristled. "He put his hand on me."

Puzzled, Alexander's eyes went from Vander to the irritated teacher, who paced back and forth on the other side of the glass, holding his wounded hand to his chest. "Did he hurt you?"

Reluctantly, Vander growled, "No."

"Were his intentions ... inappropriate?"

Guilty, Vander studied the floor. "No, not really."

Alexander sighed. "This might go a wee bit faster if you told me the story in its entirety."

"Fine!" Vander exclaimed. "I had finished my assignment early and was putting up my book when Mr. Richards came up behind me and laid a hand on my shoulder."

"And?" Alexander asked.

"I didn't like it! It's my body, mine... I don't want people touching me or thinking they can do whatever they want to just because I'm small and a nobody." Vander sucked in a quick breath, then continued, "I don't care if they look nice and have a good education, I'm not gonna let people hurt me anymore and thought it best to get my point across before he tried anything."

"So you..."

"Grabbed his hand, bent it back, and broke a few of his fingers." Vander huffed and fell back against his chair.

Alexander rubbed his chin. "Well, Vander, you most certainly know how to make an impression."

Hopeful, Vander turned to Alexander. "Why can't I just stay home and learn from the tutor like I did before?"

Taking a deep breath, Alexander leaned back. "Can I not. Not 'can't.'" Resting a hand on his cane, Alexander continued, "Vander, in the past year, you have done exceptionally well with Mr. Frederick, so well in fact, you have managed to catch up to your peers."

Eyes pleading, Vander asked, "Then why do I have to go to school? I promise I will continue to work hard and learn anything that you want me to."

Alexander offered Vander a kind smile. "Because, as smart as you are, there is more to life than mere academics."

"I know, money, but you have lots of that."

Laughing, Alexander smiled. "True. But still, money will not solve all of your problems, nor will you be able to keep it unless you learn the rules of the game."

"The game?" Vander asked, curious.

"The game of life, my boy." Alexander cast a brief look at the men in the office. "You're smart, gifted, and I dare say, have an abundance of emotional intelligence. All of which helped you survive life on the streets in Cape Town."

Vander could see that his teacher and principal's patience was waning. "So, what are you saying?"

"That, as smart as you are, and as far as you have come, you are now in a very different jungle than the one you were accustomed to." Alexander got to his feet. "I can help you navigate this new, unexplored landscape my young friend, but in order to do so, I need you to trust me and to trust the decisions I make in regard to your life here, at least until you are of age."

Trust? Was he even capable of such a thing? Mute, Vander looked up at his mentor.

Alexander got to his feet and readied himself for the oncoming battle with the two men who anxiously awaited his presence. "Ponder those thoughts while I attempt to keep you enrolled at this fine establishment." Alexander took a few steps toward the office, then turned back to him.

"Vander, you are no longer alone. You do not have to fight these battles on your own. If you would allow me the privilege, I would happily guide and protect you as if you were my own."

As much as he hated it, Vander's heart swelled with affection for Alexander. Deep down, he knew what kind of man he was, knew the dark-depraved things he was capable of, yet he could not help but feel joy in knowing he was no longer alone in his fight. This cub finally had a mighty lion to protect him from whatever force might come against him.

APRIL 29TH—12 DAYS

CHAPTER 1

DARK FORECAST

VANDER (13 YEARS LATER)

Philadelphia, PA—University of Pennsylvania—Day

YOU ARE EITHER THE HUNTER OR THE PREY. **V**ANDER KNEW this. Still, sitting there with his hands and feet bound and a shimmering surgeon's blade pressed against his throat, Vander wished he had endeavored more toward being the hunter.

Without fear, Vander peered into the ice-blue eyes of his mentor, Alexander, who stood above him with an appreciative smile. Vander knew the act of killing him was born not out of vengeance, anger, or hate. The impulse that drove Alexander was one of admiration, a desire to preserve that which he held in the highest esteem.

A look crossed Alexander's face, one that Vander had not seen before: sadness. Waves of indecision flowed from his mentor and engulfed Vander with the internal struggle that Alexander was now burdened with.

Vander was not a stranger to the sensation. Still, after living with the man for these past seventeen years, it still surprised him that Alexander was capable of this emotion, or any emotion, really. Vander could tell his mentor was as perplexed by this change of events.

Hands steady, Alexander lifted the blade from Vander's throat and took a step back. "I dare say, my boy, this is harder than expected." Vander watched as Alex surveyed the room. Everything was in place, not a detail left to chance, as was Alexander's way.

Moonlight cascaded down through the thick glass panes of the massive atrium. The humidity clung to Vander's skin, moistened it for the delicate carving that lay ahead. The world about them was lush with vegetation and bursting with vibrant colors of every array of blooms that thrived within the plant's sanctuary.

Vander was intrigued by the manner in which Alexander had managed to gain access to the museum's famous atrium, and curious as to whether he had managed to have the cameras taken out, his mentor was not as savvy with modern technology as he should be considering his opaque hobby.

As impressive as all this was, Vander was still most astonished at how Alexander had managed to acquire the rare plant that now stood watch over him. Knowing Alex's nature, Vander was no stranger to some of the most unique flowers on earth.

Picking up a cloth, Alexander began polishing his blade as he smiled over at Vander. "Vander, I'm sure you are familiar with the Amorphophallus Titanium, the Titan Arum, otherwise known as the corpse flower?"

"Yes, it is the largest unbranched inflorescence in the world." Vander was grateful Alexander had not gagged him, but then, his mentor had known that once Vander had been subdued, he would not struggle.

Pleased, Alexander continued to caress the surgical instrument. "Very good, and why is it called the corpse flower?"

It was curious that Alexander was stalling, but then, perhaps, his mentor wanted to make sure Vander knew just how special he was to him and why his death would be Alexander's crowning glory. Vander had always aspired to make Alexander proud. Sadly, his last act would be to provide Alexander with his *finissage,* his final work of art. "Once the deep-red bloom opens, the plant emits a stench much like that of rotting meat," Vander answered.

Impressed, Alexander pulled up a chair next to Vander. "Brilliant, my boy, you have always managed to impress." Gently, Alexander brushed the hair back from Vander's eyes and looked at him much like a loving father would if, perhaps, Alexander had been capable of love. "You know why I picked this flower for you?"

There were many reasons that came to Vander's mind, but he searched for the one that would please Alexander the most. "Because it is unique."

Chapter 1 — Dark Forecast

Vander gave the simplest but most complex answer. He knew the corpse flower was endangered, with fewer than a thousand left in the wild.

Though it could live in captivity, it took five to ten years for the flower to bloom, which meant, if it were lucky, it would only shine a few times in its lifetime, because, for many, they died after their very first opening. Rarer still, their bloom, as awe-inspiring as it was, only lived a short while. Once opened, it would begin to wither and collapse within twenty-four to thirty-six hours.

Vander's mind raced back to the beautiful artwork that decorated the walls throughout Alexander's home in Boston. Each of the paintings, drawings, or beautifully captured photos displayed a country in which his mentor had opened a school, hospital, or other charitable public offering.

To the unsuspecting observer, those framed works of art were a testament to Alexander's achievements, his feats of philanthropy. However, Vander knew those pictures represented something far more sinister.

Every serial killer kept trophies, at least those Vander had researched and read about, did. For his mentor, the keepsakes were represented in those works of art from the cities in which he had made his kills.

Alexander kept his trophies in plain sight, hung with pride upon the walls of his home, here in America. Within each beautiful frame, not only did Alexander have the image of the kill site, chosen with much thought and care, but also, tucked safely behind the tempered glass, sat a preserved flower, each special bloom symbolized an individual whose life his mentor had taken and preserved.

Vander never told Alexander that he had discovered his secret. He understood more than most that someone like his mentor would consider this gleaned knowledge a threat.

Wanting to prolong this moment as long as possible as well as make Alexander proud, Vander added, "You picked this flower for me because … you knew I was special, a rarity that would only shine for a little while. My life has always been encompassed by death, always looming over me in one form or another, so it was only fitting that my death mirror the same grim fate." Vander knew he was hitting the mark and wanted to give his adopted father the absolution he so desired.

Excited, Alexander nodded as his nurturing smile turned to one of bitter sadness. "You do understand Vander, you truly do."

Vander peered into Alex's ice-blue eyes, eyes that belonged to a man whom he had so desperately wanted to believe loved him, even if it was only in his own twisted way. Life had held so many possibilities for Vander, dreams he had yet to realize. Why had he allowed his admiration for this man to blind him to the cold reality that to Alexander, he had always been and always would be a trophy?

Whatever the reasons, it no longer mattered. Vander knew only too well what came next. Nightshade cried in warning as the echo of Jack's ridicule merged with the venomous hisses of the angry souls who awaited him in the void. If he had only done what was necessary, did what he knew he should have done before it was too late.

Sentiment was just as deadly as love; it clouded one's judgment and allowed it to strike you down like a venomous serpent the moment you let down your guard. Vander closed his eyes, ready to be done with this, and heard the faint scrape of Alexander's chair as he stood and pushed it back. There was no need for tears or to plead. His end was at hand, and he would face it with the same cold indifference that had allowed him to survive for as long as he had.

To allow Alexander easier access, Vander tilted his head back and looked up through the multiple square windows. The time to fight for his life was over. There was nothing left for him to do but die. Iridescent, the moon shone down upon Vander. He smiled when he caught sight of his beloved Nightshade.

A sharp sting sliced across his throat, followed by the sensation of warm, sticky blood that flowed from his jugular and soaked his neck and chest. For the last time, Vander's spirit left his body and floated upward. Nightshade dove toward him. His beloved bird greeted him just above the towering atrium. Vander gathered his beloved pet to his chest and marveled at the fact that death was not as bad as he had imagined.

Faintly, a feminine voice called to him from far away, "Vander! Hey, you all right?" The concern in her tone echoed across the great expanse between them. "I don't know. He doesn't seem to be breathing."

Torn, Vander's spirit wavered. His curiosity to watch Alexander finish the task of carving up his corpse warred with the necessity of returning to his body before his girlfriend, Christina, called an ambulance.

It took great discipline to slow your heart rate and breathing enough to allow your spirit to venture out and astral project. Vander had thought

Chapter 1   Dark Forecast

his body would have been safe where he had left it, alone in a far corner, upon a bench underneath a large tree. But obviously, his acquaintances had either stumbled upon him or sought him out.

"I don't know. What do you think we should do?" Marco Aldez, another one of his friends, asked.

Irritated that his quest to the other side was cut short, Vander cast one final glance at the scene below. With loving precision, Alexander had begun to slice through his body's soft skin. Layer by thin layer, his mentor peeled back the skin and started to mold Vander's corpse into a replica of the Titan Arum.

Disappointed, Vander closed his eyes, relaxed, and allowed his spirit to begin the journey back to his body. It would seem, at least for the moment, that his efforts to dissuade Alexander from this course had failed.

Vander spiraled through the void; he could feel the tethers that tied his soul to his body. The threads were thin, not noticeable to the human eye, but to someone who traversed this plain often, he could not only feel their pull but also see them.

Time was irrelevant in the astral world; it did not move at the same alarming rate as it did in the one where a human body was forced to move about. Nearing the campus, Vander took in the god-like view of the area.

Students milled about, music played from the band who had decided to practice outside, and numerous cars were either leaving campus or circling parking lots as they searched for a coveted space.

Nearing his form that sat motionless on the bench underneath a rather impressive oak, Vander surveyed the small crowd that had gathered about him. He would have to be more careful in the future when he took these little journeys.

"Hey ... you in there?" Christina, his cute, five-foot-six, brunette with hazel eyes, girlfriend inched closer and poked her finger into Vander's chest.

Annoyed, Vander stretched out, released his breath, and allowed his soul to drift back into his body. The weight of his flesh settled in upon him like a weighted blanket.

Feigning a lengthy yawn, Vander smiled up at the group. "Sorry, must have fallen asleep. Did I miss something?" Vander looked up at Christina, Marco, and his other zany friend, Frank Abney, who held his cell phone at the ready, just in case an emergency call was needed.

Relieved, Christina laughed. "Thank God you're all right. We thought you were dead."

Images of his desecrated corpse flashed into his mind. Forcing a smile, Vander said, "Not yet." But he soon would be if he could not find a way to alter the gruesome course that had been laid out before him.

Stepping up beside Christina, Marco, his uptight fellow student, piped in, "Sure you're okay? For a minute there, we couldn't tell if you were breathing."

Calm, Vander dusted off his shirt, flashed them a charming smile, and got to his feet. "Right as rain... those meditation classes have paid off."

"Yeah, well, they about got you a ride in an ambulance, buddy," Frank growled. "Maybe you should lay off the zone-outs when you're in public."

"I'll take that into consideration." Vander laughed. "So, was there a reason you guys are here gawking at me?"

Christina looped her arm in his. "We were wondering if you'd care to join us for a drink after class tonight?"

As much as he would like to go with his college friends and drink away the images of his future, Vander knew Alexander was due back to Pennsylvania that night and he wanted, no, he needed, to see him. "I wish I could, but I have to meet up with Alexander."

The usual name-calling and brow-beating commenced. Vander knew it was all in good fun and he laughed it off as he made his excuses. "I know, I know. I'm a loser, but rest assured, we shall drink ourselves to oblivion soon enough, I promise." Vander gave Christina a chaste kiss, then looked back at the large building to the north. "But right now, I have to get to class."

Pouty, Christina agreed. "Fine, but I'm holding you to it."

"Whatever man," Marco teased.

"Okay, but you're buying the first two rounds," Frank added.

Leaving the trio behind, Vander started toward the large building at the end of the square.

Though he had agreed to take all the required classes Alexander insisted upon—Business, Law, Foreign Relations—it was the extracurricular ones he found most interesting. Though the university had a limited track of parapsychology classes, he had signed up for all of them in the hopes of better understanding his unique gifts.

Chapter 1 — Dark Forecast

True, most of the information given in the lectures and stacks of books was pure drivel, but there were, on those rare occasions, gems he discovered that aided him in his quest.

Vander had grown much in his years with Alexander, and as his earlier visions had shown him, those years had been filled with everything he could have wished for as well as everything he had feared. Vander did not regret his decision, because he knew that above all things, he not only wanted to survive, but he also wanted the chance to thrive, and he had ... so far.

Face grim, Vander looked up at the looming building and started inside. If he could not find a way to change Alexander's mind about killing him, he would have to find a way to better see his future to alter it. Vander knew he was missing something, but what? There were calculations, methods in place, that had assured Alexander's advantage and Vander must discover what those missing pieces were.

Stepping into the classroom, Vander smiled to himself as he found his seat. As much as he hated it, he could not help himself from admiring Alexander. The man was gifted in so many ways, but the one thing Vander found most intriguing was the old man's insistent pursuit of understanding the strengths and weaknesses of those around him.

Even after everything Vander had been through as a child, he had been unable to stop himself from trusting Alexander, for the most part anyway. There were parts of himself that he would never trust to anyone else, not in this life or the next.

In the early years, Vander had shared information about his gifts, and about his struggles with them, hoping his mentor, who was better equipped with knowledge, could help him. To Alexander's credit, he had done everything in his power to aid him. Unfortunately for Vander, that much-needed education also helped his old friend gain knowledge about him. Knowledge that had, for the moment, given Alexander the upper hand.

April 29th—12 Days

CHAPTER 2

SOMETHING'S WRONG

ALAYNA

Austin, TX—Day

BROWS FURROWED, ALAYNA SAGE, A PETITE WOMAN with ash-brown hair, deep-green eyes, and an air of mystery about her, leaned against an uneven counter. With a sigh, Alayna raked her fingers through her hair.

There was a negative charge to the air that day, a bad vibe that washed over her. She had woken up that morning with a cold sense of dread, a feeling as if something bad was going to happen. Had she been like most people, she could have shaken off the dark mood without a second thought, but she was not like most people.

To distract herself, Alayna surveyed the interior of her small antique shop. She could literally feel the history, the old emotions, and the memories that lingered upon or within the various items that decorated her cozy shop. The treasures were like an old friend who happily shared their secrets with her.

The walls of the room were lined with old cabinets filled with antiques. Everything in the room was tinged with a layer of age, from the chipped paint on the furniture to the musty smell that lingered in the air. It was as if time had been frozen there, allowing a place among the relics of days long gone and which remained untouched and forgotten.

Chapter 2 — Something's Wrong

Everywhere she looked, there was evidence of another time, a reminder of how fleeting life could be. Despite all this, there was a certain beauty to it; something that made Alayna want to know more about these antiques and what they had experienced over the years. It was as if they harbored secrets between their cracks and crevices—secrets that waited to be discovered.

At twenty-six, Alayna was still directionless and uncertain about her future. She had no idea where life would take her next—the possibilities were endless, but at the same time, frighteningly unknown. Despite this uncertainty, she held on tightly to a secret hope that something better lay waiting for her just around the corner.

No matter what happened in life, Alayna knew that she must remain strong and keep moving forward. With every step into the unknown, she took one small step closer toward what awaited her.

Alayna smiled when she spotted her assistant, Hannah, outside. Hannah sashayed past the store windows, doing a funny dance while she kept a tight hold on the two cups of coffee grasped in her gloved hands. Even though it was early morning, Hannah's funny, quirky personality was alive and well and had the ability to instantly lighten Alayna's mood.

"Good morning!" Hannah said cheerfully as she bumped the door open with her bottom. "Ready for the cray-cray?"

Alayna nodded. "I will be as soon as I've had some coffee."

"Oh! Look at that... I just happen to have some." Hannah handed Alayna one of the steaming beverages. "Enjoy it before we get busy."

Laughing, Alayna took a sip. "Something tells me there isn't going to be a run on the antique shop."

Shrugging, Hannah laughed. "You never know."

A chill ran down Alayna's spine as her mouth drew into a thin line. She glanced out the window, took in the bright sunlight, and tried to push away the dark feeling that sank into the pit of her stomach. A few moments passed before Alayna returned her attention to her coffee.

Hannah fixed her gaze upon Alayna. "What's wrong?" She set her cup aside.

Despite Alayna's best efforts, she couldn't hide her unease. "Something's off."

Hannah's eyes went wide. "Something like a ghost, a natural disaster, a—"

"I don't know?" Alayna cut her off. "I've just had this bad feeling all morning and I can't seem to shake it."

Looking back at the closed door, Hannah asked, "Should we just stay closed today, lock the door and open up tomorrow?"

There was a part of Alayna that wanted to do just that. Ever since she was little, Alayna knew there was something that set her apart from the other children. It was not just a feeling—it was a dark gift that she kept hidden from the world because it made her an outcast. Her precognition and mediumship gave her the ability to see beyond what others could perceive, but it also cursed her with loneliness and fear.

Not long after hiring her assistant Hannah, Alayna had foreseen the young woman's grandmother would pass away unexpectedly. From Hannah's sweet nature, she knew her assistant would always regret not being able to say goodbye to her beloved Nana.

So, against her better judgment, Alayna had told Hannah that she needed to take the day off and go see her.

Hannah had seemed afraid and suspicious of Alayna's request, but reluctantly took the day off and went to see her grandmother. When Hannah returned from the visit, her fears seemed to have dissipated. To further reassure Hannah, Alayna had revealed her secret. In that moment, something between the women shifted, what had begun as suspicion turned to trust, acceptance, and appreciation.

Slapping a hand onto the counter, Alayna brightened. "You know what... everything is going to be fine. I'm just being weird." Coming around the counter, Alayna marched over to the door, flipped the closed sign to open, turned back to Hannah, and smiled. "I think the coffee has finally kicked in. Now let's get that new shipment unpacked."

"Want to start with that shipment we got in yesterday?" Hannah asked.

"Sure, why not." Alayna laughed as she followed Hannah down the long hallway toward the storage area.

APRIL 29TH—12 DAYS

CHAPTER 3

USUAL SUSPECTS

BRAYDEN

Austin, TX—Sunset

BRILLIANT RAYS OF ORANGE, RED, AND YELLOW LIGHT stretched forth from the half-hidden sun. Its daily journey nearing completion as it sank beneath the distant horizon. Fighting off boredom, Brayden James, twenty-six, a handsome, young detective, leaned forward and tried to peer past the intense glare cast upon his windshield. He'd been there for hours with his partner Juan Lozano, fighting off boredom.

"I cannot believe you're going to an amusement park for your honeymoon," Brayden teased Juan Lozano, his heavy-set partner.

"Trust me, it wasn't my idea," Lozano, mid-thirties, huffed.

"Admit it, you love those kiddy rides," Brayden snickered.

Lozano smacked Brayden in the chest with the back of his hand. "Look who's talking, Detective Baby on Board."

Not offended in the least, Brayden removed Lozano's hand with a smirk. "Hey, I'm not going to apologize for being mature and making detective early. Just because it took you more than a decade to accomplish that same—"

"Mature my ass! Is that why you're always pulling those dumb pranks on everyone at the station?" Lozano grumbled.

Brayden was about to give a witty reply when a sudden movement caught his eye. The antique shop's door opened. A crystal, suspended above the open sign, caught the retreating sunlight and sent a spectrum of colored lights to dance upon the sidewalk. Happy to be on their way, the couple, gift package in hand, left the store and headed toward their car parked farther down the street.

Quietly, Brayden settled back against his seat. "Think he'll make his move tonight?"

"If we get lucky," Lozano said as he took a sip of his cold coffee. "God, I hate stakeouts." Lozano made a face.

Unlike his partner, Brayden could not help but feel excited. They had been working this case going on five weeks now, and that night they just might get the break they had been waiting for. Lozano might enjoy sitting behind a desk, going over case files, but Brayden loved the field work and being out there on the job.

Eyes still fixed on the antique store, Brayden watched as a sexy brunette approached the large, double-paned windows. The Cajun beauty craned her neck as she looked first one way, then the other, as she studied the empty street. For a moment, Brayden and Alayna's gazes locked, as her emerald-green eyes met his soft hazel ones. Brayden's breath halted as she studied him, just as intensely as he had observed her. A mischievous grin curled her sultry lips as she flipped the open sign to closed, then slowly shut the blinds. Brayden released the breath he had been holding.

Lozano took notice. "Maybe you should go in for a closer look. You know, just to make sure you didn't miss anything."

Grinning, Brayden offered, "Good idea. You never know who might be helping our perp." Frowning, Brayden held up a hand. "Hold up."

Brayden watched as Jose Mendoza stepped out of the alley. The sickly figure was barely recognizable, with sunken eyes and pallid skin that reflected his former life of criminal activity. He gave a nod to two dangerous-looking men farther down the street.

He glanced over at Lozano, who nodded wordlessly in agreement; they both knew it was time for action.

The two men drew nearer to Mendoza. From his seat in the car, Brayden could tell the men were up to no good; their hard stares, hushed voices, and bulky frames all pointed to some kind of criminal intent. Mendoza's hands trembled as he offered them a package wrapped in a brown paper bag. Mendoza scanned his surroundings, ensuring that no one had noticed their silent exchange.

Chapter 3 — Usual Suspects

The large man closest to Jose took out a large sum of money from his coat pocket and handed it over to him. Though it was getting dark outside, Brayden could still make out a hint of suspicion in the man's eyes, and danger seemed to radiate from his presence.

Mendoza quickly pocketed the cash and started to turn away.

Carefully, Brayden and Lozano crept out of the vehicle and took up strategic positions behind cars across the street. Brayden's heart raced with anticipation. The stakes were high, but Brayden had faith that they could take these guys down without anyone getting hurt.

"Freeze!" Brayden called out in warning.

Eyes wild, the three men jumped into motion. The man closest to Mendoza lunged forward, knife in hand, "Damn snitch!" and stabbed Mendoza in the stomach before he made a break for the antique shop.

Withering in pain, Mendoza fell to the pavement, hands pressed tight against his bleeding gut as the other man fled down the alleyway.

Giving chase, Brayden broke for the alley as Lozano went to give aid to Mendoza. "Call for backup!"

Alarmed, Lozano pointed to the antique shop where one of the perps had just disappeared inside. "Where are you going!?"

Gun at the ready, Brayden nodded toward the alley. "Around back."

Understanding dawned on Lozano as he keyed his mic. "Dispatch, we need an ambulance and backup at the corner of Ninth and Washington."

Inching his way along the brick wall, Brayden was aware of the dangerous situation he faced. He knew that if he did not act quickly, the two women in the antique shop would be in serious peril.

Knowing that, he ignored the suspect who had made his way to the end of the alley and rounded the corner out of sight. Brayden's only mission now was to get inside that store and neutralize the threat, by whatever means necessary.

CHAPTER 4

TRAPPED

ALAYNA

Austin, TX—Sunset

Unable to hide her smile, Alayna winked at Hannah as she turned on her heels and made her way over to the counter from the front door.

"What?" Hannah asked, her interest piqued.

"I believe we have two officers on a stakeout across the street."

"And?" Resting her chin in her hand, Hannah leaned her elbow on the polished surface as she fixed Alayna with an expectant look.

"And nothing." Alayna laughed as she gave the front door another glance.

Irritated, Hannah hopped down from her bar stool and started for the door. Alayna caught her arm. "Wait." Hannah gave her a *come on already* look. "One of the men might have been a really, really hot guy."

Smiling, Hannah hurried back to her seat. "Do tell."

"There's nothing to tell. I was locking up and spotted him in a car across the street." Alayna gathered the mail that the carrier had left from the counter and began going through it.

Hannah looked over at the front door and laughed. "He must have been pretty hot."

"Oh, why is that?" Alayna asked.

Chapter 4   Trapped

"Because you didn't bother to lock the front door when you closed up." Hannah laughed.

"Ugh!" Alayna plopped the mail back on the counter and started toward the door when it flew open and banged against the doorstop. Face flushed, nose flaring, a tall, burly man raced inside, grabbed the door, slammed it shut behind him, and locked it, trapping them all inside.

The intruder's presence filled the room like a dark cloud. He scanned his surroundings, and his eyes quickly fell on them, his eyes narrowed with malicious intent. Silence hung in the air as Alayna held her breath, afraid to move.

Heart pounding, Alayna watched as the man started toward them, his presence threatening. Adrenaline surged through Alayna's veins as she noticed the wildness in his eyes and the blood-stained knife in his clenched fist.

Just a few feet from the desperate man, Alayna knew what her earlier senses had tried to warn her about. She should have taken the time to be extra careful instead of losing her senses over some guy out front. She chided herself for not locking the door behind her when she had turned that closed sign around. She knew better than to ignore her instincts.

Alayna's heart thudded in her chest as the man drew closer. His eyes, filled with rage, seemed to be searching for a target to unleash his fury on. "Hey, whatever's going on, we can figure something out to help you." She spoke in a slow, steady tone, trying to reason with him. But it felt like she was talking into a void.

The man glared at her as he continued his advance and she knew that if she didn't do something quick, Hannah's and her life would be in danger. Alayna held up both hands in a calming gesture. "We don't want any trouble," she said softly but firmly.

The intruder stopped short when he spotted the bank deposit bag in Hannah's hand. Alayna followed his gaze and sucked in a breath. Without hesitation, Alayna snatched the bag out of Hannah's hand and tossed it toward the man. "Take it. That's all the cash we have, I promise."

Sirens approached, but Alayna noticed that the man remained still and focused. He was unbothered by the growing commotion outside. He held on to his calm inner agitation while she watched as he seemed to contemplate his next move. Rattled, the man snatched up the deposit, then motioned to her with his bloodied knife. "You're coming with me."

Hannah reached for the phone. "I'm calling the police."

The crook rushed toward them. Hannah screamed as Alayna grabbed the first thing she could lay her hands on—a heavy metal lamp. Alayna swung it at the crook with all her might as he lunged toward her.

The heavy lamp landed a glancing blow to the side of the man's face, which only seemed to anger him further. "You're gonna pay for that bitch!"

As the criminal advanced, Alayna held her ground. She was not about to let him hurt Hannah or take her hostage. "You're not taking me anywhere, asshole!" Alayna said, standing her ground. "Just take the money and leave while you still can." She brandished the lamp in front of her like a weapon.

A thin trail of blood ran down the criminal's face. He reached up and angrily wiped it off, and took a menacing step toward Alayna.

Fear raced along Alayna's spine. She wanted to drop the lamp and flee. Her back was to the rear exit, if she threw the lamp at his head, it was possible that she could buy enough time to race out the back door, get down the alley, and onto the street where she could flag down the officers who had been watching the shop. But that would leave Hannah alone with this desperate man and she could not and would not do that.

Nostrils flaring, the man stood between her and Hannah. Hannah was frozen in terror, unable to run. Ready to fight, Alayna tightened her grip on the lamp. A loud creak sounded behind her as one of the old boards gave way under someone's weight. Alayna's heart lurched. *Oh my God, there are two of them!*

"Drop it, or I'll drop you!" A low, threatening growl sounded behind Alayna.

With no option left to her, Alayna dropped the lamp, held up her hands, and turned slightly to see who had broken into her store and snuck up behind her.

Relief warred with shock as she spotted the detective from earlier. The handsome detective had his firearm held out before him; his eyes fixed on the intruder as he snarled, "I won't tell you again."

Towering over her, the officer had to be a little over six feet tall. He had an athletic build, not too heavy, but muscular. Relief washed over her as the man slid one of his powerful arms in front of her and gently guided her back and behind him. He was placing himself before her like a human shield.

Hannah rushed over to her as they both retreated a few feet down the hallway, allowing the detective to handle the armed man.

Chapter 4   Trapped

Alayna watched as the officer's hazel eyes narrowed on the suspect and he motioned to the knife with his gun. "Drop it, then kick the knife away with your foot and get on the ground."

With an animalistic snarl, the intruder looked around the detective and back at her and Hannah. Alayna felt Hannah's hand strangle her upper arm as she held on tight to her.

The officer took another step toward the criminal, blocking his line of sight. "Don't even think about it!"

Unable to close the distance between himself and his would-be-hostages and with no way out, the hostile man complied. The intruder dropped the knife, kicked it away, then got to his knees, holding both of his hands behind his head.

The detective kept his weapon trained on the suspect until another man, the one that Alayna had spotted in the same vehicle that her rescuer had been in earlier, busted into the shop, his gun at the ready. "You good?"

The detective nodded to his partner and readied a set of handcuffs as his partner trained his gun on the suspect. "I'm good." The handsome officer's movements were quick and efficient. In a matter of seconds, he had subdued the criminal. His movements were decisive and purposeful, leaving no room for doubt that he had the situation under control.

Alayna felt a huge rush of relief as she watched the officer yank the crook up and onto his feet, then haul him toward the door. The detective's once-intense gaze now turned soft as he flashed her a sexy smile.

"Everyone okay?" Brayden asked.

Nodding, Alayna answered for them both. "Yes, thank you." She blushed slightly and smiled back in response. *This guy had better not be married or I will be hating on the fates that brought him into my life.*

"Let me get this guy into the back of a unit, then I'll be back to get your statements." The detective and his partner escorted the intruder out of her shop and into a waiting squad car.

Hannah leaned in and whispered in her, "If you don't get his number when he comes back ... I will."

CHAPTER 5

CATCHING UP

VANDER

Philadelphia, PA—Sunset

Just a short distance from the university, Fitler Square was not only a unique neighborhood in Philadelphia, but also one of the most expensive in Philadelphia and boasted many high-end amenities. The average homes in the area were appraised at an astonishing $1.4 million dollars, making Alexander's choice to invest in this area all the more impressive. Vander felt a sense of awe there.

Vander enjoyed the benefit of the suburb being only a short distance from the University of Pennsylvania, where he attended college.

It was the place many of the richest citizens of the city called home. Situated between Center City and Schuylkill River, the atmosphere was distinctively different from other parts of the city. Its historic architecture, tree-lined streets, and small-town charm made it a place to ponder and appreciate a serene beauty.

When Vander had first seen the house that Alexander had purchased in Fitler Square, he could not help but feel inspired. Not only did it symbolize a new beginning for him as he started university life, but it also gave his mentor Alexander an opportunity to come visit him from time to time and to explore the neighborhoods with him.

As they walked around the area, Vander noticed how vibrant and unique Fitler Square was compared to other parts of Philadelphia. There

Chapter 5   Catching Up

were quaint cafes and restaurants, small boutiques, and shops, and even a park with flowers in full bloom. It was an area that captivated both, and although they knew it would be difficult to leave when the university year ended, Vander felt fortunate to have been able to experience such a special part of Philadelphia during his time there.

His mentor, Alexander, seemed equally enthralled, often remarking on the wonderful people he had met and the interesting conversations they had shared. For Vander and Alexander, Fitler Square was more than a place—it was an experience that brought them closer together in ways they had not expected.

The Schuylkill River Trail made for a picturesque backdrop and cemented Fitler Square as one of the most impressive neighborhoods in Philadelphia. It was no wonder Alexander had chosen this as their temporary home.

Vander had grown up on the poorer side of town in Cape Town and had never imagined that one day he would not only walk through this luxurious park but also live with someone who owned a property near it.

As Vander passed by expensive high-end restaurants and the lush greenery decorating the front of the building, the smell of fresh flowers accompanied by the soft music that played from a music hall down the street once again reminded Vander of how much his life had changed from his meager beginnings.

Despite the stark contrast of his old life, Vander embraced the change. As he walked along the river, Vander smiled, content with this promising reality. He was finally living the life of abundance and comfort he had so often dreamed of and longed for as a child.

The relaxed atmosphere of the park gave him clarity and a newfound hope for what might lie ahead. His contemplative journey reminded him that no matter how dark times may seem, there could always be light found if you were willing to traverse the darkness that separated you from it.

Looking up at the lit windows, Vander smiled. It had been weeks since Alexander had come to visit and though the vision from earlier troubled him, that emotion paled in comparison to the one of excitement of conversing with his mentor.

Vander started up the stairs to the meticulously designed townhome, featuring four beds and six baths at approximately 5400 square feet. He punched in the keyless door code and stepped inside.

As always, the townhome was immaculate. Alexander had made sure every detail was attended to. High-end luxury was on display at every turn, from the roof deck hosting panoramic views of the city to the glass railings that accommodated the hot tub.

Even the kitchen had a Wolf/Sub-zero appliance package, waterfall island, built-up countertops, custom inset cabinetry, and custom white oak hardwood floors with a herringbone pattern that spanned the entire space.

Filled with delicacies was a large butler's pantry that also contained a beautiful wine refrigerator. There was designer lighting and plumbing throughout, with lavish wood trim and tons of storage. Alexander had also made sure that Vander would have his own private study.

There was, of course, a bathroom on every level, which to Vander, seemed a bit extreme considering they rarely, if ever, had guests. The crisp white walls of the townhome met with the soft, blue-gray, custom tile, and high-end windows. The modern, yet, somehow, industrial staircase had cobalt-blue, metal railings that followed it up the four stories of the building.

There was a linear gas fireplace, that, in the winter, heated tile floors and a smart home automation system. A nice, two-car garage with its own charging station attached to a private, landscaped courtyard.

Simply put, there on Delancey Street, was a sleek, modern, efficient tiny piece of heaven that they could call their own while in the charming city of Philadelphia until he completed his education.

If there had been any doubt as to whether Alexander had made it home, those doubts were chased away by the welcoming sound of classical music that played softly adding to the faint smell of a fine cigar that had recently been enjoyed.

"I had hoped you might stop by," Alexander called out in greeting as he made his way down the spiraling staircase. At seventy-five, Vander thought that his mentor would have taken advantage of the sleek elevator, that they also had the privilege of having, especially since he was descending from the top of the third floor, but he knew that Alexander wanted to stay fit and active, even with the looming threat of arthritic knees.

"Of course, I would not miss an opportunity to welcome you home." Vander waited patiently as his mentor continued his journey down the stairs. "How was your trip?"

Satisfied, Alexander smiled. "Interesting."

Chapter 5   Catching Up

"Care to be more specific?" Vander asked. When Alexander was vague, it often meant trouble. The kind of trouble that, had he not been distracted by visions of his own murder, he would have more than likely been privy to.

Laughing, Alexander's stylish, leather Oxfords landed on the final step. "How about we discuss my exploits over dinner?"

"I would not be opposed to that suggestion." Vander laughed as his stomach growled. The smell of savory meat cooking wafted into the living room from the kitchen, making his mouth water.

"Hungry as always, I see," Alexander teased as he strolled past him and led the way to the dining area.

"Afraid so," Vander agreed as he followed.

Alexander ushered Vander to the dining room where a sleek, stylish table and chairs waited amongst expensive, high-end décor. "I decided to have Phillip join us for the remainder of our time in Philadelphia."

Surprised, Vander replied, "Are you not happy with Delmonico?"

Alexander pointed to an empty seat near the head of the already set table. "He is more than capable, of course, but I thought you might want someone with a little more finesse to prepare your meals and, of course, the celebratory dinner party for you and your fellow classmates."

Vander took his seat, his senses suddenly on high alert as he maintained an easy smile. Phillip had prepared a literal feast for two. Vander's appetite grew as he watched the chef place the first part of the exquisite meal before them. The first course, a delicate yet enchanting sushi Omakase, offered an array of vibrant colors and flavors, each morsel an ode to the ocean's bounty. Truly, it was a work of art in both sustenance and beauty.

Afraid to ask, Vander took a sip of the second course which had been set before him, a hauntingly aromatic Tom Yum soup that flooded his senses with its fiery essence. Vander swallowed as he maintained his gaze downward, his eyes taking in the intricate wood grain of the table. The room was filled with a deafening silence that echoed with anticipation. Each tick of the clock punctuated the tense atmosphere, amplifying Vander's nervousness. "Now that we have finished with the simple pleasantries, I would like to hear about your trip to Austin," he finally managed, his voice calm and steady.

Alexander paused, a spoon halfway to his mouth. He let out a slow, deliberate sigh, setting down the utensil with calculated precision. His eyes, shadowed under the dim light of the room, flicked up to meet Vander's.

There was an unsettling calmness about him as he dabbed at his mouth with a napkin. "Austin," he began, his tone as rich as the Texas landscape, "was enlightening." His words hung in the air, shrouded in mystery and unspoken implications, raising the tension in the room to a nearly palpable level. The silence that filled the space afterward was heavy, each second ticking by filled with a daunting anticipation.

Forcing a smile, Vander met Alexander's gaze. "Care to elaborate?"

Philip took the bowls away and presented them with the third course, a Peking duck wrapped in a shroud of thin, crisp pancakes, a dance of sweetness and spice that unfolded on his tongue like a tale spun by the ancient masters of Beijing.

Alexander, with an undeniable glint of excitement in his eyes, leaned toward Vander. He began to unravel the tale of a new exhibition at the Blanton Museum of Art, his voice filled with wonder. "Mind you, this was no ordinary exhibit," he revealed, "but a majestic display of European paintings, a collision of antiquity and modernity, and a powerful testament to contemporary American and Latin American art."

Alexander's eyes were fixed on the far wall, but Vander knew he was envisioning it in his mind's eye. "It was more than just an exhibition; it was a labyrinth of artistry, housing the largest and most comprehensive collection in Central Texas."

As Alexander continued to describe one picture at the exhibit, Philip set the fourth course, a mystifying Korean Bibimbap, a mosaic of vegetables, rice, and meats. The dish embodied the soul and spirit of the vibrant Korean landscape.

Alexander leaned forward, fork in hand as he continued, "You see, each piece of art," he explained, "was a portal into the minds of their creators. Visitors would be transported from the vibrant energy of modern cities to the rustic charm of old European towns, then whisked away to the colorful, soul-stirring streets of Latin America. It was an artistic journey across centuries and continents, waiting to be embarked upon."

At his mentor's enthralling tales of art, Vander felt his unease begin to lift. The trip had been nothing more than an opportunity for his friend to enjoy a new, beautiful museum. "It sounds wonderful. Next time you go for a visit, I shall join you."

Chapter 5   Catching Up

Vander observed a subtle twitch in Alexander's jaw, a slight tick that danced beneath his weathered skin. It was a telling sign, a shrouded whisper to Vander that hinted at an impending storm. Alexander was hiding something, and he knew that was never a good sign.

Oblivious to the change in the room, the chief presented the final course, a sublime Matcha green tea ice cream that concluded the evening's odyssey.

Dabbing at the corners of his mouth, Alexander smiled. "I would be delighted to share that experience with you, dear boy ... just as soon as we have your graduation day behind us."

Vander heard Nightshade cry out to him in warning. Nightshade's ethereal cry hung in the air like a spectral melody, fraught with foreboding and a dark symphony of things yet to come.

CHAPTER 6

FAMILY TIES

BRAYDEN

Austin, TX—Night

Turning the corner, Brayden took in the picturesque homes that graced the peaceful neighborhood. Each dwelling was nestled back and off the street like a precious gem in the tapestry of the middle-class suburb.

Brayden, seated in his black Mustang, wound his way down the quiet streets as his mind revisited the recent, adrenaline-filled encounter at the antique shop. He smiled at the memory of the beautiful shop owner, how she stood there, defiant in the face of peril, ready to take on an armed assailant with nothing more than a small, brass lamp. It had been so odd that amidst the danger they both faced, they had shared a sense of connectedness in the turmoil, which had been both profound and unexpected.

The journey to his sister's home was haunted by Alayna's phantom presence, a reminder of the thin veil separating the safe, welcoming world he now drove through, and the harsh realities that he knew lurked just out of sight.

As Brayden pulled up to the curb, the familiar silhouette of his sister's house emerged from the shroud of darkness, a beacon of warmth and love in the cold, uninviting night. He turned the key, silencing the engine's purr, and for a moment, allowed himself to bask in the comforting silence that surrounded him. Even through the veil of night, the house radiated a sense of unspoken safety and respite. It was more than just an abode. It was a sanctuary, a testament to the bond that transcended the confines of mere blood relation. There, amidst the rhythmic chirping of nocturnal creatures and the soft rustle of leaves in the cool wind, Brayden found solace. This place, filled with the love of his sister and her family, was a haven, a refuge.

Brayden stepped out of the vehicle and into the cool night. Each crunch of gravel beneath his feet brought him closer to the enfolding warmth of the home. As he approached the front door, familiar sounds of laughter could be heard.

With a sense of calm anticipation, Brayden reached out, grasped the cool doorknob, and prepared to step inside without knocking.

As the door creaked open, Brayden was engulfed by a wave of warmth and familiarity. The smell of well-worn furniture, home-cooked meals, and the soft, comforting scent of peaches, unique to this house, filled his nostrils.

Stepping over the threshold, he was immediately met with the heartwarming sight of his sister's family. Ethan, his brother-in-law, was sprawled on the floor, trying to fend off the playful attacks from his son Hunter, as Paige, his sister, watched, a sweet smile on her face as she laughed at her son's antics. Zoey, their eldest child, sat perched on the couch, engrossed in one of her favorite books.

Quietly, Brayden settled his back against the door and took a moment to enjoy the happy scene that played out before him. *God, how I love this family. They are my world and the thing that matters most in this life to me.*

Looking up, Hunter spotted him and let out a high-pitched squeal. Brayden's nephew abandoned his playful attack on Ethan and launched himself at him. Brayden caught the little boy with ease, caught him up in a big hug, then began spinning him around in a big circle.

Spent, Ethan crawled to the couch and sat up against it. "About time you showed up, brother, I was just about to surrender to the munchkin."

Hunter giggled as Brayden staggered and pretended as if the boy suddenly weighed a hundred pounds. "Hunter, what in the world have you been eating? You weigh a ton!" Brayden dropped him onto the couch like a sack of potatoes.

Without missing a beat, Hunter bounced off the couch, landed on his feet, then launched himself at Brayden. Unprepared, Brayden almost missed catching him and struggled to hang on when Hunter squirmed in his arms. "Do it again, do it again!"

"You're like a fish out of water, kiddo," Brayden stammered as he chucked Hunter back on the couch and watched as he repeated the same action over again.

"That was fast," Brayden exclaimed.

"Uh-oh, now you've done it," Paige warned as she hurried past them and plopped down next to Ethan.

Laughing, Ethan pulled Paige into his arms. "Hunter can do that for hours."

"I'll give you five launches, kiddo, then I'm out for the day."

"Deal!" Hunter said as he fell back into Brayden's outstretched arms, ready to be thrown.

"One, two, three ... lift off!" Brayden tossed Hunter onto the couch several more times, then hurried and took a seat on the recliner before he could start another round.

"Ahhhh," Hunter whined.

"Sorry, buddy, we'll do more rocket launches next time." Brayden held up his hand, allowing Hunter to give him a high-five.

"Okay." Hunter jumped, slapped his tiny hand against Brayden's, then rushed off toward the kitchen for a drink of water.

Zoey, a few years older than Hunter at nine, had waited patiently for Hunter to have his time, then hurried over to Brayden, wrapped her arms around his neck, and gave him a quick hug. "Hi, Uncle Brayden."

"Hi." Happy, Brayden returned Zoey's hug as he smiled at his sister. "Whatcha reading?"

Suddenly animated, Zoey began chattering, "Oh, it's the best book ever! It's a true story about Lizzie and her mother who is a zookeeper; their family got attached to this orphaned elephant, who will be destroyed if its zoo is hit by bombs. Lizzie persuades the zoo director to let the elephant stay in their garden instead. When the city is bombed, the family flees with thousands of others, but they can't go the same way as the others because they have an elephant... then—"

"Zoey, don't tell him the whole story. He may want to read the book," Ethan said.

Disappointed, Zoey huffed at her dad as she turned to him and folded her arms across her chest. "Dad, I was just telling him what it was about."

Chapter 6 — Family Ties

Looking over Zoey's head to Ethan, Brayden mouthed the words, *Thank you.*

Catching her dad looking at Brayden, she spun around and looked at him. Guiltily, Brayden stammered, "It sounds great... How about we read it together sometime?"

Delighted, Zoey clapped her hands together. "Deal!"

"I hate to be the bad guy," Paige said, "but it's bedtime."

Hunter walked into the living room, a big glass in his small hands. "But I'm not tired."

"And Uncle Brayden just got here," Zoey whined.

Prepared to show a united front with Paige, Ethan got to his feet, took the glass of water from Hunter, and pointed to the stairs. "You can visit with Uncle Brayden in the morning. He is taking you to school." Ethan looked over at Brayden. "Right?"

"You bet." Brayden only got to take the kids to school a few times a month, when Paige and Ethan's schedules collided, but he was always happy to.

"But, for now, you two have got to get ready for bed." Ethan gave the kids a mischievous smirk before he sat Hunter's water down, then bolted for the stairs. "Last one to brush their teeth feeds the bunny tomorrow!" Ethan called over his shoulder.

Squeals erupted from Hunter and Zoey as they gave chase and ran up the stairs after Ethan.

"I can't believe that worked." Brayden shook his head in amazement.

Paige began to pick up the living room. "It won't work for long, I'm afraid. The kids are growing up fast."

"Yeah, they are." Brayden grabbed a few of the throw pillows and positioned them back on the couch where they belonged. Brayden could not help but feel like time was flying by. It seemed like only yesterday when Paige and Ethan had brought Zoey home, then Hunter. Before he knew it, they would be teenagers, then out on their own. He could only imagine how Paige felt.

"Hey, you all right?" Paige asked.

"What?" Brayden responded, not realizing he had gotten lost in thought. "Oh, yeah, yeah, I'm fine, just a little tired."

"Long day, huh?" Paige motioned for him to follow her to the kitchen where she poured three glasses of wine, handed him one, and took a sip of another.

Brayden swirled the liquid in his glass, knowing he was not going to escape the night without a more detailed breakdown of his crazy day. "Well," Brayden began, a slow grin spreading across his face.

Out of breath, Ethan hurried into the kitchen, grabbed his glass of wine, and asked, "What did I miss?"

"Brayden was just about to tell me about his day," Paige said.

"Awesome, must be exhausting taking down those parking meter thieves." Ethan laughed.

"Hold up, you know we only go after jaywalkers, right?" Brayden smirked, knowing Ethan loved harassing him.

"That's right, sorry." Ethan motioned toward one of the chairs. "Have a seat."

The three of them took a seat at the table, while Paige continued to eye him suspiciously and he could not help but squirm under her scrutiny. His older sister was a master at getting information out of him. "Okay, little brother. What's up? You're actually blushing, so I have to assume you've met someone."

"What!? No. What would make you—" Brayden stammered.

Ethan almost choked on his wine as Paige laughed at Brayden's sudden distress. "Busted! Who is she?"

Brayden could not help but enjoy this playful interrogation from his sister and brother-in-law. Now that he was cornered, he had no choice but to tell them the story of a drug deal gone wrong and how it had led to him saving the beautiful, green-eyed Alayna Sage.

CHAPTER 7

ALMOST FORGOT

ALAYNA

Austin, TX—Night

"**Good thing that jerk didn't get more time to** wreck the place." Hannah's words echoed in the quiet of the shop.

Alayna studied the ravaged vase, the only true victim of the criminal who had busted into her shop just over an hour before. Its broken and fragmented pieces lay strewn upon the floor, further destroyed by the heavy footsteps of the officers who came in to remove the suspect. "Or time to do something far worse."

Hannah shuddered, her wide eyes going to Alayna. "Right!" Setting her broom aside, she took a seat. "I can't believe you hit that guy in the head. What were you thinking? He could have killed you!"

She rubbed her hands up and down her arms. "That if that guy got either one of us out of here and alone someplace, we more than likely wouldn't have survived."

"You're right, it was better to make a stand here, together than be taken somewhere alone, where he might have had time to—"

"Let's not think about that, okay?" Alayna cautioned. They had both had more than enough fear for one day and she did not want to allow their imaginations to paralyze them with fear or make them afraid to be there alone in the days to come. She would make sure she was more careful in the future and ensure that Hannah also took more caution when she was opening or closing the antique store.

With a broom in hand and determination etched on her face, Hannah began sweeping up the broken china. "You're right, I would like to put my thoughts to better use." The mood in the shop seemed to brighten with each sweep and removal of the debris. "Why don't we talk about Mr. Tall, Dark, and oh-so-handsome Detective James?"

Holding the dustpan and wastebasket, Alayna looked up at her quizzical assistant and smiled. "What about him?"

Carefully, Hannah maneuvered the sharp shards into the waiting dustpan. "You know what I'm talking about," Hannah teased. "The sexual tension between you two when he was taking your statement was palpable."

Dumping the full dustpan into the trash, Alayna straightened. "Don't be ridiculous."

"You're not going to deny you're attracted to him?"

Laughing, Alayna set the trash can and dustpan down. "No, but I wouldn't go as far as to say the attraction was mutual."

Setting her broom aside, Hannah plopped onto one of the seats by the counter. "Oh, trust me, it was mutual. That guy couldn't stop gawking at you, even when he was putting that jerk in handcuffs."

A piercing alert sounded, its incessant hum vibrated from Alayna's back pocket. Still nervous from the events of the day, Alayna jumped, then calmed down as she reached into her pocket and retrieved the phone. Looking down at the bright screen, Alayna gasped in alarm.

Hopping off the bar stool, Hannah asked, "What is it?"

In a panicked voice, Alayna put a hand to her mouth. "Mrs. Richard! I totally forgot we have an appointment!" Alayna looked up at the old clock on the wall and her eyes widened. "She'll be here in less than fifteen minutes."

"Maybe she'll be late." Hannah shrugged.

Alayna fixed her with a look. "Has she ever?"

"Nope!" Both women jumped into action, putting things into place. "Hey, you go get ready. I'll handle things up here."

"You sure?" Alayna asked.

"I've got this, now go!"

Backing away, Alayna added. "You may have to stall for an additional five to ten minutes," Alayna warned.

Chapter 7 — Almost Forgot

Grabbing a nearby tea kettle, Hannah smiled. "I'll start some of her favorite tea."

"You're the best!" Alayna called over her shoulder as she turned and hurried down the hallway toward her reading room. Hannah would make sure she had the time she needed to get ready for her client.

Hurriedly, Alayna raced around the room, lighting the various candles that she had strategically placed. Catching her reflection in one of the mirrors, Alayna caught sight of her haggard appearance, illuminated by the wavering candlelight. Stomach in knots, she combed through her wild locks, her fingers trembling as she tried to impose order on her appearance. In the room, candles flickered and cast long shadows. Her usual serene disposition before working a session as a medium seemed to elude her.

Alayna closed her eyes and forced herself to tune into the calming energy of the room. She listened to the soft whispers of the wind that blew outside, the flicker of the candles, and the hushed voices of Hannah and Mrs. Richard as they drank their tea in the front of the store, farther down the hall.

Hands steady, Alayna allowed her hands to move over the cool surface of her crystal ball and took a seat. Allowing her mind to clear from the turbulent past few hours, she prepared her spirit and shielded it from any unwanted energy or vulnerable spirits that might lurk in the shadows.

When working in mediumship or with anything in the occult, one had to protect themselves because to communicate with the dead, you left yourself vulnerable and open, to not only spirits, but negative energies, dark forces, or any number of unknown things. Therefore, Alayna knew she had to take the time to prepare and leave nothing to chance.

Calming her mind, Alayna found herself immersed in the obsidian silence. She felt the pulsations of her intuitive reading ripple through the ether of her consciousness. With every rhythmic beat of her heart, she constructed a fortress of light around her soul, each brick a testament to her unwavering determination and strength.

This was not a mere flight of imagination. It was her protection, her preparation against the unseen forces that hovered in the liminal space between the physical world and the spectral realm. She knew that this sanctuary of light was not exclusive to her alone.

Many carried the same divine spark, but either out of fear or ignorance, chose to smother it. Yet Alayna embraced her ability, seeing it as a bridge to the mysterious otherworld, rather than a curse.

Little by little, Alayna felt her protective wall solidify. Its luminescence intensified in the darkness. The wall, a beacon in the vast sea of unknowing, became her sanctuary, her stronghold against the enigmatic entities that sought entry. She was the gatekeeper, the guardian of her ethereal realm. Her senses heightened, her intuition sharpened, and she began the preparation to interact with the spectral entities. As the veil between the worlds thinned, she could hear the whispers of the spirits, feel their ancient wisdom coursing through her, their stories ready to be told.

A soft rap sounded at the door. Mind calm, spirit and soul now protected, she said, "Come in." Alayna's voice sounded like a spectral whisper in the candlelit room.

Tendrils of uncertainty wafted off Mrs. Richard. Her sorrow-stained eyes flickered with the faintest trace of hope. The atmosphere was heavy and fragrant with the scent of burning sage, its smoke curled into symbols only seen by those tuned to the unseen.

Alayna's heart echoed with empathy for Mrs. Richard, for she was no stranger to the ache of a heart that yearned for a lost love. "Hello Vivian," she began, her words soft in the ominous silence. "Mack is here. He wants to tell you something." Alayna reached across the table and offered her hands to Mrs. Richard, an unspoken promise to guide her through the looming darkness of her grief.

Mrs. Richard hesitated for a moment, then took a seat and placed her trembling hands into Alayna's. Her touch was cold, a stark contrast to the warmth of the room, a physical manifestation of the chills of loss that coursed through the older woman's veins. Alayna closed her eyes and reached out with her spirit to the realm beyond the physical.

For Alayna, this was more than an intuitive reading. It was her way of offering a lifeline to those who grieved and could find no solace. In the quiet, Alayna whispered, "Mack... Vivian is ready to hear what you have to say." Silence enveloped the room. Hannah left, closing the door behind her as the air filled with anticipation.

Alayna, with her spirit extended into the realms unseen, waited. Vivian held her breath, the raw edges of her grief momentarily dulled by the whisper of hope. Time seemed to dissolve as Alayna felt the lifetime

Chapter 7   Almost Forgot

of love from Mack to Vivian flood her senses. Images of long walks in the woods, a playful Yorkie running out ahead of them, and beautiful days of Mack and Vivian spent together flooded into Alayna's mind.

A sweet, soft voice seemed to whisper into her ear as she heard Mack say, *< Tell her I love her, that I miss our walks with Tuffy. >*

The candlelight danced and encapsulated them as their two worlds merged inside this small, insignificant room. "Mack wants you to know that he loves you and that he misses the walks with you and your little Yorkie named Tuffy." Alayna could tell that her voice washed over Vivian and gave the older woman a small respite from the icy grips of her sorrow. Mrs. Richard's intuitive reading had officially begun.

· APRIL 29TH—12 DAYS

CHAPTER 8

OUTSMARTING A FOX

ALEXANDER

Philadelphia, PA—Night

Alone, Alexander wandered into his study and immersed himself in the echo of empty hallways. He exhaled deeply and watched as his breath fogged up the glass of the windowpane he looked out.

The city had come to life; tiny pinpricks of light showed from everywhere as he looked past the towering trees that stood as sentinels to each side of his townhome. He thought about the nice dinner he had spent with Vander just a few short hours before, and wondered at the mix of emotions that now plagued him.

Vander had retired shortly after their meal, stating the need to prepare for an early exam. However, Alexander knew there had been more to Vander's quick departure. Though his young friend had tried to conceal it, Alexander knew Vander's attitude toward him had shifted halfway through dinner. It had gone from one of delight to see him, and interest in his travels, to one of guarded mistrust.

Contemplating his next move, Alexander poured himself a glass of Hennessy Paradis Imperial, a brandy in and of itself the very symbol of sophistication and decadence. Taking a sip, he savored the blend of nuanced flavors, evoking notes of jasmine, orange blossom, and smoky accents. Like a specter, it was both there and not, providing a fleeting comfort to those who found solace in its depths. Yet, as Alexander tilted the bottle, the amber liquid sparkled ominously under the dim light, mirroring his internal turmoil.

Alexander took another drink of his exquisite brandy, then swirled the amber liquid in his glass. His eyes glittered with dark anticipation as he mulled over years of well-laid plans. Vander, his protégé, had proved to be a driven soul, a force to be reckoned with.

The boy's progress, his determination to succeed, was like watching a masterpiece unfold. Vander was a testament to his relentless spirit. Alexander's chest swelled with pride as he considered Vander's journey from the gritty streets of Cape Town to this new world of elegance and refinement. Vander's transformation was not only impressive, but it was also a tribute to the resilient power of his ambition. Alexander took another sip, the brandy's warmth spreading through him.

What should his next move be? Vander's sudden change in mood left Alexander with little doubt as to his young ward suspecting him of some ill intent.

As Alexander placed his glass down, the echo of the crystal against the mahogany desk reverberated and added to the symphony of silence in the room. His fingers drummed lightly on the polished wood; each tap a beat in the grand symphony of his schemes. His mind was alive, an unstoppable whirlwind of ideas and strategies.

Alexander's gaze flicked back to the untouched seat across his desk—Vander's chair. He could practically see the young man's determined posture, his keen eyes reflecting the fire that had carried him this far. From a life of squalor to the epitome of success, Vander's journey was a testament to his sheer willpower and tenacity. His adaptability was a trait Alexander greatly admired, a trait he knew was crucial in the cutthroat world that, even now, they inhabited.

As Alexander envisioned his next plan, a thrill coursed through his veins. The game was far from over, and Vander, his greatest piece on the chessboard, was poised to make his next decisive move. Alexander's pride in Vander was tinged with anticipation—the anticipation of witnessing a future champion in the making, a future king in his kingdom, or a final piece of art to complete his collection.

The boy had surprised him, yes, but he had also confirmed Alexander's belief in him. Vander was the raw diamond he had so hoped for. He had been polished, refined, and was now ready to be flaunted. He had guided Vander, molded him into the champion he had been destined to become.

Alexander was ready to play, ready to seize the victory that was tantalizingly within his grasp. He drank the last of his brandy. The fiery liquid served as a fitting metaphor for the tumultuous journey that lay ahead.

Alexander thought, Was this the beginning? Or was Vander and his journey nearing its end?

As Alexander gazed upon Vander's empty chair, a shadow rippled across his countenance. Was this the dawn of a new epoch or the twilight of their shared path? Was the game of life and death, the dance of kill or be killed, about to unfurl its cruel design? He could feel the rhythm of time coiling tighter with each passing moment. His once vibrant days, bursting with vitality and promise, were now a chiaroscuro of aged wisdom and dark contemplations.

Vander, on the cusp of inheriting Alexander's legacy, was indeed his magnum opus, a testament to his life's work. In one respect, his heart swelled with pride. Vander was so strong. Capable and ready to execute the plans that were laid out before him. Still, Alexander was also haunted by a dread that gnawed at his soul.

It was a game of success or loss, a dangerous gamble where the stakes were life itself. His twilight years were a testament to his determination, his resolve to realize his dreams through Vander. As his own life was coming to an end, would Vander be the torchbearer of his legacy? Or would he be the dusk that ushered the end of all that Alexander had strived to build?

The weight of the unknown pressed heavily upon Alexander. A sense of solemnity hung in the air as Alexander pondered the bitter irony of his predicament. His legacy, his life's work, was in his hands, ready to be molded, shaped, and prepared in one way or another.

His thoughts snapped back to the present, washed over by a wave of chilling realism. Alexander glanced at his worn hands, the veins like a roadmap of a life well lived. The choice was his to make. Should Vander succeed him, or become his last, precious work of art, thus giving the young man his own chance at immortality?

The game Alexander played was no longer just chess—it had evolved into a psychological battle, a dance of intellect, much like trying to outsmart a fox. Every move, every decision, was underpinned by a dark,

Chapter 8   Outsmarting A Fox

mysterious undercurrent. Vander's life was in his hands, his fate a mere plaything in this grim game he orchestrated.

As the date of Vander's graduation loomed, Alexander found himself entwined in a web of contemplation. His eyes lingered on the big, red circle, like a glaring eye warning of an imminent crossroads. Vander, the young protégé he had watched with a blend of paternal fondness and professional curiosity, was on the precipice of a remarkable journey.

Alexander had to outwit Vander, bend his reality, or at the very least, the young man's perception of it. The need to create opportunities where little existed was his only hope of outwitting Vander. He was now trapped in a situation of his own making. Two minds, locked in an exquisite battle of wits. One, ready to sacrifice all for sweet victory while the other was determined to find a way to survive. Time would tell who the winner would be.

No matter how much Alexander prepared, there were still unknown variables at play.

Alexander might have years of experience over Vander, but he had witnessed first-hand how the young man's paranormal gifts had literally changed the course of events, even in his own life.

Alexander, with his deeply ingrained knowledge of the ordinary and the esoteric, could hardly ignore the unorthodox shifts Vander had instigated with his concealed talents.

His years of experience, typically an advantage, seemed to pale in comparison to Vander's paranormal abilities. These inexplicable skills, an enigmatic blend of the occult and pseudo-science, had not only transformed circumstances around them but had also left an indelible imprint on Alexander's own existence.

The atmosphere around Vander had always been thick with mystery. It was a constant reminder that despite their shared history, there were parts of Vander that remained elusive and untouched, like shadows that danced on the edges of a darkened room.

Despite the chill of apprehension that gnawed at him, Alexander could not suppress the spark of intrigue that Vander's clandestine abilities invoked. Vander's talents seemed to paint an arcane canvas of possibilities and Alexander found himself teetering on the precipice of an abyss, peering into the depths where the normal and paranormal coalesce.

Over the years, Alexander had delved into the shadowy realms of pseudo-science, the occult, and the paranormal in a quest to help Vander unlock his talents. The multi-faceted journeys had led them to many obscure teachers and clandestine experts.

Some had helped, many had not, and by the age of sixteen, Vander had refused to continue the search for those so-called experts. The young man had insisted that he wanted to focus on the here and now, to work on his education and try, if possible, to be normal.

However, Alexander knew that Vander was exceptional, unique, and could no more be like the insignificant students surrounding him than he, himself, could be like those average humans in his world.

Knowing Vander as he did, Alexander knew that there was little doubt that the young man had continued to develop his gifts. How could he not? Those innate skills had ensured his survival in Cape Town, a world where otherwise, he would have surely perished.

Alexander was not concerned that Vander had kept secrets from him, for he too harbored many of his own from him. One of which an institute in Virginia, where one of the most impressive libraries on the paranormal and pseudo-science existed.

Though he had already set several distractions into motion, Alexander knew it would be wise to seek council from those working at the institute to gain insight into the problems at hand. But first, before he left for Virginia, he had a graduation party to plan!

APRIL 30TH—11 DAYS

CHAPTER 9

DAY IN THE LIFE

BRAYDEN

Austin, TX—Morning

SMILING BRIGHTLY, BRAYDEN SNUCK INTO PAIGE'S kitchen.

Grinning like a mischievous imp, Brayden tiptoed farther into the heart of Paige's kitchen, his eyes sparkling with sneaky intent. The morning sun streamed through the window, casting an ethereal glow that did little to dispel the suspenseful ambiance. Hunter and Zoey, his partners in crime, suppressed their laughter as they followed along in hushed silence.

Soon, Brayden had reached his destination: the kitchen counter, where Paige was busy packing lunch for her two young children. Inches away from Paige, Brayden slowly placed his hands on her shoulders and whispered in her ear, "Surprise!"

Paige jumped with shock, then broke out into a fit of mingled laughter and relief. Brayden's laughter was clear and ringing, echoing alongside the playful chiding in Paige's voice. "You're such a child," she said, her own laughter mixed with her children's. Hunter and Zoey clung to Brayden's legs, their eyes reflected the shimmering happiness that radiated from him.

Enveloped in the warmth of the morning's light, Brayden returned the hug from his niece and nephew, his heart filled with an unspoken love. His hands found their small heads and ruffled their hair gently in a familiar gesture of affection as he directed them back to the breakfast table. "Come on, you two," he murmured, his voice soft yet firm. "You'd better finish your breakfast."

He watched as they scampered off, light-footed, leaving a trail of laughter in their wake. Brayden treasured these moments. They kept him grounded and made him feel a part of this loving family.

Brayden snatched an apple from the counter, and rolled it in his hand, as his dark eyes surveyed the healthy contents of the children's lunches Paige had painstakingly prepared.

A playful smirk tugged at the corners of his lips. "What? No cookies, cupcakes, or candy?" his voice teased. "How are they supposed to make good trades with healthy snacks like that?"

"They're supposed to eat their own lunch, not trade it for junk food," Paige chided.

Brayden made a face and turned to the kids, giving them a wink. "Don't worry, I've got contraband for you." The children cheered as Paige punched him in the stomach.

"Don't you dare give them candy! I don't want another call from Hunter's teacher telling me he that he couldn't sit still in class," Paige reprimanded.

"Hunter?" Brayden turned to his nephew. "You wouldn't do that, would you?"

Hunter giggled as he studied the floor. That was answer enough to let Brayden know that his nephew had been in trouble after eating too much candy before. That was no surprise, Brayden knew more than likely, that sugar was likely to ignite his nephew's overabundance of energy and make him even more hyper than he already was.

"Thank you for taking the kids to school. I really appreciate it." Paige smiled up at him.

"Happy to do it," Brayden said, and he meant it. He knew that Paige had an important meeting to attend, and Ethan was still on duty at the station, which happened every so often, and he was always glad to help when needed.

"You're the best," Paige said as she closed the lunch containers. "Kids, time to go." Brayden and Paige watched as Hunter and Zoey scooped up their vibrantly colored backpacks and lunches and hurried out to Brayden's waiting car.

Chapter 9　Day In The Life

Walking Brayden toward the door, Paige teased, "So, when can we expect to meet this enigmatic Cajun?"

Brayden, caught off guard, stumbled over his words, a sheepish smile spreading across his face. "I really shouldn't have mentioned her to you," he murmured.

At a loss for words, Brayden watched as Hunter and Zoey piled into the back of his unit. He turned to Paige and asked, "Have you had one of your premonitions about her, or are you just fishing for information?"

Giving him a sly smile, Paige pushed him out the door. "Get the kids to school on time, and don't speed... You have to set a good example," she admonished lightly.

Brayden smiled in response, climbed into the car, and turned on the ignition. "You guys buckled in?" Brayden asked his two young passengers.

"Yes, Sir." He heard Hunter and Zoey both answer, but turned to verify that they were indeed buckled in correctly. Hunter and Zoey waved goodbye to their mom as he backed out of the driveway and began their short journey to their school.

Half-listening to Hunter's and Zoey's chatter, Brayden's mind wandered to thoughts of Alayna Sage. Their innocent laughter, a happy symphony, became a subdued hum in the background as the memory of her haunting green eyes consumed his thoughts. He could still feel the weight of the previous day's events, the tension and mystery that swirled around her. A smile spread across Brayden's face. *Maybe I should stop by and check on her after I drop the kids off at school, just to make sure she is all right after last night's events.*

"Uncle Brayden, whatcha thinking about?" Zoey piped in. "You look so happy."

Busted, Brayden thought as he returned his focus to the road and his passengers. "Just thinking how lucky I am to have such a beautiful niece and awesome nephew."

Hunter giggled. "Uh-uh, you're fibbing."

· APRIL 30TH—11 DAYS

CHAPTER 10

HAPPY SURPRISE

ALAYNA

Austin, TX—Day

WITH HER ANTIQUE SHOP BACK TO NORMAL, ALAYNA was busy opening her shop at the usual 10:00 a.m. time. The rich scent of old books and polished mahogany wafted through the air, a comforting familiarity after the unnerving events of the night before. As she readied to unpack one of the boxes from an early delivery, a soft jingle sounded.

The small bell above her door had chimed, a simple surprise in the quiet. Lifting her gaze, Alayna's heart skipped a beat. There, in the soft glow of the morning light, stood the tall, handsome detective who had saved her and Hannah the day before. With his dark, brooding eyes and that sexy aura of mystery enveloping him, he was a figure that was both intriguing and intimidating.

With a voice almost akin to a purr, Alayna greeted Detective Brayden. Brayden brimmed with confidence as he sauntered up to the counter where she was standing and casually rested his arms upon it. His smile was a thing of beauty as he looked up at her. "Miss Sage, I—"

"Please, call me Alayna," she interrupted.

Smiling brightly, he continued with the formalities. "All right, Alayna, I wanted to stop by and make sure that you and your staff were okay."

"We're fine. Thank you."

Chapter 10 Happy Surprise

"Is there anything else that you would like to add to your statement, or something that you might have forgotten about the incident?" Brayden added, trying his best to sound formal.

Alayna, amused, folded her arms across her chest. "The incident from yesterday, you mean? Surely you don't think my memory is that bad, do you, Detective?" Her voice was drenched in irony.

Detective Brayden inched closer, his voice dripping with sarcasm, his eyes full of mischief. "Well, Alayna, the mind does have a propensity to bury unpleasant incidents," he said, the corner of his lips curling up into a half-smile. His alluring charm was undeniable, and the attraction that hung in the air was a palpable entity between them.

Alayna, unperturbed, raised an eyebrow at his insinuation, her amusement not quite reaching her eyes. The game was on, and both were aware of it.

Leaning closer, Brayden looked into her eyes, and with mock concern, said, "You might be able to recall things clearer if you were in a different environment."

Alayna put a hand over her heart and looked at him, wide-eyed. "You mean, like maybe dinner at a nice restaurant with a detective?"

Smiling coyly, Brayden said, "That would be the best-case scenario, yes?"

She felt herself being drawn toward him, and for a moment, the only thing she could do was stare into his eyes. The air between them seemed to be charged with a strange electricity, as if daring them to take the next step.

The thought of having dinner with him filled her with excitement and trepidation in equal measure. She knew it was dangerous; after all, he was a detective, and she had something to hide. But a part of her was drawn to the danger, like a moth to a flame. She wanted to explore this unknown world with him; she wanted to see where this story would lead.

Alayna finally broke the trance-like state between them and asked, "What did you have in mind?"

"Well, Austin," voice smooth, Brayden began, "is a foodie's dream. It holds a position as one of the top 10 best 'Foodie Cities' in the U.S." His eyes sparkled.

Playfully, Alayna looked up at the ceiling and tapped her index finger to her chin. "But it doesn't have any Michelin-star restaurants."

"True, but there are still dozens of fine eating establishments in the city."

Laughing, Alayna threw Brayden a curve. "Then I suggest we go to the Peach Bar."

"Come again?" Brayden asked, dumbfounded.

"It's got a great a great Taiwanese duck roll."

Pleasantly surprised, Brayden added, "And freshly baked tomato pie sprinkled with parmesan cheese."

Alayna's eyes widened in mock surprise. "You know the place?!"

Clearing her throat, Hannah stood at the edge of the counter, awkward and uncertain of what to do next. Her eyes darted from Brayden's flustered expression to Alayna's amused one. They both watched the detective straighten and stumble back as he tried to regain his composure.

"How does seven o'clock sound?" Alayna asked Brayden, wanting to help him out of the predicament.

He offered her a grateful smile as he replied, "Perfect, I'll be by to question you then."

She nodded. "Fine, I'll be ready."

Brayden gave a curt salute before he retreated outside. Her eyes followed him through the window, and she smiled as she observed the handsome detective grinning from ear to ear as he slid back inside his vehicle with his waiting partner. It was clear from the irritated glare that the detective's partner was not happy about being left in the car, but Brayden did not seem to mind.

As Hannah joined Alayna behind the counter, her gaze flitted to the men outside, her curiosity piqued. "What was that about?"

Alayna's response was a dreamy stare toward the receding taillights of Brayden's vehicle. "It was Detective Brayden's," she began, her tone matching the flattered excitement dancing in her eyes, "cute, but awkward, way of asking me out."

Alayna allowed herself one more lingering look toward Brayden's retreating car before returning to her duties. She was eager for the night ahead and could not wait to see what surprises lay in store.

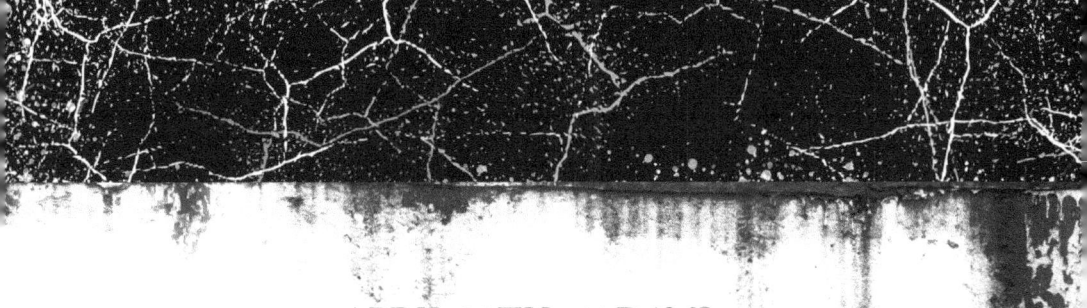

APRIL 30TH—11 DAYS

CHAPTER 11

HUMAN CAMOUFLAGE

VANDER

University of Pennsylvania, PA—Day

CLOAKED IN THE GUISE OF A TYPICAL SCHOLAR, VANDER strolled along the tree-lined paths of the vast college campus. His double major in business, a deft cover for his true interests, only helped to solidify his façade of normality.

He exchanged cordial nods with passing acquaintances. His blue eyes revealed nothing of his concealed fascination with the complex workings of the mind, and the underpinnings of criminal behavior.

To the world, he was just another student on the precipice of graduation, but beneath the surface, Vander was anything but ordinary. The art of blending in, he had mastered with meticulous precision.

As Vander continued his stroll, the campus around him buzzed with the energetic hum of college life. Yet amidst the hustle and bustle, the laughter and chatter, he remained an enigma, his true passions hidden beneath a veneer of business textbooks and financial reports.

The sun began to fade, casting long shadows that danced upon the college's historic buildings, an atmospheric echo of the secretive darkness within Vander's own heart. Every casual conversation, every exchange, was to conceal his true self.

He spotted Christina. She sat on a bench, bathed in the dappled light that filtered through the leaves of a massive tree, engrossed in one of her textbooks, *Forensic Anthropology: Decoding the Secrets of the Dead*, next to the science hall.

Vander admired her single-minded dedication to the complex and often gritty world of forensics. Her quest to solve the mysteries of humanity's last physical remains was captivating. She was studying to become a crime scene investigator, a role that required the mental agility to piece together enigmatic puzzles.

Vander noticed how the pages of her textbook were filled with notes and highlighted texts, a clear indication of her immersion in the study. The intriguing world of forensic anthropology was more than an academic pursuit for Christina; it was a calling.

As she delved into her BA in criminal justice, she was not just learning about the theoretical aspects. Each crime scene, each piece of evidence, was a story waiting to be unraveled, a truth waiting to be unearthed. And in this somber dance between life and death, Christina found her passion, her purpose.

It was far more Christina's studies than her beauty that had drawn Vander to court her. Vander had found himself fascinated by the world of forensics for more reasons than one. From his early childhood, there had sprung up a curiosity of the macabre and thanks in part to Alexander's need to continue his deadly art projects, Vander had found it best to know where murder left off and the crime investigation began.

For obvious reasons, Vander knew he could not take those classes or show too much interest in the acts of murder or in the concealing of one. Though hard-pressed not to show too much interest, Vander knew from reading about other killers, that many of those who sought to elude the police believed they could do so by gaining an education in psychology, criminology, forensics, or some other form of police investigation.

However, their odd behavior, mixed with their overzealous desire to learn all they could about such things, most often led to their discovery and arrest.

So, instead, Vander gleaned the knowledge he needed by surrounding himself with the people who were in those fields of study, and who were driven to be the best in their class. Those in his close circle loved to talk about their studies and their findings, and it went a long way in helping him gain the knowledge he needed, all without suspicion.

Through the hushed whispers of the rustling leaves, Vander watched as Christina's eyes danced over each line in her book, her brows furrowed slightly as she pieced together the intricate web of knowledge that was forensic anthropology.

He could tell, with every page she turned, that her understanding of the relationship between skeletal remains and the untold stories of the deceased deepened, and her passion intensified. Her pursuit was not simply a journey toward a BA in criminal justice but an exploration into the abyss of death, a crusade for justice for those no longer able to speak for themselves.

Such was the life of a future crime scene investigator, a dance along the fine line between the living and the dead, between mystery and revelation. It was the path Christina had chosen and Vander knew she was destined to excel.

Without looking up, Christina laughed. "Are you going to come over here, or just lurk behind that tree?"

His smoky voice broke through the quiet dusk. "I don't know. Lurking has allowed me to gaze upon your beauty. However, I do so love talking with you. So, I'm torn..." Vander trailed off, his eyes glinting with a playful tease.

He navigated the labyrinth of wildflowers, the whisper of the evening breeze making them dance in his wake. His attraction to Christina was undeniable, a visceral pull that he couldn't ignore. His admiration for her was equally palpable—her keen intellect, her fiery spirit. As he moved closer, the shadows seemed to cling to him, wrapping around him like a cloak.

Setting her book aside, she looked up at him. "Well, when you put it like that, I suppose your actions aren't quite so creepy." The air around them thickened with anticipation. His gaze lingered on her, comfortable yet full of curiosity. He was intrigued, not only by her beauty but also by her wit. He reached out, his fingers brushed against hers as he leaned in, closed the distance between them, and kissed her.

Christina cupped her hand behind Vander's neck and pulled him closer. She returned his kiss with a soft kiss of her own, a silent affirmation of their shared attraction. The kiss was sweet and lingering, an intoxicated blend of teasing and warmth that left both wanting more. The comfortable silence between them stretched on, their shared moment a testament to a growing interest in one another.

Vander pulled away and grinned down at Christina. His eyes were full of unspoken regrets, a reflection of a life that bore the weight of choices he would never be free to make with her or anyone else. A shiver of sadness threaded itself into his smile, a grim reminder of his violent origins and the dark, treacherous path he now traversed with Alexander.

Despite the cheerful façade, he could not escape the feeling that his life was a ticking time bomb, ready to detonate at the slightest misstep. He feared that if Alexander thought he might have feelings for Christina, he might do her harm to exploit a perceived weakness.

His eyes lingered on Christina, drinking in her innocence, her unblemished joy that was so alien to him. The contrast between them was stark. As if they hailed from different worlds entirely. He was the storm; she was the sunshine. Amid the self-loathing, a small part of Vander could not help but marvel at the beauty of it all.

Yet, the bitter sting of reality was never far behind. He was a haunted man, chased by ghosts of his past, living in fear of the day they would emerge from the shadows and shatter the delicate peace he had managed to find. That fear was his constant companion, an unwelcome guest who refused to leave and cast a dark shadow that loomed over every moment with Christina.

Vander yearned for an alternate reality, a different path where he was not the embodiment of darkness wrapped in a human form. However, he knew that wishes were mere wisps of smoke, fleeting and unattainable.

He was trapped in the labyrinth of his past, and no matter how fervently he wished to escape, the echo of Alexander's twisted admiration was a constant reminder that his life was not his own. For her sake, Vander knew he had to keep his fears submerged, hidden beneath a façade of smiles and laughter.

The grim portrait of his own mortality was not something he could outrun or outsmart. It was a haunting prophecy, an echo in the dark that he could neither silence nor forget. The challenge now was not just to protect Christina, but to somehow confront, and ultimately change, a destiny of his death that seemed to be set in stone.

APRIL 30TH—11 DAYS

CHAPTER 12

RESEARCH

ALEXANDER

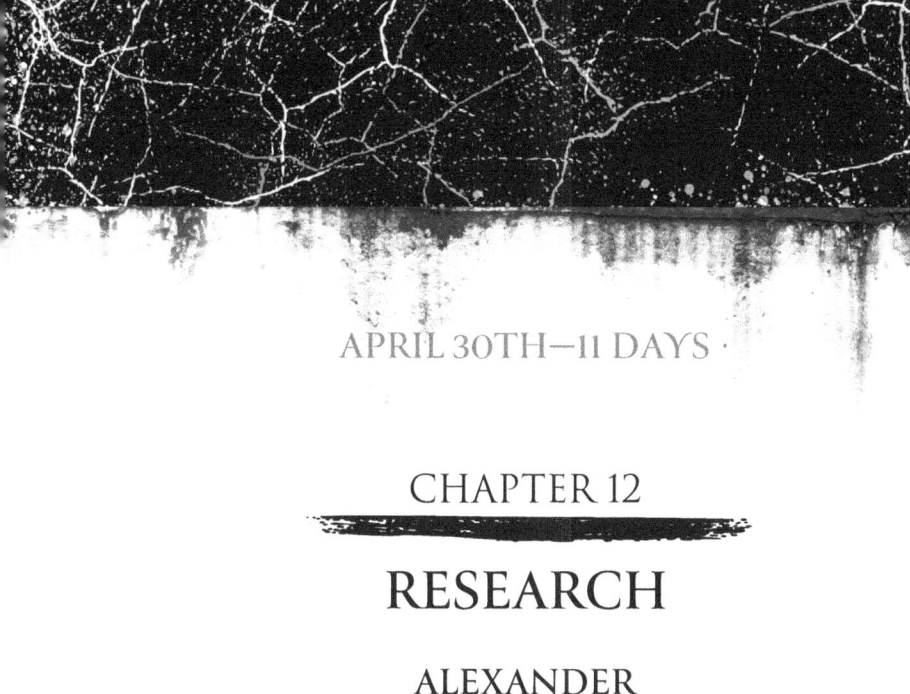

Virginia Beach, VA—Late Afternoon

After getting settled into his suite at the beautiful Cavalier in Virginia Beach, Alexander felt a rush of anticipation. His eyes were drawn to the churning waves outside the window, the storm seemed to echo the thoughts within his mind.

Ready to begin his tour, Alexander picked up the phone. Its cold, metallic tone contrasted sharply with the warmth of the room. He requested the concierge arrange transportation to his destination, the Edgar Cayce's A.R.E, Association for Research and Enlightenment, Foundation.

Alexander was resolute in his quest, convinced that he would find the answers he sought there. The murky mysteries that lay ahead did not deter him. On the contrary, they steeled his resolve. His journey had just begun, and he was determined to uncover the means to distract Vander, for Vander's own good as well as his own.

Most guests had already ventured out, more than likely, having gone to spend the day on the beach or touring the surrounding area. Alexander did not have to wait long for his driver. Within thirty minutes, he was seated comfortably in the back of the sedan and on his way.

Nestled in the heart of Virginia Beach, the journey to the Edgar Cayce's Foundation was beautiful. Established in 1931, the organization appeared as an amalgamation of the old and the new, a symbolic representation of the timeless wisdom it fosters. The facility stood with a determined stance, a beacon of research and enlightenment.

Its stone façade, weathered by years but resilient, exuded an atmosphere of solemnity, as though it whispered tales of the knowledge seekers who even now walked its halls and sought answers. The structure housed a labyrinth of rooms, each replete with vast archives of Edgar Cayce's readings and findings, a testament to the endless quest for understanding the human mind and spirit.

Stopping before the main building, the driver hopped out of the vehicle and held Alexander's door open. "Would you like me to wait for you, Sir?" he asked.

Not knowing how long it might take, but also aware that the hotel had little need of the driver for the next few hours, he said, "Yes, please. This should not take too long," as he got out.

"Very well, Sir." The driver closed the door behind Alexander.

Body still, Alexander looked up at the towering trees that surrounded the facility. Each stood as silent sentinels, their rustling leaves whispered tales of the countless seekers who had ventured to these mysterious halls in need of solace and enlightenment.

Alexander found himself enveloped by the chilling air as the limo drove away. Standing amidst the eerie silence was the enigmatic figure of Thomas Wellington, the staffer Alexander had talked with the prior evening before making his plans to visit that day. Wellington's presence was comforting, a beacon of familiarity in an otherwise alien setting.

Wellington, one of the more seasoned staffers, had extended a gracious offer to Alexander, a private tour of the premises. "Mr. Dayton, so good to have you here in Virginia."

"The pleasure is all mine, I can assure you." Alexander took Wellington's outstretched hand and shook it in greeting.

"May I show you around?" Wellington asked.

"You may indeed, Sir." Alexander tipped his hat to him as they started up the stairs.

As they toured the grounds, Wellington spoke of the true purpose of the foundation. The Edgar Cayce Foundation stood as a beacon of gracious enlightenment. Its primary purpose was to preserve, research, and facilitate access to Edgar Cayce's readings, health information, and related materials. The atmosphere resonated with intrigue and history.

Chapter 12 — Research

The air grew thick as shafts of muted sunlight seeped through the overhead panes and cast an ethereal glow on the rows upon rows of books, journals, and artifacts. Each item, a relic of research, a piece of the puzzle, curated meticulously by those determined to unravel the mysteries of existence, consciousness, and the universe itself.

With its unyielding pursuit of knowledge, the walls seemed to hum with the resonance of a million thoughts, each room charged with the palpable energy of unfolding enlightenment. A monument to Edgar Cayce's vision, the facility served in its unwavering commitment to understanding the world beyond what was seen.

Though all of it was indeed marvelous, especially for those who had all the time in the world to delve deeper into that mysterious realm, it would be a wonderful exploration, Alexander did not have the luxury of time and needed answers sooner rather than later. "Mr. Wellington, might I ask a question?"

"Of course." Wellington was eager to be of service.

"Would it be possible, here at the Institute, to help a gifted psychic learn to control and master their gifts?"

Wellington seemed puzzled by the question. "Of course, the foundation would be helpful to someone with paranormal gifts, with all of its resources, information, and classes... But it would take a lifetime, if ever, to master one's abilities."

"But you do have those who, perhaps, would be willing to take a novice under their wing and provide training?"

"A one-on-one teacher? No, I'm afraid not." Wellington offered Alexander an apologetic smile. "We do, however, have retreats and seminars, but no online training classes for groups."

Disappointed, Alexander could see that the foundation held a wealth of knowledge, a veritable trove of wisdom accrued over countless years. Such a repository should have been a treasure trove, a myriad of hidden insights waiting to be unearthed. Yet, it was as if he stood at the shore of an endless ocean of knowledge, armed with nothing more than a tarnished cup.

With a heavy sigh, Alexander turned away, his eyes lingered on the towering shelves one last time. The dust motes danced in the dim light, a visual depiction of the hopelessness that gnawed at him. The library, with its silent tomes and whispered mysteries, was no longer his sanctuary, but a mocking reminder of his predicament.

Brows furrowed at the thought of missing the opportunity to help fund the foundation, Wellington added, "But, if you, yourself were in need of a reading, or spiritual guidance, there are those of us who could provide that service," as he led him out of the building and back toward the parking lot and his waiting limousine.

A thought occurred to Alexander. He turned to Wellington. "I would not wish to put you out."

Eager to be of assistance, Wellington brightened. "No trouble at all. What might we do for you?"

"I would very much like a reading, but I want it from your best and brightest, if you would be so kind as to arrange it." Alexander might not have time himself to delve into this mystery, but perhaps one of those who had spent years working on their gifts might be of some assistance.

Proudly, Wellington puffed out his chest. "Of course, of course. We have many gifted members here. Would sometime this week suffice?"

Pondering, Alexander countered, "I'm afraid I'm only here for tonight."

"I'll get to work on an appointment right away," Wellington said, moving aside as the chauffeur went to open Alexander's door for him. "I'll call your hotel as soon as I have a time."

"Thank you." Alexander shook Wellington's hand, then sat down in the limo.

This was the world he had to navigate if he were to best Vander. A place far removed from the orderly chaos of the foundation's archives. In the depths of this urban jungle, he hoped to find an alternative, a clue, a lifeline that might pierce the fog of uncertainty. And so he ventured into the night, leaving the lifetime of information behind, armed with nothing but his determination and a daunting question still in need of answers.

APRIL 30TH—11 DAYS

CHAPTER 13

PARENTAL CONCERN

ETHAN

Austin, TX—Afternoon

ETHAN PUSHED OPEN THE HEAVY WOODEN DOOR AND WAS welcomed by a familiar, comforting silence. The exhaustion from a double shift, punctuated by an unexpected early morning emergency call, hung heavy on his shoulders, yet he found solace in the stillness that his home offered. Still alert from the adrenaline of the day's work as an EMT, he took off his muddy shoes and left them by the back door as he stepped over the threshold.

He was engulfed by a sense of gratitude, not only for the solace of his sanctuary but also for the loving family who filled it with warmth and understanding. Despite the harsh realities he faced daily, Ethan was always relieved, always happy, to return to this place. He reminded himself, despite the darkness of his work, he was grateful for the precious life it allowed him to appreciate.

Though he would love nothing better than to collapse into bed, the allure of seeing his wife Paige's radiant face acted as a powerful antidote to his exhaustion. Despite the grueling hours spent as an EMT, and the mental images of disaster and despair that often threatened to consume him, it was the thought of her that kept him grounded. Her beauty was not merely physical but emanated from the love and kindness she selflessly gave to everyone around her.

Making his way down the hallway to her home office, Ethan heard the faint traces of her calming voice as it emanated from inside the room. It was a soothing, rhythmic sound, a melodious hum that seeped through the closed door and filled the corridor with a serene aura. He paused and listened as the mellifluous tones washed over him.

Quietly, Ethan pushed open the door, the worn wood barely creaking under his touch. He leaned against the cool frame of the entryway; his silhouette distinguishable in the afternoon light that streamed in through a window at the far end of the hallway. His eyes, bright green pools that shone even brighter in the radiant sun, locked onto Paige.

Her face, illuminated by the soft glow of the computer screen, instantly lit up at the sight of him. As she concluded her online meeting, he waited, relishing the scene before him. Paige, his rock, was a steady anchor that held his world in place.

Ethan's heart warmed at Paige's smile, as the soft glow from her computer screen reflected off her hazel brown eyes. As she stood up from her chair, he moved toward her and took her into a gentle embrace, their bodies meeting in a tender dance of affection. Their lips met in a kiss, a sweet testament to their shared love. As they held each other in the silence of the room, the world outside ceased to exist, their love creating an energy so powerful that it filled the room.

Leaning back to look down at her, Ethan said, "Hi."

Resting her head against his broad shoulder, Paige sighed back, "Hi."

"How did your web-design meeting go?" he asked, his voice a hushed whisper. A sense of melancholic nostalgia enveloped the room, reflective of a time when their lives weren't so complicated. It was a moment suspended in time, an ephemeral snapshot of their relationship, a warmed heart in the gentle embrace of the past. A tender kiss of peace in the chaos, providing a sanctuary within each other's arms, a respite from the outside world.

Paige began to weave the tales of the day. "The company wants to reach out to more clients. They want to find ways to tap into a new customer base with their new fall lineup."

"Sounds easy enough," Ethan teased.

Paige punched him in the shoulder playfully. "You know it will be a nightmare."

"Yeah, but you can handle it. I have faith in you." Ethan kissed the top of her head, believing every word he said.

Chapter 13   *Parental Concern*

Hugging Paige, Ethan's gaze traveled to a drawing on the far corner of her desk. His heart clenched at the sight. It was unmistakably a creation of Hunter's, the unsteady lines and frenzied crayon strokes distinctly those of a five-year-old. Yet the imagery it depicted was far from innocent. There, in the riot of colors, was a disturbing drawing of a man wielding a gun, looming over what appeared to be a lifeless body. A chill crept up Ethan's spine, a sense of dread settling deep within him.

Ethan's entire body tensed up, an electric jolt of fear racing through his veins as he pulled away from Paige. The palpable dread cast a dark shadow over the room as Ethan snatched up the drawing, his grip tightened around the paper, knuckles turning white, as he turned to his wife. "What is this?"

Paige reached out, her hands gently removing the drawing. She began to fold it; the paper emitted a crisp sound. "Ethan, it's nothing," she cooed, trying to infuse a sense of normalcy into the chilling atmosphere.

However, the haunting image etched on the paper stayed embedded in Ethan's mind. He grappled with the daunting possibility of Hunter inheriting his mother's psychic ability. "Are you having those same visions?"

Mouth working, Paige tried to speak but could not find the words.

Gently, Ethan took Paige by both of her arms and peered into her eyes. "Paige, if you feel like you're in danger, you have to tell me, okay?"

Resting a soothing hand on Ethan's arm, Paige began, her voice shaky, "Ethan, we're fine. It's just… it's just a drawing." Paige offered him a pained smile. "You know how kids are. They get carried away with stories of their action heroes."

Ethan nodded, desperate to believe her, but he could not shake the nagging doubt that ate at his guts. "You sure? I don't want you to keep things from me, just because I don't understand—"

Paige cut him off with a quick kiss, then she pulled back, her smile bright once more as she said, "Brayden managed to show up early and get the kids to school on time for a change… without the light and sirens."

A sense of relief seeped through Ethan at the image of his children safe with their Uncle Brayden. "That's a miracle." Ethan laughed as the heavy blanket of exhaustion began to creep up on him, zapping his strength with each passing moment.

"Ethan, you're exhausted. Why don't you get some sleep before the kids get home?" Sensing his struggle, Paige guided him through the silent corridor that led to their room. Her voice, a soothing balm.

With a resigned sigh, Ethan lay down, allowed Paige to cover him up with a blanket she had grabbed from a nearby chair, and gave in to the beckoning darkness.

CHAPTER 14

NEW CASE

BRAYDEN JAMES

Austin, TX—Late Afternoon

The Austin Police Department, a fortress of law and order in the heart of the city, emanated a commanding presence. Its stark architecture contrasted the rest of Austin's vibrant cityscape.

Inside, the air was heavy with anticipation, an ever-present undercurrent of unease. Officers, lost in thought, moved through the hallways, their minds focused on files, their spirits restless, their gazes hardened by years of experience. The station served as a stark reminder of the thin line that must not be crossed, otherwise there would be a high price to pay.

At the department's nerve center sat a command room, a low, incessant hum of activity pervaded from it. Screens flickered with the rhythmic pulse of the city's life, each pixel representing another crime riddle to be solved. There were numerous maps adorned with shifting symbols and figures that tracked pathways through the city streets.

Officers pored over case files, their minds adrift, as the room shifted with a sense of grim determination.

Lost in the labyrinth of facts hidden within his case files, Brayden's world shrank to the confines of his desk; the hum of the precinct long faded into a distant murmur.

A harsh thud startled Brayden as Lozano unceremoniously plopped yet another heavy folder onto his already cluttered desk, sending a reverberated thud in the small space. "Bohannon wants to see us."

Brayden's eyes wandered to the colossal clock on the distant wall, and a groan escaped him.

Juan leaned nonchalantly against the wall. "What's the matter? Got a hot date?" His words dripped with mirth.

Brayden cut Lozano a hard look, then sighed with heavy resignation. "No need to be a smart ass," he grumbled and got to his feet. "Let's just get this done and over with."

As they made their way down the corridor, Brayden felt a knot of tension tightening in his shoulders. If his captain was calling them in this late, it had to be important, and he did not want to have to call and cancel his first date with Alayna. Taking a deep breath to steel himself, Brayden pushed open the heavy door and ushered Juan and himself inside.

Looking up at him, Bohannon, his commander and chief, sat behind a large, imposing desk. Brayden looked down at the cluttered workspace of strewn papers, cold coffee cups, and a relic phone that seemed just as frustrated to be there as its owner was. "Close the door behind you and take a seat." Bohannon's voice was laced with a mix of frustration and resignation.

The door groaned shut behind Brayden, the noise a low, irritating rumble. Juan took a seat, and Brayden shuffled toward the vacant one beside his partner.

Leaning back in his seat, Bohannon tossed a new folder onto the desk before the detectives.

"Ever heard of Jasmine Lam?" Bohannon questioned.

Jasmine Lam. Brayden knew she was a renowned artist who was mastering the art of blending contemporary with abstract in a manner that made the Austin art scene shudder with anticipation for her next piece.

Tired of waiting for a response, Bohannon chimed in. "She's an up-and-coming artist, the new darling of Austin." Brayden's mind was instantly transported back to the exhibit he had attended with his sister Paige a few weeks ago. Not that he would disclose it to anyone, but Brayden held a secret fondness for the language of colors and shapes, otherwise known as art.

Picking up the folder, Brayden opened it and peered inside. "I do know about her; I went to one of her exhibits last month."

Chapter 14 New Case

Captivated, Brayden studied the photo. The wild, untamed streaks of color that adorned the artist's hair were a juxtaposition to her piercing blue-gray eyes. He could almost see the creative fire within them, the same spark that had birthed countless pieces of renowned art. "What are we looking at here?" Brayden asked.

"As of seven a.m., Jasmine Lam will have been missing for forty-eight hours, which means, if we don't get a call from someone letting us know she has been found, she will be considered a missing person." Bohannon ran a beefy hand down his weary face. "And will become your problem."

"So, why are you giving this to us tonight?" Brayden asked. "Is it because she is a high-profile individual?"

"That, and I've got over a dozen of her people breathing down my neck."

Juan piped in. "Has she done a vanishing act before? I mean, maybe she just needed some space and didn't want to tell anyone where she was going."

"Possible sure," Bohannan agreed. "But, according to her girlfriend, brother, and the curator at the museum, that is highly unlikely."

Looking up, Brayden asked, "Was she seen leaving with anyone? Are there any possible leads?"

Slapping both hands on his desk, Bohannan got to his feet. "Gentlemen, you know what I know." Brayden could tell that the conversation was over. "Everything I have is in that file, the names and numbers of those who have contacted me. If you want to get started on the case tonight, I wouldn't say no."

With a curt nod, Bohannon sent Brayden and Juan packing. His eyes had already glinted back to stare at his monitor as he dove back into his work.

Quietly, Juan and Brayden left the office and closed the door behind them. Their footsteps echoed ominously in the hallway as they retreated to their individual desks, just a few feet apart.

With a wicked grin, Brayden slapped the new case file against Juan's chest.

"No," Juan responded, his eyes widened, caught off guard by the weight of the file that dropped into his hands.

Brayden's laughter pierced the heavy silence. "You owe me," he stated, his smile reaching his eyes. "Tomorrow I'll bring coffee and breakfast and you can fill me in on our way to our first interview."

Dark Variations

Grabbing his jacket off the back of his chair, Brayden hurried out the door.

"Damn it," Juan cursed as he wandered toward the break room to grab some coffee.

The night air welcomed Brayden as he rushed outside the station and sprinted to his Mustang. He was looking forward to this date, even more than he had anticipated. For some reason, he found himself inexplicably drawn to Alayna, intrigued by her mysterious presence.

Firing up the engine, Brayden grinned. The rumble of the engine echoed through the deserted parking lot, a symphony of power and precision that added a thrilling undertone to his excitement as he set course for Alayna's antique shop.

CHAPTER 15

FLAWED REASONING

VANDER

Fitler, PA—Evening

HAVING COMPLETED HIS LAST CLASS OF THE DAY, VANDER once again decided to walk back to the quiet townhome. The sun had slipped beneath the horizon, casting long shadows that danced mystically across the silent streets. His heart fell in sync with the rhythmic echoes of his footsteps, a stark reminder of the bonded companionship and shared experiences with Alexander that had spanned nearly two decades.

The memories, both vibrant and haunting, ebbed and flowed like a relentless sea. Yet, amidst the familiarity of nostalgia, a sense of foreboding clung to him.

His earlier interaction with Christina had drawn him back into the labyrinth of his past, a path painted with sacrifices that seemed to bleed onto the canvas of his memories. True, Alexander had been his savior, a beacon in the obsidian darkness that had been his life, but Vander had saved him many times as well over the years. They had forged a bond through the fire of adversities, saved each other from the gnashing jaws of fate, and in the process, they had indelibly shaped one another's destiny.

In the beginning, Alexander had been the one who had sheltered Vander, had helped him navigate the hidden dangers within the sophistication of this new world. It was true that Alexander had saved him from many untold missteps and imparted survival skills and the intricate subtleties of refined living.

Time, however, had also begun to eat away at Alexander, manifesting in weakened health and miss-steps regarding the stirrings of his dark nature. Vander's mentor had become careless and now made mistakes where before there had been none. Vander had been able to cover up those errors. He had done things that he feared would implicate him as well should they ever be discovered, but he had done so out of respect for Alexander.

Alexander was changing. Vander could feel it in every word, see it in every glance. He had been given a second chance in this new world and Alexander had been the one to provide it. Now, as he watched his mentor teeter on a precipice between safety and unknowable danger, Vander felt an urge to help him, just as Alexander had helped him in the past.

Vander's apprehensions revolved primarily around Alexander's more menacing aspects. These rare, yet potent, instances when his mentor would acquiesce to the inner demons that patiently bided their time. The dread figure the authorities had dubbed the Sculptor lurked within his shadow, an abhorrent beast that preyed on those who outshone their contemporaries, individuals destined for greatness, whom he ruthlessly sacrificed to his twisted whims.

These victims were not merely killed; they were sculpted through his perverse artistry, their mortal remains converted into macabre masterpieces, exhibited, and stripped bare to the world's horrified gaze.

Vander held a deep affection for Alexander. His feelings were profound, palpable, woven into the very fabric of his being. It was this respect that served as the catalyst for Vander's actions that would be unthinkable for most. In the past few years, Vander had found himself immersed in a world of deception and manipulation, using his dark gifts to cover up the mistakes that Alexander had begun to make as he aged.

It was Vander who had ensured that Alexander's miscalculations had not led the authorities to their door, nor to threaten the illusion of the virtuous life Alexander had worked so tirelessly to build.

In the corners of his consciousness, Vander dared to nurture the fragile seed of hope. Was it naivety or a desperate longing for a father's love that made him hope Alexander could care for him more as a son than as a work of art?

Chapter 15 *Flawed Reasoning*

Vander's thoughts had gnawed at him throughout his entire journey home, and he found himself standing beneath the steps that led to the townhome. The light from the doorway cast a warm glow on Vander's face, giving him some comfort in the darkness.

Vander took a deep breath as he ascended the steps, opened the door, and stepped inside.

The silence hung in the air like a discernible entity, making Vander shudder. An aromatic scent enveloped him, akin to a welcoming embrace, a far cry from the cold indifference of the stony silence. "Alexander?" he echoed into the void; his voice swallowed by the vast emptiness of the massive townhome. His only response was the symphony of kitchenware emanating from the heart of the house.

As Vander pushed the kitchen door open, he found Philip orchestrating a symphony of items over the stove, spatula in hand. The cook offered him a smile when he spotted him in the doorway.

"Why, hello Vander," Philip said. The chef bustled around the kitchen amongst clattering pots and pans. "Will any of your friends be joining us for dinner this evening?" Philip asked.

Seeing that Philip had made more than enough food for ten people, Vander reluctantly replied, "Sorry, no." Looking about the room, Vander asked, "Where is Alexander?"

Disappointed, Philip answered, "He had to leave for an unexpected business trip."

Alarm bells sounded in Vander's head. Forcing a smile, Vander asked, "Did he say how long he would be gone?"

Philip assured him, "It should only be for a day or so. Otherwise, Alexander would have instructed me to follow, bringing my culinary skills with me." Philip turned back to his meal prep.

A thought occurred to Vander. Ever since Alexander had brought him home from Africa, Philip and his driver, Thomas, who also acted as Alexander's butler and bodyguard, had been akin to Alexander's shadow. Even when they had gone on vacation, Alexander had insisted that the talented chef be in residence.

"Philip, how long have you and Thomas been with Alexander?" Vander asked.

Pausing in his slicing, Philip thought for a moment, then turned to him. "Going on thirty years now, I suppose."

Vander added, "And you and Thomas have always traveled with him?"

Proudly, Philip answered, "I dare say we have. Your guardian cannot live without us, it would seem."

There were two men who had lived with and accompanied Alexander to multiple cities, on multiple continents, and who still had no idea of the man's true nature.

Vander felt as if the floor had opened beneath him. There would be no resolution that night, and with every passing moment, it seemed more and more likely that his future, if left to Alexander, more likely than not would end with his demise.

Since he could not speak with Alexander, perhaps he could get the answers he needed from another one of his oldest friends. Dinner would have to wait. Vander had more pressing issues to attend to. "Philip, I apologize. I just remembered that I have somewhere I must be."

Without waiting for Philip's protest, Vander slipped out of the kitchen and headed for the door. He would find some place safe, somewhere quiet, to leave his body while his spirit journeyed to the other side of the veil to see Jack.

CHAPTER 16

NIGHTMARISH

ETHAN

Austin, TX—Evening

TRAPPED IN THE GRIP OF A HORRIFIC NIGHTMARE, ETHAN searched for his small son, Hunter. Sweat dotted his brow as his mouth worked in inaudible words that emerged from his strained throat as nothing more than tortured groans. *Frantically, Ethan searched through a large, faceless crowd, desperate to locate his five-year-old boy.*

In the dream, dread washed over Ethan as his shouts and cries for his son went unanswered. The blank faces of the crowd stayed fixed, their forward march a sign of their oblivion to Ethan's dilemma. Panic built with each second that passed. Ethan shoved and pushed through the hoard as he fought to reach the end of the mass that pressed in about him.

Time was about to run out, Ethan could feel it. Then, the sky began to snow; thin sheets of paper drifted from the heavy gray clouds above. Their crisp white sheets, covered in colorful crayon strokes, floated to the earth in a massive swirl like freakish snowflakes cascading out of a winter storm.

Ethan's heart sank as he reached out and snatched one of the papers from the air before him. It was a child's creation on the crumpled sheet. It bore the image of a knife-wielding man who stood before a frightened little boy. Above the child's head was a speech bubble that read, "Daddy, Daddy help me!" Ethan's hands trembled as his eyes fixed on the image.

Forcing air past the lump in his throat, Ethan called out, "Hunter?! Hunter?!! Where are you, son?!!!"

Forcefully, Ethan shoved his way through the oppressive crowd. He pushed past anyone standing in his way. The crowd mumbled and muffled through the thick skin that covered the space where mouths should have been, as eyeless faces turned toward him as if in protest. Above the indistinguishable murmur, Ethan heard the soft, comforting cadence of Paige's voice.

The comforting sound sought to bring him back somewhere, away from his desperate search, so Ethan resisted the call and allowed the churning panic to wash over him. He would not succumb to peace until he found his child and held him safely in his arms.

The outlines of unfamiliar faces swam before him and blurred into a monochromatic haze as he fought his way forward. His vision narrowed. The noises around him faded as Paige's voice pierced through the sonic wall. Ethan felt himself being drawn backward and away from Hunter. He could see him standing just at the front of the crowd. He had to reach him, or he would be lost to him forever.

Fear took hold as Ethan's heart pounded in his chest. Sweat dotted his brow, each drop a testament to the terror that now consumed him. Paige's voice grew louder in his ears as he tried to call out to his child, but found the words would not come.

Then, from behind him, Ethan heard a chilling symphony of twisted metal and shattered glass. He turned to find the crowd gone, the remnants of a horrific auto accident strewn across a ravaged highway. A tiny hand reached out of the mangled steel, bloodied and torn. "Daddy?" Hunter's frail voice called out to him.

With the path before him now clear, Ethan ran to the vehicle and slid to a kneeling stop before it. His trembling fingers brushed against the cold, deformed metal of the car door. A chill spread through him like wildfire. Behind him, unseen, Paige's voice grew louder. Her desperate cries pierced the sound of metal scrapping against stone, like an arrow, exacerbating the torment that gnawed at his soul.

Ethan knew he had to free Hunter from the pile of shattered glass and crumpled steel. He needed to find a way past the wreckage to reach his child. Without warning, the engine ignited, bursting into flames and filling the car with thick, rolling smoke. Ethan reached for Hunter's hand to just watch it disappear back inside the thick gray plums. "Hunter!"

Chapter 16   Nightmarish

Ethan found his voice. The desperation and volume of it startled him awake as he sat up in bed, drenched in sweat.

Heart pounding in his chest, Ethan fought for breath as the ghostly vestiges of the nightmare clung to him, the sensation of being pulled from his nightmare was so palpable he could still feel the heat from the fire, the sting in his lungs from the smoke.

Hands on either side of his face, Paige sat before him, her eyes searching his frantic ones. Ethan's heart rate slowed; the terror of the nightmare began to recede like a wave pulling away from the shore. Paige's face, beautiful and calm, was a beacon in the dark, a lighthouse that guided him back to reality. "Honey, it was only a dream," he heard her say, her voice a soothing melody that washed over him. "You're here, with me," she continued, each word a thread that reassured him.

The nightmare was over, but the fear of losing his son still gnawed at his conscious mind. "Where's Hunter? Is he..."

"Hunter's fine. He is downstairs in the living room playing with Zoey," she declared. Reassured, Ethan enveloped his beloved wife in his protective embrace, holding her close, trying to absorb the tranquility she exuded. The room, though physically unchanged, seemed to brighten.

After a few silent moments, Paige gently extricated herself from Ethan's arms. Her hand, tender and reassuring, caressed his cheek as she cast him an encouraging smile. "Want to talk about it?"

Ethan shook his head no, not wanting to relive the horrific dream.

"Then why don't you come down and join us for dinner?" she invited as she rose from the bed and stood before him. In her words, there was a promise of the familiar and comfort.

Ethan nodded in agreement. "Sure thing, just give me a minute," he replied, feeling the need to pull himself together.

Paige stepped back, a smile of understanding still gracing her lips. "Take your time," she said, and with that, she left him alone in the room.

Ethan watched as the door closed with a soft click behind Paige, the dim light from the hallway spilling into the room for a fleeting moment before plunging it back into shadow. He steeled himself, then threw back the covers and got out of bed and made his way to the bathroom. There, he gazed into the mirror with a resolute smile. The reflection mirrored the strength he found in the thought of his amazing family waiting beyond those walls. His nightmare became a distant memory, a specter banished by the promise of a warm evening to be spent with his family.

Splashing water on his face, Ethan drew in a few more deep breaths and dried his face and hands, then switched the light off as he headed downstairs.

The laughter that flowed from the living room was a melody to Ethan's ears. As he descended the stairs, he could not help but smile at the teasing banter that floated up to him.

It was clear that Paige had given her children instructions to set the table, and both were making a compelling argument as to why they should not be the ones to leave the kitchen for that menial task. Hunter seemed to be winning, his youthful charm too good for even his sister to resist. Ethan could only shake his head in amusement at the idea of Hunter one day representing a debate team, it was obvious that the boy was a natural. He had a way of almost always winning any argument.

As Ethan stepped into the brightly lit kitchen, happiness seemed to dance within the room. His voice playful, he asked, "Hey, who wants to help me set the table?" Laughter, the kind that only young children possess, filled the space as Zoey and Hunter, their faces illuminated, sprang from their perches on the kitchen counter, their voices intertwining in a chorus of youthful competition. "I will, I will!" It appeared that they had just needed a little encouragement to change their minds.

"Great, let's get started," Ethan ordered, his voice filled with a soft but unmistakable resonance of sweet affection. As he watched Hunter and Zoey scramble to carry out their duties. Ethan made his way over to Paige, wrapped his arms around her waist, and kissed her on the cheek. His hands, still lingering on Paige's waist, tightened ever so slightly. A mischievous smile lurked at the corners of his mouth. "What's my reward for getting the kids to do their chore?" he whispered into Paige's ear.

Paige giggled, her eyes sparkling. "Dinner," she replied cheerfully. Shifting in Ethan's embrace, she returned his smile and winked playfully. "And maybe some dessert afterward if you behave yourself."

The two of them stood in silent accord as their children finished preparing the table, enjoying this shared moment amidst the hustle and bustle.

As the echoes of their jubilant declaration, "We did it!" filled the room, Hunter and Zoey ceased their spirited scampering. They stood still, their young faces glowing with pride, their eyes gleaming with shared accomplishment.

Chapter 16   Nightmarish

Ethan walked over to the doorway and looked down at their work. It appeared a detail had been overlooked. There were only four settings instead of the usual five. "Didn't you miss a plate?" Ethan asked.

The response was a chorus of childish giggles as Paige joined them, her lips curled into a knowing smirk. "Brayden won't be joining us this evening. He's busy elsewhere."

CHAPTER 17

YOU'RE GOING WHERE?

ALAYNA

Austin, TX—Night

HANNAH STARED AT HER, EYES WIDE, WITH A SENSE OF incredulity coloring her voice. "You're not serious?" she asked, her words cutting through the thick atmosphere of the room. "Peach Bar? With a man like that?" Her tone was laced with stunned disbelief, her gaze unwavering as she waited for Alayna's response. "With all the places in Austin, a place seeped in history, luxury, and considered 'Land of the Foodies,' you suggested Peach Bar! That's laughable, well actually, it's sad."

Alayna looked at Hannah with a cryptic smile. "I have my reasons for picking that spot."

"This I got to hear?" Plopping down in a chair, Hannah crossed her arms and legs, ready to listen to Alayna's sure-to-disappoint explanation.

Alayna cleared her throat. "For one, if Brayden was one of those guys who just wanted to show off, he would have balked at the idea, which would have shown me he was probably a jerk, and I would not have bothered to waste my time going out with him."

Alayna swept a glance over to Hannah. Her friend's face held a look of puzzled amusement, the corners of her eyes crinkling in a way that screamed incomprehension. "Hannah," Alayna began. "Hang in here. I have a method to my madness." Alayna continued with her explanation, "Two, Peach Bar happens to be one of my hang-out spots, a place where

Chapter 17 — You're Going Where?

I will have friends who will step in if this oh-so-hot detective gets out of line."

In the well-lit, down-to-earth sanctuary of the Peach Bar, Alayna knew she would never be alone. The place was a rare gem in the tempestuous city. It had a charm that lured you into its warm and whimsical atmosphere. Her allies not only lurked behind the bar, as waitresses and patrons, but she also knew several members of the band who often played there on the weekends.

If, for any reason, the detective, with his smoldering gaze and polished badge, was not everything he said he was, she would be safe there. It was the perfect place to get to know someone better without putting herself at risk.

"Three, I wanted to be sensitive to his salary. You know cops don't make great money," Alayna reasoned. "And if our first date goes well, I would like him to be able to afford a second date, in case he's the type who won't let a lady pay for a night out."

Satisfied, Hannah nodded. "Okay, that all seems fair, but don't you think you're being a little overly cautious?"

The tiny bell above the shop door sounded as Brayden stepped inside. His hair, black as a moonless night, lay neatly against his forehead and accentuated his dark, hazel-brown eyes. His attire was far from ostentatious. Dressed in a simple yet sharp ensemble, he exuded an air of understated elegance. In a casual button-down shirt paired with well-fitted dark jeans, his outfit was as captivating as the man himself, perfectly suited for a casual evening out.

Alayna had to resist the urge to lick her lips. Brayden's presence was magnetizing, a dark star in a universe of ordinary, pulling all attention unwittingly toward him. His eyes twinkled with an unspoken promise in the dim light, which only added to the mysterious allure of the evening.

Brayden strolled over to them as if he had not a care in the world, then offered her a bouquet of fresh-cut flowers. *The detective is an old soul*, Alayna thought as she took a moment to admire the flowers before taking them from him. "They're beautiful. Thank you, Brayden." Alayna grabbed a nearby vase, carefully arranging them to suit her, then passed the arrangement to Hannah. "Would you mind adding some water to these?"

Happy for Alayna, Hannah took the flower arrangement, gave her a quick wink, then backed away with a smile. "Sure thing, Boss."

Gently, Alayna took Brayden's arm and steered him toward the door.

Grabbing the door with his free hand, Brayden held it open for Alayna and ushered her outside. "After you, Beautiful." The night was just beginning, and Alayna was already very happy about her decision to give the detective a chance.

As they stepped out into the night air, the stars glimmered above them like flickering, white fireflies, and the nearly full moon guided them as they made their way down the cobblestone streets. Everything around them was alive with energy and excitement, setting the stage for a perfect night.

CHAPTER 18

CLEVER

BRAYDEN JAMES

Austin, TX—Night

STEPPING INSIDE THE **P**EACH **B**AR, **B**RAYDEN TOOK NOTE of the ambiance. It was a mix of modern and rustic, with cozy indoor seating alongside a picturesque outdoor patio, ideal for social gatherings or intimate dining.

Located in the heart of Austin, the hangout was a vibrant and inviting establishment that melded the warmth of Southern hospitality with an Asian-inspired menu. It was nestled in the heart of the city and offered a unique dining experience for locals and tourists alike. With its eclectic menu that included a fusion of American and Asian cuisines and innovative cocktails, it had an unmatched vibe there in the city.

Like a hawk, Brayden observed their surroundings and missed nothing. He could see the subtle recognition in the eyes of the quiet, weathered faces that peered at them from the dimly lit corners of Peach Bar.

There was a hint of familiarity in their gaze, a spark of recognition when they looked at Alayna. He had seen the fleeting smiles she exchanged, the non-verbal cues that told a story of hidden relationships and secret histories. This was her world, and she felt comfortable in it, which made Brayden happy. He wanted Alayna to be at ease with him and to enjoy their time together.

With a knowing smile, Brayden eyed Alayna. "So," he began, raising his voice to be heard over the crowd. "Tell me, is the Taiwanese duck really that good... or was there more to this choice of fine dining establishments?"

Unashamed, Alayna flashed him a sexy smile. "What can I say?" she purred, her voice low. "It's a culinary delight." Alayna played with her drink before meeting his gaze. "And I just so happen to know a few of the people who frequent the place."

Leaning back in the booth, Brayden smiled. "I appreciate your caution."

"Really?" Alayna asked.

"Sure, even I call for backup when entering an unknown situation." Brayden took another sip of his drink, happy to put her mind at ease.

Alayna laughed in response. "Well, good. I'm glad you understand, because in today's world, a girl can't be too careful."

Leaning forward and taking her hand, Brayden caressed it with his thumb. "No, she can't because there are a lot of dangerous people out there."

Raising an eyebrow, Alayna looked down at their touching hands. "Speaking of dangerous people, and danger in general, I have a few questions for you."

Without relinquishing her hand, Brayden sat back. "Fire away." He kept his body a picture of open relaxation and his gaze held with hers.

A mischievous smirk tugged at Alayna's lips. "All right then," she began, her voice a murmur in the hush of the room, carrying the promise of open, honest communication. "Let's start with something simple. What's your favorite color?" The question echoed in the space between them, an invitation to a deeper understanding.

Brayden paused, then said, "Easy enough... purple."

"Interesting," Alayna continued, her voice a soft whisper against the weighty silence. Her figure was silhouetted against the dim light filtering through the curtains, casting an ethereal glow around her.

"Something you're afraid of?" Alayna asked.

Brayden thought for a moment, then laughed. "Butterflies," he answered.

Taken back, Alayna stammered, "Butterflies?" Unable to contain her laughter, Alayna teased. "And what, pray tell, makes you afraid of those harmless creatures?"

It made Brayden happy to see her laugh, even if it was at his expense. Trying his best to maintain a solemn expression, he added, "I know. It's

Chapter 18 Clever

sad, but they freak me out. Think about it for a minute. Those bugs are nothing more than worms with wings!"

Laughing, Alayna wrapped her shawl tighter around her shoulders. Her eyes twinkled with an expression of utter delight, a thing of beauty in the dim glow of the candlelight that danced from a small votive on their table.

Sobering, Alayna pulled her hand away, then took his hand into both of hers. "What if I were to tell you that they were harmless... that they were more afraid of you than you are of them?"

Enjoying the warmth of her hands as they held his, Brayden allowed himself to look vulnerable. "I don't know. They can be pretty scary."

"What if I could help you create a more positive memory involving those tiny creatures?" Alayna asked.

Interest puiqed, Brayden said, "I'm listening."

Playfully, Alayna caressed Brayden's outstretched hand as she said softly, "We could go south, to the forested Central Highlands of Mexico."

"I'm liking this idea so far." Brayden grinned.

"We would fly down during the migration of the monarch butterflies."

Brayden's eyes widened, his head shaking with a no, but before he could utter the words, Alayna tugged on his hand, drawing him closer as she smiled up at him. "Once there, we would step into a timeless waltz choreographed by nature itself. The air would be thick with mystery and anticipation, as we joined the canvas painted with the flutters of countless delicate wings."

Mesmerized, Brayden hung on Alayna's every word.

Breathless, she continued, "The world around us would fade into a hushed whisper, the only sound, the beating of our hearts and the soft rustle of the monarchs who had taken flight.

"We would be a part of the beautiful and spectral. It would be like nothing you've ever seen. Being there, together, amplified by the magic of each butterfly and their shared whispers and unspoken secrets. The forest, dark and enigmatic, contrasted against the subtle brilliance of the butterflies, a journey both intoxicating and unforgettable."

Breaking the spell, Alayna released his hand and smiled up at him. "And I promise, you won't have to call for backup, because I will be there to protect you."

Oblivious to the mounting sexual tension that simmered between Brayden and Alayna, the waiter unceremoniously plopped down their Taiwanese duck roll. The abrupt clatter of plates against the wooden table echoed, disrupting their intimate bubble. Brayden and Alayna exchanged glances and suddenly burst into laughter.

His voice gruff, the waiter asked, "You guys need anything else?"

Amused, Brayden and Alayna both shook their heads no while they fought to contain their laughter. The waiter stood there and glared down at Brayden expectantly. Brayden piped in. "No, man, we're good!"

Lip curled into a partial snarl; the waiter huffed and moved along.

Bemused, Brayden shrugged. "Did I miss something?" he asked Alayna.

Laughing, she scooped up part of their shared meal and prepared to take a bite. "Bart doesn't do body language; he likes verbal confirmation."

Smiling, Brayden looked up at her. "A little warning next time would be appreciated."

"Duly noted," Alayna said and handed Brayden one of the plates. "Now, dig in."

Not having eaten since the light breakfast he had eaten at his sister Paige's house early that morning, Brayden was famished. His mouth watered from the smell of the rich and savory aromas that wafted up from the large plate Bart had sat before them.

Alayna put a healthy portion of the roll on his plate, and he happily took a large bit. The flavors were amazing. Alayna was right. It was the best duck roll he had ever tasted. The fresh, crisp scallions and cucumber that served as a side were also tasty and were great for a contrasting crunch.

All too soon, dinner was complete, and it was time to leave their quaint little booth at the restaurant. The evening had been amazing; the mundane transformed into the memorable, all under the watchful eyes of Bart, the waiter.

The early evening painted West 6th Street in hues of dimmed orange and shadowy purple and cast a mysterious yet comforting glow on the quaint urban landscape. As Brayden and Alayna wove through the labyrinth of cobblestone streets, the low hum of city life surrounded them.

Their laughter, light yet hearty, tangled with the crisp air, dispelling the gloom that clung to the narrow, historical alleyways. Each shared story and quiet reflection deepened their connection, as they reveled in the simple pleasure of each other's company.

Brayden leaned in, eager and curious to unravel the enigma that was Alayna. He said in a low, steady voice, "Okay, now that you know everything there is to know about me... my work, my interests, even my

Chapter 18   Clever

irrational fear of butterflies... it's your turn." Brayden stopped and waited beneath the glow of one of the signs.

"I would like to know about all things Alayna?" A smile played on his lips as he watched her reaction in the enveloping darkness. "And don't tell me that there's nothing to know, because from where I'm standing, I can see that we haven't even begun to scratch the surface."

Clicking the unlock button on his fob, Brayden unlocked the door. Worried, he watched as her smile faded and her trembling hand reached for the cold, metallic handle of his car door. Without an answer, Alayna slipped into the cold, dark sanctuary of the vehicle and left him standing like a statue on the street, engulfed in uncertainty.

Brayden felt his heart pounding as he replayed their conversation in his mind. They had enjoyed each other's company, filled the air with laughter, and shared glances that seemed to say more than words ever could. Yet, the moment he tried to probe deeper, to understand her better, he was met with a wall of resistance.

Her lack of response left him curious and somewhat unsettled. He wanted to get to know her, to unravel the mystery that was Alayna. He couldn't help but be interested in every little thing about her, from her playful smile to her guarded eyes. *What could she be concealing?* Brayden wondered.

Getting into the car, Brayden put the key in the ignition and started the vehicle.

As the sinewy tendrils of engine noise filled the silence, Brayden and Alayna settled into the worn leather seats, their bodies subtly reacting to the familiar hum of the vehicle. Their time together had been filled with laughter and companionship, a testament to the comfort they found in each other's company.

Brayden was curious, his eyes reflecting a quiet concern as he glanced at Alayna. He wanted to know what caused the flicker of unease in her eyes; an unease that was oddly discordant against the backdrop of their earlier light-hearted banter. "Did I say something wrong?"

With a smile that did not quite make it to her eyes, Alayna said, "No, no, you didn't do anything, it's just..." She hesitated.

Suddenly, the shrill ring of his cell phone sliced through the tapestry of silence. The luminous screen displayed Juan's number, instantly putting Brayden on edge. Juan's calls were never a harbinger of good news, always bearing the weight of problems and concerns that needed to be resolved. Besides, Juan would not have bothered him that night unless it was important.

"I'm so sorry, I have to take this," he said. In the rearview mirror, the city lights danced like flickering firelight. "Detective Brayden."

Juan's voice crackled over the phone. "Hey Partner, sorry to bother you, but it's important."

Jaw tight, Brayden kept his eyes on the road, instinctively steering his vehicle toward Alayna's shop. "Define important," Brayden replied.

Without hesitation, Juan jumped into his narrative. "Our missing person just turned up dead, as in, murdered in an extremely gruesome way, dead. The chief wants us on scene ASAP."

Brayden felt a cold shiver run down his spine. Juan's words echoed in his mind, bouncing off each other to create a grim chorus. *Dead. Jasmine Lam, our missing person, is dead before we even had a chance to begin the search for her.* The chilling finality of it all was a gut punch to Brayden. "I can be back at the station in twenty to pick you up."

The knuckles on Brayden's right hand turned white against the steering wheel, matching the stark pallor of his face under the harsh glare of the dashboard lights.

"I'll let Bohannon know you're on your way." The line went silent as Brayden hung up his cell phone and returned it to his pocket.

As if from a distance, Brayden heard Alayna ask, "Brayden, you, okay? "

He was anything but okay. The news he had received had rendered him speechless. Their missing person had been found, but not as they had hoped. The harsh reality crashed down upon him. Jasmine Lam had been murdered, reduced to a cold, lifeless figure at the hands of an unseen menace. "I'm good," he answered, as if on remote control. He had to get Alayna home safely. He had to keep his focus on her until he had her safely inside her apartment.

As Brayden's car grumbled to a halt at the curb, he wasted no time. He vaulted from the driver's side with an urgency that echoed in the quiet street. His heavy footsteps pounded on the pavement as he hurried to the passenger's side.

Alayna, sensing his haste, swiftly unbuckled her seatbelt and stepped out into the dimly lit surroundings. The glow from the nearby streetlight cast an eerie glow on the scene, painting long and foreboding shadows around the deserted street. Brayden's voice broke the almost tangible silence. "Alayna, I'm sorry about…"

Chapter 18 Clever

Alayna's lips curved into a bitter smile as she gave him an understanding look. "It's okay, Brayden. You're a cop, a detective. I know you must answer those calls when they come."

Brayden escorted Alayna to her front door. The soft glow from the numerous porch lights in the complex cast a warm, inviting aura. He waited as she fumbled for her keys, the silence of the night amplifying the jingle. The door finally swung open, revealing the darkened interior of her home. Brayden followed her in, his fingers deftly finding the light switch and flooding the room in a soft, comforting glow.

The idea of leaving Alayna alone on her doorstep in the dark had never crossed his mind. It was not in his nature to abandon her until he knew she was safe, secure within the confines of her home. His duty was to ensure she was home safely, a task he intended to fulfill before he disappeared into the inky black night.

Alayna turned to him with a smoldering gaze, her lips curled into a coy smile. "Thank you for seeing me inside."

"My pleasure, and again, I'm sorry we had to cut our evening short." Brayden hesitated.

Stepping closer to him, Alayna took Brayden by the hand and pulled him against her. The soft curves of her body harmonized with his strong angles as if they were two pieces of a neglected puzzle finally finding their rightful place.

Her lips, soft yet demanding, pressed against his, a silent plea locked within their warm embrace. The lingering taste of freshly brewed espresso danced on their tongues, a bitter yet addictive symphony that echoed in the chambers of their beating hearts.

With a determination he did not know he possessed, Brayden was able to pull away, and he rested his forehead upon her head. "Damn, I wish I didn't have to go," Brayden groaned, his voice strained.

Reluctantly, Brayden backed away from Alayna's warm embrace. Sadly, he offered her an apologetic smile before he reached down and locked the door as he stepped outside, closing the door behind him. As much as he would have liked to stay behind and explore the possibilities that might have arisen, he knew his duty called him to the far more gruesome task of seeking out a cold-blooded killer.

CHAPTER 19

WHAT MIGHT HAVE BEEN

VANDER

The Veil—Night

HAVING LEFT HIS BODY IN A DARK CORNER OF THE UNIversity's massive library, Vander embarked on a journey that transcended the confines of the physical. Engaging in astral projection, his consciousness separated from his corporeal form and ventured toward the other side of the veil.

His body, left behind, was merely a shell, a tether to the world he temporarily abandoned. The ethereal plane, teeming with unseen mysteries, whispered secrets in silent echoes, enveloping Vander in its dark, atmospheric embrace.

Beyond the realm of the known, shrouded in the shadows of uncertainty, lay the other side of the veil. A paradoxical realm where the desire to move on intertwined with the inexplicable dread of the unseen. Its mystery, as alluring as it was terrifying, beckoned him to explore, yet warned him of the darkness that lurked on the fringes.

At the entrance to the veil, Nightshade waited. The bird's eyes glistened, cold and knowing, as its ethereal form shimmered in the gloom. Vander's Pied crow was no longer a creature of the earth, but a thing transcended into a spirit-being—forever bound to Vander.

Chapter 19 — What Might Have Been

Vander extended his spirit into the cool twilight air, as his spirit began to materialize within the ethereal veil. Holding his arm out, Vander waited for Nightshade to come to him. With a swift flourish of wings, the crow spirit soared high, tracing circles above him before it gracefully descended to alight upon Vander's sleeve. A greeting from the other side, a testament to their enduring friendship. Despite the spectral transformation, their strong bond was undiminished, able to transcend even the boundaries of life and death.

"Hello, Nightshade," Vander murmured, his eyes never leaving the swirling mists that danced in the ether. How Vander wanted to imagine that the crow's body was warm against his skin, but the bird was as cold as the fog that surrounded them.

Nightshade's gaze was relentless, pupils dilating and contracting in sync with the ebb and flow of the shadowy tendrils. Agonized whispers grew louder as the cries of restless spirits echoed eerily in the still air, each one a lamentation of a lost life. Yet, even still, Vander remained unwavering, his focus solely on finding the elusive Jack. Running a finger down Nightshade's feathery chest, Vander asked, "Where is our old friend, eh? Where could he be?"

Impatiently, Vander trudged through the ether, an otherworldly mist of shadows that danced around him. Nightshade worked his way onto Vander's shoulder, his presence serving as his sentinel in this realm of lost souls.

As they ventured deeper, the cries of restless spirits grew louder, a cacophony of regret and despair that filled the air. Their ghastly faces, the embodiment of untold nightmares, loomed out of the obscurity, curiously observing the one who continued to dare to tread their unhallowed domain.

Despite the chill of the ethereal realm, beads of sweat trickled down Vander's brow. The burden of astral projection weighed heavily upon him. The veil between realms shimmered, the other side holding promises of reunion and dread alike. His heart pounded in his chest, each beat throbbing with the desperate hope that Jack would indeed be waiting for him.

In the security of his sanctuary, the passage through the shimmering veil held a peculiar allure rather than dread. His form, unadulterated by the stressors of the mortal world, projected effortlessly into the astral plane, a spectral child wandering realms unseen. Yet, as he now gazed down at his diminutive, juvenile form—a stark contrast to his actual years—a cruel reality washed over him.

The act of crossing to the other side, once an effortless endeavor, was, at this time, marred by a profound heaviness. The strain of his circumstances, coupled with the ominous nature of his journey, had etched itself into his being and had forced his astral form to regress to his younger, more innocent self. The journey was indeed taking its toll. The stress engraving itself not just on his mind, but also on his spectral silhouette.

"Jack?!" Vander shouted; his voice pierced the dense fog in a manner that seemed far too vulnerable for his liking. There was a strange child-like quality to his voice, one that took him aback. As Jack's silhouette emerged from the mist, Vander could not help but feel an air of surprise. The fog rolled away, revealing Jack's familiar, comforting grin. Despite the strangeness of the situation, Vander found solace in that smile, a beacon of normalcy in an otherwise eerie atmosphere. He responded with a relieved smile, the tension in his features easing into a happy greeting. "We've got to talk."

Vander gazed at his friend Jack, who hesitated for a moment, before shaking his head with an air of finality. "What is it, Jack?" Vander's question hung in the air, a dark cloud in the stormy atmosphere. Jack's gaze hardened, his voice a low murmur filled with frustration and despair. "Vander, I can't think straight... not with the constant wailing. It's your mum, you've got to do somethin' about her. She's driving me mad!"

Vander's heart sank like a weight within his chest. His gaze dropped to the ground, the reality of the situation sinking in; his mother's incessant wailing, her countless complaints and begging had taken its toll on Jack, and his friend would help no further until Vander put an end to it. He knew what he had to do, but the thought of facing his mother now with everything else that was going on filled him with dread.

He looked up at his friend and nodded in agreement. "All right, I'll talk to her, but you stay here, all right?"

Jack huffed, "I didn't say to talk to her again, now did I?"

Sad, Vander turned and headed off on the path leading to where a place had been carved out for his mother, not long after her death. "I know. I'll do what has to be done."

That day, so long ago, seemed far removed from reality. Still, it was etched into Vander's memory like a grotesque mural. He could still feel the phantom sensation of the pills, of how he had crushed them into a

Chapter 19 — What Might Have Been

fine powder, slipped them through his trembling fingers and into the battered tin cup at his mother's bedside.

The visage of his mother, Amahle, once vibrant and full of life, had been reduced to a broken figure, near lifeless, abused and beyond repair. Her spirit, once a blazing fire, had been snuffed out, leaving in its wake a hollow shell, dead inside. He remembered holding the tarnished cup to her bloated lips, the final cocktail of mercy and inevitable doom. The path to her death had been paved with his regret, a necessary evil to spare her from the monstrous fate his father would have chosen for her.

For years, Vander found himself tormented by the same relentless dreams, reenacting his part in his mother's death. It was as if the past had woven itself into his psyche, an insistent reminder of the irreversible actions he had undertaken. His mother's lifeless body, her spirit crushed by years of abuse, had become a specter in his existence.

Vander's reality had been one where love was buried under layers of torment, kindness was a forgotten language, and peace a distant mirage, forever beyond his grasp. His father, the heartless architect of their misery, lurked in the shadows of his nightmares, a grim embodiment of dread and regret. Yet amid this dismal existence, Vander clung to a sliver of hope, a faint glimmer in the depths of darkness. That perhaps, there, in his safe place, his mother could at long last show him the love he had so longed for.

In the cloistered confines of his solitude, Vander harbored a persistent longing, a yearning for a maternal affection that was not to be. His mother, Amahle, a spectral figure consumed by her past, was either unable or unwilling to shed the shackles of her torment.

Her heart, it seemed, was perpetually shrouded in an impenetrable mist of despair, disappointment etched into every line on her face. The ghost of Lenka, the man she ostensibly loved more than herself or her son, haunted her every waking moment.

This truth had left Vander trapped, standing on the periphery. His yearning for love cast adrift on a sea of her indifference, his hopes dashed on the harsh rocks of his cold reality.

Vander stopped, his eyes going to Nightshade, who studied him intently. His gaze bore into Nightshade, the raven's obsidian eyes reflecting the turmoil within him. A chorus of emotions played out, a dance of disappointment and longing as if he was either unable or unwilling to accept the reality of his predicament.

"Wait for me at the entrance." Without hesitation, Nightshade lifted from Vander's slim shoulder and flew away into the heavy fog.

Just out of Amahle's sight, Vander waited, enveloped in the ominous gloom of the land of the In-between. His heart echoed a hopeful yet pleading rhythm, each beat a silent prayer to the gods of forgotten love and lost chances. He could almost taste the bitterness of acceptance curling around his tongue, a painful reminder of the harsh truth. His attempts to make his mother whole again, to drown both of their haunted pasts in a sea of new, happier memories, but those dreams had only been met with crushing disappointment.

It was not the cold, cryptic land that stood in their way; it was Vander himself. He must carry a strange, unnamable defect that rendered him unlovable, casting a shadow over his entire existence.

Perhaps this was the reason he now stood alone in the swirling mist, his soul aching for an unconditional love that he would never have or know.

It was hard to understand that no matter what he had done, or how hard he had tried, he could not win the love of even his own mother, who should have treasured him. This chilling realization burned away what was left of his compassion and his hope, and created a deep chasm within his heart. truth concealed in the abyss.

Amahle must have sensed him because she looked over at him. Her gaze, though soft, held a haunted emptiness that he now knew he could never fill. There was a void in his mother's soul where perhaps affection had once resided, or at least the pretense of it anyway. But now, it was filled with a harrowing sense of estrangement.

Seeing Vander in his current form, as the child of nine he had once been, gave his mother pause. "Vander?" Amahle asked, unsure.

"Yes, Mother, it's me." Hesitantly, Vander hung back because he dreaded what came next: his mother's forced smile, the placating words she had prepared, would be said followed by tears as she begged him to set her free, free to venture on into the afterlife and be at peace.

Vander spoke. His voice trembled with an emotion he would not name. "Mother, I think it's time you moved on." His words echoed, a stark reminder of his solitude. He offered a hand to his mother; her slender hand took his. Hope flared to life in her dull eyes that had once comforted him and that now only seemed to mirror his desolation.

Chapter 19   *What Might Have Been*

He knew he had to release her, to free her from her earthly bonds, and yet an overwhelming sense of dread chained him. It dawned on him then, the finality of it, the harsh reality that he would truly be alone. No family, no true friends, and only a guardian who wanted to murder him. Still, he could wait no longer. It was time. Time to let her move on, time for him to face the solitude that awaited.

Vander looked up into his mother's faded blue eyes as if searching for a sign that he was making the right decision. He saw only relief and hope there, and it began the process of turning his heart to stone. With a heavy heart, Vander led her from the sanctuary he had carved out for her so long ago, their steps making no sound in the churning mist that parted before them as they made their way to the place where he and Jack had watched countless spirits cross over.

The trip to the portal that would spirit his mother away to the next phase of her eternity seemed to take years, yet also was over in an instant. Considering he had not been ready for this moment, that he more than likely never would have been, Vander felt tears begin to well up in his eyes as he stopped short of the gateway.

Under the penetrating gaze of the radiant light, Vander's heart pounded in his chest. The rhythm echoed the passage of time that felt simultaneously eternal and fleeting. His feet traced the path to the mystical portal, each step a blend of agony and anticipation, his mother's bright smile glowing far more than the portal's strange illumination.

Amahle's happiness was evident. Her decision to cross over sealed. In that moment, Vander experienced such a profound understanding of loss, sacrifice, and the inevitable transition from one life to the next that he felt as if he could no longer breathe.

Engulfed in the radiant light, Amahle's face was a sight to behold. To Vander, she seemed not just beautiful, but ethereal, as if time itself had reversed, revealing the angelic youth she once was. The harsh burdens she bore in life, the ravages of time and suffering, seemed to fall away, replaced by a luminosity that was breathtaking. As she moved, surrendering herself to the crossing over, an unmistakable joy seemed to shine through her, and Vander knew that she was finally happy.

Without a goodbye or backward glance, Amahle stepped toward the portal, ready for her new journey to begin. Vander knew what came next. His mother's spirit would emerge from the shadows, bathed in radiant light, a phenomenon as mesmerizing as it was terrifying to the spirits that remained deep in the mist, watching.

His mother's crossing over would be a journey from the familiar into the unknown. Her passing would unfold like an ethereal dream. For her spirit, once tethered to this realm of shadows, was drawn toward the allure of new promises that awaited on the other side.

Unchecked tears ran down Vander's face as he watched the transition, tinted with the otherworldly glow, the light engulfing his mother, pure joy radiated from her features as she basked in the beauty of it all, delighted in the wonder of the things just beyond the veil of understanding.

Fleeting, his mother's form shimmered for a few seconds, then vanished in a quick flash of light.

Amahle's departure left Vander with an ache in his heart that he knew could never be filled. Though his mother had not or could not return his love, he still hoped that she was among the angels and not with his father, who he hoped, suffering in eternal torment.

Angry at himself for showing such weakness as crying, Vander angrily wiped at his tears.

What was love, anyway? A word put to a need or desire. In his experience, when a person needed or wanted something bad enough, they simply took it. His father thought he had needed his mother to have someone around to punish when life did not go his way.

His mother thought she loved her parents, at least in the beginning, when they provided for her every need. But that changed when they rejected her. Her parents, his grandparents, had proclaimed they loved his mother, but that was only until she disappointed them by marrying his father, thus ending their chance to live their life vicariously through her.

And what of Jack, his friend? Did he simply pretend to care about him because he relieved some of his boredom? Then there was Alexander. The relationship he had with him hurt almost as much as his mother's rejection.

He had done everything Alexander had asked, cared for him, protected him despite the horrible things that he had done... And even now, the mentor he had opened his heart to was at that very moment, plotting how to murder him, just to make him another one of his damned works of art.

All the questions and known and unknown scenarios alike made Vander's mind spin round and round in a vicious circle.

Chapter 19 — *What Might Have Been*

Casting a final look at the closed portal, Vander aligned himself with the agitated spirits about him, that even now, berated themselves for not having the courage to move on. Like them, Vander wanted to scream in a fit of rage, pull at his hair and gnash his teeth together. Instead, he swallowed his anger and simply backed away.

With a heavy heart, he went to look for Jack. He had done what the man asked and now it was time for him to provide Vander with much-needed answers. Hardening his heart, Vander knew no matter the cost, he would not be denied his right to live, not by Jack, not by Alexander, or even by the cruel fates themselves.

CHAPTER 20

FOUND LACKING

ALEXANDER

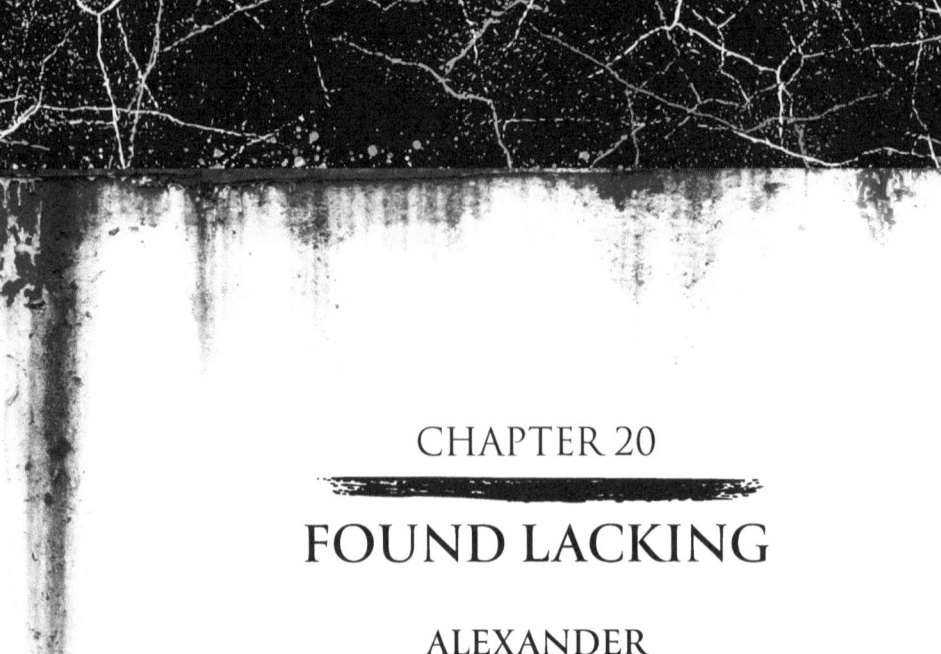

Virginia Beach, VA—Night

MIND OPEN, YET STILL RIDDLED WITH DOUBT, Alexander took his seat in the dimly lit room. The flickering candlelight cast eerie shadows on the walls, and a sense of foreboding hung heavy in the air. Wellington's enthusiastic endorsement of Rudy echoed in his mind, but skepticism gnawed at the edges of his belief.

Alexander had done a great deal of study on the pseudo-science and occult.

Emerging from the obscurity of the uncharted, Alexander plunged into the abyss of the pseudo-sciences and the occult with a voracious thirst for knowledge. He dissected the intricate tapestry of parapsychology, weaving through the tendrils of extrasensory perception and remote viewing, teasing apart clairvoyance from precognition.

His mind danced on the edge of the ethereal, toying with the cryptic symbols and enigmatic rituals that whispered of truths beyond mankind's conventional understanding. His studies spun a web of arcane knowledge, a labyrinth of esoteric wisdom that beckoned him farther into its mysterious depths.

The world of the average man's senses—sight, sound, touch, taste, and instinct—was but a mere prelude to this symphony of the unknown. His journey was not without its darkness, of course, but the shadows only

Chapter 20   Found Lacking

fueled his pursuit of enlightenment. Every psychic he encountered, each with their unique gifts and skill sets, only added more threads to the intricate mosaic of his understanding.

He, of course, had only scratched the surface of this world, but he knew he must venture farther. With each new discovery, Alexander felt more connected to the dark magic that existed beyond man's earthly realm. His passion for unlocking these secrets pushed him ever onward in his pursuit of the supernatural, and he eagerly anticipated seeing where this journey would take him. In a way, Alexander was like a kid in a candy store; each new experience was an exquisite feast of exploration that tantalized his senses and opened up new possibilities.

In truth, Alexander had traversed the foggy echelons of illusion and crossed paths with numerous psychics in his relentless search for a mentor to guide Vander. His journey took him to clandestine corners of the world, meeting with seers, each encounter leaving a trace of an uncanny revelation.

However, every expedition concluded with Vander leaving these mentors in a state of utter bewilderment, their eyes wide with shock, their hearts reverberating with newfound respect for the boy's uncharted powers. These episodes were a stark reminder to Alexander that Vander was no mere boy, but an enigma shrouded in a youthful guise, a testament to the profound depths of innate abilities he was yet to fully comprehend.

It was clear from the start that Alexander had to tread carefully, understanding fully well that underestimating the young man would be foolish. He knew in his heart of hearts that the mysteries surrounding Vander were far from mundane, and it was with this earnestness that he prepared for their upcoming acceptance or confrontation.

In the realm of the unexplained, the gifts of the psyche unfurl like ethereal whispers in the night. The most coveted of these paranormal endowments harbor unique advantages. Clairvoyance, the ability to see beyond the physical plane, grants visions of future events and insights into hidden realities.

Telepathy, the silent communion of minds, fosters an uncanny connection between beings, transcending the limits of speech. Empathy, the capacity to feel others' emotions, unveils the human heart's unspoken language. Clairaudience, the gift of hearing voices from the spiritual realm, offers guidance from celestial entities. These gifts, though mysterious, serve as beacons guiding the chosen ones through life's labyrinth.

Each psychic Alexander had encountered before held a unique array of talents, a distinct array of eerie capabilities that set them apart. But Vander was an anomaly. His abilities were not limited to a select few; they were extensive, a near-complete spectrum of otherworldly prowess.

This made Vander not only an extraordinary marvel in the psychic realm but also a formidable adversary to any who dared to cross his path. His powers were not to be trifled with, and those who did often found themselves facing consequences far darker than they could ever imagine.

Alexander knew this and was fully prepared to confront whatever might come his way. It was time for him to face the consequences of his actions, whatever they may be. Alexander steeled himself for what could be an epic clash between two equally matched forces, and he knew that no matter the outcome, it was sure to be one of the greatest battles of his life.

The confrontation ahead might well decide Alexander's fate—for better or for worse. But whatever happened, he was determined to stand strong against Vander's formidable power, if only to prove that the boy he had groomed and nurtured with such care would forever remain his student, his beautiful masterpiece, or that Vander had indeed become the master.

Alexander watched, his gaze unflinching, as Rudy, a man in his thirties, took his seat across from him. The room was filled with a palpable tension that hung heavy in the air.

Rudy's tired smile did little to alleviate the guarded atmosphere. His hands, outstretched on the table, seemed to be an offering. Alexander's emotions were locked down, a fortress against the potential intrusion of Rudy's gift, if his talents involved clairtangency. The mere thought of Rudy being able to perceive through touch was enough to give Alexander pause.

Alexander's eyes were drawn to the untouched notebook and sleek pen that Rudy revealed, an unspoken promise of secrets yet to be unfurled. Rudy's question hung in the air, a murmur in the oppressive silence. "Do you know what automatic writing is?"

Relieved, Alexander answered, "Yes, it is a form of communication associated with the mystical and paranormal realms."

He knew a great deal about this form of divination; it was a process involving the penman surrendering their conscious control, allowing an unseen force, perhaps a subconscious thought or a purported spiritual entity, to guide their hand across the page.

Chapter 20 — Found Lacking

The resulting text, often a mix of cryptic sentences and abstract symbols, was a source of fascination and speculation. It was believed that through this method, one could tap into a deeper, less tangible realm of the mind, or perhaps touch the ethereal whispers of the otherworld.

The room grew suddenly cold, the flickering candlelight cast long, grotesque shadows on the ancient stone walls. Alexander felt a shiver run down his spine, but he steadied his gaze, trying to mask his growing apprehension. Rudy, the seasoned medium, stared back at him through half-lidded eyes, his voice a low, hypnotic hum. "Prepare your mind, Alexander. We are about to venture into the unseen, the realm of shadows and whispers. Breathe and let the spirits guide us."

Alexander could have done without the theatrics because he also knew skeptics of automatic writing viewed it as nothing more than an illusion of the subconscious mind, a mere trickery of the hands influenced by one's ingrained thoughts and beliefs.

Those non-believers argued that the phenomenon was a result of the ideomotor effect, where involuntary, subconscious movements guided the hand rather than spiritual or supernatural forces. The supposed messages derived from these sessions, skeptics pointed out, often bore a striking resemblance to the writer's own thoughts, further reinforcing their stance.

Alexander watched as Rudy's psychography began. Taking the pen in his hand, Rudy placed it upon the notepad, closed his eyes, took a deep breath, then exhaled. The room was quiet for a moment; Rudy's face was a blank page. Then the candles began to flicker, the air stirred, and a deep frown burrowed into Rudy's brow as he cocked his head as if listening.

Alexander watched with an eerie calm as the spectacle of Rudy's psychography unfolded before him. Rudy's troubled expression was illuminated in the flickering candlelight, his features contorting as if grappling with unseen forces. His hand, clutching the pen, began to dart across the notepad, sketching out messages from the beyond with a frenetic energy that seemed to echo the turbulence within him.

Doubt gnawed at the edges of Alexander's calm demeanor, a shadow in his otherwise stoic countenance, as he bore witness to the proceedings, the room heavy with anticipation and an undercurrent of fear. The air grew colder, the silence of the room punctuated only by the scratching of Rudy's pen, and the candles flickered as if in response to the unseen energies being invoked.

Suddenly, Rudy's face went as white as the paper in front of him. His arm jerked unnaturally while his hand continued its feverish dance across the page. Sweat began to bead on his brow. Each droplet reflected the feeble candlelight.

The first few words he scratched out were of ominous import: murder, death, destruction—a chilling trifecta that fell heavily on the silence of the room. They were repeated, over and over, until they filled the page, each repetition growing more frantic, more desperate. Alexander watched as the darkness of the message began to consume the room.

Suddenly, Rudy jerked backward, his chair scraping on the wooden floor. His eyes, previously closed in concentration, snapped open wide in sheer terror. With a gasp, he tossed the pen away from him as if it had suddenly burst into flames. The discarded pen skittered across the table, leaving a trail of ink like the trace of a nightmare.

Alexander, caught off guard, could only watch as Rudy clambered out of his seat in panic, knocking over the chair in his haste. His reader's face was deathly pale, his eyes wide and wild, mirroring the terror that the words on the page had inspired. Alexander's breath hitched in his throat as he watched Rudy stumble toward the door, a sense of dread washing over him.

Before he could react, Rudy turned and uttered a warning, his voice barely more than a whisper.

"You should prepare yourself ... for whatever is coming." With that, Rudy fled the room, leaving Alexander alone with only the words scribbled on the page.

Alexander could not be certain if Rudy had been speaking a warning to him, or one on behalf of his previous victims? Was Rudy the mouthpiece of his past transgressions, the silenced voices of his victims that had echoed through Rudy's mind?

Alexander knew that his merely entertaining the thought of killing Vander had more than likely put his young prodigy on high alert and he was more than likely trying to devise a series of plans of his own to counter those Alexander had or would make.

Gathering his things, Alexander left the room and stepped into the night. Rudy was nowhere to be seen, probably having run all the way back to his apartment once he had fled the reading room.

The distant hoot of an owl, a lone sentinel in the macabre stillness, echoed through the night air. He mulled over the delicious anticipation

Chapter 20 — Found Lacking

that was the prelude to Vander's and his lethal dance. The game with Vander was not merely a contest of physical might, but a chessboard of the mind. Each move and countermove a step closer to checkmate. The thrill of the hunt invigorated him, the chill in the air feeling less like the cold of the night, and more like the exhilarating touch of danger.

He was ready for whatever came next and, though the hour was late, he was ready to be on his way back to Pennsylvania. He had much to do and not much time to prepare. Though Thomas would protest at returning home so late, Alexander would insist. After all, something told him that Vander would be waiting to see him bright and early in the morning.

MAY 1ST—10 DAYS

CHAPTER 21

GRUESOME DISCOVERY

BRAYDEN

Austin, TX—Before Dawn

At the door to the loft, Brayden held out his badge for the uniformed officer who guarded the door. Green at the gills, the officer said, "Gotta warn ya. It's a pretty gruesome sight in there."

Taking out his badge, Juan said, "We'll be fine." Juan mirrored Brayden's action. The cop waved them in.

Stepping inside, they found themselves in a macabre montage that instantly justified the officer's warning. The loft was a distorted reflection of reality, a testament to the bizarre and uncanny. Shadows stretched grotesquely along the walls, painting an eerie, atmospheric backdrop to the scene that lay before them.

Taken aback, Juan exclaimed. "Holly hell!"

Lost for words, Brayden was submerged in the gruesome universe that was unlike anything he'd ever witnessed. His gaze was locked onto Jasmine Lam's lifeless figure, her delicate features contorted into a grotesque slant.

Each limb, each finger, each toe bent and twisted, mimicking a bizarre floral arrangement that was both deeply unnerving and disturbingly fascinating. His senses were overwhelmed by the dark, atmospheric

Chapter 21   Gruesome Discovery

aura that seemed to seep from every inch of the room, wrapping him in a cloak of eerie silence.

No matter what he did or where he looked, the horror of this gruesome crime scene was impossible to ignore. He couldn't help but feel a sense of dread, as if the sinister presence that had been at play still lingered. Brayden could only stare and wonder how someone could have done something so twisted.

Jasmine Lam's face, pale and frozen in a grotesque mask of terror, bore the artist's finishing touch, a blood-red grimace that would haunt even the most seasoned investigator. This was not just a murder, but a dark craftsmanship that had turned the victim into a grotesque sculpture featuring her own demise.

Careful of the crime scene, Brayden made his way over to the medical examiner, Tasha Reyes. The grim reality of what had happened was becoming more and more evident. "Any ETA on time of death, Tasha?" Brayden asked. His guilt at going out on a date instead of staying at the station and diving into the case was secretly eating at him. If the artist had been killed before they had even been given the case, then his night out would no longer matter.

Visibly shaken, Tasha paused in her work and turned to Brayden and Juan. "Well, the absence of oxygenated blood flow that caused the muscle tissues to become rigid only lasts one to four days. After that, the body literally begins to eat itself."

Not understanding, Juan said, "So that means what, exactly?"

Tasha added, "That she's been dead, twenty-four, maybe forty-eight, hours tops."

Juan took a step back as Tasha's eyes returned to the lifeless body. It was clear to Brayden that the examiner's mind was already sifting through the details. Forensics was her language, and the room was a silent narrator of the gruesome tale. "But I'll need more. A lot more tests to be sure," she muttered.

Brayden fought the urge to cover his nose and mouth as he began moving about the room. The smell of decay and blood mingled with a blend of sweet floral notes. "What's that smell?"

Juan looked at Brayden as if he stripped a gear. "Seriously?"

"The flower and spice smell, you genius," Brayden chided.

"Oh," Juan said sheepishly.

Time was of the essence, and Brayden could see that Tasha was determined to get this investigation right. "It's Frangipani, also known as plumeria." Tasha continued her meticulous search for clues, scouring the area for any hint that could bring them closer to finding the killer. "It's the flowers the killer used to finish up his," Tasha motioned to delicate petals that ranged in colors from white to deep red adorning the twisted frame of the dead artist, "whatever the hell this is."

"Aren't those used in Hawaii to create lei garlands?" Brayden asked, his mind awash with questions he did not have the answers to.

"Very good, Detective James." Not many guys would know that.

"I have a sister who loves tropical flowers." Brayden thought of Paige and how horrified she would be if she saw these delicate petals put to such a gruesome task. Studying a set of flowers that dangled from the artist's deformed fingers, Brayden continued, "However, their meaning from the islands is a symbol of welcome and goodwill. I seriously doubt the killer had that message in mind when he used them."

Brayden felt Juan step up beside him, a palpable tension in the air.

They both looked at the body, a silent agreement hanging between them not to disturb the scene. Juan frowned, his brow furrowed in thought. "So, what did it mean?" Juan muttered, his words barely audible.

Tasha, wiping the sweat from her brow, gave a nonchalant shrug. "Your problem, gentlemen. You find the motive. I find the details in the aftermath," she said, her tone casual but her eyes serious.

Though Brayden and Juan had been thrust into the missing person's case just hours prior, things had changed dramatically. What started as a typical day, with the job of mundane paperwork and routine surveillance to be done, had now spiraled into a grisly murder investigation.

The weight of numerous tasks to attend to was evident. Evidence had to be gathered, witnesses interviewed, and a motive established. It was a race against the clock, and Brayden knew he would not be seeing the beautiful Alayna anytime soon. The image of her bright smile and sparkling eyes only added to the heaviness in his heart.

He and Juan had a job to do, and it was time to get started.

MAY 1ST—10 DAYS

CHAPTER 22

ENOUGH

VANDER

Veil—Night

Every muted step under Vander's feet murmured through the relentless hardening of his heart. The portal, now dormant and unremarkable, stood as a stark reminder of his mother's abandonment, her departure forever imprinted in his mind.

As the chilling winds swept through the desolate landscape, wrapping him in their icy tendrils, he vowed to take care of himself. His mother's blind love for his father had overshadowed any maternal instinct she might have possessed, leaving him alone to navigate the murky waters of his existence.

Vander was resilient. He would not falter. He would not crumble. He would harden, like a blade forged in the fierce fires of adversity, ready to carve out his own destiny.

Vander had been stupid to believe things would be different there in the land of the dead. His heart, once soft and vulnerable, was hardening like a stone submerged in icy waters. The illusions of maternal love, the fleeting moments of perceived courage, were swallowed up by the chilling reality of his mother's selfishness.

Vander often found himself lost in memories, questioning why his mother had chosen to be his shield in that isolated incident in Cape Town. Was it a momentary spark of maternal instinct, or a calculated gambit, a desperate attempt to coax his father into a rage so intense that it might extinguish her existence, a bleak escape from the perpetual void she was trapped in?

At that tender age, Vander had naively perceived her brave act as one birthed of love, a testament to a strength he believed she possessed underneath the veil of her constant fear.

But as he grew, Vander's perception changed drastically. Now, the only truth in his heart was a deep-seated dread and a slowly dawning realization that his mother had been preparing for battle all along, steeling herself to confront her greatest enemy—the monstrosity of her own life. And in that confrontation, she hoped that death would be its overwhelming victor.

As the echoes of Cape Town and his past reverberated throughout his mind, he found solace in one cold, harsh truth. He would no longer count on others to protect him. He and he alone would be his own savior, his own lion, and a lone warrior that would battle any foe that came against him.

Stepping out of the mist before Vander, Jack emerged. Jack seemed sheepish, almost guilty as he said, "I know that was hard, lad, but ... it's for the best."

Vander's gaze hardened, his jaw tightening as he stared into Jack's weary eyes. The fog around them swirled and twisted, reflecting the turmoil in his soul. "For the best?" Vander's voice was a hollow echo, resounding through the mist. His words hung in the air like a specter, a chilling reminder of the trust that once existed between them.

Jack swallowed hard, trying his best to look remorseful. But for Vander, it was too late for regrets, too late for apologies. They both knew there was no turning back.

Vander watched as Jack held up both hands, open-palmed, as if to placate him. "She was never gonna be happy here, never gonna be the mum you wanted her to be."

Vander's eyes narrowed; the fire of anger illuminated his gaze as he took in Jack's words. His fists clenched involuntarily; the ghost of her memory fresh in his mind. His voice was a low growl, a dangerous undercurrent beneath the calm façade. "She was more than just a mother, Jack. She was my world." He spat. The mood around them suddenly turned as frigid as the air about them.

Chapter 22   Enough

Jack smiled brightly. "You've got to be glad that she's now at peace and happy. Why, even the ghosts here are..."

Vander cut him off with a snarl, his rage boiling up to dizzying heights. "Just shut up! You got what you wanted!" he hissed. Vander's whole body quivered with anger, threatening to burst forth like a volcano.

There was an intensity in his gaze that could have melted iron, leaving no doubt as to what he was thinking. He took a step forward, and Jack, fear in his eyes for the first time since Vander met him, reluctantly held his ground.

The tension in the air was palpable, and Vander could feel his heart pounding against his chest. He had never felt such anger directed at another before. But the rage he felt toward Jack was a cold, hard thing that refused to dissipate. It seemed like an eternity as they stared each other down, each daring the other to make the first move.

Hands still balled into fists at his side, Vander glared up at Jack, daring him to say another word.

In surrender, Jack bowed his head and took a retreating step back. "Fine lad, okay, I won't say another word about your mum."

Eyes fixed on Jack, Vander marched around him and started down the path that would lead him out of the veil and back to the real world where his real body, the one that was in fact twenty-four years old, still waited at the library. He no longer wanted answers from Jack, he just wanted out of there and to be finished with the night.

Clearing his throat behind him, Vander heard Jack say, "So, you won't be wanting to hear about Alexander's plans after all, eh?"

Vander hesitated for a moment, then came to a stop, but kept his back turned to Jack. "What plans?" he asked, his voice barely a whisper in the wind. Jack's warning had given him pause, and despite the fury that still gnawed at the edges of his tolerance, he turned back to face the older man.

"I hate to tell ya, but right after..." Jack stalled.

Vander glared at Jack when he hesitated, his pulse pounding against his throat. Jack's voice, loaded with reluctance, started to break the silence. "But..."

Vander, his patience gone, growled, "Get on with it. I'm not playing any more games with you tonight."

Jack finally looked Vander in the eye and gave him a curt nod, then began weaving his hands before the mist. Instantly, images began to form. It was the dining room at Vander's and Alexander's townhome, but something was wrong. His friends from college were all there... but they were dead. Mangled corpses littered the room and Vander felt cold sweat bead on his forehead.

Alexander turned to his acquaintances with a twisted smile. A wine glass brimmed with a dark red wine. He was proud of his executions. Vander's stomach churned as he watched Alexander admire the scene of his destruction.

The battle lines had been drawn, and Vander could only hope that his will and determination would be enough to see him through the coming storm. He had no idea what fate awaited him, but he knew one thing: whatever happened, he would not go down without a fight. He had confronted demons before and survived, and he would do so again.

Angry, Vander walked through the twisted images, dispelling them back to the mist.

"Why would Alexander do that?" he began, his voice trailing off into nothingness, swallowed by the endless void around him. The question lingered, an unwelcome guest in the foggy expanse, as Jack watched him, wanting the explanation Vander himself sought. The atmosphere was heavy with anticipation, a dark mystery unfolding with every passing moment.

Jack shrugged. "You tell me?"

Vander's mind reached for answers, sifting through the shadows of thought and memory. He knew Alexander recognized the raw, untamed power that lurked beneath his composed façade. His mind raced back to his vision, the haunting premonition that had tingled his senses earlier. Understanding dawned, a cold, cruel reality etching itself into his consciousness.

One word echoed, rebounding off the walls of his mind—distraction. Alexander's true intentions, his real game, had been obscured, a mere smokescreen for his true objective. The looming danger was much more significant, and time was running out.

Vander said, "Distraction."

Jack smiled his approval at Vander reaching this conclusion.

"Everything he is doing is nothing but a distraction, an effort to keep me off guard so I won't recognize his true intent," Vander said, his voice barely a whisper.

As the understanding dawned, it was as piercing as the chill from the stone walls. The murder, the macabre plot of Alexander to kill his friends,

Chapter 22 — Enough

was a mere façade—a deftly designed distraction. It was not an intention. It was mere thoughts of the deed put to use just enough to create an illusion of things to come. It was an illusion of a future to cloud his perception of the future that would be.

Alexander had meticulously built a false narrative, or at the least, other moving parts that Vander must neutralize to save those around him, thus sacrificing himself. The trap Alexander had woven was both ruthless and cunning. But the true artistry, the real goal was far more sinister. Killing Vander was the endgame. It was to be Alexander's final masterpiece, the last stroke on a canvas dyed in the hues of deception and darkness.

"Alexander won't kill my friends, but he will make plans to," Vander said.

Puzzled, Jack shook his head. "Come again, lad?"

Eyes fixed on the mist, Vander looked through it and beyond. "He knows about my gifts, or at least, about many of them. Alexander will have anticipated me having premonitions about his killing me."

"True enough. So?" Jack agreed.

Vander continued, "So, knowing that I might have seen his plans, Alexander knew he would have to come up with something so shocking, a plan so terrible, that it would send me scrambling to stop him, thus I would be busy stopping one plan while he orchestrated another."

Rubbing his chin, Jack mused, "So how do ya feel about your precious Alexander wantin' to kill ya?"

"I feel marvelous, of course," Vander snarled. "And you didn't warn me about any of this because?"

"What?! You think I knew about his plans?" Jack asked, incredulous.

"You saying you didn't?" Vander asked, his eyes narrowing.

Jack threw his hands in the air, exclaiming, "I'm not God you know, nor Satan, if you be wondering. I'm not omniscient. I don't see everything all the time."

"Oh, I see. You're so busy here in the In-between that you could not possibly have had enough time to look in on something as crucial as my mentor planning my death."

"Come now, you know I always look out for ya, don't I?" Clicking his tongue against his teeth, he continued, "Which leads me to my next point. I am not saying old Alexander is gonna get the best of you, but..."

"But what!!!" Vander railed.

"What if he does end your life and you never get the chance to settle the score with Kgotso?" Jack said matter of fact.

The words hit home, stealing Vander's breath as an age-old fury burst to life within his chest. The rage that had lain dormant for so long suddenly burned hot and fierce, a harsh reminder of the retribution he vowed never to forget.

Vander's heart pounded in rhythm with the dark symphony of his resolve, each beat a testament to his undying commitment to avenge Khumalo. The bitter taste of revenge lingered on his tongue, a potent cocktail of wrath and determination, brewed from memories of torment and the icy breath of death.

The world around him melted into a mirage of shadows and whispers, a fitting backdrop for the tragic opera of his life. His path was now etched in stone, the end only a means to the beginning of his quest for justice. His eyes, a stormy sea of resolve and fury, reflected his vow—Kgotso would pay.

Memories of his sweet friend Khumalo filtered through the haze of his fury, each one a poignant reminder of the innocence cruelly snatched away by Kgotso's vile actions. They had shared laughter, dreams, and ambitions, all stolen in the blink of an eye, reduced to wisps of smoke in the wind.

Khumalo, once the embodiment of joy and kindness, had been reduced to a shell, his vibrant spirit extinguished by the monstrosity of Kgotso's deeds. Vander could still see the lifeless eyes of his friend, a sight that haunted his dreams and fueled his relentless pursuit of retribution. The memory of Khumalo's suffering, of the light fading from his eyes as he stood before that speeding bus, was a grim testament to Kgotso's monstrosity.

It was a moment forever seared into Vander's consciousness, a wound that refused to heal. The cold hand of grief gripped Vander's heart, but it only strengthened his resolve. His vengeance burned brighter, harder—a beacon in the darkness, the promise of justice for his beloved friend.

Kgotso would pay; he would ensure it, even if it was the last thing Vander did. His mind was a tempest of vengeance, a storm that had been brewing for years. The thought of Kgotso's downfall was his only solace, the only thing that could bring warmth to his icy heart. The twisted shell of a man that Kgotso had become would be shattered, and Vander would relish in the echoing sound of his collapse. Alexander's objections would

Chapter 22 Enough

not deter him; Vander was resolute. "No matter what, Kgotso will pay for what he's done," Vander declared.

Proudly, Jack approved. "Good, he's got it coming." Scratching his chin again, Jack pondered, "Still, don't know how you plan on exacting your revenge when you've got the Sculptor coming for ya?"

Eyes narrowing, Vander glared up at him. "You don't, really? Because from the time I met you, you have always seemed to know an awful lot about me and what was ahead."

A nervous laugh escaped Jack. "Well, that's because you're my friend. I make it my business to check in on you and to know what's happening."

"My friend? And why is that, Jack? Why me?" Vander asked, his voice a hollow whisper against the chill. The emptiness within him grew, a void expanded with the realization that everyone he thought cared about him seemed to want something.

Before Jack could muster a response, the spirits, once languid, now whirled in a tempestuous frenzy, their nebulous forms blurring into streaks of spectral light.

Every eye turned to the source of the disturbance—a young boy, his countenance a canvas of fear and confusion. The child, a mere wisp of five years, looked lost, an alien in the spectral realm, his presence an aberration in their ghostly domain.

Yet, in his wide, fearful eyes, Vander saw a spark, an ember of potential. He saw in the boy a kindred spirit. Perhaps, even, someone he could mentor, someone who might come to love him. A chance, Vander realized, to be the father he never had.

At the thought, Vander felt a warmth that had been absent in his life for so long. He stepped forward, drawing closer to the boy, and meeting his gaze with an expression of reassurance. The spirits around them quieted, allowing for a moment of understanding between the two strangers who came from a world not their own.

Jack's words slithered through the air, heavy with avarice and curiosity. "What do we have here?" he crooned; his tone darker than the world surrounding them. His words hung in the bleak silence, echoing off the swirling masses, heightening the sense of fear and uncertainty of the child.

"Stay," Vander ordered, his tone lethal. His eyes never left the small boy, who was cautiously peeking through the fog at them. The boy's apprehension was palpable, yet Vander approached him slowly, maintaining a calm and reassuring demeanor. His face softened into an unexpected smile, trying to convey a sense of safety.

The boy remained still, his wide eyes reflecting the flickering mist and dimly lit shadows. The atmosphere was heavy with uncertainty, but also an inexplicable sense of connection. The boy was not a spirit, yet he was there, in the place that was a bridge between the living and the dead. How curious. How utterly fascinating.

Vander, maintaining a relaxed stance, moved toward the boy with a friendly twinkle in his eyes. "Hi, I'm Vander," he said, his voice mirroring the softness of a whispered secret. As the boy's gaze shifted from Vander to Jack, a guarded expression promptly painted itself across his face. Vander's heart clenched at the sight—it was a look of apprehension, of mistrust.

His current state, which made him appear as a nine-year-old, would serve him well in this exchange. He would appear less intimidating, more relatable—a strategy to assuage the boy's fears.

"Where are we?" the boy asked, his voice trembling.

Years ago, Vander had experienced that same fear, an icy dread that crept into the marrow of his bones whenever he crossed into the spectral realm. "You're in the In-between." Vander understood the chilling welcome the spirits offered to the uninvited—a bitter greeting he didn't wish upon the boy.

The echoes of his past nightmares, many a time triggered by Jack's disconcerting presence, still lingered in the shadowy corners of his mind. The memories were a stark reminder of the ominous path the boy could tread, and Vander, bearing the weight of his own past, desired a kinder fate for the young one.

His own experiences had carved within him a resolve, as resilient as ancient oak, to ensure the newcomer would be better shielded from the malevolent spirits that lay beyond the veil.

"The what?" the boy asked, afraid.

"The In-between," Vander answered. "It's like a waiting room. Imagine standing by the shore on a moonlit night, watching the ocean waves—they're there, right in front of you, but just out of your reach.

"That's how the spirits feel on the other side of the veil. They're waiting, much like we wait for a train to take us on a journey. They're waiting to cross over to a beautiful, peaceful place, just like when we wait for dawn to break after a long night. They're waiting for the right

Chapter 22   Enough

moment to move on," Vander explained, his voice a reassuring presence in the murky atmosphere.

The boy's voice echoed in the vastness, a whisper in the darkness. "Are you a spirit?" he asked Vander, his young eyes wide with unease. The words hung in the air, mixing with the eerie whispers of the unseen spirits, creating an unnerving symphony of the supernatural. His question, while childlike in its innocence, was heavy with the fear of the unknown, the fear of the ethereal world they now found themselves navigating together.

Vander, sensing the boy's distress, smiled kindly and shook his head. "No, I'm just like you," he said to reassure him.

Confused, the boy continued. "You're lost too?" he asked.

With a slight laugh, Vander nodded in affirmation and replied, wanting to put the boy's mind at ease: "I used to be, but now, I know how to get around here. Want me to show you the way back home?"

Scared of the world around him, the boy nodded vigorously. Unapproving spirits rushed past them, crying out in anger. Vander waved them off. "Don't worry about them," he said warmly. "They can't harm us. You're safe."

Vander heard Nightshade's voice, a whispered echo that drifted from the entryway of the veil. "Follow me. Your home is this way."

Vander started toward Nightshade's call and turned to make sure the boy was following him, which he was. Vander asked, "What's your name?"

Looking back at Jack, fear etched on his small features, the boy said, "Hunter."

Facing Hunter, Vander could sense the fear in his eyes—a reflection of his own fears of rejection and abandonment. In Hunter, Vander was hoping to find someone who might understand him and accept him as a friend; someone who would not use him like the others in his life had done. He wanted to keep Hunter safe and protect him like he had wanted to be protected so long ago.

Wrapping an arm around Hunter's shoulders, Vander led him away from the disembodied spirits, away from Jack's nightmarish images, and back toward his home with the bright new possibility of friendship.

MAY 1ST—10 DAYS

CHAPTER 23

REGRETS

ALAYNA

Austin, TX—Night

WINE GLASS IN HAND, ALAYNA SAVORED THE RICH flavor of the delicious red wine, each sip a symphony of taste and aroma. She relished in the peace of her small, cozy bottom-floor apartment, its warmth drawing a stark contrast against the blanket of darkness outside. There was something comforting about being home, just a quick trip from the bustling city where her shop was located to her sanctuary, an abode that belies its urban surroundings, a small, one-bedroom apartment that is a realm of whimsy and imagination.

The air is thick with an enchanting murkiness, a peculiar veil of mystery that shrouds the space, inviting those who dared, to delve deeper. The glow of a lone candle flickers, casting dancing shadows upon the well-worn walls, adorned with peculiar charms and curiosities collected from forgotten corners of the world.

The bedroom, her haven, bathed in the soft, ethereal glow of the moon, was a cocoon of warmth. In that atmospheric refuge, every knick-knack whispered tales of adventure, every creaking floorboard sang lullabies of yesteryears, and every breath you took was a step into the dreamland of solitude and mystery. It was not just a dwelling, but a living, breathing entity, pulsating with an unfathomable and captivating energy.

Chapter 23 — Regrets

The trance-like stillness only added to the alluring atmosphere, creating an opportunity for inner exploration and reflection. Entering that world away from distraction allows deep introspection, free from the pressures and judgments of a bustling metropolis. The walls were a silent witness to all that transpired, as if they knew her innermost secrets without ever having to speak a word.

Alayna's gaze, lost in the starless night, was occasionally interrupted by the glow of the streetlamp that cast long shadows on her solitude. The evening had been surprisingly fun, filled with laughter and exciting anecdotes shared with Brayden. He was hot, no doubt, but more importantly, he was kind and thoughtful. His presence had warmed her, his words echoing in her ears, and his touches left such a tantalizing sensation upon her skin.

She had felt a companionship she had not known she was missing. But now, as she stood there alone, all those feelings were replaced by a profound sense of loneliness.

Alayna's intuition had yet again proven its worth, especially with Brayden. He was a delight, exceeding her expectations in ways she had not anticipated. Beyond his undeniable sex appeal, Brayden's thoughtfulness stood out, revealing a depth to his character that was both intriguing and compelling.

Reflecting on the evening with Brayden, Alayna found herself dwelling on the abrupt ending. Her gifts, while advantageous in many ways, often felt like a curse, making it challenging to trust others. She had the uncanny ability to see through the lies people told themselves, and ironically, the ones she wished to believe about herself.

Brayden was open, honest, and unlike any other guy she had thus encountered on the dating scene. Yet, her innate talents and past encounters had built a wall of skepticism that she struggled to lower, even for Brayden. This internal battle was one of the many reasons she found herself alone in her cozy apartment that night, contemplating the consequences of her gifts and her inability to fully trust.

Her musings continued long into the night as she tried to make sense of it all. She had always felt like an outsider, unable to form real connections with anyone because of her gifts. But something told her that Brayden was different, and Alayna was beginning to wonder if he could be someone she could share her life with. If only she could let down her well-constructed walls of mistrust, she might just be able to experience a real connection.

In the veiled intensity of twilight, Alayna found herself admitting, if only to her own heart, how much she was captivated with Brayden. The way his gaze held hers—imbued with an affection she had never known in her life—had an inexplicably comfortable familiarity to it.

She reveled in his perception of her, untouched by the knowledge of her unique gifts. Her abilities of mediumship, a secret silently carried, were kept hidden in the deepest corners of her soul, shrouded in a myriad of unspoken words and emotions.

For the time being, she preferred the calm of ignorance, a tranquil sea untouched by the storms of revelation. Alayna did not want to see that sincerity in Brayden's eyes dissipate, replaced by fear or doubt once he knew the truth.

In the veil of the night, under the cold gaze of the moon, Alayna felt the icy grip of inevitability tighten around her heart. She knew Brayden, a human hound with an uncanny ability to unearth buried secrets.

His inquisitive nature was not just a trait but his very essence, an incredible detective who could unravel the most tangled skeins of mystery. Her clandestine side business, her secret refuge, was a sanctuary where she aided the grief-stricken, and offered solace to those who sought to touch the ephemeral strands connecting this world to the next.

She wanted to spend more time with Brayden. But she knew that it was just a matter of time before he uncovered the truth about her and her special abilities.

It was time for Alayna to decide. Did she take a chance with her heart and tell Brayden the truth? Or would her fears prevail and convince her that the best path forward was to break off contact before things got too serious?

It was not a difficult decision, Alayna wanted the opportunity to have Brayden in her life, and she refused to end their relationship before it had even begun. She would reach out to Brayden in the morning and make the next move.

If he gave her another chance to go out with him, she would tell him the truth about herself. Then Alayna would let Brayden decide if he wanted to stay or walk away. It was a risk, sure, but it was one she was willing to take. She refused to be a coward and let her fears dictate her future; this time, it would be Brayden's choice.

Chapter 23 — Regrets

With that thought, Alayna finally allowed herself to drift off and dream of a brighter future. She knew that the path ahead might be rocky, but she refused to let fear prevent her from living her life on her own terms. It was time for Alayna to take control of her destiny and bravely face whatever fate had in store.

Setting the wineglass down with a faint clink against the wooden table, Alayna allowed her gaze to linger for an ephemeral moment on the paned glass. The moonlight streaming through the window bathed the room in an ethereal glow, rendering each object within a spectral silhouette.

Alayna caught a shadow moving behind her, a fleeting figure that dashed to the far corner of the room.

The tranquility she felt had been shattered by the insidious encounter about to unfold.

Hand at her throat, Alayna turned, praying that it had only been a trick of the light, but bracing herself for a possible confrontation.

Her heart lurched in her chest as she came to an abrupt halt. The color drained from her face at the sight before her. There, suspended inches above the polished floorboards, huddled in the corner, floated a mangled apparition. The spectral figure, a tormented soul, reached out to her. Its ghastly form appeared to have been bathed in delicate flower petals of white, red, and pink.

Alayna could not breathe as the spirit acknowledged her presence with a faint whisper, "Help me."

MAY 2ND—9 DAYS

CHAPTER 24

SMALL REPRIEVE

BRAYDEN

Austin, TX—Dawn

Exhausted, Brayden knew he should have gone straight home to get a few hours of sleep. The remnants of the previous night's horrific scene played like a loop in his battered consciousness, demanding his attention and robbing him of peace. But it was not the physical fatigue that he sought escape, it was the relentless haunting of his mind, the dark overtones that painted every image.

His body could withstand the lack of rest, but his soul craved reprieve, a balm for the wounds left by the images he had witnessed the past twelve hours. And so, he found himself driving not toward the comfort of his own bed, but toward the familiar and comforting presence of his sister Paige's house.

The house was nestled in a quiet suburb. It was a simple yet elegant two-story home. Paige had insisted on a home that had more warmth than beauty, thus settling on the smaller, yet sophisticated blend of red brick and striking white trim. This suburban haven showcased the perfect balance between humble charm and dignified elegance. The quiet surroundings echoed an ambiance of tranquility, making it an idyllic retreat away from the hustle and bustle of city life.

As the first rays of dawn pierced through the veil of darkness, the hushed town was still enveloped in the remnants of night. The children,

Zoey and Hunter, were probably cocooned in their dreams, oblivious to the world stirring outside. But Ethan, his brother-in-law, was a creature of dawn. Even in the dim morning light, Brayden could picture him awake, embracing the day with open arms.

Brayden's lips curved into a smile, a warmth spreading through him. Ethan was more than a brother-in-law; he considered him his brother. Ethan not only loved his sister Paige with an intensity that was palpable but also embraced him as part of their family.

Ethan made Brayden feel like he truly belonged and had created a true sense of brotherhood. The dawn's early light seemed metaphorical to Ethan's influence in Brayden's life—a beacon of acceptance, love, and a sense of belonging.

The conversations they shared, the memories they created, and the bond that was growing between them had filled Brayden with a sense of belonging. Ethan's presence in his life brought him a trove of emotions, and Brayden was grateful for it.

Startled out of his musings, Brayden blinked as he found Ethan, his brother-in-law, tapping on his car window. In his hand, Ethan brandished a rolled newspaper, which he waved with an infectious grin. "You staking out the house? Or have you come for breakfast?"

Brayden couldn't help but laugh as he rolled down his car window, the sudden interruption bringing an unexpected happiness to his morning. "That depends. Are you cooking? Or is my sister?" Brayden teased.

Ethan stepped back to let Brayden out, his response coming in a conspiratorial whisper. "I'm on cooking duty today, so your stomach is safe."

Brayden slapped a hand on Ethan's back, his laughter ringing out in the morning air. "I'm telling Paige you said that."

"Go ahead... I'll just deny it," Ethan teased with a playful wink. Ethan motioned for Brayden to follow as he led him toward the house.

Still laughing, Brayden and Ethan came into the kitchen like two rambunctious kids. Their merry laughter echoed off the walls, filling the room with the contagious spirit of camaraderie.

Sitting at the kitchen table, drinking her first cup of coffee, Paige put a finger to her lips. "Quiet! You want to wake the kids?" she warned, her voice carrying an undertone of amusement.

The sight of Brayden and Ethan, acting as if they were afraid, brought a glow of affection to her eyes. She observed as Brayden, trying hard not to laugh, tiptoed his way to sit next to her. Meanwhile, Ethan, his face a picture of exaggerated caution, passed her the morning paper.

Turning, Ethan headed to the cabinets and began pulling out pots and pans with the utmost care.

From the floor above, the sound of children's excited footsteps thundered and reverberated through the home like a chorus of joyous heartbeats. Brayden, Ethan, and Paige paused, their conversation momentarily forgotten, as they listened to the cacophony.

The footsteps echoed like tiny hailstones rapidly striking the floor. The children were no doubt excited, perhaps in a hurry to join their favorite uncle, Brayden. It was a sound that brought smiles to their faces, a cheerful reminder of the innocence and exuberance of childhood.

Paige put her cup of coffee to her lips and scolded Brayden, "Uh-oh, you've done it now!"

Teasingly, Brayden glanced at the back door and grinned. "Should I make a break for it?" His eyes sparkled with mischief.

Ethan chuckled, balancing his cooking duties with a stern, yet affectionate, gaze. He replied, "You wouldn't dare?" His tone, though feigned with exasperation, was filled with appreciation. "I'm not going to be the one who tells them you snuck out of here before they got down here."

Brayden grinned. "All right, I'll keep them. You just do your thing with that French toast. I'm hungry!" Brayden conceded.

Despite his weariness, Brayden sprang up from his seat and positioned himself strategically a safe distance from the closed door. His stance resembled that of a catcher poised behind home base, ready to embrace the charge of the exuberant little ones.

In a flash, both kids burst through the door, banging it against the far wall. They spotted Brayden and launched themselves at him. Brayden allowed himself to be tackled by Hunter and Zoey, cushioning their fall with his body as the three of them collapsed onto the floor in a pile of giggles.

Amused, Paige watched from the sidelines, allowing the kids to enjoy their victory before calling them off. "Okay, okay. Enough roughhousing. Let Uncle Brayden up and go get dressed!"

Despite their groans of protest, they reluctantly stopped their attack, gave Brayden a departing hug, then ran off to their bedrooms.

Chapter 24 — Small Reprieve

Brayden sat up, taking in a few labored breaths, trying to recover. "I was thinking about having kids. But I'm afraid I'm already too old for them. Where in the world do they get all that energy?"

Paige helped Brayden to his feet as Ethan sat a pan of fluffy French toast, eggs, and sausage on the table.

Brayden's fatigue, which he had been keeping at bay, finally manifested itself physically, as his body swayed into Ethan.

Ethan reached out and steadied Brayden with two firm hands on his shoulders. "Hey, you all right?" he asked, his voice suddenly full of concern.

Brayden avoided Ethan's stern look, attempting to mask his fatigue. "Those kids are stronger than I thought," Brayden said, trying to shrug off Ethan's worry.

Ethan and Paige exchanged a worried glance as Brayden took his seat with more force than he had intended. Paige poured Brayden a tall glass of orange juice and handed it to him. "Did you get any sleep last night?"

"Sleep is overrated." Brayden took a big swig of the cool orange juice.

Paige placed plates and utensils around the table, a pattern of meticulous arrangement she had grown accustomed to. Meanwhile, Ethan, with a dishcloth wrapped around his hand for protection, carefully lifted the tray of freshly baked biscuits from the oven. The aroma of the biscuits quickly filled the room, a comforting scent that made their morning routine feel complete. He set them down gently, careful not to burn himself.

Eyes wide, Brayden surveyed the large spread. "Wow, is your whole fire station coming for breakfast?"

Laughing, Ethan said, "I'm used to cooking for a big crew."

"Obviously." Brayden smiled.

Paige hugged Ethan from behind. "Don't worry, he takes the leftovers to the station. His guys make sure that nothing goes to waste. Isn't that right, honey?"

Giving Paige a quick kiss, Ethan moved past her, grabbed the butter and jelly, and put them on the table. "It is. I'm lucky if the food even makes it past Ramiro to the kitchen some days."

Looking down at Brayden, Ethan could not help but observe his tired eyes, as he scooped up some eggs and piled a healthy portion onto his plate, "Paige said you had a hot date last night, is she the reason you're running on fumes?"

Brayden smiled. "I wish, but no. I got a call from work. Just left the crime scene about an hour ago."

"Oh no! You didn't blow it with the shop owner, did you?"

"What? No!"

Paige shook her head, that knowing, unapproving look on her face. "You didn't leave her sitting alone at a restaurant while you went off to answer a call?"

Ethan stopped gathering the food and studied Brayden with concern. "Bro, seriously?"

Defensively, Brayden sat up, ready to plead his case. "I swear, this time, it wasn't my fault. Well, not completely," Brayden admitted, with a hint of regret.

"Go on," Paige encouraged.

"I showed up on time, flowers in hand, like you told me. I made the appropriate amount of small talk before escorting her to my car." Brayden's eyes were distant, dreamy as he recalled his time with Alayna. "The date was going well. Great, actually."

Intrigued, Ethan took his seat. "So far, so good."

"We were having a really good time at the Peach Bar—"

Offended, Paige interrupted, "Peach Bar?!"

"Hey, that's where Alayna wanted to go, so I obliged." Brayden thought for a moment, then continued, "Matter of fact, she wanted to go there in order to be in familiar territory with people around her that she already knew."

"Oh, smart. I like her already." Paige smiled.

"Besides, what's wrong with the Peach Bar?" Brayden asked.

Paige rolled her eyes and waved an irritated hand at Brayden. "Continue."

"Alayna was easy to talk to, funny, a smart-ass at times, but you know, in a good way." Brayden laughed. "She also loves Taiwanese duck roll in case you need to know that for any future reference."

Brayden's smile faded as his voice dropped to a softer tone. "But as my luck would have it, I got a call." His gaze fell to his hands, fingers clenched around the cold glass of orange juice.

Incredulous, Paige asked, "So, you did rush off and leave her sitting alone in the restaurant?!"

Offended, Brayden corrected her. "Of course not." Lost in thought, Brayden added, "We cut our date short. I drove Alayna home, made sure

Chapter 24 — Small Reprieve

she made it inside all right, then headed to the station." Brayden did not tell Paige or Ethan about the chaste kiss or the awkward silence that came after he had asked Alayna about herself.

Paige flashed Brayden a reassuring smile. Her eyes, full of appreciation and concern, spoke volumes. "You'll have another chance to see her," she said, her voice weighed heavy with thoughtfulness. "Matter of fact, why don't you invite her over here for dinner?"

"What?" Brayden asked, startled.

"You can't be serious?" Ethan asked, at the same time Brayden did. Both men looked at one another, then back at Paige.

"It's a great idea, don't you agree? This young lady needs to see that there is some normalcy in your life." Ethan choked on his coffee; Brayden laughed.

"Wait a minute, you want me to try and convince Alayna that I have a normal life by bringing her here?" Brayden said, trying his best not to bust out laughing.

Smugly, Ethan took another sip of his coffee. Paige playfully slapped Ethan on the back of the head. "What did I do?"

"I'll deal with you later, mister." Paige put a hand on Brayden's shoulder. "Bring her over for dinner next week. Ethan will be off then, so we can all meet her." Paige gave Ethan a warning glare. "We will all be on our best behavior."

The corners of Brayden's mouth turned upward, his expression mirroring the comfort he found in Paige's words. "Great, so I have nothing to worry about," he replied confidently, reassured by her unwavering faith in him.

Brayden managed to summon a smile as Hunter and Zoey, dressed for school, barged back into the room with the joyous abandon only children possessed. Zoey, the more organized of the two, settled back into her chair after strategically placing her backpack near the backdoor, ready for a swift exit when it was time to go. Hunter, however, had other plans. A crumpled drawing clasped in his small hands, he bounded up to Brayden, his eyes shimmering with youthful enthusiasm. "I made something for you," he declared, his voice ringing out with innocent pride.

Making sure his expression was filled with excitement, Brayden studied Hunter's latest work. Though it was messy, Brayden could tell the picture was a depiction of Brayden and Alayna's night out. There was even a misspelled Peached Bar on the large sign above them and the small booth that they had shared.

Trying to mask his surprise, Brayden stammered, "Wow, this is great! Thank you, little buddy." Brayden's gaze slipped over to Paige, his expression guarded. It was not the first time Hunter had drawn a picture of something Brayden knew the child could not have seen or known about.

There was no mistaking the details in the drawing—the tilt of his head, the way his hands rested on the table, the exact curve of his smile. More disturbing than this mirrored likeness was the specter of a woman opposite him.

Alayna. Hunter had not met Alayna, yet there she was in vibrant color, her beauty captured in the innocent scrawl of a child's hand. It was an eerie paradox. A chilling realization dawned on Brayden—Hunter might be like his mother, Paige, possessing an uncanny knowledge that belied his tender years.

Brayden's gaze was fixed on his sister, Paige. Her eyes danced with a nervous energy, a spark of trepidation that flickered each time they wandered over to her husband, Ethan. "Hunter, darling," Paige's voice was strained, "your breakfast won't eat itself."

Hunter took his seat and began to pour a hearty helping of maple syrup on his French toast.

Brayden began to fold the paper, but Ethan snatched it away and began studying it. "I want to see Hunter's work." Ethan's smile faded as he took in the details of the drawing.

It felt like an eternity before Ethan's gaze softened. He forced a smile and returned the paper to Brayden. "Hunter, you are quite the artist." The tension in the room eased.

"Thank you, Daddy." Hunter beamed.

Brayden was acutely aware of Ethan's discomfort, his unease palpable whenever something emerged that hinted at Paige's, or what appeared to be Hunter's developing, abilities.

Not long after Ethan and Paige had met, she and Brayden had agreed not to discuss her gifts in front of Ethan. This pact was a protective shield crafted out of love and concern for Ethan because they both knew that anything to do with the paranormal upset him.

Though the drawing, even though a child had drawn it, was still a perfect portrayal of last night's date, Brayden could not help but be relieved

Chapter 24 — Small Reprieve

that it had not been worse. There was no telling how Ethan would have reacted if Hunter had seen or drawn images from last night's crime scene.

Was the closeness he shared with Hunter somehow drawing him into his world? And if so, what did he need to do to shield him from it? He loved this family and would never in a million years cause them harm or distress. It would crush him if he found that just by being close to him, he was subjecting Hunter to things his young mind should never see.

Brayden had suddenly lost his appetite; he would talk to Paige about these troubling thoughts when they were alone and not at risk of being overheard by Ethan. "Hey guys, I hate to eat and run, but I've really got to get some sleep." Brayden stood, Ethan rising with him.

"I can pack up some stuff for you to take with you?" Ethan offered.

"No, no. I'm good. But thank you."

They said their goodbyes and before he knew it, Brayden had stepped outside into the morning sun. He could hear the happy banter in the house behind him, but forced himself to walk away and get into his car. The brilliant light seemed to mock his inner turmoil, splashing its carefree radiance over a world that, for him, had turned dark.

The echoes of the previous night's events reverberated in his mind, their gruesome details clawing at his consciousness like a relentless specter. His eyelids felt heavy with the weight of exhaustion, but he feared that with much-needed sleep, there would also be vivid nightmares of the victim and her elusive killer.

God, he hoped he was wrong about Hunter. Prayed that he was, because if he was not, he knew he would have to put some distance between them to ensure he was not exposed to the nightmarish world he sometimes found himself in. He loved his sister and her family and would do anything to protect them, even if it meant staying away from them himself.

MAY 2ND—9 DAYS

CHAPTER 25

GOOD MORNING

ALEXANDER

Philadelphia, PA—Dawn

BATHED IN THE NASCENT GLOW OF THE DAWN, ALEXANDER found his spirits soaring. A delicate porcelain cup was cradled in his hand. The steamy tendrils of his imported English tea danced upward, intertwining with the somber notes of the morning. As he sipped, the rich undertones of the brew seemed to entwine with the crispness of the morning air, creating a symphony of flavors that reverberated through his senses.

A traditional continental breakfast of freshly baked croissants, their flaky exterior hiding a soft, buttery heart, sat alongside an array of cold cuts and selected cheeses. As the morning sun continued its ascent, the breakfast remained untouched on the mahogany table while Alexander read over the morning trades, his face a mask of indifference as he studied the stock reports, the coded language of profit and loss.

The room was filled with an uncanny silence, broken only by crinkling paper and the occasional clink of the teacup against the saucer.

Alexander reveled in his solitary morning sacrament; a somber dance choreographed by the stillness of the new day. The ritual, a palliative lullaby, whispered promises of serenity and tranquility, setting a slow, unhurried rhythm that echoed in the hollows of his existence. His eyes,

Chapter 25 — Good Morning

accustomed to the gloaming, savored the ephemeral moments of twilight as the world around him began to stir from its nocturnal slumber.

Sunlight streamed through the window, bathing the small breakfast nook in a blanket of golden warmth. It was an amazing day, bright in its promise, much like a summer's day before the building storms. Despite the serenity, there was an underlying current of anticipation, a prelude to the storm that Alexander himself had set in motion.

He sat there, sipping his tea, the sweet notes of brown sugar lingering on his tongue. It served as a momentary distraction from the events of the previous night. The room, a peaceful sanctuary to the busy streets below.

Two days prior, Alexander had received information from his informant. Information that would help him surprise Vander later that day over lunch, when he would be in one of his hangouts with his fellow classmates.

It was important to his plans that he catch Vander off guard, to disrupt his normalcy to keep him off-balanced. Alexander would, of course, make his intrusion into Vander's world in the politest way, making sure his actions were not obvious to Vander's associates, though he had no doubt, Vander would take it as the threat he intended.

Thinking back on his time with Vander, Alexander thought of the great care he had taken to mold the young boy into the fine young man he had become. Vander was a gentleman, a man with great potential, and a person with an unyielding drive. If he were fair, he also had to give credit to Vander, for he, too, had not wasted a single opportunity, nor had he failed to learn from the lessons he was taught.

And still, even after all these years, Vander found ways to surprise Alexander from time to time, an enduring testament to his unique spirit. It was that realization that continued to form the unwanted question that kept repeating in Alexander's mind. *Why am I so driven to end Vander's life?*

Alexander was torn between two schools of thought. On one hand, he harbored a deep curiosity, almost akin to a long tranquil river, about Vander's potential. Could Vander rise to the occasion, stepping into the big shoes left behind, and commandeer the empire that Alexander had painstakingly constructed? Yet, on the other hand, Alexander was gripped by a sense of serene apprehension, much like a placid lake ruffled by a sudden breeze. Was he about to entrust his lifetime's work to capable hands, or was he setting it on the path of uncertainty?

Alexander sank into the peaceful sanctuary of his thoughts, contemplating the crossroads that had presented itself. Would he allow Vander, his protégé, to continue to strive for an incredible future, a path laden with the thrill of achievement and the risk of failure?

Or should he transform Vander into a timeless piece of art, immortalizing him in the zenith of his youth, thereby creating his final masterpiece for the world and gifting Vander with his own touch of immortality, a work of art that would never be forgotten?

The decision weighed heavily on Alexander, like an artist's palette laden with a myriad of colors, each representing different paths Vander's life could take.

He quietly gazed around him, taking solace in the stillness that filled his home and wrapped him in a cocoon of peace. He let the tranquility lull him into a deep, meditative state as he pondered on his wisest course of action.

Alexander was pulled from his musings by the soft sound of footsteps descending the staircase. As he refocused on his surroundings, his gaze met Vander, who had just arrived at the landing.

Vander's calm demeanor remained unruffled despite the early hour, as he moved with a serene grace, his movements echoing the peaceful sanctuary of their abode. He offered Alexander a small nod, a silent greeting, before he made his way over to the breakfast table and joined him. "Good morning," Vander said in greeting.

"Good morning to you, my boy." Alexander motioned for Vander to take a seat. "I hope you had an enjoyable evening."

Curious, Alexander watched as Vander made himself a cup of tea. Steam wafted up from the delicate china cup, the scent of the brew mixing with the lingering aroma of the freshly baked bread that still sat untouched upon the silver tray.

Vander's movements were unhurried, a slow, deliberate dance of pouring, stirring, and finally lifting the cup to his lips. The room fell silent except for the soft clink of the porcelain and the faint rustling of Vander's robes.

Alexander studied him, his gaze intent, trying to decipher the thoughts behind those enigmatic eyes. The morning light illuminated Vander's features, accentuating his youthful determination and adding a touch of mystery to his profile.

Chapter 25 — Good Morning

Vander strode over to the window, his cup forgotten on the table. Outside, morning had come and with it, the sounds of rushing cars, muted conversations, and hurried footsteps on the street below.

Alexander watched as Vander looked down at the busy street for a few moments, seemingly lost in thought. Alexander wondered what he must be thinking. Had Vander received a premonition last night in his dreams about his possible plans for him? Or was he simply distracted by the thoughts of his upcoming graduation? Alexander could only guess, for Vander remained silent, his face an unreadable mask.

Alexander was no stranger to the silence; he found a sense of comfort in it. As the morning light wove its way through the cracks of the barely open window, illuminating the dust particles hovering in the air, he knew something was weighing on Vander's mind. Vander remained perched by the window, his silhouette outlined by the rising sun, his thoughts imprisoned within a fortress of solitude.

Trust for Vander was a rare commodity, dispensed sparingly, if at all. However, Alexander understood the nature of the young man and respected the boundaries Vander had established.

Alexander, his cup of tea now cold, set it aside and braced himself for the silence, patient and unwavering. The light in the room slowly grew brighter, and the cracks within Vander's armor began to show. Alexander could sense that something was stirring beneath the surface, a deep truth that Vander would soon reveal. *Today,* he thought, *is going to be an interesting day, indeed.*

Alexander watched as Vander drew in a deep, measured breath. His shoulders rose and fell with the rhythm of his breathing, displaying a calm façade that belied the stormy sea of thoughts undoubtedly swirling within him. Alexander couldn't help but admire Vander's ability to present an unbroken front despite the chaos that life often threw his way.

Alexander had always admired Vander's frankness and honesty, his fierce determination in spite of life's hardships. He could see that Vander was now struggling with something deep within himself, something he was having trouble expressing. "Vander, whatever it is, you can tell me," Alexander said, hoping this would give Vander the freedom to express whatever it was that troubled him.

Vander's deep blue eyes searched Alexander's face, a storm of emotions brewing within them. His gaze was an abyss, mirroring the turmoil he felt inside. "Last week, you asked me what I wanted for a graduation gift."

Alexander was taken aback by the depth of emotion he saw in Vander's eyes. He had never seen him so vulnerable before, yet his face still showed strength and resilience. For a moment, Alexander felt a small wave of panic rise within him. If Vander had foreseen his plans for him, the ones where he would immortalize the boy within his own grand, one-of-a-kind masterpiece, would he now be ready to plead for his life?

The realization sent a wave of panic rippling through Alexander, a sensation as foreign as it was concerning. Could he deny the plea if Vander voiced it? The oncoming darkness within his soul was relentless, its shadowy tendrils feeding upon the need to complete his life's work.

Alexander cared for Vander as much as he cared for anything in his life. Yet, this passion of his, the one that had driven him since childhood, demanded he finish this last masterpiece before he, himself, met his own end.

Breath held, Alexander waited. Vander came to stand before him, framed by the golden haze of the morning sun, his silhouette casting a long, menacing shadow. His arms rested behind his back, a posture of formality that belied the chilling statement he made next. "I want Kgotso dead," Vander simply said, his gaze locked onto Alexander, "by my hand before I graduate next week."

The words hung heavy in the air, their dark intent reverberating between the two men. Alexander was both relieved and alarmed at the same time. He had promised Vander years ago that he would have his revenge on the rogue Cape Town officer. Alexander kept his promises, but if he let Vander go now, he might lose him to the very vengeance he sought.

Alexander knew he could not deny Vander his vengeance. A vengeance seventeen years in the making, rooted in the sins of a man named Kgotso. A man who, like a lurking predator, had preyed upon the innocence of Cape Town's most vulnerable.

Vander had watched, helplessly, as Kgotso rose through the ranks, ascending to the helm of the Cape Town precinct. "I suppose you have a plan?" Alexander said, knowing all too well the seething resentment that Vander harbored.

Alexander understood that Vander would never rest until Kgotso was made to pay for his crimes, even if it meant risking everything, including their friendship. The vow he had made to Vander was not to be taken

Chapter 25 — Good Morning

lightly, and Alexander would honor it, even if it led him down a path from which there might be no return.

His eyes were cold as Vander answered, "I do."

Tapping his finger against his lips, Alexander thought it over for a moment. Vander was indeed intelligent and resourceful, an intricate combination that bolstered his chances of successfully returning from his mission undetected. The words Vander had uttered hung in the air, wrapping the room in a thick veil of tension and anticipation.

There was something chilling about Vander's demeanor, a sense of readiness that eclipsed all doubts. Alexander found himself entrusting Vander with the task, a decision borne more from a debt of gratitude than anything else.

He owed it to Vander, after all. A twisted semblance of a smile played on Alexander's lips as he gave his assent. "Provide me with a list of things you need, and I shall ensure you have everything," Alexander assured his young ward.

With those words, Vander's eyes lit up like two stars in the dead of night. His solemn face was replaced with a look of elation and hope, one that stirred something deep within Alexander's chest. He watched silently as Vander nodded, then turned on his heel to prepare for his trip back home to Africa.

As Alexander watched Vander ascend the stairs, a sardonic smile curled on his lips. He was more than happy to honor his word to Vander, gratifying the young man's thirst for vengeance.

Not only was it a promise long overdue, but this gift also served as a much-needed distraction for Vander. It offered Alexander the precious time to finalize his own intricate plans, undisturbed and unobserved. The air was electric with anticipation as he envisioned the imminent party and the departing masterpiece he had in store.

With Vander occupied elsewhere, he retreated to his study, his heart thrumming with a strange, dark joy. *Today,* Alexander thought, *will be a wonderful day indeed.*

CHAPTER 26

LIKE NO OTHER

BRAYDEN

Austin, TX—Day

After picking up Juan from his nondescript apartment building, Brayden and he made their habitual detour to the local corner vendor, a grizzled old man who poured them the strongest coffee this side of the city.

Their day had only just begun, but the dark tendrils of the case already wrapped around them. The crime scene, having been picked clean by the forensics team, awaited their discerning gaze. It was time to dive deep into their investigation, a puzzle that required their keen intuition and years of experience to decipher.

Every piece of evidence held an untold truth, every clue a small beacon in the overwhelming darkness. At the center of this intricate maze, lay their key to understanding exactly who Jasmine Lam was. It was time for Brayden and Juan to comb through every aspect of her life, her patterns, her secrets, and to interview anyone they could who had been close to her.

Once the crime scene tape had been lifted, it was the police detectives' job to embark on the journey of piecing together the crime, where every clue, every piece of evidence, had its own story to tell. The officers' journey often began at the nucleus of it all, the victim. Their life, habits, friends, associates, jobs, their daily encounters all served as a roadmap to a possible suspect.

Chapter 26 — Like No Other

Most times, the detectives assigned to the case had to notify the family of their victim's misfortune. Lucky for them, due to the notoriety of this latest victim, their captain had taken on that uncomfortable task.

After their initial visit to the crime scene, they had returned to the station to do a quick briefing with Bohannon. Brayden and Juan asked their questions, took down notes, then gathered their case files with a sense of urgent determination.

Well over an hour into studying the provided materials, Brayden tossed his folder aside. "I'm going down to the lab."

Focused on a report, Juan waved him off. "Let me know what you find out."

"Copy that," Brayden said as he pushed away from his desk.

It was quiet in the precinct that day; few officers milled about, with most of them having already left for their daily tasks on the streets or out in the field. Brayden did not pass any of his comrades on his journey to the lab-slash-morgue and found the silence unsettling.

Stepping inside the brightly lit room, Brayden was met with the heavy scent of antiseptic.

Brayden soon discovered Tasha, engrossed in her analysis, and tirelessly sifting through the gruesome remnants extracted from Lam's body. A symphony of methodical clicking and whirring resonated from her equipment, forming a discordant backdrop to the grim examination.

"Find anything interesting?" Brayden asked, startling her. "Sorry."

Recovering, Tasha raised her head and scoffed. "Interesting, yes. Helpful, no," she replied. Tasha sighed. "It would appear, that after draining the victim's body of blood, carving her up, breaking her bones, and twisting her up like an exotic bush of paradise, the killer actually used the victim's blood like glue to stick the flowers to her."

Brayden had thought he could not have been more horrified by the crime scene than he already was, but Tasha had just proven that theory incorrect. He could not believe the depravity of this killer, and he shuddered at the thought of what Lam's final moments must have been like. The image that had been painted by Tasha was dark and sinister. "Guess that explains why we didn't find her in a pool of blood."

"Indeed, this not only indicates a high level of proficiency but also a certain level of audacity," Tasha added, her cool tone echoing eerily in the quiet room. "Our suspect operates with clinical precision and leaves no trace, almost as if challenging us to catch him."

A shiver ran down Brayden's spine, the full weight of the situation sinking in. Their adversary was not just dangerous but also incredibly intelligent and had more than likely been practicing or had killed before. "How much you want to bet that this wasn't his first kill?" Brayden asked Tasha.

Tasha nodded slowly; her gaze fixed upon the evidence before them. "I would take that bet," she murmured, shaking her head sadly. "Evidence would suggest that he is proficient, and more than likely has done something like this many times before."

Brayden closed his eyes and took a deep breath, allowing himself a few moments to reflect on what they knew. He had spent so long trying to make sense of it all, but the truth was far darker than he could have ever anticipated. Taking his time, Brayden allowed himself to come to terms with what it meant.

Not wanting to assume anything, Brayden asked, "What about the pattern? The meticulous placement of bones... could it be some sort of ritualistic element?" His voice trailed off. The question hung in the air, adding another layer of mystery to the already unnerving case.

Tasha shook her head. "It's hard to say. It's almost as if the killer wanted to send some sort of message, but I can't make out what that message might be." She paused, a crease forming between her brows in thought. "I'm afraid we'll have to wait until we get more evidence before we can understand."

Brayden's hand lingered on the cool metal of the door handle. "You think our killer is a male?" The question hung in the air, echoing in the stillness.

Tasha nodded, her eyes locked on Brayden's, her voice steady. "Yes. The killer's hands were large, skilled, and extremely strong to do what he did." The room descended back into silence, with only their thoughts for company.

Brayden pulled on the door handle, gave Tasha a nod, then stepped out of the room and back into the empty hallway.

Moving swiftly back down the long corridors Brayden thought about the case and knew that it was not uncommon for a detective to collaborate with local, state, or even federal law enforcement agencies if he believed there was a possible trail of victims that might extend beyond their precinct's boundaries. Though he did not want to believe there were other victims like Jasmine Lam, his gut told him there was more to this case than all of them had previously believed.

MAY 2ND—9 DAYS

CHAPTER 27

DANGER AHEAD

ETHAN

Austin, TX—Day

DRESSED IN HIS EMT UNIFORM, A PATCHWORK OF PRECIsion and practicality, Ethan carried supplies to his waiting ambulance in one of five large bays. Each piece of equipment, a lifeline in the wilderness of unpredictability, had a tale to tell, stories of lives saved, of narrow escapes, and of silent prayers answered on lonely roads and busy highways.

As he closed the doors of his rig, Ethan spotted his partner and fellow paramedic.

Donut in hand, Ramiro Quezada, a kind-hearted and ever-jolly Hispanic man in his mid-thirties, looked at Ethan with his usual wide grin. "Looks like I arrived just in time. You've already done all the heavy lifting," he teased, his eyes twinkling with friendly mirth.

Ethan knew that despite his light-hearted humor, Ramiro never shied away from his responsibilities, always pulled his weight, and was considered by all, an asset to their team.

Ethan considered himself lucky to have Ramiro as his partner. "Oh, don't worry, I've left plenty of work for you, my friend." Watching Ramiro devour his donut with gusto, Ethan felt his stomach growl. "You better not have eaten my cinnamon roll buddy, or there will be hell to pay."

Offended, Ramiro put a hand to his heart. "I'm hurt, amigo, that you would even think I would do such a thing."

"Are you kidding me? There's no thinking about it. Around here, you eating my pastry is darn near a daily occurrence." Ethan chuckled and started for the break room. As he passed Ramiro, Ethan patted his partner on his plump belly. "Besides, you need to be under that two-hundred-and-fifty-pound mark at your next weigh-in," he said, his tone full of good-natured ribbing as he snuck past him. "Or they are going to strap you to that treadmill."

Ramiro growled and gave Ethan a light shove. "I can't help it. I have big bones!"

Entering the hallway, the smell of freshly brewed coffee greeted Ethan as it wafted through the air, a scent that immediately brought a comfortable familiarity to the start of his shift. The break room was the crew's hangout, a place where they could take a moment away from the intense pressure of their jobs and share stories and laughter over inside jokes.

Even the worn-out sofa in the corner, with its lingering impression of countless tired bodies, was a testament to their shared memories in this room.

"Morning Ethan," Shane Curtis, the youngest member of the team, greeted him. Shane was brimming with energy, even in the early hours. Buster Duran, the firehouse veteran, gave a nod of acknowledgment from his corner, his eyes heavy but alert. Eric Avila, the fearless hotshot, was already gearing up, ready to dive into the day's work. Across the room, Lu Guillen, the level-headed team member, was checking equipment, his calm demeanor a constant.

The only one missing on this shift was their fire chief, Michael Ganaway, who was no doubt poring over reports in his office. Julie Reyes, their dispatcher, still radiant in her mid-thirties, was also there, savoring her coffee, adding a sense of normalcy to their morning routine. There were, of course, other women who served as EMTs, paramedics, and fire crew, but for some reason, they were not on this shift that day.

Ethan rummaged through the cabinet, his fingers finally closing around the familiar ceramic handle of his personalized mug, the words "World's Coolest Dad" emblazoned across its side.

Smiling, he poured himself a cup of coffee. It was going to be another long day, but at least he had his second family there at the station with him, which helped it to feel like his home away from home.

Chapter 27 — Danger Ahead

Ethan loved his job and loved the crew. Even with all their differences, they were close and always had each others' backs. Not to mention that they had the coolest jobs ever. After all, how many people got to spend their days helping people and saving lives?

Just as Ethan was about to ask Buster about the intriguing book he was engrossed in, an abrupt ring from his back pocket interrupted their conversation. He pulled out his phone, recognizing the number instantly. It was Paige, his wife. There was a pang of regret as he remembered their rushed goodbye that morning. He'd left her with nothing more than a quick, chaste kiss, too preoccupied with Hunter's drawing to indulge in their usual morning routine.

Ethan knew it was not fair to Paige; she had not asked for her son to be burdened with those unexplainable gifts any more than Hunter had asked to receive them.

Deep down, Ethan wished he could be more accepting of their strange abilities and less fearful of them and how they affected their lives. It was uncharted territory, a part of his wife and son that he did not know how to navigate.

Putting the phone to his ear, Ethan stepped out of the break room and back into the hall.

"Hey, honey. Do you have a minute?" Page asked, her voice troubled.

"Of course. What's up?" Ethan asked, his voice warm and comforting. He leaned against the cool wall of the hallway, his posture relaxed. The murmured buzz of his comrades faded into the background as he focused on the conversation and was instantly concerned when Paige did not answer him.

His sense of unease grew as a knot formed in his stomach. "Babe?" he said, trying to maintain a calm he did not feel. He knew Paige had a knack for sensing things, but the timing of her premonition, just after the unpleasant incident with Hunter, was unnerving. Ethan couldn't help but feel guilty. He wondered if his earlier outburst had contributed to her present anxiety. He loved Paige, despite the mysteries that often surrounded her, and he wanted to reassure her.

"It's okay. Whatever you need to say, just say it."

Paige's voice was trembling as she replied, "Please be careful today on any call you might get. I've had this really bad feeling all morning and can't seem to shake it."

Ethan forced a chuckle, trying to lighten the mood between them. "Paige, everything is going to be all right. You're just nervous because I acted like an ass this morning. I'm sorry for freaking out." He felt a sense of relief as he spoke the words. It was important that she knew how sorry he was for his uncharacteristic behavior.

As Ethan held the phone close to his ear, he could hear Paige's breath catch on the other end of the line. A silence dropped between them, a silence that was as heavy as it was profound, laden with emotions that words could hardly capture. Then, he heard Paige's voice, faint but clear, whisper the sweetest words, "I love you, Ethan." It was a sentiment that echoed in his heart, a sentiment he reciprocated with all his being. "I love you back, Beautiful."

He could hear Paige's anxiety through the phone, and he knew what she was asking of him. "Remember what I said and be careful, okay? I don't know what I'd do if anything happened to you."

Wanting to reassure his wife, Ethan said, "I will. Promise." Finally, with a quiet goodbye, they severed the connection.

As Ethan returned his cell phone to his pocket, the station's alarm sounded. As the piercing alarm echoed through the station, an icy chill swept through Ethan. The ominous code reverberated through the speakers, the warning more chilling than the alarm itself. "10-33, Active Shooter." This, the most dreaded of all the codes, he knew would set in motion a series of events that would test all their skills, courage, and resolve.

The door to the break room erupted, spewing forth a wave of firemen, their faces shrouded in grim determination. They surged past Ethan like a current of urgency, their boots thudding in a synchronized rhythm that echoed ominously in the vacant hallway.

Ethan, caught in the undertow, found himself yanked from his momentary stupor. His heart pounded fiercely against his ribs as if trying to escape the foreboding dread that filled the air. Paige's words, now a whispered ghost in his ear, sent an icy chill racing down his spine, "Please be careful today."

As he and Ramiro vaulted into their ambulance, trailing the fiery tail of the fire truck, the world seemed to slow, each second heavy with a portentous silence.

MAY 2ND—9 DAYS

CHAPTER 28

LUNCH WITH FRIENDS

VANDER

Philadelphia, PA—Noon

With his morning classes completed, Vander found himself navigating the university's pathways, each step carrying him closer to Christina's dorm. The early afternoon was warm, but mild as he navigated across, his mood bright and upbeat despite the dark task that lay before him.

There, his troubles with Alexander seemed like a distant memory. University life had proven more worthwhile than his high school years, an era smeared with the awkward hues of adolescence. It was as if the campus had been a crucible, melting away the insecurities of youth, leaving behind only those matured by the fire. Those who clung to their childish ways were sidelined, ignored, left to the mercy of their own solitude.

That afternoon, he was meeting his acquaintances for lunch, a thought that filled him with a sense of peace. Each footstep was a beat in the rhythm of his pre-graduation celebration, a song that he was eager to share with his comrades.

Their meetup would also serve a much-needed purpose. He would need to deliver his final term paper to his classmate, David, for him to turn it in while he was away in Africa. With such a massive class, Vander had no doubt his teacher would not miss him, thus, once his paper was turned in, his instructor would assume he, himself, had been present, and he would not have to worry about failing to meet the necessary requirements of the class.

Rounding the corner, Vander was pleased to find Christina was already there waiting for him, she sat at the top of the steps leading into the building which housed her and her fellow roommate.

A ripple of laughter echoed from Christina. "You're two minutes late," she declared, her voice a playful taunt. "So, you're buying dinner."

Surprised, Vander looked down at his watch. "Really, I thought I was right on time," he stated. Even though he was, however, on time, he was happy to allow Christina her small victory. "Very well, but you will have to sit next to Wanda".

The mere suggestion of having to endure the incessant chatter of their mutual friend set Christina to roll her eyes dramatically. "Ugh, fine, okay, but be prepared for me to be irritable the rest of the afternoon!"

With a deep sigh, Christina gathered her things and started down the steps. With a playful smile, she handed her things to Vander to carry, then looped her arm in the free one Vander offered.

It did not take Vander and Christina long to get to their destination.

Dim Sum House by Jane G's, situated in the heart of University City, was a culinary gem that offered an array of delightful dim sum specialties. Stepping inside, Vander embraced the ambiance. Its modern decor was cozy and welcoming, creating a comfortable space for patrons to enjoy their meals while enhancing their dining experience.

Vander's classmates had made a wise choice in selecting this restaurant for its extensive array of dishes. The menu boasted everything from delicate steamed shrimp dumplings to fluffy barbecue pork buns, all meticulously prepared with an attention to detail that underscored the chefs' skill and authenticity. Vegetarians were not left behind, with a wealth of options prepared with equal flair. The quality and flavor of each dish were rooted in traditional.

More importantly, Vander thought, this popular hangout offers affordable pricing which attracts college students, particularly those from the nearby University City, thus making it a favored hub for casual hangouts, intense study sessions, or a well-deserved respite from the rigors of academic life.

Spotting their boisterous group at a large table in the back, Christina and Vander weaved their way through the labyrinth of busy waiters, crowded booths, tables, and chairs. The air was thick with laughter and

Chapter 28 — Lunch With Friends

the buzz of conversation, fueling their happy spirits. With wide, welcoming smiles, they approached their friends, ready to dive headfirst into the joyous chaos.

Vander slipped into his designated seat at the table-end, an unspoken spot of power that his companions unconsciously surrendered to him on many occasions. It was an easy act of forgetfulness, a comforting illusion that Vander was just an ordinary young man, wrapped in the same blanket of optimism and future dreams that his friends so brightly wore.

But Vander, under the jovial façade, was a stranger to his own life. The laughter, the camaraderie, and the hopeful chatter as they all discussed their future seemed alien to him. After all, in a few short days, he may not have a future at all, for more than likely, he would be dead.

Having known what to order long before he and Christina had arrived, Vander let his gaze sweep over the faces of the men and women he had called friends for most of the time he had been at the university.

Each person had been carefully chosen, a piece in his intricate camouflage that Alexander had so brilliantly taught him how to create.

There was David Sierra, the business major, with his mind always on numbers and strategies. Jonathan Nesmith, the economics student, his analytical brain always ticking. Marco Aldez, who was engrossed in finance, his eyes constantly following the flow of money. Christina, with her fascination for criminal forensics, was a striking contrast, while Stephanie Hernandez, who studied psychology, was ever serious and observant.

Frank Abney, the computer information and systems expert, was a wizard in the digital realm. Lastly, there was Wanda Stout. A nurse in training, she was Frank's shadow, an addition he had not planned for, yet who was still intriguing in her own right.

Each one of them held an interest that Vander couldn't pursue himself, for reasons only he knew. Each one, a camouflage, a friend, a piece of the puzzle that helped him explore avenues to a future he was still trying to build.

Vander watched, his eyes tracing the waitress as she wound her way through the busy room. Her smile was bright, blissfully unaware of the chill that had suddenly filled the air. Her laughter preceded Nightshade's shrill call. Of course, only Vander had heard his precious bird, and thus the others sat oblivious to the sudden warning cry that had instantly set his extra sensory senses to attune to his surroundings.

The room seemed to hold its breath; the clinking of silverware against plates halted mid-bite and conversations hushed into anxious whispers. Vander knew something had changed, an unseen peril had entered their midst, sensed only by the ominous avian harbinger and himself.

Pen and notepad in hand, the waitress stopped at their table, her laugh lines becoming more pronounced as she readied herself to jot down their orders. Vander's gaze slid to Alexander, who nonchalantly strolled up beside her.

Alexander was resplendent, a perfect picture of charm and elegance, yet Vander knew that beneath that polished exterior lurked a heart as cold and ruthless as a winter night.

"Please forgive my intrusion." Alexander turned to the waitress, an apologetic nod to her as he continued. "Would you mind if I spoke to your patrons for a moment before you take their order?"

Easily manipulated, the waitress tucked her notepad and pen away and motioned toward the kitchen. "Not at all. I'll go check on everyone's drink and be back in a few minutes."

"Thank you so much," Alexander said as he turned his eyes to the group. An uneasy silence settled over the table as Alexander's eyes studied each of them in turn. Vander felt a shiver run down his spine as he met Alexander's gaze and held it. "Dear Boy, I hope I haven't embarrassed you? I was dining with an associate and just happened to see you come in. I wanted to drop by and introduce myself to your friends."

A knowing smiled tugged at the corners of Vander's lips. *Oh, how Alexander loves his games.* He knew his mentor would no more frequent this restaurant than he would one of the cheap franchises that sat on every busy corner in America. He was up to something.

Not wanting to make this any more awkward than it already was, Vander stood and began the forced introductions. "Not at all."

Alexander, his face bright, stood there like the perfect gentleman. "Everyone, I would like you to meet my guardian, Alexander Dayton." Vander could not help but notice the curious glances amongst his friends as he began to introduce them. "Alexander, this is David Sierra, Johnathan Nesmith, Marco Aldez, Christina Wallace, Stephanie Hernandez, Wanda Stout and Frank Abney."

Despite the palpable tension, Vander forced a smile, attempting to dispel the building unease. He could not shake off the feeling that Alexander's presence had somehow altered the room's atmosphere.

Chapter 28 — Lunch With Friends

Delighted, Alexander straightened, one hand casually draped over the opulent handle of his cane. A thin smile danced on his lips; his eyes gleamed with a curious type of mirth that seemed out of place. "It is so wonderful to finally meet some of Vander's friends."

Not wanting to be rude, his friends all gave a form of greeting to Alexander with smiles all around. Vander knew there was more to this chance meeting and remained standing, his eyes on Alexander. "I appreciate you dropping by. I'm glad you had the opportunity to meet everyone."

"The pleasure was all mine, I assure you." Alexander offered Vander a polite nod as he turned toward the door. "Oh, dear, I almost forgot," Alexander exclaimed as he paused.

Vander had to fight to maintain his smile and resist the urge to fix narrowed eyes on his mentor as Alexander's hand rummaged within his coat pocket and emerged with a cluster of stark, white envelopes, their pristine surfaces starkly contrasting with the dark room. The gold-etched invitations glinted in the dim light, an ominous representation of a supposedly joyous occasion. "I was going to ask Vander for a list of names and addresses to which to send out these invitations," Alexander said, the corners of his lips curling into a smile. "But seeing as how you are all here, I hope you wouldn't mind taking one of these now and saving me the trouble?"

"Sure thing," David said and was the first person to take an invitation.

Happy to oblige, the group extended their hands to Alexander and accepted their invitations one by one.

"Wonderful!" Alexander said with delight. "Again, thank you for your time and I hope to see you all next week." With the formalities concluded, Alexander tipped his hat to them and started off, his cane echoing with a soft thud against the wooden floor as he made his way to the door. "I'll see you at home later," Alexander called over his shoulder, his voice bouncing off the austere walls, leaving an eerie echo that merged with Nightshade's fading call.

"Did anyone else feel a chill when he walked up to our table?" David sounded off first, his usually jovial voice now laced with an underlying note of unease.

Vander, suddenly quiet, could only nod in agreement. His supposed sanctuary had been infiltrated right in the middle of the day. Vander had thought this place was off his mentor's radar, but now he knew he was wrong.

Christiana, mesmerized by Alexander's sophisticated manners, seemed oblivious to the undercurrents he had caused. "There's something captivating about him," she murmured. "Why haven't you introduced him to us before?"

Little did they know, they were all prime targets for Alexander's perverse amusement. Vander had kept his worlds apart not out of shame, but out of a desperate attempt to protect them. And now, the nightmare Jack had shown him had a very real possibility of coming true.

As the waitress hurried back to their table, a halo of light from the solitary overhead lamp seemed to dance across her worn apron. Her pen was poised, ready to take down their orders. Taking his seat, Vander made a reasonable excuse. "Alexander travels a great deal. There really has never been a good time for introductions."

Turning to Vander, the waitress asked, "What can I get for you?" Vander set aside his fear and forced a smile.

"I'll have the Dragon and Phoenix," he stated, his voice steady. The dish was a medley of jumbo shrimp and dark chicken meat swathed in the fiery embrace of General Tso's sauce, crowned with the crunchy regalia of walnuts. One of his favorites, but unfortunately, Vander had just lost his appetite.

Each member of the group followed suit and placed their orders. The moment their orders were complete, a sense of camaraderie washed over the group again. They raised their glasses in a toast to friendship and their soon-to-be graduation. Amidst the clinking of cutlery and the hum of chatter around them, they reveled in shared stories and hearty laughter.

The waitress was soon back with their meals, the steaming plates and aromatic smells wafting up from their table. Digging into their meals, their conversation flowed naturally from one topic to another, touching on everything from current events to childhood memories.

Suddenly Wanda exclaimed, "Did you guys hear about the body they found in the art district down in Austin, TX?"

Time stilled as Vander, his fork halfway to his mouth, paused. Alexander had just been to Austin and had enjoyed a few days admiring the various museums that the city had to offer.

Christina, having heard and studied tales of dozens of corpses, seemed bored. "Why would we? Unless, of course, there was something special about the killer or the body they found."

Chapter 28   Lunch With Friends

Wanda leaned in close, her gaze intense. "They said it was some up-and-coming artist," she whispered, her voice breathy with excitement. She continued, "They found her in her studio. Her body was twisted up like some weird sculpture and covered in flowers."

MAY 2ND—9 DAYS

CHAPTER 29

MAKE THE CALL

ALAYNA

Austin, TX—Late Afternoon

Exhausted from her sleepless night, Alayna heaved a sigh of relief as she locked the doors of the shop and flipped the open sign to closed with a heavy sigh. Already, she could hear the sure-to-be heavy rush hour traffic that had begun to worsen quickly after she had said goodbye to her last departing customer.

Wanting to be alone, Alayna had sent Hannah home early, and sensing her unhappy mood, her assistant had more than happily obliged.

Wearily, Alayna went back to the locked door. She wanted to be sure she had not made the same mistake she had a few days prior of forgetting to fortify the entry.

A wistful smile tugged at Alayna's lips as she pondered how beautiful the paradox of life could be, while also wondering how exhaustion could, many times, bring about a sense of peace. Even then, when she faced a crossroads. Should she stay the course or take a chance at a new beginning? It was an intimidating thought, filled with uncertainty but also promise.

Absorbed in thought, Alayna straightened a few items on the shelves and allowed her mind to wander. She had come a long way since setting up her shop over three years ago. She had taken risks, made mistakes, and

Chapter 29 — Make The Call

celebrated a great deal of success, all of which had eventually brought her to this point in time.

Going over to the counter, Alayna found the card that Brayden had left. She turned it over in her hands, the solid weight of the thick cardstock a comforting presence. His name, Detective Brayden James, was printed in stark, no-nonsense letters, a number neatly inscribed below. It was a tangible link to the man who had unexpectedly become her and Hannah's savior, a reassuring symbol of safety in turbulent times.

As she traced the embossed letters with her fingers, Alayna could not help but ponder the surreal turn of events that had created this quiet moment of introspection.

Decision made, Alayna picked up the phone, and a sense of certainty washed over her. She dialed Brayden's cell. Each tone of the dial echoed in the empty room. The phone rang a few times, creating a rhythmic tension that hung in the air.

The moment Brayden answered, his voice resonated through the speaker; a deep, sexy cadence that was uniquely his. "Detective James, how can I help you?"

The sound sparked a smile on Alayna's tense face. "Hey Brayden, this is Alayna Sage. Is now a good time to talk?"

Listening, Alayna heard Brayden stumble over his words. "Oh, hey... yeah, yes, now is a great time. How can I help you?"

The melodic tone of Brayden's voice sparked a smile on Alayna's face, a silent acknowledgment of the bond they shared and the conversation that was about to unfold. A subtle hint of anticipation hinted at her words as she asked, "I was wondering, if you weren't busy, maybe you could swing by my shop after work. I could make us something to eat?"

There was a brief hesitation, a moment where time seemed to slow and the world hushed, waiting for Brayden's response.

On the other end, Alayna heard Brayden's partner goading him. "The lady asked you a question. Say something!" His voice was hushed.

"Don't you have something to do?" Brayden's harsh reprimand was heard, even though Alayna could tell he had his hand over the receiver.

Trying to play it cool, Brayden's words to her were measured and tentative. "Sure, yeah, I would be happy to. I could stop by in a couple of hours?"

A couple of hours, Alayna thought, a small price to pay for the joy that was likely to follow. "That would be great. See you then," she said, a smile in her voice as she hung up.

With a spring in her step, Alayna moved toward the small room at the back of the shop, where an assortment of different attires was carefully organized. She softly hummed a tune, lost in thoughts of the evening that lay ahead. Her mind was riddled with a blend of anticipation and curiosity. *What should I wear tonight? Should it be charming and elegant, or more casual yet chic? Casual chic, of course. We will be dining here in the little kitchen at the back of my shop. No need to be fancy.*

She opened the door and carefully surveyed her options. Taking a few extra minutes to ponder upon each option, Alayna eventually chose the perfect outfit for the evening. A simple yet sophisticated dress perfectly matched with her favorite pair of heels.

Alayna hummed to herself, a happy melody that resonated through the hushed stillness of her quaint room. The notes weaved and echoed within the confined space. As Alayna slipped into her silk dress, a spectral harmony joined her happy tune, a ghostly serenade that seemed to ripple in the night.

Uninvited, the chilling whisper of the entity lingered on the edge of Alayna's senses, a dissonant note in her solitary symphony. Its presence something she sought hard to ignore, yet its flickering presence was as relentless as a faulty light switch that threatened to shatter the veneer of a normal evening.

Frustration etched on her features, Alayna swiveled around, her gaze locked onto the spirit that hovered ominously before her. The desolate apparition shimmered in the air, its ghastly pallor casting an eerie glow in the dim light of the room.

"I told you," Alayna's voice echoed in the hollow silence, a tremor of exasperation threading through her words, "I don't know how to help you." It was a stark truth, hanging heavy between them.

She hadn't known the woman in life and as far as she knew, Alayna had no ties that connected her to this mournful spirit that sought her aid. She had received no calls from any client in which someone else might have wished to engage with this departed soul, so what did she want her to do?

Chapter 29 — Make The Call

If Alayna could not find the connection that had brought this tormented spirit into her life, she would be unable to help her or show her how to move on.

CHAPTER 30

TROUBLE AHEAD

ETHAN

Austin, TX—Day

WITH HIS PARTNER RAMIRO, ETHAN CROUCHED LOW behind their ambulance. The piercing sirens ripped through the air, their clamor echoing off the decaying apartment buildings that rose before them like a group of bedraggled giants.

Their breaths were shallow and rushed, each one sucking in the acrid smoke and exhaust that filled the air. The police unit closest to them sat abandoned, its door swung open like a grim invitation. The flashing lights danced and twisted upon the vehicle. Their department's fire unit, with its windshield a shattered testament to the onslaught they faced, had retreated to a safe distance a few blocks away.

When Ethan and Ramiro had first arrived on scene, the two officers were already down, one struggling to crawl back to the perceived safety of his unit. His movements had been labored, each breath he took a painful effort.

The other officer had been pinned behind a vehicle that had been parked haphazardly nearby, trapped like a deer in the headlights of an oncoming storm.

Ethan could feel the palpable fear that hung in the air, the dread of knowing that the next bullet fired could shatter the precarious balance

Chapter 30 — Trouble Ahead

between life and death. The stark reality of the situation was a chilling reminder of the thin veneer that separated order from chaos in this world.

At first, Ethan held out hope that the wounded officer on the ground had not taken a direct hit, that his Kevlar vest had protected him from a life-threatening injury. But as more shots rang out, the officer, having already suffered being hit by a couple of bullets, was struck again. This time, however, the 556 round from the AR-15 tore through his damaged vest and pierced through to the officer's chest. Ethan had watched helplessly as the cop screamed in pain, fell to the ground, then went silent.

Sporadic, the gunfire continued to erupt from the third floor of the dilapidated apartment complex. Ethan's gaze went from one officer to the other. The man by the parked car only had a flesh wound to his leg. If he did not succumb to shock, he should be all right, at least for the time being.

More important was the officer who lay unconscious on the street. The man was losing blood fast, and without immediate intervention, he would not make it. A sense of helplessness washed over Ethan as he peered into the back of his rig, wishing he had something more along the lines of offense to join the firefight. He did not wish to harm anyone, but if he could lay down some cover fire, at least they could get to the injured officer without being shot.

Ethan understood that a paramedic's role extended beyond mere medical assistance; they were the first line of defense in precarious situations. Whether it was a car accident, a domestic dispute, or a natural disaster, the responsibility of a paramedic involved ensuring their own safety as well as that of others. This involved quick decision-making, gauging the situation effectively, and implementing measures to prevent any further harm.

However, Ethan also understood that his role was fundamentally to save lives, not to engage in combat. They did not carry guns, tasers, or even a good baseball bat. Instead, they were equipped with protective gear such as Kevlar vests to shield themselves. Despite the lack of offensive tools, he was outfitted with the knowledge and equipment to stabilize patients, create order amidst chaos, and navigate dangerous situations.

His protective gear symbolized his commitment to the cause, a shield to fend off harm, not a weapon to inflict it. Ethan's courage was defined not by his capacity for violence, but by his unwavering dedication to the preservation of life in the face of danger.

Ethan watched as the officer, close to the cop bleeding out on the asphalt, bravely fired back at the armed perpetrator who held the higher ground. The scene filled Ethan with a profound feeling of helplessness. The wounded officer was fading fast, his life hanging in the balance. Ethan's mind raced with calculations, his gaze shifting between the bleeding cop, the officer returning fire, and the looming threat on the high ground.

If he timed it just right, when the officer was laying down suppressive fire, Ethan might have a window of opportunity to dash into the street, pull the wounded cop clear, and drag him back to the waiting ambulance. Beside him, his partner Ramiro watched, his eyes wide and incredulous as he saw the gears turning behind Ethan's determined eyes.

As Ethan tightened his Kevlar vest, ready to chance the hail of bullets, Ramiro let out an exclamation of disbelief, "Don't even think about it."

Ethan made his decision. With no time left to spare, he took off running as soon as the officer opened fire. Fearless and resolute, Ethan's only thought was to save the cop who lay bleeding in the street. It was a mission that could cost him his life, but Ethan was determined to see it through.

As Ethan ran toward the fallen officer, he felt something whiz past, dangerously close to his head. He willed himself not to consider that the passing object could very likely have been a bullet from the shooter's rifle.

"Get your ass back behind that ambulance before he blows your head off," the defending officer yelled as he fired two more rounds.

Trying to stay low, Ethan grasped the wounded officer by his shirt, a sharp pain suddenly tore through his arm, making him momentarily lose his grip, then with new determination, Ethan snagged the man and dragged him back behind the ambulance as a bullet ricocheted off the side of the rig. Using their bodies as shields, both he and Ramiro covered the wounded officer.

Looking up, Ethan spotted a fleet of armed vehicles rumbling down the street toward them. The units thundered past them and took up a strategic position in front of the ambulance. The SWAT team deployed swiftly and began to secure the perimeter.

They held their assault rifles at the ready, the ominous barrels aimed unflinchingly at the suspect's apartment. Amid the tense standoff, orders for the suspect to surrender echoed through loudspeakers, ricocheting off the surrounding buildings. However, Ethan and Ramiro didn't let that

Chapter 30 — Trouble Ahead

diversion distract them from their mission. Instead, they used the distraction to get to work, and to do what they had gone there to do.

Ethan's hands moved swiftly and precisely, his years of experience guiding his actions. First, he and Ramiro cut away the officer's bloody shirt, revealing the raw wound left by the gunshot. Stripping the injured officer of his vest, they exposed the site to assess the damage.

A chest gunshot wound was especially dangerous and required immediate attention. Their primary aim was to prevent further harm to the officer. The use of a chest seal was critical, designed to prevent outside air from entering the chest cavity, thereby reducing the risk of a life-threatening tension pneumothorax.

While awaiting further medical intervention, the paramedics had to ensure the patient was positioned on his injured side to facilitate breathing and prevent blood from filling the uninjured lung. Ethan and Ramiro performed these steps quickly and efficiently, their hands steady despite the chaotic scene unfolding around them.

The urgent need for transport was palpable. The officer, gravely injured, was rapidly losing blood. Each second ticking by was a heavy weight, pushing him farther away from survival. He wouldn't last long in that state; they had to get him to the hospital, and soon.

A trauma center was their only hope, and Ethan was determined to deliver him there sooner rather than later. The captain of the SWAT team, amidst the chaos, issued a final request to the assailant, a desperate plea for the violence to end. But the shooter's reply was one of gunfire, echoing through the streets.

The officers took shelter as the gunman unloaded his weapon on them. Once the gunman had fired his last round, there was a moment of silence, then Ethan heard a single shot ring out.

The radio crackled to life with a simple call, "All clear".

Ethan knew what that meant; the threat had been neutralized, and the gunman was now dead. At that moment, Ethan felt relieved yet burdened by the responsibility on his shoulders to get the officer to safety.

With the immediate danger dispelled, the atmosphere in the ambulance was a flurry of activity and raw urgency. Ethan and Ramiro, their hands steady despite the adrenaline surging through their veins, immediately began administering lifesaving procedures to the wounded officer. "Ramiro, get us to the hospital." Ethan issued the order.

Ramiro did not hesitate as he hopped into the driver's seat. "How do I get past this train wreck?"

The officer's partner, his hand pressed up against his bleeding leg, hobbled to the open mouth of the rig and asked, "He gonna make it?"

Hands covered in blood, Ethan held pressure on the officer's chest as his blood began to seep into the sheets on the gurney beneath him. "He might if we can get him to a hospital in time."

Face grim, the cop nodded as he shouted to Ramiro, "I'll make a path. Follow me!"

"Wait! You need medical attention," Ethan yelled. But the officer was already across the street.

Ramiro buckled his seat belt as the officer shouted orders to the SWAT team to move their rigs. Ethan kept his focus on his patient as the ambulance lurched forward.

The officer's partner, having now assumed the role of both protector and pathfinder, darted ahead of the ambulance, weaving through the chaos to create an unobstructed route for them. Amid the blaring sirens and frantic communications over the dispatch radio, Ramiro kept his attention on the officer's vehicle ahead, following it closely as they sped away from the crime scene.

Pain seared through Ethan's shoulder and radiated down to his arm as he fought to maintain pressure on the man's wound. His once clean white shirt was now drenched, soaked through with crimson.

Thin lines of blood trickled down Ethan's arm and pooled onto his hand that he had pressed against the officer's wounds. An involuntary curse slipped past Ethan's lips as he realized that he had been shot. "Damn it!"

Startled, Ramiro shot him a concerned look. "What? What's wrong? He crashing?!"

"No, no, everything's fine… just focus on the road," Ethan quickly assured Ramiro. He did not want to distract his partner. The speedy, perilous journey to the hospital amidst the heavy, unforgiving traffic was dangerous enough.

The last thing Ramiro needed right now was to know that his partner had taken a bullet.

CHAPTER 31

UNBELIEVABLE

BRAYDEN

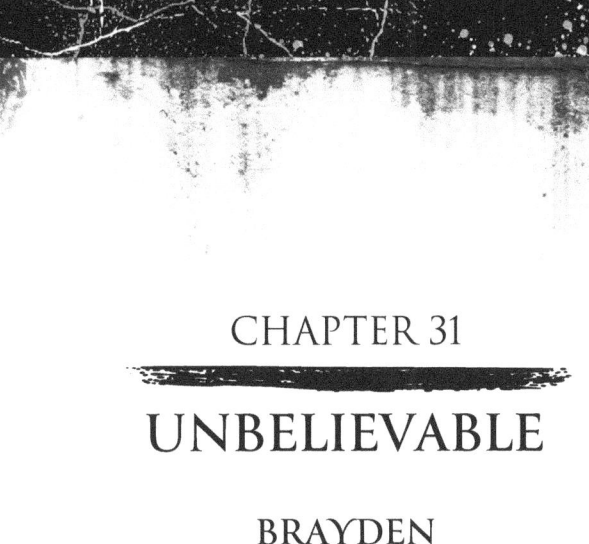

Austin, TX—Day

Brayden and Juan had spent the morning navigating their way through a throng of interviews, tirelessly piecing together the details of Jasmine Lam's life. Amidst the mass of testimonials from friends, family, and associates, one common thread emerged—Jasmine was well-loved. Her kindness and her artistic talent, revered. Despite their extensive investigation, they found no discernable motive.

After a disappointing morning, Brayden and Juan found themselves scanning the internet and information from the national archives. Their investigative journey had led them there, searching for hidden clues of past crimes. Amid trial records, newspaper clippings, and old letters, they hoped to uncover some overlooked detail about Jasmine Lam.

Frustration etched on his face, Brayden forcefully clicked out of the search engine. The sterile glow of the computer screen did nothing to illuminate the answers they so desperately sought. He raked his fingers through his hair, the tension in the room wrapping around him like a shroud. "We're looking in the wrong place," he muttered.

Juan, ever the rule-follower, merely shook his head, his gaze never leaving the screen. "Follow procedure man, stick to the checklist. We'll solve this," he said, his voice as monotonous as the ticking of the clock on the wall.

As Brayden's mind whirled, a sense of foreboding hung heavy in the air. He felt the cold touch of the unknown pressing against the walls of his mind, hunting for a different perspective, a fresh angle. The silence was deafening, punctuated only by the rhythmic tap-tap-tap of the rain that fell on the windowpane, a grim metronome to his racing heartbeat.

Brayden cursed to himself, "Shit!"

Juan jumped, startled at Brayden's sudden outburst. "You strip a gear?" Juan asked.

Grabbing his cell phone, Brayden began scrolling through his contacts. "We need to contact the NCAVC."

Juan looked around the busy squad room, and in a harsh whisper, Juan asked, "You serious? You calling the National Center for Analysis of Violent Crimes?"

Finding the number he was looking for, Brayden picked up the receiver on his desk phone. "I am. They should have been our first call after we found Lam's body." Brayden knew as part of the Federal Bureau of Investigation, their knowledge and expertise would serve as an invaluable asset.

"Listen, Brayden, even if you do get a hold of someone, and they actually listen to you, I doubt they will be able to do anything to help," Juan warned, his voice doubtful.

Brayden flashed his partner a knowing smile. "That might be true *if* I didn't personally know someone working in the upper ranks with the bureau."

Shaking his head, Juan mused to himself. "Why am I not surprised?" Folding his arms across his chest, Juan glared at Brayden. "This isn't another woman you've slept with, is it?"

As the sound of a muted ring echoed, Brayden cast a sidelong glance at Juan, his voice a low, gravelly whisper, "No, now shut up."

As they waited for an answer to Brayden's call, their gaze was drawn to a flurry of activity as a crowd grew near the captain's office. Juan turned to Brayden. "What's going on?"

Brayden's response was noncommittal, as his eyes stayed fixed on the gathering officers. "I don't know."

Suddenly, the call was connected to a woman's voice mail. "This is Agent Chantal Robinson. Please leave your name, contact number, and case identification number and I will get back to you as soon as possible." The beep that followed was sharp and jarring.

Chapter 31 — Unbelievable

Brayden rose, his eyes fixed on his captain, who had just emerged from his office and left a message. "Yeah, Chantal, this is Brayden James. Please call me back. I've got a case here in Austin that could use your expertise."

Curious, Brayden hung up the phone and gestured to Juan. "Come on. Let's see what's going on."

Joining the ranks of their fellow officers, Brayden and Juan waited as Bohannon held up a hand, his silhouette cutting an imposing figure against the harsh neon glow of the precinct. The room fell silent as their gazes fixed on Bohannon. "Officer Gutierrez... Jessie Gutierrez..." Bohannon's voice was gravelly, and he struggled with the officer's name.

Bohannon continued, "Was shot and injured. I just got off the phone with his partner, Officer Sanchez. Gutierrez is still in surgery. He took two bullets to the chest. The doctor said he is in critical condition, and they are doing everything they can, but I'm not going to lie to you. It doesn't look good."

Brayden felt a cold rage fill him. Gutierrez was one of their own. He, like the other officers beside him, wanted justice for their fallen comrade. A ripple of murmurs spread throughout the room. Brayden and Juan were just two among many.

"Damn it," Marvin Garcia barked. His eyes, hardened by years on the force, flickered with an anger that made the air feel charged. "What the hell happened?"

Reluctant, and afraid of giving out incomplete information, Bohannon kept to the known facts. His voice was a low rumble as he cleared his throat. "At approximately 0930, Officer Gutierrez and Officer Devore responded to a domestic at Saint Ed, a neighborhood near the edge of town." Bohannon paused, his brow furrowed as he continued. "Upon arrival, the two officers came under heavy fire. At which time they called for backup and Officer Devore took a round in the leg. He is out of surgery and recovering in a standard room and being held overnight for observation.

"Gutierrez was hit multiple times. Two rounds from the suspect's AR-15 were able to penetrate his vest and punctured his lung." He shifted uncomfortably. "Medics and fire units were on scene, and able to administer aid until help arrived."

Brayden felt a sense of unease wash over him. Ethan could have been on that call, and in danger, along with his fellow officers.

Bohannon assured them. "The suspect was neutralized by a member of SWAT shortly after the first shots were fired and Gutierrez was treated at the scene, then later transported by ambulance to Dell Seton Trauma Center." The news brought some relief, along with curses mixed with cheers at the death of the suspect who had injured one of their comrades.

From behind Brayden, he heard officer Sanchez ask, "I heard one of the EMTs working on Gutierrez took a bullet. That true?"

Reluctantly, Bohannon's gaze met Brayden's. The air hung heavy with the weight of unspoken words, the silence a suffocating fog. Brayden could feel the gaze of his captain pierce him like ice that invaded his soul.

For a moment, it seemed as if Bohannon held his breath. The deafening tick-tock of the clock on the wall echoed as Brayden felt the floor begin to sway underneath him as he waited for his captain's delayed response.

Finally, Bohannon spoke, his voice heavy. "While Gutierrez and Devore were still under fire, one of the paramedics, at great risk to his own life, rushed into the street and pulled Gutierrez to safety while Devore returned cover fire."

Voice shaken, Brayden asked. "Sir, you didn't answer Sanchez's question."

Bohannon grimaced. "All we know at this time is that paramedic Ethan Williams was in fact injured in the altercation. At this time, I do not have news on his condition."

A knowing look pasted between Brayden and his captain, heavy with unspoken words. The police station suddenly felt colder, its shadows deeper. As Bohannan's stern lips pressed together, he gave Brayden a curt nod; it was permission, a release for Brayden to go check on both his fellow officers and his brother.

The case would have to wait. Brayden turned swiftly; his shoes echoed ominously on the worn-down linoleum as he ran back to his desk and snatched his jacket and his keys as Juan trailed behind him.

"You want me to come with?" Juan asked, his voice gentle but firm. He and the other brethren at the station knew how much Ethan meant to him; Ethan was family. Brayden shook his head. "No." His gaze shifted to Juan's for a moment, imploring him to understand. "You stay here," Brayden said in a resigned voice. "Keep working the case, and I'll let you know what I find out."

CHAPTER 32

TOLD YOU

ETHAN

Austin, TX—Night

ETHAN'S EYES FELT HEAVY, AN UNCOMFORTABLE WEIGHT pressing down on them as he fought to wake up. The world beyond was a blur, an indistinguishable swirl of colors and shapes that made no sense. Sounds were muffled, distant echoes, as if he were underwater and striving to break the surface. Yet, through the fog of confusion, a persistent hushed stillness hung in the air, a solemn silence broken only by the soft, rhythmic beeping of machines. As his eyes at last opened, Ethan found himself waking to the sterile, cold ambiance of a hospital room.

The sight of Paige holding his hand was the first clarity in the storm of his senses. Her face, pale as untouched snow, seemed to starkly contrast the fear that dwelt in her eyes, which brimmed with unshed tears.

Brayden stood nearby, as an immovable guard at the other side of his bed, his face grim. Ethan struggled to lift his head to look at Ramiro, who sat in the corner chewing on his nails.

"Ethan?" Paige asked, quickly getting to her feet as she brushed the hair away from his eyes. "Hey, honey. How are you doing?"

The air in the room was heavy with concern, and Ethan could feel it pressing down on him like a weighted blanket. His voice weak, he asked, "I'm good. Is everything all right?"

A nervous laugh escaped Paige as her voice broke into a sob. "Yeah, yeah, everything's fine, honey."

"Good." Ethan's voice was strained, burdened from his recent bout with anesthesia. Confused, Ethan tried to sit up, then thought better of it when pain tore through his wounded shoulder. "What happened?" His words echoed in the quiet room that was disturbed only by the hum of the monitoring machines he was hooked to.

Brayden swallowed hard and forced out a nervous laugh. "You don't remember?"

Ethan struggled past the fog of the medications he had been given and looked up at Paige. Her eyes glistened with unshed tears as she clung to his hand.

Across the room, Ramiro's grin appeared more frightened than comforting. "Man, you gave us quite the scare. What the hell were you thinking?" His voice resonated in the quiet.

Suddenly, Ethan's soft brown eyes widened, and memories of the shooting rushed back to him like an unstoppable train. "Oh ... yeah," he murmured, the realization sinking in.

Images of the injured officers seared themselves into Ethan's mind. The agony in his shoulder pulsed rhythmically. As he attempted to rise, he was thwarted by Brayden. His brother-in-law placed a gentle but firm hand against his good arm, trying to quell his escape.

"Take it easy. You don't want to mess up the doctor's work, do you?" Brayden said in his low, soothing voice.

Ethan complied, more from the waves of pain and dizziness that assaulted him than from Brayden's firm hand. "How are the two officers?"

Brayden took a step back and smiled down at him. "I just came from Devore's room. He's the one who got shot in the leg. He is going to be fine. They're keeping him overnight for observation."

Afraid to, but unable to stop himself, Ethan asked, "And the other one, with the chest wound?"

Ramiro came to stand at the foot of his bed. "He made it out of surgery and is in the ICU. He is still critical, but thanks to you, he has a fighting chance."

Relieved, Ethan allowed himself to relax against his pillow. His body felt heavy and weighed down by his injuries and by the sheer exhaustion that came after the prolonged use of adrenaline he had used during the

Chapter 32 — Told You

shooting incident. "Good, he's tough. He will pull through." Ethan tried to fight the lull of sleep, but continued to struggle to keep his eyes open.

Gently, he felt Paige's soft lips press against his cheek. "I thought I told you to be careful," she whispered, her voice laced with a blend of concern, relief, and a hint of worry. As she rested her forehead against his, Ethan closed his eyes, allowing himself to relish this moment. More than ever, Ethan was aware of how quickly life could be snatched away from you.

Ramiro cleared his throat, giving a subtle warning that instantly drew the attention of Ethan and the others. Ethan's eyes tried to focus on the door as it swung open to admit the doctor and Captain Ganaway.

The doctor, a stern man with a surprisingly gentle touch, wasted no time in his examination. His gaze was sharp, his hands skilled as they probed gently at Ethan's shoulder. His words, when he spoke, were clear and informative, eliminating the uncertainty that had been hovering with those surrounding him. "The bullet went straight through your deltoid with minimal injury to the surrounding tissue."

Ethan's brows furrowed. That report defied everything he knew about injuries from that caliber weapon. "That's great, but also unexpected. I thought it would be a lot worse, considering the usual damage from an AR-15."

Appreciative of Ethan's knowledge, the doctor commented, "You know your injuries."

"I should. I've seen enough of them." Ethan grimaced.

Nodding, the doctor agreed. "Normally, that kind of weapon destroys the tissue, twisting and turning through the flesh, leaving the veins, muscle, and soft tissue like ground beef. However, in your case, the bullet went straight through, made a clean path. Probably due to the long distance the bullet traveled and perhaps from going through a wall or another structure close by before it hit you?" The doctor straightened and smiled down at him. "Either way, you're a very lucky man."

In pain, but trying his best to conceal that fact, Ethan asked. "So, when am I being discharged?"

Laughing, the doctor shook his head. "Let's see how you do for the next couple of days."

"Days!" Ethan exclaimed.

Ganaway stepped up beside the bed. "You lost a lot of blood Ethan and took a serious hit. Do what the doctor says, and you'll be back to work soon enough."

Taking in Ethan's pained expression, the doctor added, "I'll tell the nurse to bring you something for the pain." The doctor closed Ethan's chart, slid it back into the slot at the end of the bed, and smiled at Paige. "Keep him out of trouble ... if you can."

Giving Ethan one of her looks that usually sent the children scurrying, she nodded. "I'll do my best." Now he knew why the kids ran for cover when she gave them that look. *Man, am I going to pay for this later.*

Brayden laughed. "I can't believe you got shot before I did."

Horrified, Paige glared at her brother. "Seriously?!"

"What?" he said to Paige before leaning over and poking a finger at Ethan's bandaged shoulder. "And with an AR-15, man!"

From the end of the bed, Ramiro began singing Ethan's praises, ignoring the warning look from Ethan. "Dude, you should have seen him. Ethan was like, 'We can't leave him on the street, he's gonna die.' I was like, 'Are you crazy?' Bullets were flying, ricocheting off our rig, off the street. But no, Ethan gives me this look, like, 'I'm going to save him... don't try to stop me!' Then like that," Ramiro snapped his fingers, "Ethan bolts, runs right into the firestorm, grabs the cop by the shoulders, and drags him back behind the ambulance with me where he starts cutting his shirt off and doing triage. It was awesome!"

Currently more afraid of Paige than facing a firing squad, Ethan did not dare look at her. "Ramiro is exaggerating. I was never in any real danger."

Brayden laughed. "Says the man lying in a hospital bed with a gunshot wound."

At that very moment, Ethan wanted nothing more than to throttle his brother-in-law. "Don't you have someplace to be?" Ethan growled.

Ethan was sure Brayden was about to come back with another one of his smart-ass remarks when he suddenly stammered, "Oh crap, I do, actually!"

Relieved, Ethan breathed a sigh of relief. "Thank God."

"I told Alayna I would stop by after work. When I heard about Ethan, I totally spaced it."

The throbbing of his injury was really starting to get to him. What Ethan really needed was for everyone to go home so he could be alone and writhe in pain. Casting a look at the clock Ethan encouraged, "It's not too late to get your ass over there."

"I can't leave you," Brayden argued.

Chapter 32   Told You

Laying his head back, Ethan closed his eyes. "Oh yes, you can, and you should, because I'm about to press that call button and see where those pain meds are. I need some sleep and I can't get any with you guys standing there gawking at me."

Worried, Paige put a comforting hand on his shoulder. "Ethan's right, you guys should go. I'll stay and make sure he behaves himself."

Reluctant, Brayden held his ground. "Maybe I should take the first watch."

Ethan groaned and reached for the cup on his tray. "Don't make me throw this, you know it will hurt me a lot more than it will hurt you," Ethan warned with a half-smile.

Ramiro snagged Brayden's arm as he said to Ethan, "Stay out of trouble until we get back." Tugging on Brayden's arm, Ramiro nodded at the door. "Come on, let's give these two some space."

Brayden resisted. Paige sat down next to Ethan and smiled up at him. "We'll be fine. I promise."

Giving in, Brayden backed toward the door after Ramiro. "Call me if you need anything, I mean it."

"We will," Paige assured him just as Ethan smirked and spoke.

"No, we won't."

Needle in hand, the nurse walked past Brayden and Ramiro as they exited. "Doctor Evans asked me to give you this for the pain."

Relieved, Ethan settled back. "Thank you."

"You're welcome," she said as she administered the medication straight into his iv.

Within seconds Ethan felt the drug washing over him. It was a balm to his battered body.

The bed shifted slightly as Paige carefully stretched out beside him and nestled up against him. As sleep began to overcome him, Ethan wrapped his good arm around Paige's shoulders, letting a profound peace envelop him. With Paige snuggled up against him, he could feel the soothing rhythm of her breath and the softness of her hair against his skin.

Each breath they shared became a melody, their hearts beating in perfect harmony, creating a symphony of love that resonated within his soul. The intimate moment, comforted by the warmth of his wife, was Ethan's sanctuary, a place where all worries ceased to exist.

CHAPTER 33

WHAT WOULD YOU LIKE TO KNOW

ALAYNA

Austin, TX—Night

WITH THE FOOD HAVING LONG SINCE GONE COLD, Alayna could not help but feel a sense of disappointment. She had put so much effort into preparing a wonderful meal and creating a cozy ambiance, hoping for an enjoyable evening. But as she looked at the untouched plates and the candles that had melted down to small pools of wasted wax, she felt a pang of sadness.

The excitement and anticipation that had filled her earlier had dissipated and had been replaced with a quiet sadness. She was just about to turn off the lights and head home when she spotted Brayden, standing in the doorway, his face apologetic as he silently mouthed the words. *I'm sorry.* Alayna should have been angry but could not help but smile at how handsome and childlike he looked.

Taking her time, Alayna strolled over to the door, opened it slowly then silently beckoned him inside. She knew that coming there was a huge step for him and she wanted to make sure he felt welcomed and comfortable. When he finally stepped into the room, she could see the emotion in his eyes, the combination of relief and hope clearly visible.

Chapter 33 — What Would You Like To Know

A pained expression washed over Brayden's face as he took in the table and ruined dinner that she had prepared for them. "Alayna, I am so sorry. I can go get us something else."

Motioning to the cold food, Alayna smiled and gently nudged the plate toward Brayden. "What, you don't like cold pasta *aglio e olio*?" she inquired, her eyes twinkling with mirth.

Brayden let out a hearty laugh. "What?" he echoed, slightly bemused. Alayna patiently explained, "It's a classic Italian dish, a simple combination of pasta, olive oil, minced garlic cloves, red pepper flakes, and a zing of lemon zest. Voila! Dinner for two, in under 20 minutes." Her hands gracefully gestured as if painting the recipe in the air.

Brayden couldn't help but grin at her enthusiasm. Moving in close, he commented, "Twenty minutes, huh? You really pulled out all the stops, didn't you?" His tone was light, full of amusement, and a touch of admiration for her culinary skills.

Taking Brayden's hand in hers, Alayna guided him into the small but cozy kitchen. She all but purred, her voice thick with promise. "You see Brayden, the magic of this dish lies not just in its taste, but in its transformation over time."

Brayden, intrigued, pulled her close, wrapping a firm arm around Alayna's waist. "It is?" he asked, his eyes reflecting his curiosity. Just as Brayden leaned down, a spark of anticipation between them, Alayna playfully pulled away.

Turning with a dancer's grace, she grabbed the two plates from the table. "It is indeed," Alayna affirmed, her voice a seductive whisper. "Let me show you." With a smile that could light up a room, she slid the first plate into the small microwave on the counter and hit the start button. The soft hum of the microwave in the background added a rhythmic soundtrack to their intimate culinary exploration.

Alayna, with a playful smile on her face, reached for a bottle of red wine that had been sitting on the kitchen counter. Holding it with care, she passed it over to Brayden, a subtle jest in her voice as she said, "Here, make yourself useful." Brayden, always up for a challenge, happily took the wine and began the task of opening it.

Alayna then put the second plate of pasta into the microwave, never stopping her teasing as she said to Brayden, "There are two glasses on the table."

Brayden grabbed the glasses and filled them with wine as Alayna returned the reheated meals to their proper place on the table. With a flourish, Alayna picked up a fresh candle and lit it, the warm firelight danced in her eyes as she said in a low, seductive voice, "While we eat... maybe you can explain to me, why you are so late."

Pulling her chair out, Brayden allowed her to take her seat, then he carefully pushed her chair in. Brushing her hair aside, Brayden leaned in and whispered in her ear, "I promise you'll forgive me. It was for a really good reason."

He straightened and took his warmth and charm with him as he went around to the other side of the table. Brayden's reason more than likely had something to do with one of his cases. Putting her napkin on her lap, Alayna fixed Brayden with a knowing look. "Let me guess, you got another call from the station and just couldn't say no."

Smiling, Brayden shook his head no as he unfolded his napkin and followed her lead. "Nope."

"You were saving a cat that got stuck in a tree?" Alayna teased.

"What? No. Detectives don't do those kinds of things?" Brayden said, feigning being offended. "That's for the patrol officers to do."

"Then what could have possibly kept you?" Alayna teased as she took a slow sip of her wine.

Though she could tell Brayden was searching for something witty to say, his expression became serious and slightly pained. "Actually, I was at the hospital ... because my brother-in-law was shot."

Alayna had to swallow her wine in an attempt not to choke on it. "What?!"

"He's a paramedic," Brayden said as an explanation.

"Wait, what? Why would someone want to shoot a paramedic?" she asked, flabbergasted.

He took a long drink of his wine, which told Alayna the event upset Brayden far more than he wanted to admit. He took a moment, then continued, "Well, the guy wasn't shooting at Ethan, per se. The gunman had shot two of our officers and had them pinned down when Ethan decided to play the hero and run into the street where the officer with a chest wound was bleeding out and he was shot dragging the cop to safety."

"My God, is he okay?" Alayna asked.

In answer to her question, Brayden took another drink of his wine. Then set his empty glass aside. "He will be. Lucky for him, it went clean

Chapter 33 *What Would You Like To Know*

through his shoulder. He just needs a little time to heal, then he will be as good as new."

Alayna could feel his worry and fear clear across the table; it rolled off him in nerve-riddled waves. She was not sure if Brayden was saying those things to assure her or himself. It was obvious he loved his brother-in-law a great deal, and he was worried sick about him. "Shouldn't you be at the hospital with him and your sister?"

Brayden slapped a hand on the table and laughed. "Would you believe they threw me out?"

"What?" Alayna gasped. "Why would they do that?"

Studying his silverware, Brayden sobered. "Actually, they didn't. I mean, they did, but it was only because Ethan needed to rest and Paige knew he wouldn't sleep if she didn't make all of us leave."

"I would understand if you wanted to go," Alayna offered, wanting to do whatever she could to help.

Looking up at her, Brayden smiled, then took her hand in his. "Thank you, but right now, there is no place that I would rather be." He lifted her hand to his lips and kissed it softly, then rested it back on the table. "Now, let's try this amazing twenty-minute meal before it gets cold ... again."

Returning his warm smile, Alayna picked up her fork. "You got it."

MAY 3RD—8 DAYS

CHAPTER 34

NOT FORGOTTEN

VANDER

Cape Town, Africa—Day

The clock was ticking, and Vander, unflinching, had wasted no time. After Alexander had so graciously offered to his book flight, Vander had opted for the most direct path possible—a non-stop flight to Cape Town, courtesy of South African Airways.

There had been the quick flight from Pennsylvania to New York, where Vander departed from the heart of America, New York's JFK, knowing that he would find himself stepping onto African soil fifteen or so hours later, depending on the jet stream, arriving around 8:00 a.m., close to the day's beginning. Cape Town International Airport, the third largest on the continent, would be his landing point.

It was not just an airport, but a symbol of Africa's grandeur, a premier destination for tourists and VIPs alike. Its reputation gleamed as brightly as the awards that adorned its metaphorical mantle.

For Vander, sleep had become a ghost, an elusive specter that flickered at the edges of consciousness but never fully materialized. His mind was a vortex of dark thoughts, swallowing up the tranquility that sleep offered. The black, rolling waves below mirrored his restlessness, endless and fathomless. As the plane touched down in Cape Town, the first light of dawn infiltrated the city's narrow alleys, casting long shadows that danced over the cobblestone streets. Yet, for Vander, the darkness was far from over.

Chapter 34 — Not Forgotten

Bathed in the dim cabin light, Vander clutched his carry-on with an air of quiet mystery. The sleek leather bag, an extension of his persona, carried the means with which he would end Kgotso's life. He shot a final, appreciative glance at the first-class stewardess, her gracious service still resonating with him. With a nod, he stepped into the aisle, leaving behind the cocooned luxury of the plane, and disembarked the safety of the plane.

Had Vander been anyone else, his pursuit of Kgotso would have been a maze of complexities, a dance with shadows. A normal person would have been forced to employ a legion of private investigators, spending countless hours and resources to trace the crooked cop's movements, habits, patterns... But Vander was anything but normal.

His peculiar abilities allowed him to transcend the boundaries of conventional surveillance. He could unfailingly follow Kgotso, tracking his every move with an uncanny precision that no investigator could match.

Over the years, Vander did not merely watch; he studied, he calculated, patiently biding his time for the ideal moment. He knew with chilling certainty when and where to strike, pinpointing the moments when Kgotso would be most vulnerable. The game of cat and mouse was not a game to Vander; it was a dance he had mastered, navigating the darkness with an unsettling grace.

Among the myriad of gifts Vander possessed, remote viewing was particularly intriguing. This uncanny skill, like a spectral eye capable of crossing the boundaries of time and space, allowed Vander to keep a watchful eye on Kgotso undetected. He was able to delve into his life, study his habits, his fears, and his dreams, all without leaving a trace.

This extraordinary ability was not limited by physical barriers, nor did it adhere to the conventional laws of nature. It reached into realms beyond, gathering elusive information, and yet retained Vander's anonymity. The police investigators, who might later seek to find the reasons behind Kgotso's gruesome death, would find no answers, no clues, no motives behind Kgotso's downfall because Vander's involvement would remain undetectable.

But Vander's gifts were not without their own consequences. For as long as he was able to elude detection, his actions remained unchecked and unfettered. With no one to answer to, the darkness in his heart had a chance to grow unchecked, until it became strong enough even for him to fear its power.

In the unlikelihood that suspicion was to fall on him, Vander was prepared. He had planned meticulously, weaving a story that was as plausible as it was tantalizingly elusive. He would claim a sentimental journey, a pilgrimage to the resting places of his parents before the onrush of the real world post-graduation.

Vander would ensure he was seen by the right people, a well-chosen bouquet of flowers cradled in his arms, his face a perfect tableau of sorrow and nostalgia. His path would meander, but purposefully so, each interaction, each calculated conversation, cementing his alibi. And then, with the appropriate show of solemnity, he would make his visit to the graves, a lone silhouette against the vast African sky—a poignant picture of a dutiful son paying respects.

Emerging into the Cape Town International Airport terminal, Vander cleared the doorway, then stopped to take in the nexus of vibrant cultures. The terminal hummed with a symphony of foreign tongues, intermingling to form a hauntingly beautiful chorus of human connection.

The smell of strong African coffee danced through the air, mingling with the exotic scents of spices from lands afar. Shadows grew longer, creeping across the polished terminal floors as the sun rose above the horizon. This African gateway, a hub of international transit, was a testament to the mystery and allure of the continent, drawing explorers from all walks of life, their stories yet to unfold.

The pressing tick of the clock echoed in Vander's ears, a constant reminder of the transience of his time here. His every heartbeat played in sync with the relentless rhythm, marking the fleeting moments that remained. The daunting inevitability of his departure hung heavily in the air, a somber sousaphone in the symphony of his journey.

Before long, another plane would be carving its path through the heavens, ferrying him across the expansive, unending stretch of the Atlantic. But, despite the grim circumstances, a maleficent smile unfurled across Vander's face, casting an ominously intriguing aura around him.

With a confident, knowing glance, he caressed his leather bag, the thrill of imminent adventure sparking a devilish glint in his eyes. Time may have been a ruthless adversary, but Vander knew precisely where to commence his dance with the ticking enemy and precisely where to begin his quest for vengeance.

Chapter 35 — Nice Room

he just wanted to make her feel safe, reassure her that no matter what, she was safe with him.

He stepped forward and placed his hands on Alayna's shoulders. "I'm sorry. When I'm nervous, I tend to say stupid things."

Unsure, Alayna looked up at him but remained silent. Brayden smiled, then gently pulled her close and hugged Alayna to him. "I promise, open mind and open heart. No matter what, I'm not going anywhere," Brayden whispered; the words tinged with a newfound understanding.

Brayden felt a small sense of relief, his eyes softening as Alayna returned his gaze with a faint smile that hinted at a shared understanding.

The tension that had built up within him evaporated; he was grateful he had not quashed this delicate moment of revelation. Alayna's fear of rejection, her trepidation about sharing this psychic, mystical facet of herself, was something he understood intimately. His sister, Paige, lived in a similar cryptic world, a fact unknown to Alayna.

As Alayna led him by the hand to the small table, he complied without hesitation, an unspoken promise of support in his actions. Across the table, Alayna settled into the seat opposite him, their connection resonating in the space between them, filled with intrigue, acceptance, and the promise of new-found love.

Her eyes flickered to Brayden, a silent understanding passing between them. "They're as much a part of me as my own heart." Brayden's intent gaze did not waver, his curiosity and protectiveness evident. She knew he was sincere; his actions so far had proven as much. And in his eyes, she saw an acceptance of her revelations, a readiness to delve into the unknown with her.

Quietly, Alayna began, "Ever since childhood, I've been blessed and cursed with these abilities. I saw things, things other people could not see." Alayna picked up the long lighter on the table and lit the lone candle between them. "I also knew things about people, how they were feeling, where they had been."

Her eyes flickered to Brayden, a silent understanding passing between them. "Their true intentions." Brayden held Alayna's gaze, if she was able to read him, then she should know that he had always been completely honest with her, she would know that in his heart, he only wanted to know more about her, to shield and protect her from any harm, real or imagined, that might find its way to her.

Dark Variations

Wanting to put Alayna's mind at ease, Brayden said, "Alayna, your ability, this gift you possess, it's intriguing, and it's rare. You channel spirits, you connect the living with the departed. That's not something everyone can do." He paused, then continued, "It might be scary. It might be beautiful. But it's you, the one I'm falling for." His voice echoed sincerity and acceptance.

Alayna's eyes widened in surprise, yet a glimmer of relief was apparent. "Brayden, are you... are you really okay with this?"

He gave her hand a reassuring squeeze. "More than okay, Alayna. I think it's incredibly brave and compassionate of you to use your gift to help others, to ease their grief. It's part of what makes you, you. And I wouldn't want you any other way."

He gently kissed her hand and smiled.

Alayna felt a warmth spread through her. The realization that this unique gift of hers was accepted and appreciated by Brayden. She had found someone who could accept both the beautiful and scary aspects of her ability, someone who would love her for all she was worth. Smiling back at him, Alayna knew without a doubt that she had found the one.

Brayden was about to reveal a part of himself that he had long held close. His hands, still trembling slightly from the sudden rush of adrenaline, hung in the air as he sought the right words. "Alayna," he began, his voice steady despite the tumult inside him. "I understand more than you know. I grew up with someone similar to you, so I understand."

Suddenly the candle between them toppled, and hot wax spilled onto the velvet-covered table. Brayden's reflexes kicked in and he snuffed out the flames before they could spread any farther. Alayna flipped on the light switch as Brayden started to ask if she was okay, but his words died on his lips when he took in the fear in her expression.

Alayna's eyes were fixed on a space behind him, and Brayden slowly turned to look at the empty space. He knew she was looking at something that he could not see. "What is it?" he asked softly, taking in Alayna's pale face.

Brayden took a step closer to Alayna, a mixture of concern and curiosity painting his features. "Hey, it's okay," he assured her, his voice a soothing whisper against the oppressive silence. His eyes, filled with unwavering determination, locked onto hers. Alayna, her eyes wide with fear, rushed into his arms, then she buried her face against his shoulder.

Chapter 35   Nice Room

Brayden felt the warmth of her breath through the fabric of his shirt as she spoke. "Brayden... Oh my God, you have no idea what she looks like." Her voice quivered as the words left her lips.

He looked back at the empty space by the table. "It's all right," he said softly.

Reluctantly, Brayden loosened his grip around Alayna, allowing her to gracefully pull away from his sturdy arms. Her body was still shaking, tangible proof of her fear and confusion, but she forced herself to stand tall, a beacon of resilience amidst the uncanny. She dared to look past him, her eyes piercing through the air, focusing on the unseen apparition that haunted her presence. "I'm sorry," Alayna's voice trembled, a mixture of regret and fear. "That was cruel. I didn't mean it."

Brayden stood there, a silent observer of her one-sided conversation. He knew her apology was not meant for him but for the ghost that he could not see. He watched her take a deep, shaky breath and step forward, inching closer to the invisible specter. "I don't know what you want from me?" Alayna's voice trailed off, her words hanging in the air, unanswered. "No one has come to..."

Suddenly, a spark of realization lit up Alayna's face, startling Brayden. Her eyes widened, full of newfound understanding, as she turned to look at him. Overwhelmed with curiosity and a sudden unease, Brayden couldn't help but ask, "What?" His voice echoed in the room, a question that hung heavily between them, waiting to be answered.

Uneasy, Brayden watched as Alayna's eyes traveled back and forth between him and the unseen spirit. His heart pounded in his chest, matching the rhythm of the uncertainty that clouded his thoughts.

The knowing look Alayna fixed him with held a mysterious acceptance, a silent understanding of what was to come. "The woman with the broken, twisted body covered in delicate pink, red, and white flowers," Alayna started, her voice barely a whisper, "she's here because of you."

MAY 3RD—8 DAYS

CHAPTER 36

LIFE IS GOOD

KGOTSO

Cape Town, Africa—Day

Cloaked in smug satisfaction, Kgotso planted himself at his customary spot in the heart of the bustling Punjabi kitchen. As he situated himself at his usual table, a small spectacle of familiarity amid the intoxicating aromas and fervent chatter, he began his customary observation.

With a keen eye, he watched tourists and locals alike, their faces a vibrant tapestry of life that weaved itself before him. The staff, always alert to his presence, had his table prepared for his late morning arrival. It was a silent testament to his importance. Kgotso relished this small triumph, a milestone in his relentless quest for significance in the chaotic city.

Kgotso's gaze returned to the menu. It was a canvas of myriad curries and presented its patrons with an intoxicating challenge, almost akin to a cryptic puzzle. It urged one to choose their preferred level of spiciness, to decide between the earthy comfort of rice or the subtle bite of cauliflower.

The specials, meanwhile, whispered tales of exotic goat curry, the dangerous allure of swordfish curry, and a curry carrying the secrets of freshly foraged mushrooms.

Having already placed his order by phone before he came, Kgotso sat back, allowing the dim murmurs of the restaurant and the distant clink of glasses to wash over him.

Chapter 36 — Life Is Good

The room was steeped in a sense of anticipation as he watched the waiter navigate through the low-lit labyrinth of tables toward him. Hidden in the shadows, the plate was a mere silhouette, but as it was placed before him, the vibrant hues of his chosen curries emerged. The sampling was a well-crafted tableau of culinary artistry. Kgotso leaned in, letting the tantalizing aroma envelop him, a heady blend of spices that promised an explosion of flavors. His first bite was a slow, deliberate movement, a moment savored in silence. In that instant, the world felt better than good; it was an intoxicating dance of taste and satisfaction.

Life is good. Kgotso smiled. The city of Cape Town danced in the distance, casting long shadows from the mid-morning sun. They whispered of his journey from oblivion to at long last, being someone who was well known.

He had accomplished much in his career and was now respected in not only Cape Town but in other communities along the coast. His days of patrolling the shitholes of Cape Town and dealing with the rift-raft that littered the streets were over.

Of course, his rise to power had not come without its price. Not long after the debacle with the Sculptor case, there had risen up such a cry from Interpol at losing one of its best and brightest, that a task force had been formed for one singular purpose, to cleanse the treacherous corruption of Cape Town's law enforcement.

Back then, there were more officers who resembled criminals than those who chose a good conscience and high morals. In his younger years, Kgotso had been the embodiment of the very menace he was sworn to combat. He was one of the many crooked cops, whose names were whispered in hushed tones and avoided in polite conversations. His reputation was a chilling reminder of a time when law enforcers turned into lawbreakers, a time when the guardians were also, more often than not, the predators.

Fortunately for Kgotso, he had close ties to someone who had been put on that task force. Someone who knew if Kgotso went down for his evil deeds, so would he. This confidante, his brother in crime, danced the same perilous dance on that tightrope of law and anarchy. It was he who had alerted Kgotso of the investigation and of those who threatened to shatter their clandestine world.

Kgotso had taken this knowledge and manipulated it into a cloak of deception. A veil that hid his illicit activities and served as a shield against any consequences. The evidence of his crimes, no matter how minute, was systematically destroyed—any clue that could lead back to him was meticulously erased.

His transgressions remained hidden, as silent as the voices he had stifled. Those who had dared to oppose him, or even held the potential to testify to his wrongdoings, were silenced.

Even more sinister was that Kgotso had framed any individual who posed a threat to his rise to power, their reputations tarnished by the ill-gotten gains he so skillfully attributed to them. Once again, Kgotso used the law to his advantage, turning it into a twisted game, where he assured himself the victor.

Thus, Kgotso's actions were a reinforcement of his opinion that power could be obtained and maintained through deceit and manipulation.

With his newfound status, there was a need to erase any trace of his deplorable past, to wipe the slate clean. In the shadowed corridors of the Cape Town orphanage, the once trusted priest met a gruesome end at Kgotso's hands. This brutal act was not born out of spite or hatred, but out of necessity.

The priest knew far too much about Kgotso's unspeakable arrangements, his vile satisfaction sought in the innocence of children. If left alive, the man would have been a ticking time bomb, certain to cast Kgotso into the heart of a storm that would lead to his incarceration and, ultimately, his death at the hands of indignant fellow inmates.

Now, Kgotso had to find other ways to channel his reprehensible needs. He ventured out of the insular city and soon found himself in places where no one knew him or his heinous past. With money and power as his companions, he was free to indulge in whatever perverse pleasure he wished, if it kept him far from home.

Yet, for all the money and power Kgotso now had, he could never completely rid himself of his darkest desires. He had to exercise caution and moderation in his pursuits, fully aware that if he were to indulge too often, it would eventually be his undoing. But the need still gnawed at him like an insatiable beast. It was a small price to pay for the status and prestige he held in abundance.

The only things keeping Kgotso from complete ruin were the boundaries of his own control. If he could remember that, he would remain on top.

Chapter 36 — Life Is Good

With his meal complete and his stomach contentedly full, Kgotso tossed his crumpled napkin and loose cash onto the worn wooden table. The subtle clink of coins on the table's surface echoed in the crowded room as he scooted his chair back, rose to his feet, and prepared to leave.

The still air was suddenly disrupted as a large man, adorned in a finely tailored suit, stumbled into him. Kgotso staggered back, the surprise etched on his face as the stranger's large hands shot out to grip his shoulders, keeping them both from tumbling over.

In the midst of the chaos, Kgotso found himself locking gaze with a pair of deep, cerulean blue eyes. Deeper than the ocean, they stirred a sense of familiarity within him. An apology spilled from the stranger's lips. "Forgive me. I must have lost my footing." His voice was soft and quiet in the busy atmosphere of the restaurant.

Kgotso, still caught by those eyes, uttered, "It is all right, no harm done." He stared intently at the stranger. "Do I know you?" Kgotso asked, their bodies straightened, a silent agreement to steady themselves.

Flashing Kgotso a brilliant smile, the stranger answered, "It would be unlikely, for I've just arrived in Cape Town this morning."

Suddenly suspicious of the chance encounter, Kgotso questioned, "Oh, business or pleasure?"

"Both," the man said, his demeanor relaxed, his expression open to Kgotso's scrutiny.

The elegant man gave him a curt nod, then took a step back. "Again, apologies." As if noticing a spot on Kgotso's uniform, the man frowned, then his hand reached out, his fingers dusted off Kgotso's lapel, then brushed off his lower arm. "Oh dear, I hope I haven't ruined your uniform with my brandy." Kgotso looked down at an ugly burgundy stain. At about that time, a sharp pain stabbed into his forearm. Kgotso yanked his arm back, surprise etched on his dark features. The stranger's hands lifted in a gesture of innocence, his fierce blue eyes wide with confusion. "Apologies, I was merely trying to…"

Kgotso's gaze fell to his arm, a thin line of red blood betraying the scratch he'd received. The stranger followed his gaze, horror washing over his handsome features as he looked at his expensive watch—the metal edge slightly bent and likely to have been the cause of the injury.

"I can have that looked at," he stammered, but the restaurant's manager was already rushing over, concern furrowing his brow as he tried to assess the situation. Kgotso, not wishing to be the center of attention, reassured both men that he was fine and needed to return to work.

The stranger, still apologetic, asked once more if Kgotso was all right. Assuring him that he was, Kgotso slipped out of the restaurant. Outside, he couldn't shake off a sense of familiarity. Something about those fierce blue eyes struck a chord within him, leaving him with an unwavering sense of déjà vu as he returned to work.

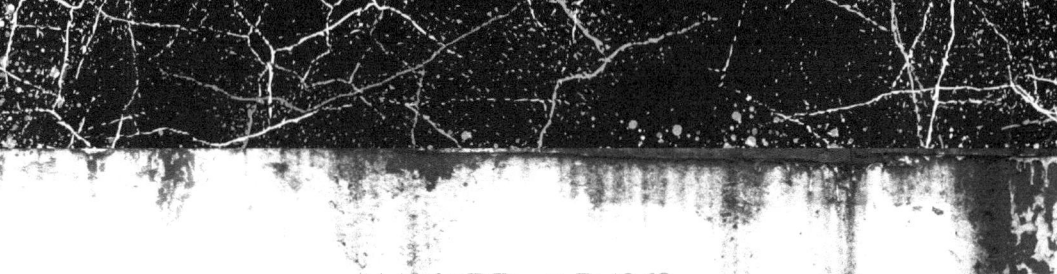

MAY 3RD—8 DAYS

CHAPTER 37

GONE BUT NOT FORGOTTEN

PETER

London, England—Day

PETER O'REILY SAT IN HIS OFFICE, ENSNARED IN THE WEB of hushed whispers from his past life. The once bustling corridors of international crime and justice were replaced by the serene silence of academia. The thrum of adrenaline, the chase, the danger, all replaced by the tranquil hum of fluorescent lights and the rhythmic ticking of the wall clock. His past seemed distant, fleeting.

The alleys of Peter's mind, once well-lit and bustling with clarity of purpose, now lay shrouded in an impenetrable fog of despair and uncertainty. What once echoed with the anthems of justice and courage was now filled with a deafening silence, punctuated only by the haunting whispers of regret.

Shadows danced in these forgotten corners, each a chilling remnant of his past, a chilling reminder of Erin and the life they once shared. The pain of her loss served as a relentless shadow, turning his once vibrant city of thought into a desolate landscape, an echo of the man he used to be.

In his role as professor, Peter had been given a chance to start anew, but he found the door to his old life barred. He felt a deep sense of guilt and regret for having left behind the world he had once served. He was unable to escape the ghosts of his past, as if they had become a part of him; an ever-present reminder of what could have been.

The days passed like blurred flashes in Peter's mind, each one filled with the same oppressive dread. He spent his days in a state of quiet desperation, struggling to reconcile himself with his decision and find peace within the darkness he now called home.

As the weeks passed, Peter found himself slowly beginning to accept what had happened in his life. He was able to take solace in the knowledge that he was still making an impact, one that may not be as grand or far-reaching, but was no less important.

It was only then that he found his way out of the alleys of his mind and back into the light. He had given up one life to make a difference in another, and in so doing had reclaimed some semblance of peace within himself.

He had found his strength once again, and with it, a renewed sense of purpose. Peter chose that moment to make the most of his second chance, determined to use what he had learned and apply it in whatever way he could.

He was no longer an agent but an academic, one who could take the knowledge from his past and help guide others through their own dark alleys.

He had once believed that justice was best served through punishment, but now his focus was on understanding and preventing crimes before they happened. He poured himself into the work, giving lectures and offering insight to his students, all to bring a little light to the darkness of the world.

With this new sense of purpose, Peter moved forward, determined to make the most of his life and bring about a brighter future for those who would come after him. He had learned that sometimes you must give up one life to create another, and he was determined to make this one count.

He began teaching classes on criminology, exploring different theories, and offering fresh perspectives on how society could work to better prevent crime. He also found ways to help those who had been affected by the criminal justice system, providing counseling and resources for those trying to rebuild their lives after an unfortunate experience with the law.

With his newfound strength of purpose, Peter was able to face the darkness in his mind and embrace a new life of service. Though he still struggled with thoughts of what could have been, Peter was now able to look forward with hope. He no longer needed to be defined by the

Chapter 37 — Gone But Not Forgotten

tragedy that took Erin's life. Instead, he chose to take what was left of his, and forge something better from it.

On slow, quiet days, like that day, Peter would sit in his office, and remember his old assignment and desk that sat across from Erin's. He would remember the piles of notes and case files that had littered their desks and her bright smiles as she sat going over each detail, scribbling each hastily written hypothesis, a testament to her determination and her relentless pursuit of justice.

Erin's desk was always cluttered with cold coffee mugs and dog-eared crime novels. It was on such days, amidst the silence and memories, that Peter felt the weight of her absence the most.

Erin's life had been taken by the very monster she had sought so vehemently to catch, and he was haunted by that fact as much as he was by his inability to save her from herself. Erin, despite her best efforts, had been outsmarted and overpowered by the monster after she had gone after him alone.

He thought of all the possibilities, of what might have happened if only she would have trusted him, trusted the other officers, someone would have been there to help her.

No matter how badly Peter wanted to forget, the image of Erin's death was forever frozen in his mind. The first time he had witnessed the crime scene, he had been forced to spend hours looking over Erin's corpse, trying to make sense of the senseless.

The nightmare didn't end there. He had to relive that horrific night in photos weeks later, each one a stark reminder of the tragedy he had borne witness to. The questions from his superiors echoed in his head, a constant cacophony of confusion and blame. But how could he explain something that he, himself, couldn't comprehend?

There simply was no explaining Erin's death. He had been forced to accept the tragedy and move forward in life.

At the time of Erin's death, Peter had been so shell-shocked that his mind had reeled from the grief and confusion. He had worked on autopilot, trying to keep one foot in front of the other, to focus on the evidence while his heart bled out its sorrow.

His mind had not been clear, his vision clouded by a veil of pain so profound that logic and reason had no place. Which now left a nagging sensation at the back of his mind.

If Peter had been able to look at the crime scene objectively back then, he would have seen the discrepancies. The man the African authorities had labeled as the Sculptor could not be the man Erin and he had pursued across continents; it could not have been Rex Helmsworth. It was as if Erin's murder scene had been staged to perfection.

Rising from his well-worn desk, Peter ambled over to the diminutive window that overlooked the sprawling campus. As was typical for London at that time of year, the sky was a monotonous gray, the clouds densely woven like a woolen blanket.

Encased in that profound gloom, he found his mind wandering back to the turbulent weeks following Erin's demise. He had, against all directives, delved headfirst into the Sculptor case, driven by a deep-seated conviction that Rex Helmsworth, contrary to popular belief, hadn't committed the heinous crimes.

As the evidence pointed elsewhere, Peter followed its trail, a decision that led him down a path fraught with official reprimands, restraining orders, and heated disputes. Eventually, faced with the stark choice between dismissal and resignation, Peter opted for the latter, his focus unwavering on the pursuit of truth.

Rather than marking a bittersweet ending, however, his departure only deepened the mystery shrouding Erin's death. With little to no progress in her case and his own detective work having come to an abrupt halt, he had no choice but to accept that perhaps his suspicions were nothing more than a product of his grief-stricken mind.

Moving away from the window, Peter had one final thought. Draped in the soft glow of the solitary desk lamp, he found himself reflecting on the inexhaustible quest for knowledge that had driven him all these years. The unanswered questions that once ignited his passion had now become an unending maze of uncertainty. He surveyed the papers strewn across the desk, the ink-filled proof of hours upon hours of meticulous work left before him.

The phone on his desk came to life, its muffled ring piercing the heavy silence of the quiet room. A sense of dread filled Peter as he reached for the receiver; the room was too quiet, his thoughts too loud. He was desperate for a reprieve from the relentless march of his troubled thoughts. Lifting the phone to his ear, he greeted the caller, "Hello, this is Professor O'Reily. How may I assist you?"

Chapter 37 Gone But Not Forgotten

A woman's professionally sounding voice answered from the other end of the line. "Is this Peter O'Reily? The agent who used to work for Interpol."

His legs went weak, and Peter slumped into his chair as his hand gripped the phone tight. "Yes," he managed to stammer.

"Sir, this is Agent Robinson from the FBI special unit department here in America. If you wouldn't mind, I'd like to ask you a few questions about the Sculptor case."

CHAPTER 38

GOING HOME

KGOTSO

Cape Town, Africa—Day

KGOTSO HAD BEEN AT THE OFFICE FOR LESS THAN AN hour when the first insidious wave of nausea rocked his body. He had been ensnared in the monotonous drone of his subordinate, a hapless officer, recounting the grim details of yet another murder case for over an hour.

As the officer's words continued to buzz in the stale office air, Kgotso's internal battle with his unraveling stomach began in earnest. A raw, animalistic growl ripped from his throat as he abruptly halted the officer's morbid monologue.

Kgotso lurched to his feet with a sudden, jarring movement, he was forced to clutch the edge of his weathered desk, a lifeline against the vertiginous onslaught that threatened to send him spiraling back into his chair.

The officer, caught off guard, managed to stammer out, "Sir, you all right?"

Kgotso could only respond with a low, guttural growl. "No," he managed to grit out between clenched teeth. "That damn place gave me food poisoning." The words hung heavy in the room, casting a chilling pall over the otherwise mundane office, adding another layer of menace to the officer's grim reality.

Chapter 38 — Going Home

Kgotso fought to steady himself as his world spun like a drunken top. His breath was ragged, a symphony of short, harsh notes reverberating in the small room. "I'll sort this case out later," he muttered, his voice gruff. "Now get out! I need to get home."

The officer shifted uncomfortably, his concern evident. "I could drive you," he offered, his voice filled with an undercurrent of worry. His eyes, flickering with unease, searched Kgotso's face for acknowledgment, or a sign of acceptance.

Kgotso's nostrils flared as he absorbed the officer's words. A hard, icy look froze his features, a silent declaration of refusal. "Not necessary," his voice thundered, louder than Kgotso had intended. His throat tightened. A knot of resistance against the rising tide of nausea, Kgotso added, "I'll manage. I will be back in the morning."

The officer nodded; his concern replaced by a mask of professional detachment. Kgotso pushed past the man, his steps unsteady, each footfall a battle against the merciless pull of the sickness that was battering him.

Kgotso stepped out into the squad room. A torrent of silence crashed down as dozens of eyes locked onto him. An icy dread seeped into his veins and threatened to immobilize him. The mere thought of losing control in front of his subordinates was unthinkable. Yet, his stomach twisted and turned in rebellion, a cruel reminder of the traitorous meal he consumed.

As the painful cramps slowly receded, Kgotso seized the moment of respite. His voice echoed through the room, a clear command cutting through the tension, "Get back to work!" He did not wait for a response. Instead, pivoting on his heel, he stepped out into the scorching embrace of the African sun.

The heat was a tangible force, oppressive and unyielding, sweat cascading down his brow. Squinting against the glare, Kgotso scanned the vicinity, his attention focused on locating his vehicle.

Kgotso spotted his small, black SUV a few yards away. In the searing heat, the vehicle miraged on the horizon, a phantom rising from the dust-choked earth. Each step toward it was a battle, a painful victory against the gnawing agony in his guts. His heavy footfalls stirred the parched earth, the swirling dust a testament to his torturous journey.

As Kgotso finally reached the SUV, his world tilted dangerously. He leaned against the vehicle, trying to quell the nauseating wave threatening to unravel him. The vehicle's metal surface seared his hands like a branding iron, causing him to recoil.

Undeterred, he fumbled for the fob clutched in his fist, activating it with a shaky press. Yanking the door open, he collapsed onto the baked seat, the sweltering heat inside adding a fresh level of torture. As he succumbed to the unbearable pain, he made a silent vow. Once he recovered, he would find the cook at that cafe and make him pay.

For Kgotso, the short journey to his home had been akin to a solitary journey through the netherworld. Each wave of pain was a brutal attack, a relentless onslaught that had him battling against the raging tide of traffic and the sea of oblivious pedestrians, their lack of sense to steer clear of the road only adding to his anguish.

Driving in his police unit, he was a recognizable figure, one who couldn't afford to lose control and run down the very citizens he was sworn to protect, no matter how foolish they seemed. Eventually, he reached his sanctuary, his abode, a meticulously maintained house in a prestigious neighborhood. With every ounce of strength sapped, he somehow managed to lock the door behind him, trudge to the bathroom, and purge the pent-up torment of his stomach.

The journey may have ended, but the night was far from over. Kgotso stared at himself in the mirror, his reflection a distorted image of pain and frustration. He had lost a day at work, and by the looks of it, would need to forfeit another to recuperate from the stupid ordeal.

Rinsing out his mouth, Kgotso spotted a tinge of red staining the otherwise pristine white porcelain of the sink. The bitter taste of iron lingered on his tongue, an unwelcomed reminder of the violent illness he battled.

He speculated that the crimson hue was an aftermath of the meal that had triggered his bout of sickness. The memory sent a shiver down his spine, a chilling echo of the torment he had endured.

Despite the weakness that clung to him, Kgotso willed himself to the kitchen. The cool touch of the glass in his hand brought a sense of normalcy, and the tepid water he drank, paired with a few crackers, seemed to soothe his unsettled stomach.

Feeling marginally better, but still having his strength drained, Kgotso sought the comfort of his couch, surrendering to the allure of rest. The room seemed to darken around him, the atmosphere heavy with the silent promise of the impending night.

CHAPTER 39

MUCH TO DO

VANDER

Cape Town, Africa—Day

VANDER HAD BEEN BUSY SINCE LANDING IN CAPE TOWN. The city was teeming with life and vibrancy, yet under its picturesque façade, Vander knew there were secrets waiting to be unearthed.

Time was a luxury he did not have. Alexander, the ever-detailed planner, had scheduled a four-day sojourn. But Vander, consumed by his relentless pursuit of knowledge, planned to wrap everything up in a mere forty-eight hours. He could almost hear the tick-tock of the clock echoing in his mind, the pressure mounting as he raced against time, his heart pounding in sync with the rhythm of urgency.

He intended to be airborne and en route back to America before Alexander could even suspect he had returned home. The stakes were high and for Vander to gain the advantage, he needed to hit the ground running in Philadelphia. Every second mattered in this intricate game of wits and will.

Vander had made sure to be seen checking into his luxurious suite. His calculated actions were a meticulous strategy, as he let his presence be known to all. The fiery-haired reservation clerk, the bellboy straining under the weight of his luggage, even the concierge who had arranged for his leisurely dinner just blocks from where he knew Kgotso would be.

Dark Variations

Each move was deliberate, underlined by the implicit message Vander sent with every interaction. His words to the driver were a pointed promise, "I will call when I am ready," before he disappeared into the restaurant. Inside, the heat of the day was barely tempered, clinging to his skin like a second layer. His order was placed, the meal savored, while Vander waited patiently for Kgotso to do the same in his own time, at his own place.

The anticipation simmered inside him, a thrilling counterpart to the oppressive heat outside. Every moment was worth the wait.

Once Vander's meal had been completed, he rose from the table with a placid demeanor that masked his sinister intentions. He made his way toward the cafe, then to Kgotso's table, his steps measured but seemingly aimless. Vander had wagered on Kgotso's fading memory, a gamble that now seemed to be yielding dividends.

As he moved closer to his oblivious target, Vander "accidentally" stumbled, skillfully orchestrating a minor scratch on Kgotso. It was a well-orchestrated act. A very small, carefully concealed syringe released the deadly poison into Kgotso's veins. In the dim light of the room, it appeared nothing more than a trivial accident. As Vander had regained his footing, he could not help but feel a cold satisfaction seep into him, knowing full well that he had delivered a death blow to Kgotso.

Vander had watched Kgotso hurry out of the cafe, his face scrunched up in thought. More than likely, Kgotso was trying to figure out why Vander seemed so familiar and if that small incident had indeed been an accident. After Kgotso had gone, Vander called his driver and went back to the front of the restaurant where he had been dropped off and waited.

Once he was back in the air-conditioned car, Vander had asked if the driver would mind stopping at a strip mall where he could make a few purchases. The mall, of course, was across the street from Kgotso's police station.

Allowing Vander the opportunity to stroll through the various stores as he kept watch. Sooner than expected, Kgotso stumbled out of the station, looking disheveled and exhausted. Holding back a smile, Vander watched as Kgotso struggled into his vehicle and swerved through traffic before disappearing.

With a few small purchases and the two large bouquets of flowers in hand, Vander returned to the hotel's guest car and asked to be taken to the graveyard where he now stood at the large entrance.

Chapter 39 — Much To Do

Vander had walked past myriad gravestones, each a silent testament to a life once lived. The cemetery, their current dwelling, had numerous homeless souls tucked away in every hidden crevice, the forgotten and ignored of society. He caught sight of one such man rising from his makeshift tent, a spectral figure seemingly in quest of a corporeal form started toward Vander.

A man of humble origins, Vander usually held a softer side for such misfortune, but it was not a day for empathy. Locking gazes with the pitiful man, Vander fixed him with a venomous stare. The man stopped, recoiled, and slithered back into his shadowy abode. A silent flap of canvas closed him off from the world and away from Vander's heated glare.

Continuing, Vander proceeded on his predestined journey, a path he had tread countless times in his dreams. Staring down at the headstone, an icy wave of anger spiraled in his soul. The names etched into the stone read Lenka Masozi & Amahle Masozi, forever binding his mother to his father; in life, in death, and in whatever spectral plane their souls now resided in.

Vander knew that had it not been for Alexander, his fate as well as his parents' resting place would have been vastly different.

Alexander's kindness had spared Vander's parents from the indignity of a pauper's grave, the cold anonymity that befell those left to the mercy of society's indifference. Because of his mentor, there was no mass grave for them, no void in which Vander would not have had a place in which to direct his grief.

Instead, there was a headstone, a quiet testament to their memory, and a personal grave where he could lay his sorrows. Yet Vander found little comfort in these meaningless gestures. The grim truth was his parents were not there. Their bodies had long since surrendered to the relentless march of nature, their essence vanished into the ether.

The ritualistic visits to their grave felt hollow, a macabre dance with decorated dirt. Trust, he realized, was as elusive as the love he yearned for, its existence as ephemeral as the supposed paradise beyond the veil of life. For someone like Vander, the notion of love seemed as unlikely as walking the clouds in heaven.

Vander's gaze remained fixed on the sun as it began its descent, casting long shadows that danced upon the cold, granite tombstones. Time was a luxury he could no longer afford to squander amidst these specters of death, these forgotten souls who had breathed their last beneath the cruel indifference of the cosmos.

His thoughts turned to Kgotso. He could almost feel the venom coursing through the veins of his adversary, the sweet, slow burn of his impending demise. His heart pounded with dark anticipation as he set off toward Kgotso's home, a place soon to be a stage of suffering, a theater of torment.

It was there that he would bear witness to the grand finale, a death as gruesome as it was well-deserved, a symphony of pain, a ballet of degradation.

CHAPTER 40

SOMETHING'S WRONG

KGOTSO

Cape Town, Africa—Night

STRONG CHILLS WRACKED KGOTSO'S BODY. THE ICY TENdrils of the chill seemed to reach into the very marrow of his bones, a torment as relentless as the ticking of a clock. Each convulsion of cold sent new waves of agony through Kgotso's frame, turning his body into a battlefield where he was losing.

The eerie silence of the room was broken only by a low, pitiful moan. A sound so filled with suffering, it seemed to seep into the very walls. Kgotso's foggy mind struggled to place the source of the heart-wrenching sound until, with a chilling realization, he understood it was his own voice echoing back at him.

A feeble attempt to sit up sent his world into a dizzying spin, his body rebelling against him. His fever-ridden mind swam in confusion and terror, the moan increasing in volume, a stark soundtrack to his plight.

Suddenly, nausea surged within him, a volcanic force demanding escape. With a Herculean effort, he stumbled off his couch and lurched toward the bathroom. The world tilted dangerously as he barely made it to the sink before his stomach purged itself, leaving him weak and trembling.

With one hand hanging onto the sink for support, Kgotso used the other to flip on the light switch, then to turn on the water. The harsh, sterile light of the bathroom made his reflection in the mirror a ghostly apparition. With his head bowed low, he scooped up a handful of water, its coldness a sharp contrast to the warmth of his bloodied mouth. He swished it around, grimacing at the metallic flavor that tainted it.

With a grim determination, he spit out the tainted water, recoiling as it splattered against the porcelain sink, a violent explosion of crimson. The sight of his own blood, bright and horrifying, splashed across the white sink and floor seemed unreal, yet the taste of it in his mouth was undeniable.

His gaze found its way back to his reflection in the mirror. Looking at himself, he pulled his lips back, revealing his bleeding gums. The sight was as shocking as it was unexpected. His teeth, once white and healthy, were now framed by a grotesque red line that seemed to bubble up at the gum line.

He ran a lone finger against his teeth, smearing the red stain in a futile attempt to wipe it away. But as he watched, a new line of blood welled up, seeping from his gums like crimson tears. "What the hell?" he mumbled to himself; the words barely audible over the drumming of his own heart in his ears.

Kgotso's vision was a blur, a vague smear of reality that lacked distinction. He glanced downward, his eyes reluctantly focusing on the sink and the water that rushed from the tap. The sight of crimson lines bleeding into the clear fluid, transforming it into a murky pink vortex that twisted down the drain, was a grotesque spectacle.

His mind, wracked with chills and an all-consuming pain, struggled to process the scene. Despite feeling drained of all vitality, a pressing urge emerged from his body's depths. He shuffled toward the toilet, clumsily undid his pants, and started to relieve himself. Kgotso's terror peaked as he saw his life essence, blood, streaming into the bowl. His outcry, "Fuck! What is wrong with me?!" was less a shout and more of a pained, animalistic growl.

There was more blood than piss coming out of him. When the crimson stream finally abated, Kgotso staggered back to the sink. The cold porcelain against his skin was a harsh reminder of the grim reality he faced. His hands shook as he reached for the faucet, the metallic squeak of the valve echoing ominously in the stark silence of the room.

Gathering his wits, he yanked the towel from its hook, the fabric rough against his pallid skin. His reflection, a morbid spectacle in the

Chapter 40   *Something's Wrong*

dimly lit bathroom, stared back at him, a man marked by an unseen menace. But he had to brave the stares, and endure the whispers, for he knew he must seek help.

A wave of dizziness washed over him as he clung to the sink, cold porcelain a grounding anchor in a sea of panic. He looked up, his gaze meeting the mirror once more. Thin rivulets of blood trailed down from his nose, his eyes, and his mouth, painting a terrifying tableau. His image, distorted by this nightmare, shocked him to the core.

As Kgotso stumbled out of the bathroom. The world around him took on a dark, surreal quality. Another bout of violent nausea assaulted him, a monstrous wave threatening to smash him against the jagged rocks of his own frailty.

With an involuntary shudder, Kgotso fell to the ground, his body curling into a tight ball as he writhed upon the cold tile, each convulsion a distinct echo in the eerie silence. After a few excruciating minutes that stretched out like a lifetime in purgatory, the pain ebbed some, a retreating tide leaving behind the wreckage of a once vibrant man.

Desperation spurred Kgotso to make it up onto his hands and knees. A chilling realization crept over him—he was no longer able to drive himself to the hospital. His survival rested on an emergency call and a much-needed ambulance.

Kgotso had to get to his cell phone. Like a wounded animal, he mustered every bit of energy left in his shaking body. His chills, fever, pain, and fatigue were relentless adversaries, yet he pressed on. Each inch toward the table felt like a mile, yet each inch was a symbol of Kgotso's fierce determination.

Upon reaching the table, he hoisted his weakened frame up, his hand trembling as he reached for his lifeline. However, his fingers found not the cool metal of his cell phone, but the rough texture of old magazines and newspapers. "Whaaaaat? Where is it?" Kgotso rasped, his voice a painful whisper.

Suddenly, a figure detached itself from the shadows by the kitchen door. Stepping into the dim light, the handsome stranger from the morning emerged, his presence adding an unexpected twist to Kgotso's desperate search.

Kgotso's feverish brain struggled to process the chilling reality. The man, dark and foreboding, stood in his sanctuary, his home. An icy dread crept up Kgotso's spine as he caught sight of his phone cradled in the stranger's hand. It was then that Kgotso understood, his weakness, his fever, it wasn't natural. This man from the cafe was a poisoner in the guise of a stranger. But why? The answer was as elusive as a wisp of smoke in the wind.

The rich timbre of the stranger's voice was threatening, yet also held an allure, a command that demanded Kgotso's attention despite his debilitating state. "You know what has always troubled me most about Cape Town?" he began, an eerie calm to his voice.

With a wolfish grin, Vander reveled in the sight of Kgotso's turmoil. His eyes glinted in the scant moonlight. He shifted languidly in the shadows, his silhouette a distorted caricature against the flickering glow of a distant streetlight. "That help could be so close, yet so ... unattainable."

MAY 4TH—7 DAYS

CHAPTER 41

WITCHING HOUR

VANDER

Cape Town, Africa—3:00 a.m.

CALMLY, VANDER SQUATTED BEFORE THE COFFEE TABLE, his eyes cold and unyielding, locked with Kgotso's. "Did you know there are varying beliefs across many cultures in regard to the witching hour?"

Rattled, Kgotso's eyes widened in fear. "What?"

Vander nodded. "It's true. In Western lore, it is said that mirrors should be covered during this time to prevent spirits from entering our realm." Vander looked at a far wall, his eyes fixed as if he were simply telling a bedtime story. "In Eastern traditions, it is believed that ringing bells can ward off evil entities."

Kgotso's fingers clung desperately to the polished wood, betraying his façade of indifference. His knuckles whitened as they strained to maintain their hold, the only tangible evidence of his internal turmoil as Vander returned his hardened gaze upon him.

"Yet others suggest avoiding crossroads, as these places are known as meeting places for witches and demons." The dim light of the room flickered and cast eerie shadows to dance on Vander's impassive face. "It's an hour in which the mind is lulled into a trance-like state, amplifying the auditory hallucinations of the night. The ticking of the clock, the creaking floorboard, the wind rustling the trees. It blurs the line between reality and the paranormal and embeds itself into the realm of nocturnal nightmares."

Inside, Vander felt the calm slipping as his anger rose to the surface. He wanted to stay enveloped in the unusual tranquility, to show no emotion to the man he had hated for so long.

He was in the same room with the monster who had dogged his every step as a child. The one who had extinguished so many lives, including his innocent, childhood friend Khumalo. Vander felt no empathy, no sympathy, and most certainly no form of compassion for Kgotso. What he did feel was a strange mix of rage, justice, and closure that brought him a sense of peace.

"What did you do to me?" Kgotso croaked, his voice a tremulous whisper.

Vander knew that anyone else would have been horrified at the sight of Kgotso. A ghastly transformation had taken over the man. His skin had bloomed into an eerie shade of indigo beneath his dark brown complexion. Thin rivulets of blood traced a path from his tormented eyes, nose, and mouth. Yet Vander remained unperturbed, his eyes riveted on the horrific spectacle, an unsettling delight playing at the corners of his mouth.

Tilting his head, Vander peered down at the gruesome aftermath of the administrated toxins. The outcome was exactly what he had anticipated. With a chilling calm, Vander posed a question, "Did you know, drop for drop, Boomslang venom possesses the most potent venom of any snake in Africa?" His chilling words hung heavy in the air, adding to the atmosphere's dark and sinister undertones.

Losing his grip on the table, Kgotso's fingers slipped. He almost fell to the floor, then fumbled to regain his hold and held on for dear life as he struggled for breath.

Vander straightened. "The amount of venom required to kill a human is so small that it can barely be seen with the naked eye," he continued his explanation.

Realization finally dawned on Kgotso as he spat, "You're Lenka's brat!" The insult failed to hit its mark; Vander remained unfazed.

"Of course, the Boomslang is unlikely to bite a human, because they are back-fanged, with their short fixed fangs far back in their mouths," Vader retorted.

Chapter 41 Witching Hour

Letting go of the coffee table, Kgotso, weakened by the venom that coursed through his veins, struggled to crawl back to the couch. "Give me my phone!" he demanded, his voice muffled as he spat past the pooling blood.

But Vander simply glared down at him. His gaze never wavered from Kgotso's agonized form. The room was steeped in a chilling silence, save for the sporadic gasps of pain from Kgotso. Each wince, each grimace, was a grim testament to the insidious power of the Boomslang venom coursing through his veins.

Vander's tone was eerily calm. "Such a fascinating creature. Its venom, hemotoxic as it is, works slowly, gradually undermining its victim's life force." His eyes glinted with a macabre fascination as Kgotso's suffering intensified. "The true tragedy," Vander continued, "is that the poison masks its deadly intent behind hours of deceptive calm. By the time the unsuspecting victim realizes the gravity of their plight, their fate is already sealed."

Vander turned, found a nearby chair, and took a seat, his movements casual yet purposeful, as though he were a puppeteer pulling strings. "Fortunate for some," he started, a knowing smirk on his face, "there is a monovalent anti-venom made especially for Boomslang envenomation. It's kept here, at the South African vaccine producers."

Kgotso's face contorted into a snarl as he spat out words of defiance. "You will never get away with this!" His voice was thick with rage.

A picture of tranquility, Vander leaned back in his chair. "Another interesting fact," he began again. "There was a physician in America who documented his own death from the bite of a Boomslang. No one knows why he did not seek medical help... perhaps it was because the man, like you, knew that help would not have arrived in time to save him."

Vander's eyes held a gleam of sick joy as he proceeded, "Indeed, the unfortunate physician chose instead to document each grotesque symptom as it took hold... extreme nausea... violent vomiting... relentless chills... a fever so high it could scorch the sun... bleeding from his eyes, nose, mouth... an agonizing hell no mortal should endure."

Kgotso's eyes widened with horror, his breaths ragged and heavy. The spasms of pain racked his body and seemed to coincide with Vander's dark narration.

Ignoring Kgotso's discomfort, Vander smiled, his voice a sinister taunt. "Most believe he suffered one of the most excruciating deaths conceivable. His final entry was made less than twenty-four hours after the serpent's fatal kiss. Not much time, wouldn't you agree?" Kgotso's labored breathing became the only sound in the still room.

Vander watched, his gaze as cold as a winter moon as Kgotso lay there, defenseless, his body trembling from the deadly venom that coursed through his veins.

Vander's voice held a final note of cruel satisfaction. "The physician was found on the floor," Vander came to the end of his tale, "bathed in sweat, unable to talk or communicate in any way. He was rushed to the hospital, where he was pronounced dead less than twenty-four hours after his unfortunate incident with the snake."

As Vander's narration came to an end, Kgotso's eyes widened in horror, his gaze fixed on the cracked ceiling above, filled with a pain that was more than physical.

Getting to his feet, Vander fastened the button on his blazer. His eyes, devoid. "I would have liked to have given you a smaller dose," he continued, his voice a chilling whisper in the oppressive silence, "in order to prolong your suffering."

Vander paused, cocked his head, closed his eyes, and smiled as he listened to Kgotso's ragged breathing. "But unfortunately," Vander said coolly as he looked down at him. "I have pressing business back in the States."

With gloved hands, Vander placed Kgotso's only tool of communication, his lifeline, his phone, upon the sleek surface of the TV, ensuring it remained safely beyond the desperate reach of the failing man.

Voice, void of emotion, Vander said in parting, "Enjoy your final moments, Kgotso, for I can promise you, the hell that awaits you is far worse than anything you have suffered thus far."

With a satisfied nod, Vander strolled toward the backdoor, stepped into the pre-dawn hour, then quietly closed the door behind him, leaving Kgotso to his impending doom.

MAY 3RD—8 DAYS

CHAPTER 42

HOME AT LAST

ETHAN

Austin, TX—Night

It had taken far more arguing than Ethan would have liked to convince his doctor to release him from the hospital. He knew that he should have stayed another day or two for observation. Still, he was a paramedic, and unlike many other patients, he knew the signs to look out for in case of trouble. He was young, well relatively so, strong, and the gunshot wound miraculously had done far less damage than any of them had expected after they had gotten him into surgery.

If he had any trouble, he would know it and have Paige or one of the guys get him back to the hospital if needed.

At first, Paige had been angry with him, scolding him about being as bad as a doctor and refusing to let the professionals handle his care, but after some serious debate, he had won her over and she reluctantly agreed to take him home and promised the doctor that she would keep him out of trouble.

Now, with his head resting against the headrest, Ethan found himself sinking into a half-sleep state, his consciousness meandering between sleep and waking. The song on the radio intertwined with the humming of the engine to produce a lullaby-like rhythm that kept tempting him toward slumber.

The exhaustion mixed with his throbbing shoulder and pain medication had left him struggling to stay awake.

Paige's sweet voice, laced with concern, sounded as if from far away. "I should have never agreed to bring you home. I knew it was too soon to leave the hospital."

Ethan stirred. "I'm just snoozing. I'm fine." He assured her with a small smile that he hoped belied his fatigue. For Ethan, being out of the hospital, on their way home, was a balm to his weary soul.

"They should have at least kept you until morning. Who releases a patient at seven o'clock at night? Seriously."

Eyes closed, Ethan fought to listen to his wife, wanting to convince her he was well enough to have been released. "Paperwork takes forever, so that happens more often than you think. If I wasn't okay to leave, they wouldn't have sent me home."

"You're not fooling me for one minute, mister. I know you. You wore the staff down and wouldn't stop complaining until they kicked you out." Paige warned, "So if you try anything you're not supposed to ... I'll have Ramiro put you back in an ambulance and haul you straight back to that hospital."

Laughing softly, Ethan wanted to look alert, but already felt his eyes drifting shut. "I won't... best behavior, promise." *Dang it.* His voice sounded slurred and weak.

"Uh-huh," Paige grumbled. "And just so you know ... I'm still mad at you for scaring the hell out of me."

"I'm sorry," Ethan said. He knew he could not promise her that he would not do something like that again, because if given the same circumstances, he would.

"You can make it up to me by behaving yourself at dinner tomorrow night."

Puzzled, Ethan tried to make sense of that last statement. *Why would she say that?*

Paige added, "I had told Brayden to invite Alayna over for dinner, before you were shot of course, but seeing as how you are feeling so much better."

Ethan knew the last part of her statement was meant as a dig, trying to goad him for his rebellious attitude that had won him his freedom from the hospital, and though he knew he should have come back with a smart-ass remark to reassure his beautiful wife that he was, indeed, okay, he could not resist the overwhelming urge to drift off to sleep as the car journeyed toward home.

MAY 4TH—7 DAYS

CHAPTER 43

PLANE TO CATCH

VANDER

Cape Town, Africa—Morning

Having breezed through security, Vander found himself at his gate sooner than expected, affording him the luxury of a leisurely breakfast. He savored the crisp bacon and fluffy scrambled eggs, comfort food that was a stark contrast to the dark deeds he had left behind. Vander was next in line to board his flight to America, a voyage that seemed more symbolic now, a journey not only across physical distances but emotional ones as well.

He had carried the toxin of his hate for Kgotso so heavily, like a second skin, that even the act of breathing had become laborious. Now, however, the weight had vanished, leaving Vander feeling strangely light, almost giddy. Kgotso, the source of his torment, was now nothing more than a discarded husk, bleeding, rotting, a pitiful end for such a formidable enemy.

The sense of euphoria had Vander pondering, *Is this what Alexander feels after each life he claims?* Was it the satisfaction of a promise kept, or the intoxicating power of having another's life dance on the strings he pulled?

Putting his best mask forward, Vander appeared a man of calculated charm and mysterious demeanor, as he made his way onto the aircraft, greeted by the sly smiles of the two stewardesses welcoming travelers onto the aircraft.

Their glances held an allure, an unspoken promise of the adventures that lay ahead. He reveled in the attention, relishing the thrill of new conquests on the horizon. His fondness for Christina was undeniable, but Vander was no fool. He knew that love, like everything else in his life, served a purpose—one that Christina had fulfilled.

He had foreseen the inevitable end, the mutual disengagement that graduation would bring, as they both found themselves submerged in the demands of life and new careers. It was a harsh reality, but one Vander had already accepted, even as he mourned the impending loss. Christina had served her purpose, and soon, he would have no further need of her. Such was the stark, unforgiving truth of Vander's existence as he stepped into the welcoming embrace of first-class luxury.

Vander took his seat, then turned his attention to the small window looking out at the city. The once familiar skyline now seemed alien, a stark reminder of a past he could never reclaim. With his parents gone and Kgotso now dead, a grim realization washed over him. Vander knew that he would never again step foot in the country of his birth. This melancholic thought hung heavy in the air, casting a shadow over the remnants of his past life. His future, what was left of it, lay before him back in America. An unsettling silence filled the room as Vander acknowledged the irrevocable end of this part of his life. This part was over, done, and there were no other reasons to return. The finality was comforting, yet chilling. A new chapter was waiting to be written. Even if it was dark and uncertain, Vander also found it irresistibly compelling.

As the announcement ceased, a shiver ran down Vander's spine. The stewardess, with an eerie calmness, sealed the entrance, the metallic click echoing through the confines of the aircraft. It was a sound as final as a tomb door closing, casting a pall over the once-buzzing cabin. Vander could feel the weight of the journey that lay ahead, a fight not just against Alexander, but against his own haunting fears. It was a battle for survival, every moment shrouded in a murky cloud of uncertainty. This was no ordinary flight; it was a journey into a storm of unknowns.

Vander had lost four days to this journey. He had departed Philadelphia at dusk on May 04, with the clock already working against him. Losing a couple of hours to drive to the airport soon morphed into another hour when he had been ensnared in the masses as they worked their way through

Chapter 43 — Plane To Catch

security. Once aboard the plane, fourteen more hours were swallowed by the gaping mouth of the journey across the ocean. Touchdown in Cape Town had stolen an additional eight hours due to the time difference.

It had already been early evening by the time Vander checked into his hotel. The poison, a concoction that he had been hard-pressed to obtain, had been forced to wait in its vial another night before being delivered to Kgotso's arm mid-morning the following day. The cost of time had been high, a full day spent as Vander had watched Kgotso succumb to the lethal venom. Now, as he embarked on the journey westward, the aircraft wrestled against an obstinate jet stream. It would take an additional sixteen to seventeen hours before he landed back in the concrete jungle known as New York.

Vander knew that by the time he landed, went through customs, and drove back to Philadelphia, it would be nightfall. Representing another lost day. Graduation was on May 13, giving him less than five days to figure out not only how he was going to survive the plans Alexander had for him, but also how to navigate the firestorm that his mentor had created by murdering the artist in Texas.

Notepad in hand, the stewardess stopped beside him. "Sir, is there anything I can get for you?"

Most people would feel helpless in Vander's unsettling predicament, trapped in a metal tube coursing through the sky. But Vander was different, unique in a way that defied ordinary comprehension. His psychic gifts, a beacon in the sea of mundane existence, provided him with a different set of possibilities. "Could I trouble you for a pillow and blanket? The time difference has really done a number on me."

The stewardess placed a gentle hand on Vander's shoulder and returned his smile. "Of course, I'll be right back."

While his body might remain strapped in the aircraft seat, his soul would be undeterred by those trivial constraints. His psychic gifts, a beacon in the sea of mundane existence, provided him with a different set of possibilities.

The stewardess returned. "Here you go."

"Thank you," Vander said as he took the items and settled in. As the cabin lights dimmed, Vander perceived the unseen gateway that would soon open for him, leading to an ethereal journey parallel to the aircraft's course. While his body appeared to sleep, his soul would traverse a different realm and garner the invaluable insights he so desperately needed.

MAY 4TH—7 DAYS

CHAPTER 44

GETTING TO KNOW YOU

ALAYNA

Austin, TX—Night

ALAYNA WAS NERVOUS TO BE MEETING BRAYDEN'S FAMILY for the first time. Growing up, she had always been close to her single mother, who was more like a cool best friend than a traditional parent. As she stepped into his sister Paige's welcoming home, it almost felt surreal—like something out of a movie.

Her nerves only seemed to intensify as they all sat around the dinner table. Alayna couldn't help but fidget with her napkin, her hands trembling ever so slightly. She was thankful when Brayden reached down and placed his warm hand over hers, offering a reassuring squeeze.

It had only been two dates, yet there she was meeting the family. It seemed crazy, but at the same time, it felt right. As she looked up into Brayden's warm brown eyes, she felt a sense of safety and peace wash over her. This was real, this was happening.

Despite her nerves, Alayna couldn't help but feel grateful for Brayden's strong presence beside her. He made her feel loved and supported, even in an unfamiliar situation like meeting his family. And as the night went on, she found herself laughing and bonding with his family, feeling more and more at ease.

In spite of telling herself to keep her guard up, Alayna found herself relaxing and enjoying the evening. The twinkle in Brayden's eyes and the warmth of his smile were contagious. She laughed more that evening than she had in a long time. Even Brayden's brother-in-law, who had initially been somewhat standoffish, seemed to thaw as the evening progressed. A ball of energy, Hunter asked his mother, "May I be excused?"

Paige nodded, her eyes sparkling with affection for her son, "Of course, but come right back, okay?"

Without any hesitation, Hunter dashed toward the stairs. "Yes, Ma'am."

With her unique abilities, Alayna could sense something different about Hunter. She had never met someone like him before. His tiny form was enveloped in a brilliant aura with hues of blues and purples. It was breathtaking and a bit … unnerving. Hunter was different, that much she knew. He was an old soul, unlike any she'd encountered before. A pang of anxiety crossed her mind as she contemplated whether Hunter had begun to display signs of his abilities yet. It was a frightening yet thrilling thought. Just how special was this child named Hunter?

"So Alayna, I've got to ask… Why in the world did you agree to go out with Brayden?" Ethan's question took Alayna out of her musings. His tone was light, but there was a hint of genuine curiosity in his eyes.

Alayna blinked, taken aback. She looked at Brayden, who was smirking in amusement, then at Paige, who was trying to hide a smile. She felt her face flush slightly under the scrutiny. "Well," she started, her voice a bit shaky. "Brayden… He's different." She glanced at Brayden; his smirk was replaced by a surprised expression. "But I'm broke and his offers of free food were too good to pass up."

Ethan laughed and leaned back in his chair, apparently satisfied with the answer. Brayden's surprised expression slowly morphed into a smile.

"Thanks a lot, big brother," Brayden said sarcastically.

Paige elbowed Ethan in the ribs, and he added, "I'm just saying, Alayna might not be a good judge of character, that's all." Ethan teased, though there was a hint of protectiveness in his tone. Alayna smiled at the playful banter between the family.

Alayna watched as Paige tried to hide her concern as she asked Zoey to go check on Hunter. "Zoey, would you go see what's keeping your brother?" Like the little lady she was, Zoey nodded and excused herself from the table and started toward the stairs. Just then, Hunter, papers in hand, came hurrying down the stairs.

"Ugh," Zoey exclaimed as she spun around and sat back down.

Excited, Hunter raced past his mom and Zoey and scrunched himself in between Brayden and Alayna. "I made you something." Alayna could feel Brayden's instant tension as he forced a smile.

Taking the paper from Hunter before Alayna could see it, he asked, "What ya got, buddy?" Brayden's smile wavered for a second before he was able to maintain it. "That's really something."

Curious, Alayna tried to see the paper, but Brayden began to fold it. Hunter snatched it away from him and handed it to Alayna. "It's for her, too... You're supposed to share." Alayna couldn't help but snicker at how the little boy had just schooled Brayden. Taking the drawing, Alayna looked at it. Instantly, she understood Brayden's reaction.

Within the crude lines, Alayna could tell that Hunter had attempted to draw the murdered artist who had visited her shop, the same scene that Brayden had described to her. *Brayden did not discuss these horrible cases with his family, did he?* Unable to mask her shock, Alayna looked up at Brayden.

"Hunter has really bad nightmares sometimes," Brayden said as a form of explanation.

Sadly, Hunter asked, "You don't like it?"

"Oh, no, buddy, it's great." Brayden picked Hunter up and sat him on his lap. "Thank you," Brayden said as he tried to look at the drawing as if it were nothing more than a puppy chasing a butterfly.

Ethan reached his hand out to Brayden. "I'd like to see the picture Hunter drew for you." All humor had left Ethan's voice, his eyes were guarded once more.

Reluctantly, Brayden handed the paper to Ethan. Ethan looked down at the horrific image, his jaw clenched as a slight tremor passed through him. Without looking at Brayden, Ethan cast Paige a knowing look and handed her the paper as he got to his feet.

"Okay, kiddo, time for bed." Ethan took Hunter from Brayden, not meeting his or Alayna's eyes as he hugged Hunter to him. It was as if Hunter could sense Ethan's mood and did not protest, but instead, laid his head upon his daddy's shoulder. "You too, Zoey."

Zoey protested, "But I'm three years older than him!"

Playfully, Ethan put a hand on Zoey's head and shook it gently. "Then you can stay up and help me read a couple of stories to Hunter."

"Ugh!" Zoey rolled her eyes, losing her ladylike composure and reverting to the beautiful child she was. "Fine, but I get to pick them out."

"Deal," Ethan said as he started toward the stairs. "I'll be back in about twenty minutes," Ethan told them as he and the children left the room.

Confused, Alayna asked, "What just happened?" Brayden studied his hands for a moment, then looked up at his sister Paige.

Paige assured Alayna with a soft smile. "Hunter sometimes sees things, like events from the past or future, and it can be overwhelming for him."

Brayden chimed in, "And for Ethan, he doesn't like anything that he can't explain."

Puzzled, Alayna asked Paige, "But you're psychic."

Paige fixed Brayden with a look and raised an eyebrow. "You told her?"

Brayden shrugged. Alayna jumped to his defense. "He wanted to put my mind at ease regarding my gifts. And, even if he hadn't, I would have known as soon as I met you." Alayna smiled. "You're very intuitive. Anyone sensitive to these things could easily tell."

Reluctantly, Paige handed Brayden Hunter's drawing. "It's true, I am... But Hunter, he..."

"Is different," Alayna added.

"Yes, he is showing signs of precognition, clairvoyance, and I don't know what else." Paige took a deep breath, then fixed Brayden with a look. "Has that already happened, or do you think it will?"

Grimly, Brayden took the paper, gave it one last look, then folded it and placed it in his pocket. "It took place days ago. Juan and I have been assigned the case."

Alayna could tell that Paige's face had paled and from the look on his face, Brayden had, too. "Paige, what is it? What's wrong?"

Eyes fearful, Paige looked up at the empty staircase, then leaned in toward them. "Hunter isn't the only one having nightmares. I've been waking up to the same dream for four nights in a row now. But I can't make sense of it. Its all jumbled, fragmented." Paige shook her head and dropped her head into her hands. "Ethan has convinced himself that Hunter is having night terrors."

Wanting to comfort Paige, Alayna put a hand on her arm. "What do you believe?"

Paige looked at her with such raw pain that Alayna had to resist the urge to cry herself.

"It's okay, sis, we're here for you," Brayden encouraged.

Paige tried to smile, an attempt to shake off her worried expression. "That if Hunter's dreams are anything like mine, I know why he is so afraid. I feel so helpless. I don't know how to help him," Paige confessed.

"Sis, we'll figure this out, I promise." Brayden reached across the table and took her hand.

"Tomorrow, after school, why don't you and the kids come by my shop?" Alayna offered.

"No!" Ethan said from the doorway. "I don't want you or my children exposed to this nonsense."

Getting to his feet, Brayden tried to reason with his brother-in-law. "Ethan, I know you—"

"It's late, you should go." Ethan did not wait for their reply. He started for the kitchen and began to clean.

MAY 4TH—7 DAYS

CHAPTER 45

MOMENT SHARED

BRAYDEN

Austin, TX—Night

QUIET MOST OF THE WAY HOME, BRAYDEN WAS WORRIED that Alayna misunderstood Ethan's behavior and his abrupt ending to the evening. "I'm sorry about tonight."

"It's okay," Alayna assured him.

"Ethan's one of the best people I know. He loves my sister, and is always patient to a fault with the kids." Brayden laughed. 'Heck, Paige is the one who disciplines the kids when they misbehave because Ethan doesn't have the heart to."

Turning into her apartment complex, Brayden glanced over at Alayna. She nodded. "I understand. He's worried about his family and is very protective of them."

"He is. Before Ethan and Paige had Zoey, I used to think a momma bear was the most dangerous creature to run into, but after seeing how Ethan looks after his family, I would bet on Ethan." Brayden parked his car and killed the engine.

Unbuckling her seatbelt, Alayna turned to Brayden. "It's okay, Brayden. Anyone with eyes could see Ethan's crazy about his wife and kids. I understand his fear, his frustration, and I'm a stranger. Plus, not knowing how to help his own family when he is saving the lives of others almost every day, I can't imagine how frustrating that must be for him."

"You do get it." Brayden laid his head back against the headrest. "You're amazing. You know that."

Alayna rewarded his compliment with a sexy smile. "You have time for a drink?"

"I'll make time." Brayden took the keys out of the ignition. He was still waiting for a call back from Chantal to see which way his investigation needed to go. Hopping out of the car, Brayden went around to the passenger's side and opened Alayna's door. It might be old-fashioned to open the door for a lady, but he did not care. He was an old-fashioned kind of guy and he was glad Alayna did not mind his need to be chivalrous.

Alayna took Brayden's hand, her fingers gently intertwining with his, a silent promise of support and companionship. The soft, warm glow of the apartment lights cast a delicate sheen on her face, accentuating her features and lending her an ethereal beauty. Brayden, although nervous, could not help but be captivated by the sincere tenderness mirrored in her eyes.

When Brayden had picked her up, she had met him outside of her private sanctuary. As Alayna poured them a drink, he walked around the simple one-bedroom apartment, taking in the details. Her sanctuary whispered of Alayna's earthy spirit. The air smelled of sage and Palo Santo. The hardwood floors were adorned with a large beige-and-stone-colored rug. Honey-hued macrame wall hangings intertwined with lush, verdant plants graced the corners, crafting a symphony of nature indoors. Each piece of furniture, each trinket, and each artifact seemed to tell a story of adventure, love, and spiritual exploration—a testament to a life lived in harmony with the earth. The aura of tranquility and peace that permeated the space was a gentle reflection of a woman anchored to the earth, guided by the stars, and in tune with the rhythms of nature.

Alayna handed him a Negroni. Brayden looked into Alayna's eyes, finding a hint of mischief glowing in them. He took the glass from her, his fingers brushing gently against hers, the contact sending a subtle thrill through him. "What is this?" he asked, his voice soft, almost a whisper.

The playful glint in her eyes sparkled brighter as she twirled the decorative orange peel around her finger. "A Negroni. A concoction of gin, Campari, and sweet red vermouth over ice. Garnished with a twist," she explained, her words flowing like a sweet melody.

He watched her as she took a long, slow sip of her drink, her eyes never leaving his. Brayden raised the glass to his lips, the aroma of the

Chapter 45 — Moment Shared

cocktail teasing his senses. He took a sip, savoring the unique blend of flavors. It was good, exceptionally good. His eyes met hers again, a soft smile playing on his lips as he drained his glass, the taste of the Negroni lingering on his tongue, just like the tender moment lingering between them.

Alayna took Brayden's glass and set it down gently on the coffee table, the soft clink barely audible in the quiet room. It was as if the world around them paused, holding its breath at this intimate moment. Alayna turned to Brayden, her eyes shimmering with the soft glow of the room's ambient light. She moved closer, her arms wrapping tenderly around his neck. Their faces were inches apart, their breaths mingling in the space between.

Then, as if guided by an unseen force, their lips met in a kiss that was as profound as it was gentle. Brayden's heart soared as he held her close, the warmth of their bodies a soothing balm to his soul. The world outside ceased to exist. All that mattered then was Alayna in his arms, their hearts beating as one. And in that moment, he knew without a doubt that he would do anything to protect that woman and keep her safe. For that was more than a fleeting passion; it was a bond meant to last a lifetime.

Brayden felt Alayna pull away from him, his heart throbbing in the quiet spaces between the beats. He wanted to protest, a hitch in his breath betraying his longing. Yet, instead of words, Alayna placed a single, silencing finger against his lips—a tender barrier to his unspoken thoughts.

Her eyes, pools of mystery under the soft light, held a seductive promise. In a whisper as soft as silk, she invited, "I'd like to show you my room if you have a little more time?" The question hung in the air, an invitation to an enchanting realm.

Brayden's heart fluttered, his thoughts a whirlwind of anticipation. Alayna, choosing to let her actions speak louder than words, gently took his hand and led him down the short hallway. Brayden, caught in the undercurrent of her allure, surrendered willingly and followed her without a second thought.

MAY 4TH—7 DAYS

CHAPTER 46

TROUBLED

ETHAN

Austin, TX—Night

ETHAN COULDN'T SLEEP. AS HE LAY THERE, STARING INTO the darkness, his mind whirled with thoughts of Brayden's new girlfriend. The way she looked at Paige and Hunter earlier that evening remained etched in his memory. He had seen an unspoken promise in her eyes, an eagerness to extend her psychic abilities to help them. The concern was not about her intentions, but the unfamiliar path she was inviting them to tread. He felt a pang of guilt for not being more open-minded, for letting his skepticism cast a cloud over their evening. But his heart ached with the purest form of love for his wife and children and his only aim was to protect them. Yet his mind wrestled with the question—was he doing more harm than good by shielding them from this potential route of help? The silence of the night offered no answers, only amplifying his inner turmoil.

Ethan looked over at his sleeping wife, her chest gently rising and falling with each tranquil breath. A soft smile crossed his lips as he stroked her hair, the silken strands slipping through his fingers like precious threads of gold. Her serene face, bathed in the pale moonlight, was a sight more beautiful than any sunset or starry night sky. His world, his purpose, his love, all wrapped up in the woman who lay peacefully beside him. Her presence was a soothing balm to the hardships of his demanding

Chapter 46   Troubled

job, her unwavering understanding and support his stronghold. In her, he had found his home, his completion.

Slipping out of bed, Ethan quietly opened the door and tiptoed down the hall to the children's rooms. His heart was a tender knot of concern and love as he peered into Zoey's room, where she lay peacefully amongst her army of stuffed animals, a remnant of their bedtime stories. Moving onward, Ethan crept into Hunter's room, where the quiet rhythm of his son's breathing filled the silence. In those moments, the depth of his love for his children was overwhelming, their innocent slumber a poignant reminder of life's precious simplicity. They were his world, gifts of love from his beloved Paige, and Ethan treasured every moment with them.

Ethan wanted this same kind of life for Brayden, his younger brother-in-law. He wished for Brayden to be blessed with the joy of finding a loving partner, and of experiencing the unique happiness that fatherhood brought. Ethan's heart held a special place for Brayden, a corner filled with brotherly love and concern. Yet, as he watched Alayna, he couldn't help but feel a sense of disquiet. Brayden was a beacon of light, always quick with a smile or a witty retort, his intelligence shining in every conversation. However, Alayna was a mystery. She was an enigmatic puzzle, her eyes haunted, her demeanor guarded. Ethan couldn't shake off the feeling that she was concealing a part of herself, not just from him, but from everyone around her. This nagging uncertainty etched lines of worry onto Ethan's face, for he wanted nothing but the best for his brother, his friend, Brayden.

Rubbing his jaw, Ethan thought back on the evening. Ethan was more than happy to give Alayna a chance, despite the storm of apprehension brewing within him. However, when Hunter had passed yet another one of those unsettling drawings to Brayden, a chill ran down his spine. The chilling sketch etched into his son's paper was a horrific image that made his protectiveness surge like never before. This mysterious "gift" that Paige claimed she and Hunter possessed was an enigma wrapped in a paradox. A tender concern filled his heart, his love for his family amplifying his inherent caution. He yearned to understand, but found himself lost in a maze of uncertainty.

Because he loved Paige and wanted to understand her, Ethan delved into the realm of psychic abilities with a sense of tender intrigue, fueled by his affection and his quest for understanding. His research, however, led him into the shadows of uncertainty and skepticism. It was like navigating a labyrinth with no definitive conclusion, a realm often dismissed as pseudoscience. Yet, what he could comprehend and even relate to was the concept of intuition—that gut feeling which, in one way or another, everyone experienced. However, what troubled him deeply was Paige's conviction that she and Hunter were not just intuitive, but precogs, plagued by visions of events yet to happen—events often of a distressing nature. This was something he felt powerless against, and it gnawed at him, the lover, the protector, who could not shield them from these unseen, unpredictable horrors.

Ethan's heart clenched at the familiar sound, a soft, distressed sound that tugged at the deepest strings of his paternal instincts. He quietly moved toward his son's bed, each step heavy with concern yet feather-light to avoid disturbing his troubled sleep any further. The room was dim, the nightlight casting long shadows that flickered like ghosts across the walls. As he reached the edge of Hunter's bed, he gently brushed a lock of hair from his son's forehead, his touch as soft as a whisper. His voice, usually strong and steady, was tender as he murmured soothing words into the hushed silence. "It's okay, Hunter," he reassured, "Daddy's here."

His little face dotted with perspiration, Hunter looked up at Ethan, his troubled mind still clinging to sleep. "I'm sorry, Daddy. So sorry."

Ethan sat on the bed next to his little man. "Hey, hey, it's okay, little man. You're just having a bad dream. Everything's okay." Ethan cupped Hunter's tiny face in his strong hand as his thumb stroked the worried frown from Hunter's forehead.

Tears formed in Hunter's eyes as he came fully awake and sat up. "Don't hate me, Daddy."

Shocked by Hunter's words, Ethan felt like he had been punched in the gut. "Hunter... I could never hate you."

Hunter sprang into his arms and held onto Ethan like a lifeline. Ethan held Hunter close and rocked him. "What's this all about, kiddo?"

Muffled, Hunter kept his face buried in Hunter's shoulder. "I don't know how to stop it."

Ethan strained to hear Hunter's muffled voice. "I don't know how to stop it." His voice, barely more than a whisper, was lost in the fabric of Ethan's shirt.

The depth of Hunter's vulnerability was palpable in those words, laying bare an internal struggle that left Ethan's heart aching. But the weight of the moment was not lost on Ethan. "Hunter," he began, his

Chapter 46 Troubled

voice a soothing balm against the raw pain in Hunter's admission. "It's okay. It's not your fault," he reassured, the gentle rhythm of his words underpinned by a deep, unchanging love. "I love you just the way you are, okay?" His arms tightened their hold, a silent promise of unwavering support. "We're going to figure this out together, okay?"

MAY 5TH—6 DAYS

CHAPTER 47

NEEDED CALL

BRAYDEN

Austin, TX—Morning

After making love to Alayna for hours, Brayden had drifted off to sleep, with her cradled gently against his chest. Their hearts were beating as one, rhythmically creating a sweet symphony of love. The serene silence of the night was interrupted by the soft buzzing of his phone. Glancing at the clock, he noticed it was 2:15 a.m. Whoever was calling had better have a compelling reason. With careful effort not to disturb Alayna's peaceful slumber, Brayden shifted slightly. He reached for his phone, answered, and whispered with a tone of concern, "Detective James."

Brayden heard the familiar voice of Agent Chantal Robinson, with the FBI back east, come through on the other end of the line. "Brayden, I hate to bother you so late," Chantal's voice came through, a hint of regret seeping into her tone.

Despite the physical distance, her concern was palpable. Brayden, however, found comfort in the sound of her voice, a reminder of the world outside his intimate bubble with Alayna. "No worries, I've been waiting for your call," he responded, his voice a gentle whisper in the quiet room.

He glanced down at Alayna, her peaceful form curled into the crook of his arm, her hand resting on his bare chest. A tender smile tugged at

Chapter 47 — Needed Call

his lips, a testament of the love he held for her. As he listened to Chantal on the other end of the line, he stroked Alayna's hair softly, careful not to wake her.

"I did some research in regard to your current case," Robinson continued in a hushed tone, sensitive to the harsh reality they were discussing. There was a poignant pause, significant enough to make Brayden worry about what came next. "There has not been another case like yours within the States," she added, her voice heavy with concern.

Brayden's shoulders slumped in defeat. He had hoped that Chantal would unearth a connection to his case. "But," Robinson's voice grew louder, infusing determination, "there have been several similar murders that Interpol had been tracking across the globe."

At this revelation, Brayden sat bolt upright, a surge of energy pulsating through him. "What?!" he exclaimed, his mind reeling at the implications.

Startled, Alayna jumped up with him. "What? What's wrong?" she stammered, her wide eyes reflecting her growing concern.

Brayden placed a gentle hand over the receiver as he flashed Alayna an apologetic smile, his eyes brimming with reassurance. "Sorry, I've got to take this," he murmured, his tone soft, yet edged with a hint of urgency. As Brayden slipped out of bed, phone still pressed to his ear, he struggled to get dressed, his movements a clumsy dance of haste and necessity. Alayna, nestled in the sea of covers, watched him as he slipped into his pants. "Go on," Brayden said to Chantal.

"As you know, the FBI often works with local and state law enforcement agencies when a crime falls under federal jurisdiction, but we also help when local law enforcement agencies request assistance," Chantal said matter-of-factly.

Brayden tugged his shirt over his head, and let out a deep sigh, his heart echoing the same heaviness. He ran his fingers through his tousled hair, his mind racing. "Consider yourself requested."

Chantal continued from her end of the line. "As a federal law enforcement agency, we have a wide range of investigative tools and resources at our disposal, which would be more effective with your very complex crime." Her voice was gentle, the concern palpable even through the phone line. She took a deep breath, the pause filled with unspoken worry. "But in this instance, I believe we need to reach out to Interpol as well." She let the words hang in the air.

Taken aback, Brayden flashed a worried look at Alayna, his eyes filled with tender concern. Holding the cell phone to his ear, his voice was a gentle whisper. "Interpol? Are you serious right now?" The love in his gaze was unmistakable, even as worry flooded his features.

"I've already put in the call. There was some case, started over twenty-five years ago, that was closed about eight years after that. They thought they had caught their serial killer," Chantal explained.

Brayden did not want to alarm Alayna, but knew she was already involved thanks to his victim's ghost. "And you think they may have been wrong?"

"It's either that or you have a copycat killer in Austin." Chantal hesitated.

Brayden knew Chantal was a straight shooter. If he were honest, the agent was downright brutal with her honesty most of the time. His heart pounded in his chest, the unease gnawing at his gut was a clear indication that something was amiss. Maintaining an intellectual and matter-of-fact tone, Brayden cautiously turned his back to Alayna, subtly shielding her from the potentially disturbing information that Chantal might reveal. His voice carried an edge of concern as he posed his question to Chantal. "What are you not telling me?"

Hesitantly, Chantal continued, "Interpol lost two of their best agents in pursuit of the Sculptor. If, indeed, he is still alive and killing, you need to be careful. Extremely so, Brayden." Chantal warned, "No Lone Ranger shit... got it?"

Brayden nodded, a sense of dread washing over him. "Understood."

The muscles in Brayden's jaw tightened further, a visible manifestation of his growing unease. His gaze, often sharp and focused, was becoming hazy with concern for Alayna. The situation necessitated a calculated approach, a balance between personal emotions and professional duty. The killer they were hunting was no ordinary criminal, his intelligence matched by his ruthlessness, making Brayden's task all the more challenging. The stakes were high, and the slightest error could turn the tables against them. "Yes, Chantal, I heard you," Brayden managed to reply, his voice betraying an undertone of worry that he usually masked with his easy humor.

"Good. Now listen. You keep tracking down those leads in Austin," Chantal added.

Puzzled, Brayden asked, "What are you going to do?"

Chapter 47 — Needed Call

With an intellectual, yet matter-of-fact tone, she explained her plans. "I'm in London now, trying to locate the man involved in the Sculptor case when the assumed culprit was presumably apprehended. Later, this individual stirred up quite a controversy within Interpol's ranks, claiming they had the wrong suspect in custody. My intention is to gather his insights before we decide to navigate the standard procedural routes."

Brayden nodded, understanding the gravity of the situation. This was a case that had caused waves in the international law enforcement community, and it seemed like they were still far from solving it. They needed all the help they could get, especially from someone who had insider knowledge.

"Keep me updated." The phone went silent.

Brayden watched as Alayna got to her feet, her actions marked by the grace of a dancer. The flicker of understanding in her eyes reflected the resignation of their shared circumstances. Brayden hung up the phone, its cold, metallic edge a stark contrast to the warmth of the room. The device found its customary place in his pocket, a silent harbinger of the outside world's demands. "I'm sorry. I've got to go," he directed toward Alayna, his voice tinged with a layer of regret.

Alayna's response was wordless, her arms enlacing his waist in a gentle embrace that spoke volumes about their unspoken bond. The departure was as swift as it was necessary, Alayna leading him through the familiar maze of her abode and back to the front door.

Brayden, overcome by emotion, pulled Alayna closer, his heart echoing the reluctance to let the night cease. Their lips met in a kiss that was a poignant mix of passion and despair, a silent vow etched into the ephemeral canvas of time. As they parted, Brayden's hands stayed, framing her face as he locked eyes with her. His voice, a touch husky, resonated with genuine concern. "Alayna, promise me you'll lock your doors and windows. I need you to be extra cautious, please." His words, as straightforward as they were heartfelt, were a testament to his growing apprehensions.

Brayden waited for Alayna to answer.

"Always," Alayna assured him as she gently pushed him out the door. "You do the same, handsome," she said, flashing him a flirtatious grin. As the door shut behind him, the unmistakable sound of a lock clicking into place echoed down the hall. A sense of satisfaction washed over Brayden. His next course of action was clear: he would return home, take a swift, refreshing shower, and then promptly make his way back to the station.

MAY 5TH—6 DAYS

CHAPTER 48

TAKE A MINUTE

VANDER

Veil—Morning

HIS THOUGHTS WERE A WHIRLWIND, EACH ONE A TEMpestuous cyclone hurtling into the next. Boundless and formless, his spirit roamed the astral plane, a phantom adrift in an ocean of cosmic energy. Nightshade's call rang out, a spectral siren song that echoed through the ethereal emptiness around him. It was a lure, a "come and see" whispered into the night, a beacon guiding him back to the veil that separated this world from his physical reality.

Despite the fatigue that weighed on his soul, Vander was drawn to the call; his heart tethered to the bird's haunting melody. The airplane and his corporeal shell bound for New York felt both a million miles away and yet, paradoxically, within touching distance.

He could feel the pull of both worlds, a tug-of-war in his very being. The weight of his human responsibilities pulled him back to consciousness, and the allure of the astral plane urged him to stay a little longer. But Vander knew he couldn't ignore Nightshade's call. He had to return, even if it was only for a moment. For in that place, in between the realms of the living and the dead, Vander found a sense of calm. A quietness that eluded him in his waking life.

Beneath the inky cloak of the cosmos, Nightshade extended its obsidian wings, casting spectral patterns that danced upon the veiled

Chapter 48 — Take A Minute

mists of the netherworld. Vander's spirit, unburdened by corporeal shackles, found an eerie comfort in the bird's austere gaze. It was a gaze that held millennia of wisdom, its intensity as penetrating as the chill of the afterlife itself. A shared silence fell between them, a silence that spoke of unspoken recognitions, of memories long past, and of a reunion that transcended life and death.

Reaching his hand out, Vander's energy field stretched forth in greeting, undulating like a spectral serpent in the mist. It weaved its way through the ether, a luminous wisp seeking out Nightshade's spirit. Upon contact, the energy transfer commenced; it was an almost palpable connection, akin to a gentle caress against the bird's glossy feathers. This ethereal touch, silent yet potent, bore an affection. "What is it, my friend?"

Nightshade cocked its head as if contemplating Vander's question. Then, without a sound, the raven spread its black wings wide and soared through the brooding entrance to the veil and into the mist. Vander followed without hesitation. Moments later, Vander's eyes widened as they fell upon the subject of Nightshade's interest.

Alone and afraid, Hunter sat huddled within the swirling mist, his small body curled into a tight ball, arms wrapped tightly around his knees with his head tucked against them, trying his best to hide himself from the scary world around him.

Interested, Vander took note that the spectral observers kept their distance from the child. They lingered on the fringe, lurking in the shadows, silent as the grave—a blissful quiet that they had never shown him. *How very curious?*

Quiet, as if not to disturb the boy, Jack made his way to Vander, sporting that damn smug grin on his cocky face as he made a few short gestures with his hands and created a thick wall of fog between them and the boy to conceal them. With a sigh, Jack nodded toward the area close by where the child was. "Isn't it a shame?"

Vander clamped down his jaw. As much as he hated to, he needed to let this stupid game play out. He needed all the information he could glean, be it from Jack, his visions, instincts, ghosts, or from whatever source he might gain it from. "What?"

"Oh, just that your new friend also happens to be related to the people trying to bring ya down."

Vander's eyes narrowed on Jack, even as his heart thundered inside his chest. Even though he wanted to deny that accusation, he knew, deep down, he always knew, that the child was somehow connected to the visions of the detective and the psychic, or at least, one of the psychics he was working so hard to block.

Eyebrows raised, Jack smiled. "Ahhhh. You already know. Good. What about the ps—"

"Two psychics, who are assisting the detective in Austin?" Vander answered.

Confused, Jack shook his head as if to clear it. "You saying there are two of them?"

"You didn't know?" Vander asked, suspiciously.

Holding up a hand to his heart, Jack answered, "I swear it, I only knew about the boy's mum." Jack rubbed. "I can't believe it! One seer in and of itself would be a rare thing indeed, but having two such rare individuals along with you... Well, now, that's unimaginable."

Weary, Vander wished he could go back to a simpler time. Those brilliant years when he and Alexander were comfortable friends, a time when his mentor and he shared the dream of a bright future, and not the one where his death had been meticulously planned. "Not if the one orchestrating those events knows both your strengths and weaknesses."

"Alexander?" Jack asked.

Jaw tight, Vander let a fresh wave of rage wash over him. "It was not chance that put Alayna Sage on a direct course with me. Looking back, I discovered my mentor put this part of his plan into motion over a year ago."

Mouth agape, Jack stammered, "Looking back in time? How in the bloody hell could you do that?"

"You did not honestly believe you were the only one with secrets, did you?" A cruel smile twisted the corners of Vander's full mouth. "While you and Alexander have been busy playing God with my life, I took every opportunity, every moment I could spare to perfect my gifts, to discover their limits, and to push past them... all with one purpose in mind."

Jack swallowed hard as he took an involuntary step back. "Which is?"

"To survive ... by any means necessary." Vander's ice-blue eyes fixed on Jack and held him with their cold intensity.

Nonchalantly, Vander flicked his hand and watched as the mist rolled away. Spirits fled his sight and from the look on Jack's face, Vander could tell that his old friend had instinctively wanted to join them.

Chapter 48 — Take A Minute

Voice low, Vander motioned to Hunter. "No one, and I mean, no one, is to go near him."

"Yeah, yeah... I'll make sure we all keep our distance," Jack sputtered.

Turning his attention to Hunter, Vander dismissed Jack. "I'd like for you to do one other thing for me."

"Yeah?" Already backing away, Jack's eyes cut to the path offering the quickest escape.

"Keep an eye on my old friend Peter O'Reily. I need to know what he is up to." Vander sighed, wishing this could all be over and knowing it was anything but. "Alexander has played his hand masterfully. It is far beyond four-d chess and has me pulled in dozens of directions, each with shifting outcomes. If you truly wish to help me, you will keep me informed on whatever path he chooses to take."

With a wink and a smile that did not quite reach his eyes, Jack bowed. "Consider it done, my friend."

"Thank you, you may go." Jack needed no further encouragement, which Vander was grateful for considering he needed to talk to the child alone and undistracted.

Hovering overhead, Nightshade circled once, twice, before he, too, retreated. He flew back to the entrance of the veil, the boundary line between the world of the living and this spectral realm. There, Vander knew he had perched, once again, the silent sentinel between the two realms.

Vander took a step toward the child, then paused, his tall, brooding silhouette casting a long shadow. Vander realized that the child would not recognize him in his current form. It was fortunate for him that Hunter still hid his face in his folded arms and had not seen him yet.

To Hunter, Vander would be a stranger in this form, a shadowy figure of dread. Vander closed his eyes, briefly allowing a flicker of vulnerability to cross his hardened features. Pushing past the nagging pull of exhaustion, he delved deep within himself, searching for the innocence he once held. Gradually, Vander's imposing figure shrank, his features softened, and the darkness receded, replaced with the youthful visage of his seven-year-old self.

Gently, Vander called out, "Hunter? What are you doing here?" Looking up at him, Hunter's eyes, wide with a child's curiosity, reflected the spectral glow of their surroundings. As Vander watched Hunter get to his feet, he noticed an eerie familiarity, a mirror image of Vander's own ghostly past.

"I... I don't know," Hunter stammered, his voice barely a whisper. There was a haunting innocence in his confusion. It tugged at Vander's hardening heartstrings. A connection, though profound, bound them in what seemed to be a shared purgatory of the unknown.

Vander felt an inexplicable urge to shield the boy, to guide him through the labyrinth of their shared fate. It was a feeling he couldn't quite understand, but one that felt right, nonetheless. For in this mysterious existence of shared psychic gifts, perhaps Vander could help this lost child. And maybe, just maybe, Hunter could find solace in the presence of someone like him who understood his otherworldly struggles.

Inching closer to Vander, Hunter asked, "Did you have a bad dream too?"

"A bad dream?" Vander echoed the question.

Hunter stopped a few feet in front of Vander, the thick fog rolling over their small feet. "I did. It was bad. I tried to wake up but..." Scared, Hunter looked around at the entities who had started to draw close.

Vander had sensed the spirits' agitation upon his arrival and was not surprised to see them begin to stir. "Found yourself here instead." Hunter nodded. Vander motioned for Hunter to follow him out of the mist. "That happens to me sometimes too."

Chasing after Vander, Hunter gladly followed. "It does?"

"Yes, do you know why?" Vander asked, looking over at Hunter who had caught up with him.

Shaking his head, no, Hunter did not speak, so Vander continued, "Your nightmare is more likely a vision."

Confused, Hunter stopped. "A what?"

Vander leaned in close to Hunter and smiled as if he were sharing a secret with his best friend. "A vision is like a dream, Hunter, but it's a special kind of dream about things that haven't happened yet," Vander tried to explain in simple terms.

"You know how when you play with your toy cars, you can imagine the races they might have? It's a bit like that," Vander continued. "When I have one of these special dreams, it's like my spirit decides to take a little adventure time-traveling into the future. Sometimes, the things it sees can be a bit scary, like a big thunderstorm, and so it comes back here, to the In-between."

Chapter 48 Take A Minute

Guiding him on, Vander smiled. "This is a safe place, like your cozy bed, where your spirit can think about what it saw before returning to your body. Just like you'd come home and tell your mom about your adventure at the park."

Hunter's eyes widened as he listened, trying to understand this new concept of visions. "But why does your spirit go back to your body? Can't it just stay here?"

Vander smiled patiently. "Well, just like you have to eventually leave the park and come home for dinner with your family, your spirit has to return to your body so you can wake up and continue living your life. But it's like a little break for the spirit to go on these adventures and come back with important information."

Hunter nodded, trying to make sense of it all. "So, your spirit is like a superhero?" he asked excitedly.

Vander chuckled. "I suppose you could think of it that way, Hunter. My spirit is a bit like a superhero, going on secret missions to gather information and help me understand the future."

Hunter's eyes lit up with wonder as he imagined himself as a superhero too, with his own special powers. Vander smiled, knowing that this explanation had helped Hunter understand visions in his own unique way. "So, why don't you tell me about your nightmare? Maybe I can help you figure it out."

Hesitantly, Hunter played with his hands. "It was about my uncle Brayden. He's a cop. He arrests people who do bad things."

Up ahead, Nightshade's shrill made them both jump. Vander's mind raced. Hunter's Uncle Brayden could not be the same detective hunting Alexander, could it? That would be insane, even in his world. "Is your uncle a detective?"

"Uh-huh, and the man he's after does really scary things and wants to hurt my uncle." Hunter's voice was barely above a whisper as he spoke. His little lip trembled as he added, "I love him and don't want the bad man to hurt him."

Images flashed through Vander's mind as new possibilities and dark outcomes surfaced. Alexander, Vander's mentor, had set one course for Hunter's future, yet Vander found himself questioning whether he could forge a better one? But no matter which path he chose, it seemed inevitable that Hunter would suffer loss. The question was, how could Vander best help Hunter navigate the impending storm?

Vander looked at Hunter, his heart heavy as he observed the trust gleaming in the boy's eyes. It was a trust Vander feared he might shatter.

In the cruel game of fate, could Vander do what was necessary to secure his own future, even at the cost of Hunter's innocence and happiness? The weight of the impending decision hung over Vander like a dark cloud, casting long shadows on what lay ahead.

Ultimately, it would be Vander's mentor who held the power to shape Hunter's world and determine their fates. As the pieces fell into place, Vander couldn't help but wonder if this was all part of Alexander's twisted plan and recoiled at the thought that Alexander could, in fact, be that cruel.

Vander felt the tug of his body that sat unconscious in a plane about to land in New York. With a sparkle in his eyes, Vander asked, "Hunter, do you want to learn a super speedy way to get back home? It's like a magic shortcut."

Hunter's face lit up like a firefly in the dark, his eyes wide and full of curiosity. "I do!" he responded, his voice filled with excitement.

Suddenly, they heard Nightshade's call in the distance. Vander's face broke into a grin, and he took off like a rocket, calling back to Hunter, "Let's see who can reach the entrance first!" Leaving the scary mist and the angry ghosts behind, Hunter followed Vander, his little feet silent as he hit the unseen ground, and sprinted after his friend.

Vander would soon return to his corporeal form as his airplane began its ominous descent. But for now, his mission was far from over, the task of guiding Hunter's spirit back to its rightful place awaited him.

Once they arrived at Hunter's house, Vander would take every precaution to guarantee the successful merging of spirit and body for the boy. Then, while there, Vander would explore the dwelling. Vander would familiarize himself with its layout and secrets, which would better equip him to deal with Detective Brayden James, Paige Williams, Alayna Sage, and Alexander.

MAY 5TH—6 DAYS

CHAPTER 49

GOT A MINUTE?

ETHAN

Austin, TX—Morning

MEMBERS OF THE DEPARTMENT CALLED OUT TO ETHAN, their voices echoing through the vast expanse of the precinct. "Salutations, Ethan!" Garcia intoned, with a wry twist to his mouth. His words, despite their casual tone, bore the unmistakable imprint of respect. He continued, in an almost teasing manner, "Please make sure you're on duty if ever I encounter a bullet."

A symphony of applause and cheers erupted, sweeping through the room like a swift current. Amidst this cacophony, Ethan appeared somewhat taken aback, his discomfort evident in the way he averted his gaze and made a reluctant gesture of acknowledgment.

Concerned, Brayden knew Ethan would not come to the station unless something was wrong. Ethan was a man of quiet valor and an unassuming character; he always shirked the spotlight. His place, Ethan often argued, was not in the glow of commendation, but rather in the trenches of duty, his actions a silent testament to his commitment. Therefore, Brayden could safely infer that whatever brought Ethan there must be significant.

Wanting to spare Ethan from all the unwarranted attention, Brayden intervened, raising his hand to silence the boisterous officers. "Enough guys," he announced with a dry chuckle. "I have to deal with this man on a daily basis. Don't make his head swell any bigger than it already has." His jest was meant to dispel the growing tension, to redirect the focus from the visibly uncomfortable Ethan. "I mean, it's not like he took a bullet saving one of our own, right?"

The room erupted in laughter and a new wave of cheers, seemingly interpreting Brayden's banter as a playful addition to the ongoing celebration. However, Ethan fixed him with a pained look, his expression a stark contrast to the jubilant atmosphere.

Brayden watched as Ethan maneuvered his way through the crowd with a stoic grace that belied his discomfort. The congratulatory pats and playful hair ruffles seemed to press down on him more heavily than physical blows might have. His expression, an attempt at a gracious smile, carried an undercurrent of distress that was not lost on Brayden. When Ethan finally made it to his desk, he made a request that was more of an appeal. "Could I talk to you for a minute?" he asked, seeking refuge. "Outside please?"

Aiding Ethan's escape, Brayden conducted an expert crowd management maneuver. He addressed his fellow officers with a mix of authoritative command and fraternal camaraderie. "Gentlemen, give Ethan some space," he uttered in a firm but gentle tone. His words were coupled with a gentle wave of his hand, signaling a retreat. The underlying humor in the situation was not lost on Brayden. He knew Ethan would more than likely smack him later for it, but he could not resist the urge to guide him out of the squad room like a distinguished guest. Brayden led Ethan to the front steps of the station, carefully navigating through the throng of officers.

Once outside, Brayden turned to face Ethan, his eyes twinkling with mischief. Ethan's irate expression did nothing to lessen Brayden's amusement. "When I'm better, you're so going to pay for that," Ethan warned.

Brayden leaned up against the exterior of a nearby police unit, a slow smirk spreading across his face as he shrugged nonchalantly. "Worth it," he chuckled.

Running a hand down his face, Ethan sighed. Brayden could see that Ethan's eyes held a certain heaviness that was not just the result of physical fatigue—it was an echo of worry, a telltale sign of internal conflict. "What's the matter, Ethan?" Brayden inquired. "Is something wrong with Paige, with the kids?" Ethan's hesitation added to Brayden's growing unease.

Chapter 49   Got A Minute?

Brayden watched as Ethan's expression hardened. "It's about your girlfriend."

That was not a topic Brayden had anticipated. "Alayna?" he queried, his voice echoing the surprise he felt. Ethan, with a face etched in grim determination, nodded in affirmation. "Yes."

A knot began to form in Brayden's stomach, an instinctive reaction to Ethan's disapproval.

Brayden could feel himself growing tense as Ethan spoke. "I try to be patient with Paige and Hunter's gifts, try to understand this unexplained intuition they have. But, since Paige spoke to Alayna, she has been jumpy, nervous, agitated." Ethan fixed Brayden with a look. "I don't want Alayna feeding into Paige's hyper-vigilance, heaven knows she has enough to worry about with the two of us as it is."

"Alayna just wanted to help, she would never—" Brayden's words were cut off as Ethan jumped in.

"Look, I won't tell you who to see or who to be involved with." Ethan cautioned. "I just ask that Alayna not encourage my family to follow her down into this mystical, magical world of hers, okay?"

Brayden's shoulders slumped. "I'll ask, but, Ethan, that's who Alayna is. I can't ask her to change just because you're afraid of something you don't understand."

Ethan's lips pressed into a thin line. "Brayden, this is my family, I have to do what I feel is best for them."

Brayden retreated a step. "So, what? If I refuse to stop seeing Alayna, I'm not family anymore?"

Ethan was torn, Brayden could see that, but he could also see his resolve. "That's not what I'm saying. You know we love you."

Defensive, Brayden argued, "Alayna is only trying to help."

Firm, Ethan shook his head. "We don't need or want that kind of help."

"We, or you Ethan?" Brayden challenged.

Ethan stiffened. "I'd better let you get back to work." Sadly, Ethan turned to go.

Brayden did not want to leave things like that. He and Ethan had never disagreed on anything significant before. "Ethan... I'll talk to Alayna. In the meantime, please reconsider. She might be the only one who can help Paige and Hunter deal with their unique gifts."

Brayden wondered, *If Ethan can't accept Alayna, it will take its toll on our relationship.* His brother-in-law's abrupt departure, marked with a curt nod as his only farewell, was a painful affirmation of the growing rift between them.

As Brayden watched Ethan disappear down the street, the unspoken question hung heavily in the air. Was he prepared to live estranged from his family if they could not accept Alayna?

"Detective Brayden?" a familiar voice called from behind him.

Surprised, Brayden watched as Chantal Robins approached him with an unknown gentleman trailing behind her. His call to the FBI for additional information must have raised some red flags for them to send one of their best agents all the way to Austin, TX.

Brayden quickly forgot about Ethan as he extended his hand to Chantal. "Agent Robinson, I'm a little shocked to see you here in Austin." Chantal took Brayden's hand and nodded to the older gentleman. "Detective James, this is Peter O'Reily… He was one of the lead agents assigned to the Sculptor case seventeen years ago."

Taken aback, Brayden shook Peter's hand. "Agent O'Reily, from Interpol?"

"Yes, but please, just call me Peter." Peter straightened, a weary smile on his weathered features. "And as far as Interpol, I'm afraid I am no longer with the agency, nor am I an agent or officer of any branch of law enforcement."

Puzzled, Brayden looked back at Chantal. "Then, why are you…?"

"To shine some light on the case." Nodding toward the precinct, Chantal continued, "Is there someplace we can talk in private?" The agent held up a large satchel and motioned toward the large twin doors. "It would be helpful to have a place to set up. The sooner we get started, the better. Time is not on our side."

Face grim, Brayden started up the stairs, with Chantal and Peter close behind. "Follow me." Brayden could sense the thick, unspoken tension as the three of them went inside. Brayden would have to clear an office for their investigation with his captain first, which he knew would not be a problem. This was a high-profile case, and Bohannon would be more than happy to lend whatever resources necessary to resolve this investigation.

Grateful for a quiet place to spread out, Brayden, Chantal, and Peter began setting up. In the dim light, they began shuffling through the old case files that lay scattered, their worn edges echoing with horrific tales as they rested upon the worn counters and desks.

Chapter 49   Got A Minute?

Each file represented a cryptic puzzle piece in the labyrinthine web of the case, whispered secrets of sins long past, yet intrinsically tied to the present investigation. The scent of aging paper and ink mingled with the cold austerity of the room and created an atmospheric testament to the unceasing pursuit of truth.

As the three of them poured over each file, they found themselves lost in a sea of faces, testimonies, and evidence, in shadows of forgotten victims who seemed to still plead for a closure they had not been granted, their souls crying out from beyond the veil.

Reluctantly, Peter confessed, "I never believed Interpol had caught the real killer," as he ran a hand down his weary face. "Throughout our investigation, my partner Erin insisted our killer was a man of means, of refinement." Peter fought to maintain his stoic demeanor, but suddenly, his façade began to crumble. The horrors of the past seemed to weigh heavily on his mind as he reluctantly spoke about his doubts regarding Interpol's actions.

As he spoke, his voice became low and almost haunted, as if the words alone brought back painful memories. It was clear that the case had deeply affected him, and his inner monologues revealed a mind struggling to make sense of it all.

Hesitantly, Brayden asked, "Then why did you stop?"

Defeated, Peter shrugged. "After losing Erin, in the most horrific way possible… I was lost, you see. There was a part of me that wanted to believe we had found the man responsible." Peter hesitated, his mind searching for answers. "After a while, after I had the chance to clear my mind… I pondered upon the case, upon the inconsistencies, and knew that we had been fed a convenient narrative that, unfortunately, the agency was not willing to dispute." Stuffing his hands into his pockets, Peter turned and stared out the window.

There was no doubt in Brayden's mind that Peter's world had gone darker after losing his partner. It was obvious that Peter O'Reily not only cared about his late partner Erin Reese, but had also loved her. The new murder had torn open old wounds for the retired agent, and his thoughts were probably consumed by memories of Erin—her smile, her laughter, her warmth. But now, all of that was gone, replaced by a cold emptiness that seemed to seep into every corner of his being.

Brayden could not shake the feeling that Peter was right. There was more to Erin's death. His eyes fixed on one of the numerous reports,

Brayden said, "It says here that none of the victims had been found near the kill sites."

Peter nodded. "That is correct."

As they studied the reports in front of them, a sense of unease settled over Brayden. The lack of evidence at the previous crime scenes added to this already ominous investigation.

Brayden tossed the folder onto the stack. "And that during yours and Agent Reese's investigation, you only found one victim per region. The victims were of various ages, non-similar in looks, both male and female."

"Also correct," Peter concurred.

Brows furrowed, Brayden fixed Peter with a look. "None of the victims shared occupations, interests... Were there any similarities?" Brayden studied the contents of the folder, pored over each detail, and pondered its significance. He couldn't shake off the feeling that there was something connecting all these seemingly random victims.

"We need to collaborate with other departments, dig deeper into their backgrounds," he said as a plan formed in his mind. The darkness surrounding these cases was suffocating, but Brayden was determined to shed some light on it.

"If you are looking for a commonality, I can tell you, after years of researching, there is only one that has been accepted by the authorities," Peter added.

"Which is?" Brayden asked.

Pipping in, Chantal answered, "That each victim, in their own way, was remarkable in one form or another."

Understanding dawned on Brayden. "My artist, the victim here in Austin, was exceptional." To Brayden, this proved that their cases were indeed connected. The victims all shared a sense of uniqueness, whether it be in their talents, skill sets, looks, or leadership qualities. "Even so, it doesn't make sense that the Sculptor would wait seventeen years to strike again. She was exceptional, but no more than any other up-and-coming artist." Brayden posed the question to both past and present agents, "So why her? Why now?"

Chantal took a seat. "Could be a copycat, a sicko that was fascinated by the case."

"Unlikely," Peter chimed in. "Erin, Agent Reese, and I had also entertained the possibilities of a copycat many years ago. We even thought that perhaps there were two killers working in tandem at one point in

Chapter 49 — Got A Minute?

our investigation, but in the end, we knew that there was only one perp, one meticulous monster."

Taking a deep breath, Peter fixed Brayden with a look of steel resolve. "Serial killers who choose to take on a partner inevitably get caught." Peter walked over to the window, stuffed his hands into his pockets, and stared down at the street. "No, our killer is far too clever to let anyone in on his secret, but, thankfully for us, I believe he has made a critical error."

Mind racing, Brayden jumped to his feet. "Wait a minute, you had said that there was only one similarity that the authorities accepted in the case."

Peter smiled, "Correct."

Brayden returned his smile. "But there is another one, isn't there? One that your supieriors would not look into?

Reaching into his sachel, Peter retrieved a worn folder and tossed it onto the table before Brayden. Brayden reached for it, Peter held a hand over it. "I must warn you, if you decide to follow me down this path, it might very well end both of your careers, it most certainly cost me mine."

Intrigued, Chantal sat up and reached for the file but Brayden beat her to it. Brayden began scanning the pages. There were numerous photographs of build sites, dozens upon dozens of crews, each from different ethinticities. Puzzled, Brayden handed several of the pages he had scanned over to Chantal. "Okay, you've got me, what's the connection?"

Chantal began looking over the images, her brow furrowed. "Are you saying our victims were each killed at a construction site?"

Face grim, Peter shook his head. "No."

Brayden looked up, confusion marring his face. "Then, what's the connection, what am I missing?"

Turning his attention back to the window. "The one clue that my partner, Erin Reese tragically unearthed and had not shared." His expression stoic, Peter turned back to the two detectives. "There was an organization, a philanthropist, if you will, present in each country, at the time of each of the Sculpter's murders."

Taken back, Brayden stammered. "Wait, what?"

Alarmed, Chantal leaped out of her chair, causing it to scrape backward on the concrete floor. "No way, there is no way Interpol would not have looked into something like that."

Bitter, Peter grabbed a chair and plopped into it. "Oh, believe me Agent Robinson, given enough excuses, loopholes and turning of a blind eye, they most certainly would and in this case, did."

Trying to take all of this information in, Brayden drew in a deep breath and dove in. "Okay, all right, bring me up to speed here. What are you saying, that you suspect someone with this organization?"

Peter took the file from Brayden, flipped through several pages then pulled out a photographe of a younger, Alexander Dayton and tossed it onto the table. "Not just anyone, I believe that the founder himself is responsible."

Chantal laughed as she threw her hands up into the air. "Oh, okay, now I see why they fired you."

"I don't follow?" Brayden said.

Pointing down at the photograph of Alexander she smirked. "Alexander Dayton is one of the richest men in the world. He has started dozens if not hundreds of outreach programs all over the world, I'm talking schools, hospitals, clinics, food banks just to name a few."

Nodding, Brayden agreed. "Okay, sure, the guy sounds like a saint and like someone who has better things to do than carve up exceptional people ... then we look at his team, people on the work sites—"

"No!" Peter growled as he slapped a hand onto the table. "I've done the research. As far as his team is concerened, Dayton always hired a different group, it was part of his finding new up-and-coming talent from universities to put together initiatives. In each country he hired locals to help boost their economies."

Getting it, Brayden sat down and looked Peter in the eyes. "So the only common denominator was Alexador Dayton himself?"

"Yes." Satisfied, Peter leaned back in his chair.

"You know how crazy that sounds, right?" Chantal added, not yet convinced.

A bitter laugh escaped Peter. "I dare say I do. But, while going through Erin's files that she had stashed away at home."

Both Brayden and Chantal gave each other a look. Peter shrugged, "We had been in a serious relationship before going to Africa." Sad once more, Peter looked down at his hands. "I knew a few of her idiosyncrasies... she had a habit of scribbling down note after note and stuffing them in a folder that she kept in her bedside table. Most of the notes I found were too confounding for me to decifer, however, there were two pieces of evidence that I was able to decern."

On the edge of his seat, Brayden leaned forward. "And they were?"

Eyes burning with determination, Peter met Brayden's gaze. "Scribbled on a note pad, Erin had written the initials, AD, private lessons, Yorkshire, England, Henry Moore at the age of nineteen."

Not getting it, Chantel asked. "It's a stretch, but, yeah, AD could be Alexander Dayton, but who the hell is Henry Moore?"

Jaw tight, Peter looked back at Alexander's photo. "A sculptor who pioneered a new vision for modern sculptors, one who was inspired by the human body and someone that Alexander Dayton followed with a fervid passion."

Brayden could tell by the look in Peter's eyes that this man would not stop until the monster they hunted was brought to justice. It did not matter whether Peter had a badge or not. He was going to find Erin Reese's killer and Brayden knew he was willing to do whatever it took to help him.

CHAPTER 50

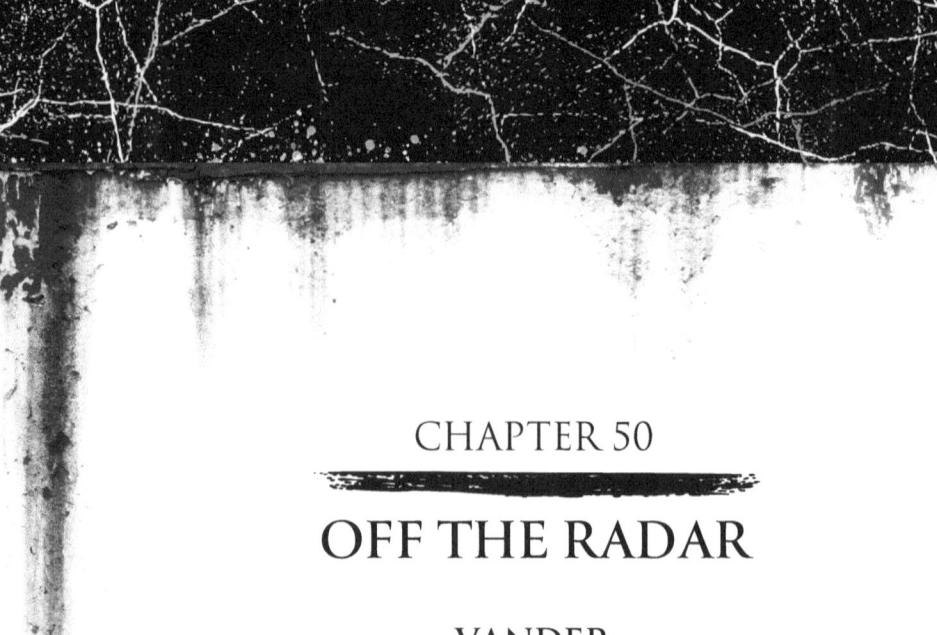

OFF THE RADAR

VANDER

Philadelphia, PA—Night

Like most times after a prolonged astral projection, Vander felt a deep exhaustion seep into his bones. The overseas trip had been a marathon of sensory overload, a surreal voyage that had stretched his physical and mental endurance to its limits. Usually, he was able to return to a location where he had left his body, but on this journey, he was left to rely on the silver cord that kept the soul tethered to his body to return safely, since it too, had been traveling through time and air.

His quest had left him reeling, and he felt the full weight of its aftermath in every cell of his body. It was a palpable drain on his energy, one that left him struggling to complete the short hour-and-a-half drive from the airport to a car rental return center he had chosen just a few short blocks from the university.

Still fighting the heavy weight of exhaustion, Vander stepped outside of the busy terminal and allowed the cool night air to wash over him.

Though he would like nothing more than to make his way back to his dorm or, better yet, back to his cozy bed at the townhome, Vander knew he could not afford himself the luxury. He had allowed Kgotso to die far quicker than he would have liked, all to buy himself a few precious days' head start.

Chapter 50 Off The Radar

There was little doubt Alexander would be monitoring his travels to and from Africa. That was the main reason Vander had decided to abandon his original return flight to seek an earlier departure. The last-minute fee had cost him a hefty sum, but it would be well worth it if it fooled Alexander into believing he was in Africa when, in fact, he was unraveling the plans his mentor had made for him back in Austin.

Of course, if Alexander had not been distracted elsewhere, Vander knew the man would have been monitoring all returning flights from Africa as a precaution. Alexander was resourceful, brilliant, and cunning, so Vander was not going to make the mistake of underestimating his mentor.

It was imperative that Vander continued to work as if Alexander knew his every move and that he continued to do what was not expected, no matter how dark or unpleasant the tasks before him became.

All of which led him back to the problem at hand. Just in case Alexander had indeed been keeping watch for his return, Vander had taken the necessary steps to have it appear as if he had returned to New York, rented a car, drove straight back to Philly, and returned to campus.

Vander had even gone as far as to have one of his classmates ready to turn in his term paper the next day. Since there were so many students in the class, the professor would not miss him, or notice his classmate submitting his papers. Thus, giving the appearance that he was present at school, hopefully long enough for him to get to Austin and back before Alexander knew any better.

Casting a sideways glance at the security camera a few feet away brought Vander back to his current dilemma: Austin was a long way from Pennsylvania, so he had better find a ride southwest, and soon. Vander knew there would be records of him returning the car, so on the off chance his actions were ever questioned, he would walk toward the campus until he was out of sight of the cameras, then he would make his way to a part of town where the crime was high and camera footage was scarce.

As he walked down the darkened streets, stepping in and out of shadows cast by the few working streetlights, Vander felt calm, at peace. Long ago Alexander had taught him that when you were the hunter, the night and its welcoming darkness were an asset, a protective camouflage that allowed you to move in and out of areas without detection. He also knew he was a more dangerous predator than those who hunted those narrow streets.

Just a few short blocks away, Vander knew of a shady neighborhood, one in which camera systems were not only discouraged but regularly destroyed. There he would find a driver willing to take him southwest for a handful of cash, no questions asked. He just had to make sure the thug's car was sound enough to make the long journey.

Somewhere along the way, of course, he would have to dispose of the driver before the driver worked up the courage to murder him. What was that old saying, "Honor among thieves?" In Vander's world, there was no such thing. People who exploited others and made their living from taking from those weaker than themselves, could not be trusted.

As Vander made his way down a dark and narrow street, he felt the ill intent shimmering off a large man who hid within a cramped stairwell up ahead. The man was sizing him up, deciding on his best plan of attack as he watched Vander make his way up the street.

It was almost midnight, and though people still scurried like rats up and down the street, no one seemed to care or want to be bothered with what was more than likely about to happen. Which, of course, suited Vander just fine. He was not in need of being rescued.

Resisting the urge to smile, Vander crossed the street and headed straight for the man cast in shadow. There was someone the authorities would not bother looking for when he went missing.

A small, crimson circle glowed as the man took a long drag on his cigarette, and stepped into the light. "You lost?"

"No," Vander answered, calmly.

Casting a wary glance about them, the man stepped into the light. "You looking to score or some'ng?"

Offering the hoodlum a smile, Vander held out one of his hands, trying his best to look harmless. "More along the lines of something." Vander could see the man was on edge. He did not know whether to run, stab him, rob him, or do all three in quick succession. "I was hoping you could help me with a ride to Texas," Vander said, as if simply asking for directions.

This further agitated the man, who hunched up and started waving his arms. "Damn, you high or just fuckin' stupid?!" the man sputtered.

"I am willing to pay you a thousand now and a thousand dollars once we reach our destination." His request left the man dumbfounded. He

Chapter 50 — Off The Radar

stood there with his mouth hanging open in stunned disbelief. "I believe that is a far price for a few days of your time, is it not?"

"If you got that kind of money, why don't you take a plane, train or hire a rich ass chauffeur?"

Vander could tell the wheels were turning in the thug's muddled brain. "I have some business that requires a level of secrecy and need to be discrete."

The man's eyes narrowed. "You got the law or someone after you?"

"The less you know, the better," Vander offered. "If you're afraid of the risk you might encounter, then perhaps I shoul—"

"I ain't afraid of shit!"

Good, Vander knew he would hit a nerve. Thugs who grew up on the streets were forced to continuously prove their strength, commitment, and more importantly, their lack of fear, a fact that Vander would use to persuade him to take this job. "Excellent!"

Sensing the other gang members, curious about the strange encounter, beginning to close ranks and make their way toward them, Vander knew the exchange needed to reach a conclusion soon or he would have more problems to contend with. "Then we have a deal?"

Nervously, the thug scanned the street, started down the stairs, and stopped a few inches before him, trying his best to look intimidating. "A thousand now ... a thousand when I drop your ass off?"

Vander gave him a curt nod. "Yes."

"Be a lot easier to take that fancy watch of yours, your cash, and just leave you here bleeding on the street?"

Not wanting the crook to lose face with any of his homies that might be close enough to hear, Vander countered, "True, however, whatever I might currently have in my possession, you would most certainly have to split among your friends." Vander motioned to the group that was beginning to gather close by. "The other half of the money is waiting in Texas, so, if you agree to drive me there, you will not only have the full payment and perhaps the watch if you prefer, but you would also have no need to share your fee."

This gave the man pause. His nostrils flared as he drew in a deep breath, peered out at the other members of his gang, and weighed his decision. Vander knew he had already won. If this man did not own a car that would make the trip to Texas, he would most certainly steal a vehicle to make it happen.

"Fine, meet me at the corner market on 5th street in ten." The man shoved past Vander and started for his friends. "If you're late ... deal's off."

Since he planned to go straight to the meeting point, Vander knew he would be ready and waiting.

Having a driver would allow Vander to take a short trip to the astral plane and offer Paige Williams and her new friend Alayna Sage one final warning to stop looking for the man responsible for the artist's killer. If they chose to ignore it, well then, he would have no choice but to protect himself and Alexander by any means necessary.

Amidst the constant flux of potential realities, Vander had traced the labyrinthine strands of the future, past, and present with one goal in mind: to analyze a myriad of possible outcomes. Each strand he traversed offered a distinct narrative, a unique culmination of decisions, much like the diverging paths in an obscure forest.

A choice once made, seemingly leading to a desired destination, could unexpectedly veer off, steering him in an unanticipated direction. Sometimes, the pursuit of a safer, more promising path led him right back to the very beginning, leaving Vander lost and stranded, yearning for the elusive safety that remained frustratingly out of reach.

Vander knew that had Alexander merely planned to kill him, he could've easily thwarted such a plot. But the stakes were higher now, murkier. With the brutal murder of the artist in Austin, TX, Alexander had spun another twisted strand into the futuristic chaos that lay sprawled in front of Vander.

The act of violence was not just a message; it was a calculated move in a deadly game of chess. As the clock ticked, Vander's time to alter his looming fate was dwindling, and Alexander's actions piled obstacles before him like a daunting mountain.

As night enveloped him, Vander knew that another day was quickly slipping away, leaving him with a mere four days until his graduation ceremonies commenced.

Graduation, a moment that should have been full of elation, of triumph, now bore the grim shadow of his potential end. His mouth, usually curved in a charming smile, now formed a grim line, hardening his youthful features.

A recurring thought echoed in Vander's mind, *I have the right to survive.*

MAY 6TH—5 DAYS

CHAPTER 51

A PEEK BEHIND THE CURTAIN

ALAYNA

Austin, TX—Day

WANTING TO PUT PAIGE AT EASE, ALAYNA HURRIED over to her with a bright smile. "Paige, I'm so glad you were able to come!" Paige forced a smile as Alayna took her trembling hand into hers, Alayna was surprised at how cold Paige's hands were and immediately felt sorry for asking her to come, this was much harder on her than she had expected. Alayna just wanted to help Paige. She had not intended to upset her or cause her alarm.

Alayna's determination was unwavering. She would not rest until she unlocked the mysteries that haunted Paige and helped her overcome them. Her resolve only grew stronger as she saw the fear in Paige's eyes. She knew that this was more than just a simple case of nerves.

Concerned, Alayna asked, "You all right?"

Paige straightened as she nodded. "Yes, sorry. I just hate lying to Ethan."

It was obvious how much Ethan and Paige loved one another, and Alayna knew it must be hard for her to go against his wishes. Alayna watched Paige's face turn into a mask of determination. "We don't have to do this, you know. I would be just as happy if we went out for a cup of coffee and talked about the weather," Alayna offered, wanting to make sure to give Paige an out if she wanted it.

"No, I want to do this. I need to do this," Paige told Alayna as she cast a weary look down the long hallway that led to Alayna's psychic reading room.

Alayna gave Paige's hand a firm squeeze, smiled, then walked over to the shop door, turned the open sign to closed, and locked it. "All right, follow me." Alayna led the way to the room at the end of the hall, ready to guide Paige to the answers she sought.

As Paige followed her to the back room, Alayna could feel Paige's turmoil. It was obvious she was afraid, but from what Brayden had told her earlier, Paige must be more afraid of not knowing the truth than of discovering what her dreams might mean.

"How long have you been having these nightmares?" Alayna asked as she opened the door to the small room. Right after she had received Paige's call, she had left her assistant to manage the store and had set about preparing the room for her arrival.

Not only did Alayna need to help Paige relax and get into a meditative state, but she also had to prepare herself mentally to guide her new friend. Alayna had been diligent as she prepared for Paige's arrival. Amid the dim light, splintered rays of light filtered through the windowpanes, casting an ethereal glow on the worn furniture.

In the center of the table, there was a constellation of flickering candles, their determined flames casting long shadows that danced upon the walls. The scent of smoldering sage filled the air, its purifying scent a silent testament to the careful preparations. Alayna followed Paige's glance as she spotted two thick pillows that sat within a thick ring of salt. "That's for our—" Alayna began.

"Protection," Paige finished. "I've read about it. You use it when you plan on going into a deep meditative state or if you plan on trying to astral project. Is that what we're going to try to do?"

"It is, if you're okay with that," Alayna said. "But, no pressure, if you're not ready for this."

Head held high, Paige walked over to the pillows. "No, I'm ready. I need to figure this out." Alayna watched as Brayden's sister removed her shoes, then carefully stepped into the ring of salt and took a seat on one of the pillows. "I need to figure this out. I don't know how, but I know Brayden, and maybe even the rest of my family, is in danger, and I'm going to do something about it."

Chapter 51   A Peek Behind The Curtain

 Offering Paige a reassuring smile, Alayna removed her shoes, stepped into the circle, took a seat before her new friend, and held out her hands. "Then let's begin."

MAY 6TH—5 DAYS

CHAPTER 52

COULDN'T HURT

ETHAN

Austin, TX—Day

ALL THE WAY TO THE FIRE STATION **ETHAN** COULD NOT shake the feeling that Paige had purposely agreed to letting him check in at work just to get rid of him. Sure, he had been driving her nuts just a couple of days after being released from the hospital, and when she suddenly agreed, he should go to the firehouse to check in with his crew, he had not hesitated.

But now, after a twenty-minute drive to work, he had found time to think about Paige's change of mind. Though it was possible it was a simple case of him wearing his wife down and her relenting just to get a couple of hours of peace, it was also possible that Paige had agreed for other reasons.

Ethan knew his wife, understood her little idiosyncrasies, and he could tell that something was troubling her. She had been on edge ever since he had walked in on her and Alayna discussing her nightmares. Nightmares that seemed to be coming on a regular basis these days.

At 10:00 in the morning, the traffic was light compared to the hectic school and work commute time between 7:00 a.m. and 9:00 a.m. and Ethan was thankful for that, especially considering his mind kept wandering and the pain in his shoulder throbbed from use.

Chapter 52 Couldn't Hurt

Sitting still was not one of his strengths, even when it was quiet at the station, he always found things to do, whether it be restocking his rig, sterilizing their gear, washing the units, cleaning the bays, or volunteering to cook, which he was far better at than most of the guys at the firehouse.

When he was home with his family, there were also a lot of things to keep him busy. All of which he loved. He helped Paige with the cooking and cleaning and loved his time aiding the kids with their schoolwork, playing games, or attending one of their activities. So, to be sidelined by a gunshot wound had been less than ideal.

It warmed Ethan's heart that his family and friends had been so loving, concerned, and attentive, but all the attention also made him extremely uncomfortable. Used to being the one to take care of others, he was not as equipped to be taken care of himself, which led back to his driving to the station far sooner than his doctor or boss would have allowed.

However, Ethan knew he could get away with showing up at the station if he did not clock in and try to do any real lifting or intense work. But there was nothing wrong with checking in, maybe supervising the other guys while they worked, right?

Turning into the parking lot, Ethan felt a sharp pain radiate down his arm. "Damn it!" Though he felt as if he was ready to return to work, his body was still in violent disagreement. He would have to remember not to use his injured arm to make those turns, at least for a little while longer.

Careful not to make the same mistake, Ethan cautiously maneuvered his truck into one of the parking spaces at the far end of the lot, put the vehicle in park, and killed the engine. Catching his reflection in the rearview mirror, he noticed a few beads of sweat dotting his brow.

Logically, he knew he was pushing it. There was a reason the doctor had sidelined him for the next four weeks. Even though he had been extremely lucky with that high-caliber gunshot wound, his body was still reeling from the shock of the injury and blood loss.

A deep frown creased Ethan's forehead as he remembered the worried look on Paige's face and how her body had trembled when she had crawled into his hospital bed and let him hold her close. It gnawed at him that he had caused Paige that fear and worry. He wanted nothing more than to protect her, to protect his family.

Ethan scooped up his cell phone and stared down at it. Maybe he should call Paige? She had been distracted, he would say, even flustered this morning and abrupt with getting him out the door.

Taking a deep breath, Ethan rested the phone on his thigh, rested his head back against the headrest, and closed his eyes. "Page just needs a little time," Ethan murmured to himself. Paige's behavior could be due to his brush with death.

He felt bad about it, but in truth, if given the same choice, he would most likely do the exact same thing. It was his job to save lives, even if that meant putting his own life at risk sometimes

Ethan adored Paige and loved everything about her, her determination, free spirit, creativity, and the way she cared for him and their children. He even found her mysterious, adventurous nature alluring. There was nothing he would change about her and never wanted to do anything to stand in her way or to hold her back, even if that meant the things she did at times unnerved him.

Stuffing his phone in his pocket, Ethan got out of the truck and headed toward the station.

The back door to the station burst open as two firemen came rushing out. Ramiro, his EMT partner, rushed out and tossed the contents of a large bucket after them.

Laughing, the two firefighters rushed behind Ethan just as the cold water splashed safely a few feet away. "Ramiro! What the hell are you doing?" Ethan yelled, looking down at the water that narrowly missed him.

Relieved, Ramiro put the bucket aside and waved. "Thank God you're here. I'm on KP duty tonight and these morons threatened to hose me and the kitchen down if I even attempted to try and cook."

"Oh man, seriously?" Ethan grumbled to the men who still cowered behind him.

Shane put a hand on Ethan's good shoulder. "With you out of commission, we had no choice but to put him in the rotation."

No longer afraid of getting soaked, Buster hurried past them. "Yeah, Ethan. This is all your fault."

From the doorway, Ramiro called, "What the heck are you doing here, anyway? Aren't you supposed to be home resting?"

Leaning in, Shane whispered, "Maybe you can be on standby to pull the alarm just in case things get out of hand?"

"I heard that asshole!" Ramiro called.

Feeling better than he had in days, Ethan smiled and started for the station. "I was, but thought I would come down here to make sure you didn't send the crew to the hospital."

Chapter 52 — Couldn't Hurt

Smiling brightly, Ramiro held the door open wide, allowing Ethan and Shane to enter. "Just for that, you're peeling all those freaking potatoes."

Holding his arm up as if it was broken, Ethan grinned. "I don't know. I may not be up to it."

Ramiro slapped Ethan on the back of the head. "Get your ass in here and shut up... I'm sure we can find something for you to do."

Happy, Ethan followed the crew back to the kitchen. It was great to be back amongst his co-workers and the station and to have a sense of normalcy. He could deal with the unknown and all of its mysteries later.

MAY 7TH—4 DAYS

CHAPTER 53

UNSPEAKABLE

VANDER

Austin, TX—Night

HIDDEN WITHIN THE EMBRACE OF A LARGE, SIX-FOOT hedge that ran the length of the house, Vander watched Hunter. The boy sat on the back porch, unaware of the danger that lurked nearby, blissfully engrossed in his game of ball and jacks. The innocence of Hunter's play juxtaposed the impending doom that was about to splinter the tranquility of the household.

Vander, cloaked in shadows, moved stealthily toward the side of the house, guided by his knowledge of the conveniently open window. This unguarded portal would grant him entry into the sanctuary he was about to desecrate. The lives of Hunter's father, mother, and sister Zoey were precariously balanced on the edge of the blade concealed beneath his leather jacket.

This family's demise was not a matter of choice for Vander—it was a necessity. A necessity that would shatter Detective James, thus, buying Vander the precious time he needed to deal with Alexander and unravel the case that the detective had built against his mentor. Silently, Vander cursed Alexander and the damning trophies he had kept from his kills, because those trinkets, if discovered, would annihilate them both.

As Vander prepared himself mentally to extinguish the innocent lives inside, he knew there was no turning back. That night, he would

Chapter 53   Unspeakable

transform into the same monster he had been so quick to defend as a child and so ready to admire as a young adult. In that moment, more than any other in his life, Vander wished that someone kinder, with more normalcy, had come into his life earlier to show him a better way.

Feeling the cold steel pressed close to his skin, Vander knew that Jack, who was no doubt waiting in the ether to witness this horror, would be so proud of what he was about to do. Taking a moment, Vander pressed his body up against the house and stifled the bitter laugh which was rising in his throat. *Jack, my guardian in the mist. What a fucking joke!* As it had been with Alexander, Vander had been so grateful for the smallest morsel of kindness, that when Jack had offered to be his friend, made him feel as if he was not alone in that strange land of the In-between, Vander had been grateful, so much in fact that he had allowed Jack to share the horrors that delighted the older man, even when they had sickened him.

It was not until his senior year in high school that Vander learned who Jack really was. Well, not his true identity, exactly, for those in that long-ago history and even those alive today did not know who he had really been. Shrouded in mystery, his figure loomed large in the annals of crime. Still, they had given him a name in those days, a moniker to personify the dread he invoked. All of Europe had uttered it in hushed whispers, a chilling sobriquet that had echoed down the centuries—Jack the Ripper.

How ironic... Vander found himself musing, cocooned by the unrelenting darkness of his reality, *to be shepherded through life by not one, but two, embodiments of malevolence.* Under the spectral guidance of Alexander, the Sculptor, his mortal mentor, with hands forever stained in innocent blood, and that demonic entity from the astral plane, a monstrous aberration from a realm beyond comprehension. His destiny seemed etched in shadows, his fate forever intertwined with the grotesque and the macabre. An irony, indeed. A cruel joke fashioned by the gods themselves, perhaps, that he was doomed to replicate their monstrous natures, his own innocence lost in the murky depths of their dread-filled tutelage.

Vander knew that there was no point in rehashing his options. His decisions had been etched in stone; his course solidified in the shadows of his intentions. He would extinguish the lives of Ethan, Paige, and Zoey Williams. This chilling path, as harsh as a winter gale, was the sole avenue leading to the outcome he ached for with every fiber of his being. Yet, in this world of darkness and retribution, one ray of redemption existed: Hunter. He would spare Hunter from the grim fate of his kin. The reason for such mercy was more than just strategy, it was an echo of his own yearning. Vander saw himself as the guardian angel Hunter needed, far superior to the likes of Alexander and Jack. In Hunter, Vander saw a chance to be the father figure he himself had craved, to rewrite the narrative of his own forsaken past.

Vander locked away his conscience, succumbing to the primal instinct of survival that had begun to consume him. Silently, like a shadow merging with the darkness, he slipped through the open window and into the unsuspecting tranquility of the house. His piercing gaze drifted toward the stairs leading to the sanctuary of the upstairs, a forbidden path he was about to tread. He could almost hear the innocent laughter of Zoey echoing from her room, a sound he wished he didn't have to silence. The plan was simple, as ruthless as it was. He would be as merciful as possible, sparing the child the terror of prolonged fear. The mother, Paige, would inevitably rush to her daughter's aid, drawn by the distressing scene, and he would extinguish her life in a swift act of forced cruelty. Vander had no desire for this. He was no monster, delighting in the despair of his victims. They were good people, undeserving of the grim fate. Yet, in this twisted world, it was necessary. Necessary, but not enjoyable. An evil he had to manifest, an act he had to perform.

Silently, Vander started for the stairs. Each step taken was a symphony of whispers echoing in the quiet. The plush carpet underfoot muffled his movements as he navigated the labyrinth of shadows that cloaked the beautiful middle-class home. With every creak of the wooden frame, the house seemed to breathe in the darkness, a living entity aware of the looming threat. He was no longer Vander, the familiar friend, but the monster that Jack and Alexander had always hoped he would become.

MAY 7TH—4 DAYS

CHAPTER 54

INNOCENT

HUNTER

Austin, TX—Night

ABANDONING HIS JACKS, HUNTER TOOK HIS PET BUNNY out of its cage and set it down in the back yard to play. Hunter lay on his stomach, so near to the soft, innocent creature that their mesmerizing gazes locked in an unspoken dialogue. The soothing glow of his home's windows painted a stark contrast against the inky blackness of the night, their warmth a distant echo in the chilly darkness.

Petting the bunny, Hunter mused, "Sorry Mommy won't let you inside." Hunter looked up at the house and sighed. Hunter was surprised his mother had not come to fetch him since it had grown dark. "But you did chew up her carpet."

When his mom had picked him and Zoey up from school, he could tell that something was wrong. She had smiled, said that everything was all right, but he could tell she was upset. Otherwise, his mommy would not have allowed him to play outside after dark by himself. Maybe she had seen the man in her dreams too and was afraid he was coming.

Hunter knew that his mommy had gone to see Brayden's friend Alayna. He had seen it in his dreams. Alayna was special, just like he and his mommy were, and Hunter had hoped that she would be able to help them, otherwise, bad things were going to happen, and he knew that he and his mom did not know how to stop them on their own.

From the worried look in his mommy's eyes, Hunter feared that she did not get the answers they needed from Brayden's friend and that it was already too late for them to prepare for the bad man who was on his way there.

A breeze stirred the leaves overhead as an eerie silence fell upon Hunter.

Picking up his rabbit, Hunter slipped the bunny back inside the shelter of its cage. With his tiny hands still on the cage, he looked transfixed at his house.

The world around seemed to stand still, as if time itself had paused. The old house in front of him, with its towering walls and dark windows, looked like a monster from his nightmares. He felt a shiver run down his spine. His little heart pounded in his chest like a drum, going faster and faster with every second that passed. His small hands clenched tight around the bars of the rabbit cage. He looked at the bunny inside, its nose twitching nervously. He wished he could hide in its cage too, away from the big, scary house. But he knew he couldn't. *I have to be brave,* he told himself, *like the heroes in my bedtime stories.*

From within the house, a muffled scream and breaking glass echoed in the still night air, curdling Hunter's blood. The five-year-old froze, his small heart pounding like a drum in his chest. The back door, only steps away, beckoned him to safety, but then a large, intimidating shadow cut across the lit window, snuffing out the inviting glow. Suddenly, the house plunged into darkness, and fear gripped him tighter.

But he had to be brave for his mom and Zoey. Swallowing hard, Hunter forced himself to climb the steps. His mind flashed back to the marbles—his marbles—their glassy surface gleaming under the afternoon sun. With a newfound determination, he scooped them up, their cold hardness giving him some comfort, and stuffed them into his pocket.

He had seen this in his dreams; a bad man chasing him. He would lead him away, away from his mom and Zoey. With that thought anchoring him, Hunter, as quiet as a mouse, snuck back into the bone-chilling, dark house.

MAY 7TH—4 DAYS

CHAPTER 55

LISTEN

ETHAN

Austin, TX—Night

At the fire station, Ethan found he was ready to go home much sooner than he had anticipated. He hated to admit it, but the doctor and Paige were right. His body needed more time to heal, whether he wanted to admit it or not. He started walking toward the exit, eager to get home to his family. However, before he could reach the door, his partner Ramiro called out to him, "You aren't going home already?"

Rubbing his injured shoulder, Ethan grimaced, but did not stop. "According to the doctor, I'm not even supposed to be here."

Stunned, Ramiro stopped; his beefy hands landed on his hips. "What?! You told the captain you were good for light duty."

Ethan smirked, knowing that he was technically right. "That's right. I did. He doesn't have to know the doctor disagrees with me." He shrugged nonchalantly.

Ramiro couldn't help but laugh at Ethan's audacity. He leaned in and whispered to his partner and friend, "I could so rat you out."

Ethan poked Ramiro in the belly playfully. "If you do, I'll tell our captain, you were the one who ate his slice of chocolate cake."

Ramiro's eyes widened in alarm. He knew better than to mess with Ethan when he had the upper hand. "You wouldn't?!" Ramiro exclaimed, his tone bordering on panic.

Ethan raised an eyebrow, a mischievous glint in his eye as he confirmed Ramiro's fear. "Oh, I would."

Ramiro growled in frustration. "Fine... Okay, go on home to that beautiful wife of yours. Don't you worry yourself with your poor, helpless family here, about to be poisoned by my cooking." Ramiro tried to play it cool, but the thought of not having Ethan's help in making their favorite dish was enough to send him into a slight panic.

Suppressing a laugh at Ramiro's pained expression, Ethan threw up his hands in frustration. "Ramiro, I've shown you how to make that chicken spaghetti a dozen times. It's not rocket science!"

"Why don't you make it a dozen and one and I'll owe you?" Ramiro pleaded, his eyes filled with a mix of desperation and hope.

Ethan, however, remained unmoved. He reached for the door, firm in his decision. "No," he said bluntly.

Ramiro, not taking it as the final verdict, sprang up and blocked Ethan's path, leaning against the door. "Come on, man, you'd be saving lives," he implored, his voice thick with sincerity. Their standoff was interrupted by a sudden yank to the door that supported Ramiro. Ethan's partner tumbled backward, and Ethan, swift in his response, grabbed the front of Ramiro's shirt, regretting it instantly.

A sharp pain tore through Ethan's shoulder, causing him to release Ramiro and suck in a sharp breath. The sudden release sent Ramiro tumbling backward into Brayden's arms. Brayden, quick to recover from the chaos, couldn't help but tease, "Coming or going, buddy?"

Regaining his posture, a flustered Ramiro retorted, "Neither!" With a gentle shove, he pushed Brayden away. "Brayden... Don't you know how to knock?"

With a laugh, Brayden responded, "I do... but it tends to ruin the element of surprise."

"As if you're going to find your killer here at the station," Ramiro argued, his voice laced with sarcasm.

Trying to mask his pain. Ethan smiled, his eyes glimmering with a mischievous light despite the discomfort etched on his face. "Well, if you had waited until after dinner, Brayden," he managed to tease, "I'm sure you would have found another food-poisoning killer here."

Chapter 55 — Listen

Offended, Ramiro bristled and retorted, "Shut up, Ethan." Yet, there was a friendly lilt in Ramiro's voice, making it more of a brotherly jab rather than a harsh rebuke.

Feeling Brayden's scrutinizing gaze, Ethan tried to straighten. Yet, he quickly realized that was a bad idea when his hand slipped from the door facing and he stumbled back into the wall. Brayden caught him by his good shoulder and steadied him.

"Whoa, you all right?" Brayden asked, his concern replacing his earlier amusement.

Wanting everyone's attention on something besides him, Ethan sniffed the air, a teasing crinkle forming on his nose as he cast a sidelong glance at Ramiro. "Something burning?" The words were out before a sly grin could fully form on his face.

Eyes wide as saucers, Ramiro shot a panicked look toward the kitchen before bolting toward the door at the far end of the room. "Oh crap! The spaghetti!" His voice echoed down the long hallway as he disappeared.

Ethan and Brayden shared a hearty laugh, the sound echoing in the large room. "I can't believe you're letting him cook again," Brayden commented, disbelief etched in his features.

"Trust me, it wasn't my idea," Ethan replied, his smile tinged with a hint of disbelief. He shrugged, turning toward Brayden, who now had a look of concern.

"Seriously, you sure you're okay? I was surprised when Paige told me you weren't at home." Ethan was touched by the look of brotherly concern on his brother-in-law's face.

Touched, Ethan smiled. His gaze drifted over Brayden's shoulder, finding Alayna outside, casually leaning on Brayden's car. The sight of her effectively dimmed his smile, making him uneasy. "Why is Alayna with you?"

Ethan stiffened as Brayden reached out, his hands held up in a placating gesture, trying to bridge the widening chasm of fear and suspicion. "I know how protective you are of Paige, the kids, but you can trust her, she just wants to help."

Taking a deep breath, Ethan relaxed,. "Little brother, how much do you really know about her? I mean, you just met her a couple of weeks ago?

Just as the words left his mouth, Alayna, with fear etched on her face, rushed in and seized Brayden's arm, her voice a panicked whisper. "Brayden... We've got to go, we've got to go now!"

Taken back, Brayden instinctively reached out to Alayna. "What is it? What's wrong?" he said, his voice full of concern.

Suddenly, the station alarm blared, its intense ringing echoing throughout the large bay. Ethan, beyond weary, frustrated, and on his last nerve, ran a hand down his haggard face. There would be no going home.

The dispatcher's voice crackled over the loudspeaker, "All units requested at 902 West Aspen, injuries unknown... officers en route."

Hearing his home address, Ethan turned horror-filled eyes to Brayden and saw that his brother-in-law's face had gone pale. The dispatcher's voice echoed again, cold and impersonal, "All units requested at 902 West Aspen, injuries unknown... officers en route."

For a few seconds, it was as if time stood still, punctuated by the surge of adrenaline that coursed through Ethan's veins. Around the trio, the station's crew scrambled out of the kitchen, dorm rooms, and hallway, each making their way to their assigned units in a flurry of urgency. Last out the door was Ramiro, who dashed toward his and Ethan's ambulance.

A silent understanding passed between Ethan and Brayden, each grasping the gravity of the situation. Brayden grabbed Alayna's hand and dragged her along behind him as he dashed to his waiting car just as Ethan bolted to his ambulance and shoved Ramiro aside. "I'm driving," he announced, his voice a blend of dread and determination as he slammed the driver's door shut. Ethan knew that in an emergency, every second counted. He had to get to his family.

Ethan fired up the ambulance as Ramiro hopped inside. Worried, Ramiro swallowed hard, his eyes flickering to Ethan. "902 Aspen... Isn't that your place, Ethan?" he asked, voice barely above a whisper, the question hanging heavily between them. A cold wave of realization washed over Ethan.

Fear gnawed at his insides, his gaze glued to the bay doors, mentally urging them to lift faster. "Yes," he managed to grit out, his voice hoarse, the seconds ticking by with agonizing slowness.

As the gap widened, barely enough to fit the ambulance, Ethan floored the accelerator, hurtling the ambulance out of the station like a bullet. Behind him, the remaining fire trucks, their lights slicing through the darkness, roared to life and gave chase.

CHAPTER 56

NOT A HERO

HUNTER

Austin, TX—Night

FOOTFALLS SOUNDED ON THE FLOOR ABOVE HUNTER AS he stopped at the foot of the stairs. The house, usually so warm and welcoming, suddenly felt cold and alien. Hunter felt frozen at the foot of the stairs, his gaze fixated on the topmost step. The darkness seemed to grow deeper with every passing second. There was a muffled rending noise from upstairs. It was like the monster in his imagination, and it gnawed and tore at his courage. Hunter willed himself to move, not toward the stairs, but away from them. Quietly, he tiptoed into the living room, his small hands shook as he picked up the phone and dialed 911. *Uncle Brayden can help, can't he? Even superheroes need help sometimes,* Hunter thought.

A loud dial tone reverberated and Hunter slammed his hand over the receiver, his eyes wide as he peered back at the dark stairway.

Muffled, the operator said, "911, what is your emergency?"

Above Hunter, the footfalls abruptly stopped. The house fell silent, so silent that he could hear his own heartbeat thumping in his chest. Clutching the active phone tightly, he shoved it deep within the thick cushions of the couch, his small hands trembling. Uncle Brayden's words echoed in his mind, "If you're ever in trouble, dial that number." Unable to speak, he remembered to not hang up the phone. Instead, he left it buried in the couch, hoping that help would come soon.

Fearful, Hunter started up the dark stairs, his small heart racing. The house echoed with silence, intensifying the sense of unease that gripped him. He paused at the landing; his tiny hand clutched the banister tight. Little beads of sweat trickled down his forehead as he approached Zoey's room. The door was open and, fearfully, he peered inside. The sight that greeted Hunter was a stark contrast to the usual warmth of Zoey's room. The cute stuffed animals and dancing ballerinas could not alleviate the dread that seeped from the room's corner. There, bathed in an eerie dim moonlight, sat Zoey in a rocking chair, her usually lively eyes were now vacant and fixed.

Hunter's mind raced as he took in the crimson lines that ran paths down Zoey's bloodied sleeve and onto the doll cradled in her arm, its dress soaked red. He trembled. Hunter wanted to run away, to scream for help, but he was frozen in place, his fear holding him captive.

Body quaking, Hunter turned and spotted the killer from his nightmare. The man, his face obscured in shadow, studied Hunter, making him shudder. The mysterious figure's gaze was cold, emotionless, and seemed to penetrate Hunter's soul. Fearfully, Hunter reached into his pocket, his fingers closing around the cool, hard marbles—his only weapon. The marbles, small and insignificant as they were, provided a glimmer of courage as the giant figure inched closer. The intruder then spoke. "You're supposed to be outside." His voice was heavy with a South African accent. It echoed ominously in the silent room, sending chills down Hunter's spine. Despite the fear coursing through him, Hunter detected a strange familiarity in his voice, but he could not figure out why. His mind was a whirlwind of thoughts, but finding the source of that familiarity seemed impossible.

The killer stalked toward Hunter, his presence looming like a dreadful nightmare. As Hunter backed toward the stairs, his heart pounded in his chest like a drum. His eyes widened as he spotted his mother, Paige's lifeless body. The sight sent an icy chill down his spine, freezing him to the spot. The man, noticing Hunter's shock, cunningly stepped in front of Paige, blocking the horrific sight from the small boy. Confused and scared, Hunter looked up at the killer who kneeled just a few feet before him. The man, with black hair and piercing blue eyes, offered a warm, unsettling smile. His voice, frighteningly calm and smooth, echoed in the

Chapter 56 Not A Hero

silent room. "I was looking for your father. Is he home?" The words hung heavy in the air, striking more fear into Hunter's already terrified heart.

Perched for flight, Hunter watched as lights swirled and sirens wailed in the small hallway. The towering man stretched out his hand, which was smeared in a horrifying crimson. "Come, Hunter, it is time to go," the man's voice echoed, a sickly sweet poison meant to lure him. But fear made Hunter shrink away, and the man lunged for him.

Trembling, Hunter's tiny fingers curled around the cold, hard stones in his pocket. With a quick, desperate move, Hunter jerked his hand free and hurled the marbles onto the floor beneath the man's feet. The man's fingers clawed at Hunter's sleeve, caught it, and yanked Hunter back against him. Hunter struggled and felt himself begin to fall as the man slipped on the marbles and tumbled backward, taking Hunter with him.

On the floor, in a panic, Hunter jerked his arm free and fled. Hunter could hear the man as he struggled to regain his footing. His small feet pounded on the stairs as he tried to put as much distance between himself and the killer as possible. The world spun around him in a dizzying whirl of terror and swirling red lights. The stairs seemed to stretch on forever, a mountain that he could never hope to conquer. But he didn't stop, he couldn't. Fear propelled him forward, driving him toward the front door and freedom.

Bursting out the screen door, Hunter's heart raced as he searched for a place to hide. Frantic, Hunter scurried around the backyard, his eyes darted from one hiding spot to another. Finally, he spotted a shrub nearby and launched himself into it, hoping to conceal his small frame. Terrified, Hunter curled into a tight ball and buried his face in his arms.

Muffled, Hunter sobbed, tears streaming down his face as he rocked back and forth. "I'm so sorry Momma, Zoey. I'm so sorry." Hunter's cries were muffled by his hands pressed against his mouth, as if he could hold in all the pain and guilt that threatened to consume him.

Hunter's friend from the In-between had been wrong—he was not a superhero. He could not use his stupid powers to save people, and now his worst nightmare had come true.

Filled with self-blame, Hunter's mind raced with thoughts about how he could have prevented the tragedy. His dad would hate him now too, wouldn't he? Hunter hated himself for not being able to use his powers when it mattered the most. He felt stupid and useless. His mom and sister were gone, and he now, could not do anything to bring them back.

Hunter's heart felt shattered. He buried his face deeper into his arms and forced his mind to shut out the lights, sirens, and shouts from the rescuers and allow the shock to his body to wash over him.

MAY 7TH—4 DAYS

CHAPTER 57

TOO LATE

BRAYDEN

Austin, TX—Night

MIND REELING, BRAYDEN SLAMMED THROUGH THE back door of his sister's house. Brayden's body shook with rage, shock, and disbelief as each turbulent emotion fought for dominance. Brayden's senses had become hyper-aware of the now grotesque familiarity surrounding him. The once welcoming scent of his sister's home was replaced by the metallic taint of blood, the air heavy with an unnatural stillness.

Every creak of the timbers, every gust of wind against the siding felt like a mockery, a cruel parody of the tranquil life that once was. The house, a mausoleum of gut-wrenching memories, whispered horrors that he dared not acknowledge. Despair clawed at his soul as the anguished cries of his heart echoed in the silent, oppressive night.

Brayden collapsed against the wall of the house. How could the world outside remain oblivious to the atrocity that had just unfolded within these walls? How could the stars still twinkle innocently in the inky abyss above? How could anything be normal? For Brayden, the universe had irrevocably shifted—chilling darkness had descended, swallowing the light, leaving only the haunting echoes of a life forever altered.

Inside the house, Brayden had watched helplessly as Ethan had fought against the other officers ordered to secure the scene. Brayden had raced after Ethan as he stormed through their line, rushed up the stairs, and kneeled next to Paige's body. Ethan had torn the sheet away from her, gathered her up in his arms, and held her close.

Knowing it was too late for his sister, Brayden had gone to Zoey's room. Juan had met him in the hallway, begging him not to go into the room. Like Ethan, Brayden would not be denied access and had shoved past Juan. He wished to God he had not. The image of Zoey's blood-soaked form would haunt him for all eternity. *What kind of monster would murder an innocent child?*

Branden had been so shell-shocked by seeing his sister's and Zoey's bodies, that he had not even fought Juan when he took him by the arm and led him out of the room, guiding him down the stairs, and opening the backdoor for him, telling him to take a minute to gather his thoughts.

In a daze, Brayden watched as Ethan staggered outside. Tears streamed down his stricken face, his EMT uniform covered in Paige's blood. Voice thick with grief, Ethan called, "Hunter? Hunter?" Ethan's cries went unanswered.

Ethan's partner Ramiro reached out tentatively to Ethan, his hand wavering. Even from the porch, Brayden could see the raw torment etched on Ethan's face, a mirror of his own hollow despair.

Ethan's voice, usually so sure and strong, was nothing more than a brittle whisper carried away by the wind. "Hunter. Where are you, son?" His plea hung in the air, a lonely echo in the vacuum of their shared nightmare. Ethan crumbled to the ground; his body quaked with anguished sobs.

Quietly, Juan stepped outside and stood next to Brayden. If Brayden wanted to help find the man responsible for this, he had to compartmentalize. He had to pull himself together. Straightening, Brayden steadied his nerves and leveled his gaze at Juan. The most crucial thing now was to find his nephew. "Did you find Hunter?" Brayden asked, terrified of the possible answer.

Lost for words, Juan shook his head no.

"God ... please," Ethan's plea echoed and reverberated through the desolate night.

Heartsick, Brayden watched Ethan weep openly, his body wracked with sobs. "I'm begging you. I'm begging you ... please don't take them all." Ethan's plea hung heavily in the air, the silence his only answer.

Chapter 57 — Too Late

Tears welled in Brayden's own eyes and blurred his vision. He dragged the back of his sleeve across his face, a futile attempt to stem the tide of his own grief, as he wiped away his tears and made his way down the stairs toward Ethan. He had to be strong for his brother-in-law. He had to put his own grief aside and find the strength to help Ethan through this tragedy.

Coming up behind Ethan, Brayden reached out, laying a hand on Ethan's shoulder. Ethan responded as though he had been burned, violently jerking away from Brayden's touch. His growl was low, filled with a warning, "Don't! Don't you dare touch me!"

His words echoed in the night; the fury bubbled within him, clashing with the grief that was etched deep into his features. As Ethan rose to his feet, he turned to face Brayden, his eyes alight with a rage that Brayden knew needed an outlet. It was a rage that Brayden was willing to bear, not out of obligation, but out of a deep-seated love for Ethan, a love as profound as that shared by brothers. Despite the venom in Ethan's words, Brayden stood his ground, ready to withstand the storm for Ethan's sake.

Brayden forced himself to remain still, each word hitting him like a punch as Ethan snarled at him, "You did this!" The accusation, heavy and heart-wrenching, caused Brayden to stagger back. He felt crushed, the gravity of Ethan's blame pressing down on him relentlessly. Their bond was built on years of shared memories and brotherhood. Now, it seemed to be tearing at the seams.

"Ethan, please," Brayden pleaded, his voice raspy with unshed tears. He needed his brother, the shared comfort of their bond, now more than ever. But his pleas seemed to fall on deaf ears.

Suddenly, Ramiro entered the fray, attempting to get between the two brothers. "Ethan… Please, don't." But his pleas were met with a fist. Ethan, lost in his anger and grief, shoved Ramiro aside without a second thought, and snagged the front of Brayden's shirt, their faces only inches apart.

As if torn from his soul, Ethan spat the words into Brayden's face. "You brought that murderer into our lives… you might as well have killed them yourself!" The words tinged with a grief so raw that it was tangible. Ethan drew back, his fist clenched and ready to slam into Brayden's face.

Brayden, swallowed by guilt and regret, welcomed the imminent pain, craving for it to jar him out of this horrifying nightmare. But the anticipated blow never came.

Instead, the soft, tremulous voice of Hunter, his nephew, pierced the tense air as he called out, "Daddy?!"

Ethan's hand froze mid-air, his rage momentarily subdued as he turned to his son. Hunter stood there, dirt and twigs clinging to his hair and clothes. His tear-streaked face looked up at them with such despair that Brayden thought the child would crumble to ash right there in front of them.

At the sight of Hunter, his young son, Ethan sucked in a shuddering breath and released Brayden. The relief was palpable, yet intertwined with a lingering sense of apprehension. Overjoyed that Hunter was okay, Brayden watched as Ethan, hesitant yet determined, moved toward Hunter. But the reunion was short-lived; shell-shocked, Hunter backed away from his father. Ethan, overcome with emotion, took note of Hunter's fearful gaze that was fixed on Ethan's bloody uniform.

Ethan knew his child was in shock and proceeded with caution. "It's okay... it's okay... Hunter." He spoke softly, trying to ease the profound fear in Hunter's eyes. Brayden found himself holding his breath as Ethan methodically began to unbutton his shirt, then removed the stained reminder of the violence, and tossed it aside. Thankfully, Ethan's white undershirt had not shared the same fate as his thick uniform, which helped to reassure his traumatized son.

"Daddy's here... You're safe," Ethan cooed as he gently scooped Hunter up into the safety of his arms. Ethan hugged Hunter to him and collapsed to his knees. "You're safe now," he whispered, his voice trembling with emotion. Ethan cupped Hunter's head in his hand, his fingers tracing the contours of the child's face, and held Hunter's cheek to his. The rhythm of their shared breathing punctuated the heavy silence as he began rocking back and forth, a solitary tear tracing its way down his cheek. In the midst of their shared grief, a father and his son found solace in their connection, a poignant reminder of the unbreakable bond between them.

Fighting back his own tears, Brayden could only watch as Ethan cradled his son in his arms. The sight of them together was both heartbreaking and heartwarming, a reminder of all that they had lost but also everything that still remained.

Brayden was about to go, his heart heavy with the weight of unsaid words and unexpressed emotions. However, a soft, guilt-laden whimper from Hunter halted him in his tracks. "I'm sorry, Daddy." Hunter's voice was barely a whisper, a fragile echo in the somber silence.

Chapter 57   *Too Late*

The confusion on Ethan's face mirrored Brayden's own as he pulled away, trying to reassure the young boy. "None of this is your fault."

Through Hunter's tear-choked denial, a firm, "Yes, it is," sent a shockwave through Brayden, causing him to stiffen.

Ethan looked over Hunter's head at Brayden, his glare accusatory. The look his brother-in-law gave him seared into Brayden's soul. It was an unspoken blame that would forever be a chasm between them. Brayden felt an icy dread in his heart. He knew then that Ethan would always hold him responsible for the tragic loss of Paige and Zoey. To Brayden, their absence was as profound and painful as the loss of his beloved sister and niece.

Brayden's heart broke at Hunter's unwarranted shame. The boy, overcome with emotion, ducked his head into the crook of Ethan's shoulder, his small voice barely audible as he confessed, "But Daddy, I knew he was coming." Breaking, Ethan held Hunter tight as he let his tears flow unchecked.

A thought slammed into Brayden's fragmented mind. Alayna had said Hunter had the gift of foresight, had warned him that Hunter's fears might be warranted. Knowing there was nothing more he could do, Brayden cast a final glimpse at what remained of his family, wishing more than anything that he could have protected them from the horror. All he could hope for now was that he would find the monster responsible for this carnage and bring him to justice.

Quietly, Brayden slipped out of the backyard and made his way to the front of the house. Before he dove into the evidence, he had to find Alayna and ensure that she was safe.

· MAY 7TH—4 DAYS ·

CHAPTER 58

KNOWN BETTER

ALAYNA

Austin, TX—Night

ALAYNA FELT HELPLESS AS THE CHAOS UNFOLDED ABOUT her. The relentless surge of sirens and lights that blinded her was overwhelming, creating an audible and visual cacophony that seemed to mirror her inner turmoil. The crowd of onlookers had slowly crept onto the scene from their homes, drawn out by the escalating commotion. Each flashing light seemed to pulsate in sync with her pounding heart, each siren's wail echoing her internal scream. The once familiar, peaceful façade of Ethan's and Paige's house was now an alien landscape, encroached upon by the invasive presence of urgency and despair. Helplessness clung to her like a second skin, a stark and painful reminder of the delicate thread by which life hung.

God, please let them be okay. Alayna sent up a silent prayer. If something had happened to Paige, or to the children, she would never forgive herself. This was her fault for guiding Paige to the astral plane, for helping her look into the darkness and see the monster who was stalking Brayden.

Alayna's heart raced as she waited. The once peaceful atmosphere of the home now felt haunted and ominous. Shadows danced around her, playing tricks on her mind and making her wonder if she was being watched. She couldn't shake the feeling that something terrible had happened.

Chapter 58   Known Better

Alayna's mind raced back to Paige and her session. It had taken over an hour for her to help Paige relax her mind enough for her to slip into a peaceful enough state to allow the mind to explore the visions and nightmares that were plaguing her.

As Alayna delved deeper into Paige's troubled subconscious, she couldn't shake off the overwhelming feeling of being watched. The atmosphere in the room had changed—shadows seemed to dance around the corners and a chill hung in the air. But Alayna was determined to help Paige, no matter what challenges she faced.

For hours, they worked together as Alayna guided Paige through her visions. The images were haunting, but Alayna refused to let fear take over. She knew that it was the only way for Paige to find peace and break free from the nightmares that were tormenting her.

Sharing the visions Paige had experienced, Alayna could tell that Brayden's sister was right. The sinister specter that haunted their steps was not just a figment of her imagination, but a very real threat who lurked in the shadows.

Alayna's determination hardened as they drew closer to the answers they sought. She would not rest, not until they had unmasked the monster that dared to terrorize them.

The darkness hid and twisted his visage from their view, but Alayna's relentless spirit was not so easily defeated. She encouraged Paige to delve deeper into the abyss, prepared to go for as long as it took, until they found themselves face-to-face with their tormentor.

Then something terrible and unexpected happened. The tall figure in the mist turned to them, his face obscured, but the weight of his gaze heavy on their spirit forms. *How is this possible?* Alayna had thought.

Deep and threatening, the man's voice issued a warning. "Go back, do not seek to find me again or there will be consequences." Alayna had felt Paige's hand tremble in hers and found that she too was shaking. In their current form, on the astral plane, he should not have been able to see them, but he did!

Determined, Alayna issued her own warning, "We aren't going anywhere, asshole!" Though she tried to sound brave, her voice quivered. There was a pause, a few seconds as the three of them stood frozen in the midst. Then, out of nowhere, a raven dove at her and Paige, breaking their concentration.

In a flash, they were hurled back and into their bodies, with the man's final warning echoing after them. "So be it." His voice was a low, guttural growl.

As they regained control of their bodies, the resolve in Alayna's eyes was unbreakable. She knew that there was more to this man and his warning than they could have ever imagined. If it had been up to her, she would have immediately gone back in and sought him out. However, Paige was rattled, visibly shaken, and had said she had to go. She had to pick her children up from school and get home before Ethan got back.

It tore at Alayna to watch Paige go in that state, but she knew there was nothing she could have done at that moment. Now, looking up at the house, she wished she had never agreed to help Paige look into her visions, or at the very least, had pretended to agree not to go after the monster in the mist.

As each precious moment slipped by, Alayna felt an overwhelming sense of despair seeping into her soul. The absence of precognitive abilities, unlike Hunter's, amplified her sense of helplessness. Each eerie warning and ominous sketch conjured up a mirage of forthcoming calamities she feared she was unequipped to prevent. The specter of dread loomed large, casting a shroud of sorrow over Alayna as she grappled with the reality of her inability to shield Brayden and his family from the threat that loomed over them.

Through the press of people, Alayna spotted a patrol cop hurrying to his unit. A knot tightened in her throat, her heart pounding like a drum in her chest. Each beat echoed the urgency of the moment. She pushed her way through the crowd, her determination fueled by a mix of fear and desperation. The murmur of the onlookers became a distant hum as her focus narrowed to the figure in the uniform, the gate to the information she desperately needed. She had to know what was going on in that house, had to confirm that everyone was all right. The uncertainty was an unbearable weight, a tidal wave of emotion threatening to pull her under.

A few feet shy of reaching the officer, Alayna was abruptly drawn back into a cruelly tight grip. Her heart hammered in her chest as the tall figure wrapped his arm securely around her waist. The whisper of her captor's breath against her ear sent chills down her spine as he issued a stern warning. With a grief-stricken heart, she remained silent, her body trembling from the shock and the overwhelming fear that consumed her.

Chapter 58 — Known Better

Alayna could almost hear the cruel smile in his voice, a chilling symphony of mockery that sliced through her heart like a cold blade. "Alayna, with all of your amazing gifts, I am surprised you did not see me coming," he taunted, his voice a deep timbre, velvet-smooth, with the hint of a foreign accent.

Every instinct Alayna had warned her that she was teetering on the precipice of despair. The man who held her was more than just a physical presence; he was a manifestation of her deepest fears, an embodiment of the dark shadows that had lingered in the corners of her existence. His grip was as cold as ice, a chilling reminder of the loss she had endured, and the void that had been left in its wake. Every line of Hunter's haunting sketch was etched into the man's face, a cruel caricature of the remorseless predator that had been stalking them.

Alayna's body shook with involuntary tremors, a chilling manifestation of the fear that seemed to infiltrate every fiber of her being. She peered helplessly at the chaos around her—officers and firefighters bustling around with an urgency that only heightened her sense of dread. Brayden was somewhere in that melange; she was certain of it. Her heart ached in its desperation to find him. The man's voice, grating and merciless, broke through her thoughts. His words, whispered into her ear, were a cold, cruel taunt, "I'm afraid your lover and his friends are too busy to be of any help to you currently." He sneered. A solitary tear—a testament to her terror—trickled down Alayna's cheek. The man was relentless. "Why don't we go somewhere quiet, where we can talk," he suggested, his tone laced with ominous undertones as he pressed a sharp blade to her throat.

Alayna knew she could not go with the man. The very idea was a deathly whisper that sent chills down her spine. She could feel her heart pounding in her chest, like a wild drum echoing in the silence of her fear. The faceless crowd moved around her, oblivious to her ordeal. The sharp blade at her throat was an icy promise of imminent doom, the cold steel an unwelcome reminder of the hopelessness of her predicament. The bright blue uniforms of the police felt miles away, their presence nothing more than an ironic tease. The thought crushed her—a terrifying paradox of vulnerability in the midst of protection. Alayna stood there, the world a blur around her, grief and panic intertwining in a dance that left her breathless.

Fear should have overcome Alayna, but it didn't. Instead, a fiery rage ignited within her, a spark of defiance that wouldn't be extinguished.

As the calloused hands of the beast dragged her farther away from Brayden, her pillar of safety, and the nearby officers, she refused to succumb to despair. The icy chill of the night air, the menacing growl of her captor, none of it could douse the flame of her determination. In her heart, a promise was forged—she would not let this be her final night, not at the mercy of this monster.

Her mind, a whirlwind of thoughts and plans, began plotting her escape, turning her fear into a weapon of survival.

CHAPTER 59

CAN'T BE HAPPENING

BRAYDEN

Austin, TX—Night

After searching for Alayna at Paige's house and being unable to find her, Brayden had gone to the only other logical place he had hoped to find her. With each pounding of his fist against Alayna's door, his panic rose. He had to know if she was in there, had to know if she was still alive. If the monster who had killed his sister and niece had somehow gotten his hands on her?

Brayden, unwilling to wait for backup, hurled himself against the obstinate barrier that separated him from Alayna. His heart pounded in sync with the reverberating crashes, each impact sending a shockwave of dread through the onlookers. The door finally gave way beneath his desperation, splintering open with a hollow echo that seemed to mirror the hollow sensation gnawing at his insides. Brayden's voice, husky with fear, echoed through the now open doorway, "Alayna!" His call met with silence, a haunting, ghastly silence that filled the room like a thick, choking fog.

Dread washed over Brayden as he surveyed the chaotic scene. Alayna's once cozy and familiar apartment was now a chilling tableau of destruction and mayhem. A lamp lay toppled over, its light forever extinguished, echoing the sinking feeling in Brayden's heart. Broken furniture was strewn haphazardly, a silent testament to the violent struggle that had taken place. Each shattered piece seemed to pierce his soul, a stark reminder of the tranquility and warmth that had once pervaded those rooms. His hand, trembling, reached for the light switch, casting a harsh, unforgiving light on the scene of desolation.

Brayden drew his gun, his hand trembling slightly as he gripped the cold metal. The silence within the apartment was deafening, amplifying the thumping of his own heart in his chest. "Alayna," he called again, his voice echoing through the desolate rooms. His throat tightened, the name tasting like despair and fear. The absence of her response hung in the air, a haunting reminder of the uncertainty he was facing. But he had to push through, for her, for them. Despite the overwhelming dread, Brayden held on to the flicker of hope that he would find her, alive and unharmed.

Meticulously, Brayden went room to room, each scene a savage exhibition of Alayna's violated sanctuary. A sense of profound loss washed over him, as if each shattered trinket and toppled bookshelf amplified the brutal reality of her absence. The silent rooms echoed with the ghosts of shared laughter and whispered secrets; the memories now tainted by the chaos that had overrun her once peaceful retreat. A wave of sorrow threatened to consume him as he fingered the crushed scarf, the delicate fabric a stark contrast to the brutality of its treatment. The scent of Alayna's perfume lingering on the silk was a cruel reminder of their stolen moments, of a time when joy and love filled the rooms instead of the desecration he now faced.

Brayden felt his legs give out beneath him as he collapsed onto the cold, unforgiving hardwood floor. His heart pounded in his ears, a deafening metronome ticking off the seconds in this new reality where Alayna was gone. A reality he refused to accept. He could still feel the echoes of her laughter, the warmth of her hand in his, and the love she radiated. But now? Now there was only cold emptiness. The possible loss of Alayna was a blow too great, a torment he was not prepared to bear. Despair washed over him like a tidal wave, threatening to pull him under. Despite his strength, he felt himself fracturing under the immense weight of his grief. The world was ripping at the seams, and he didn't know how to sew it back together.

Mind reeling, Brayden just sat there, eyes glazed over with a pain only those who've loved and lost can truly understand. The room around him, once filled with life and laughter, now lay in shambles—a chilling echo of the vibrant soul it once housed. Every shattered trinket, every scattered

Chapter 59 — Can't Be Happening

paper seemed to scream Alayna's name, weaving a silent symphony of the chaos that had once been their shared happiness. His heart pounded in sync with the heavy boots thudding up the stairs, a harsh reminder of the reality he was still struggling to comprehend. What once was, was no more. And as he sat there, amidst the remnants of a life he no longer recognized, Brayden felt a part of himself crumble too.

From somewhere deep within the echoing expanses of the apartment, Juan, Brayden's partner, called his name. His voice reverberated through the empty rooms, bouncing off the high ceilings and landing with a thud in the pit of Brayden's stomach. "Brayden?" Juan's voice trembled, a mix of desperation and confusion seeping through. "Brayden?! You in here?" Those words hung in the air, hollow and haunting, their echo refusing to fade away. And yet, Brayden remained silent. Grief had silenced him, its heavy weight pressing down on his chest and making it hard to breathe. He could not will himself to answer Juan, couldn't even muster the strength to get to his feet. He just sat there, frozen like a statue, overcome with emotion.

Juan's voice echoed through the stale air of the room. "Brayden?" The name fell like a weighted whisper, laden with concern and the gravity of untold stories. It sounded closer this time, pulling Brayden out of his forlorn reverie. Brayden's gaze lifted, landing on the slightly ajar door. Through it, he saw the silhouette of Juan—a familiar figure who carried both authority and empathy in his stride. As their eyes met, Juan froze, his face a canvas of complex emotions. It was a blend of relief, concern, and compassion—a silent acknowledgment of the shared pain. Juan glanced over his shoulder, gesturing to the officers behind him. "Give us a minute, secure the scene," he ordered, his voice carrying the weight of command yet gentle in its undertone. With a final nod at them, he turned back to Brayden, closing the door behind him—a barrier against the world outside, leaving just the two of them in the room's somber silence.

Mutely, Brayden looked up at his partner. His eyes, swollen and red from the shed and unshed tears, silently communicated a story of loss and despair. The ache in his heart was as tangible as the silence filling the room, a silence so profound it echoed in its emptiness. His lips quivered, attempting to articulate the maelstrom of emotions coursing through him, but words eluded him. His partner, a silent spectator to Brayden's torment, understood the profound grief that no words could express or console.

Brayden felt the weight of Juan's hand, a firm yet gentle presence on his trembling shoulder. His breath hitched as he tried to suppress sobs, his heart heavy with the raw sting of loss. His gaze darted nervously around the remnants of Alayna's life, each shattered piece a cruel reminder of his earlier loss. Juan's voice broke through his musings. "Brayden. Hey, hey, look at me," Juan ordered softly.

Lifting his gaze to meet Juan's warm eyes, Brayden found solace in their shared sorrow. Brayden watched as Juan fought fiercely against his own surge of emotions, striving to offer comfort. Juan's voice, although steady, betrayed a hint of a tremble as he said, "Alayna is not here. She was not at the shop. There is a good chance that she is somewhere safe, just waiting for things to calm down." The words hung in the air, their echoes resounding with the unspoken hope that they held. Brayden clung onto them, desperate to believe that Alayna, the woman he cherished, was still breathing somewhere safe on this Earth. The shadow of grief and loss clung to him, threatening to pull him under, but the raw emotion in Juan's words kept him afloat.

Brayden listened to Juan, his words echoing in the cavernous room. "I've had them put a CLEAR alert out for Alayna." A sense of urgency hung heavily in the air. Juan straightened, his resolve etched in the hard lines of his face. "Everyone in the city is out there trying to find her." A moment passed, then Juan extended a hand to Brayden, his words sharp, pushing through the fog of despair. "Now get off your ass and help us find your girl."

Gratitude welled up in Brayden, a small ray of hope in the dark abyss of his grief. He took Juan's hand and rose to his feet, steadying himself against the tidal wave of emotion threatening to swallow him whole. If there was even a sliver of a chance that Alayna was still alive, he would move heaven and earth to find her.

Brayden swallowed hard, the bitter taste of grief giving way to a burning anger. He channeled the wrath, the raw emotion, into a flint-hard resolve. His voice, when it came, was steady. "Tell me about the evidence they've gathered so far?"

CHAPTER 60

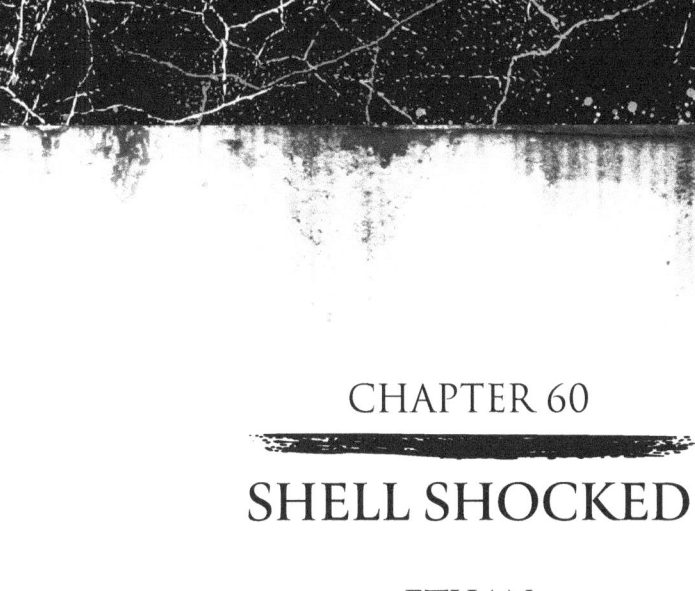

SHELL SHOCKED

ETHAN

Austin, TX—Night

ETHAN DID NOT REMEMBER THE RIDE TO THE HOSPITAL or even walking into the emergency room. The only thing he could think about was that he still had Hunter, his precious five-year-old son, in his arms and no one was going to take him away from him.

Even though Ethan's mind was clouded with a thick fog of confusion and exhaustion, there was one thing that remained crystal clear—his determination to protect his son, no matter what.

Ethan felt like he was in a dream state. Somewhere in the back of his mind he remembered that his partner Ramiro had been there, guiding him and Hunter through the large, sliding doors of the hospital and carefully maneuvering them into a quiet room all the while, as he had refused to let him take Hunter from him.

Holding his five-year-old son Hunter tight against his chest, Ethan knew his child had stopped crying. His son was more than likely in shock and needed to be examined by a doctor, but he just could not force himself to let anyone take him from him.

The world around Ethan seemed to exist in a muffled hush. A thick fog had wrapped around him. Time had slowed, each tick of the clock echoed in the hollow of his chest. Ethan's mind was a battleground. It clashed with the calm of the room and the gruesome reality of the trauma he and Hunter had just experienced.

It was as if he were trapped in a chilling nightmare, one that he could not awaken from. A sense of cold dread settled in his veins, as his body began to tremble, and despite his best efforts, his teeth began to chatter. Logically, Ethan knew he was in shock, a force that gripped him so tight, that he feared it would never let him go.

Mind reeling, Ethan was stuck in a reality he could not recognize. Paige and Zoey were gone, ripped away from him by a faceless monster. The world was different. He was different. It was an atmosphere of darkness and unknown that he now found himself lost within, an aftermath of trauma that left his world forever altered.

From what seemed far away, a voice called to Ethan, "Ethan, honey, it's your mom, Feebee. Please, let me hold Hunter while Ramiro helps you get cleaned up." In response, Ethan hugged Hunter tighter to his chest and his son let out a whimper due to being held too tight.

Mind struggling to catch up to his new reality, Ethan shook his head, trying to clear it as he looked up at the large clock on the wall. It was after 10:00 p.m., his mom lived over an hour away and should have been in bed by then. "Mom, what are you doing here?" Ethan's own voice sounded strange in his own ears. *Why can't I get a grip on myself?*

Stroking Hunter's hair, Ethan watched as his mom slowly reached out to him as if she was afraid he would break and run if she moved too fast. "Honey, the doctor needs to check you and Hunter out. Would it be all right if he took him?"

In response to her question, Ethan heard himself growl in response. "No!" He had lost his wife and his daughter; he could not risk losing his son too.

He felt Hunter stiffen in his arms and emit a muffled cry. "Daddy, you're hurting me."

Horrified, Ethan immediately loosened his grip on Hunter and put a comforting hand to his face. "Hunter! I'm so sorry... Are you okay?" Ethan took note of the fresh tears in his son's eyes.

"Ethan, dear, why don't I hold Hunter, just long enough for you to change into some clean clothes?" Looking down at himself, Ethan cringed at the blood that covered him and that had smeared onto the side of Hunter's face. It was obvious Hunter was not okay. How could he be after all that he had been through?

Chapter 60 — Shell Shocked

Unsure what to do next, Ethan looked up and scanned the worried faces of everyone who had crowded into the examination room. Hunter's pediatrician, the on-call doctor, trauma nurses, Ramiro, his captain, and his mother. A shudder ran through Ethan at the sight of his mother's grief-stricken face. She had always been there for him, had always made things right when he was young, and was the one he still went to for advice and counsel.

At that moment, under the harsh, brilliant lights and smell of antiseptic, Ethan knew there was absolutely nothing his mother or anyone else could do to set things right. All he could do was allow the people who loved him and Hunter to help them find their way through this nightmarish landscape to whatever future they still had.

Hand shaking, Ethan held it out to his mother. "Mom, would you stay with Hunter while I get cleaned up?"

Fighting back tears, Feebee took hold of Ethan's hand like a lifeline. "I won't let him out of my sight." Reluctantly, Ethan allowed Feebee to take Hunter from him. Hunter went to his grandmother without a fight and allowed her to cradle him in her arms.

Solemnly, Ramiro stepped back and allowed Ethan room to exit the small sterile room. "I brought some clean clothes for you from the station." Ethan could tell he was trying hard to speak past the lump in his throat. "The nurses said you could use the shower down the hall." He nodded, not knowing what else to say.

Casting a final look back at his mother, she gave him an encouraging nod as she quietly rocked Hunter. "We'll be right here when you get back, promise." Reluctantly, Ethan backed out of the room, turned around, and followed Ramiro down the hall.

As hard as it was, Ethan knew he had to be strong for his son. He had to go on, even though he felt as if his soul had been decimated. There was nothing he could do for Paige, or for Zoey, so he sure as hell was going to make sure nothing happened to Hunter. No matter what he had to do to protect his son, he would do it.

CHAPTER 61

NO REST FOR THE WICKED

VANDER

Texas/Arkansas State Line—Night

EXHAUSTED, VANDER HAD DRIVEN THE RUSTED, STOLEN car he had inherited from the thug back in Philadelphia down the narrow, desolate dirt road. The headlights, flickering intermittently, illuminated the path ahead in patchy intervals, casting long, grotesque shadows that danced eerily on the uneven surface. Up ahead, standing in stark contrast against the moonlit sky, rested a dilapidated barn, its wooden façade weather-worn and teetering on the brink of collapse.

Drawing on the last of his waning energy, Vander parked beside the ghostly structure, its shadow swallowing the car whole. He needed a few hours of fitful slumber, a brief respite from the relentless pursuit before embarking on the next leg of his perilous journey home.

Had his idiot driver not been so intent on killing him once they had reached Austin, it would have been nice to have had a chauffeur on the way back so he could have rested. But, unfortunately, as he had anticipated, the man he had hired to take him to Austin had spent the last five hours of their journey contemplating how he was going to kill his client.

Of course, Vander had not been worried. He knew his driver would not make a move until he had all his money. That was why Vander had promised him that they would stop at the first ATM they reached in

Chapter 61   *No Rest For The Wicked*

Austin, where he would happily withdraw the remainder of the fee he was owed.

As they had neared their destination, Vander had taken note of his driver as he showed signs of withdrawal. Sweat beaded his brow, his hands shook, and he went from burning up to freezing and had grown more and more irritable and slightly irrational.

Understanding the junkie's needs, Vander offered to pay for the man's fix and urged him to seek out a neighborhood where he could take care of his need before they sought out an ATM, reasoning that it would help the driver feel better for his return trip to Philadelphia. Since the man was in so much pain from his need, he never thought to question Vander's motives.

Soon enough, they were in a shady part of town, with the same broken-down apartments, abandoned houses, and window-barred businesses that found a way into every American city. His driver found a guy hanging out in front of a shady nightclub, approached him, and made his transaction.

Desperate for the pain to stop, Vander had watched the driver take the drug, as his dealer made a fast get-away. A slow, satisfied smile curved the corners of the thug's face. The high hit him with lightning speed, as if on a cloud. The driver took one step, then two before his eyes rolled back in his head and he hit the street, face first, without any signs of trying to stop the fall, his heart already slowing as the lethal dose of Fentanyl did its work.

Sliding over into the driver's seat, Vander started the car as he watched his driver take his last breath. The lethal dose of Fentanyl had done his work for him. Vander knew this outcome had been in his favor. Fentanyl was killing people by the thousands in America, a sad and alarming fact that no one seemed interested in changing.

Another bonus: in his hurry to get his fix, the driver had left the keys in the ignition, saving Vander the unpleasant task of searching for the keys on the man's dead body, which could have left him vulnerable.

With his driver dealt with, Vander had gone straight to the Williams' home and had put his plan into action. He had given the psychic and her friend one last opportunity to stop searching for him, to stop looking for Alexander, but they had stubbornly refused. Thus, leaving him no choice but to deal with them in the most brutal way imaginable.

Vander knew that the detective was just as stubborn as the two women who were searching for him. The only way to change the course of events that Alexander had put into motion was to cause so much pain, so much chaos, that the search, at least in his direction, came to a brutal halt. What he had done had sickened him. True, he had done horrible things in the past to survive, but he had never actually done the killing himself, had not taken a blade and watched the life drain from a body.

Vander had killed them quickly, mercifully. Only after they had died had he mutilated the bodies to cause the detective more grief and anguish. It had been necessary, but distasteful to him. Still, knowing how easy it was for him to justify taking the lives of those people should have troubled him far more than it did, which was perplexing.

In his quest to survive, he was willing to do anything. Maybe Jack and Alexander were right. Maybe he had been a monster all along and had just been denying the fact.

Fate had forced Vander's plans to change as often as the shifting shadows in the deepest corners of a forgotten alleyway, driven by the persistent hum of uncertainty that echoed in his mind. He was a puppeteer of fate, his every decision sending ripples through the fabric of his prospective destinies.

Yet, the more he tried to manipulate the looming specters of the future, the more they twisted and contorted into grotesque parodies of his intended outcomes. It was a chilling dance of cause and effect, and Vander was caught in its unrelenting rhythm, forever teetering on the precipice of the unknown.

Vander did not bother to lock the car doors, a somewhat reckless act that spoke volumes of his current state of mind. His body slumped against the car's worn leather interior, the chill of the night seeping through the thin metal frame.

His eyes, heavy with exhaustion, scanned the desolate surroundings one last time before slowly surrendering to the allure of sleep. The car, a solitary silhouette against the backdrop of the pitch-black night, sat silently—an eerie monument to his solitude.

His breath fogged up the windows, obscuring the outside world, wrapping him in a cocoon of eerie tranquility. The events of the past seven days, grueling and relentless, seemed to fade into a distant echo as he closed his eyes and let the welcoming arms of oblivion pull him into its embrace.

MAY 8TH—3 DAYS

CHAPTER 62

NOT GOING

PETER

Austin, TX—Morning

READY TO BE ON THE WAY TO PHILADELPHIA, PETER hurried up the steps to the police station, ready to meet with Agent Chantal and Detective James. Upon entering the room, Peter could tell that the atmosphere in the squad room was heavy with tension, so much so that he could not help but feel as if an eminent threat were just out of sight. He knew Chantal, Brayden, and he were getting close to finally getting the answers they had been searching for.

Peter's thoughts raced as he stood in the center of the squad room, his eyes scanning his surroundings in search of his colleagues. They each were determined to solve this case and bring justice to all the victims of the Sculptor.

With each passing moment, Peter's determination grew stronger. He would not rest until they had uncovered the truth and put an end to the darkness that had plagued him for far too long. He knew it would not be an easy journey, but he was willing to do whatever it took.

The tension in the room was palpable, but Peter refused to let it consume him. Instead, he channeled it into his resolve and the energy he would need to see the case through. They were on the brink of a breakthrough; he could feel it.

Peter spotted Chantal making her way toward him.

The atmosphere around them felt heavy, as if a dark cloud of foreboding had descended upon them. Peter's heart began to race as he noticed the determined look on Chantal's face. Her eyes met his with a grim intensity, and he knew that something was terribly wrong.

"What's wrong? Where's Detective James?" Peter asked.

Peter could tell Chantel was exhausted as she leaned heavily on a nearby desk. "Detective James won't be joining us." Peter's heart skipped a beat, if James was not going, something horrible must have happened to him. "His sister and niece were murdered last night."

"What?" Taken aback, Peter struggled for words. "What happened? Is it related to the case?"

Lips pressed into a thin line; Chantal shook her head. "I don't know all the details; the investigation is ongoing."

Peter knew this could not be a coincidence, not with everything they had learned and the lead they were about to pursue. "What about Philadelphia?"

Straightening, Agent Robinson adjusted her holster and fixed him with a determined stare. "I'm getting on that plane, with or without backup, and you are welcome to join me." Robinson strode past Peter. Not wanting to be left behind, he hurried after her.

MAY 9TH—2 DAYS

CHAPTER 63

ACT NORMAL

VANDER

Philadelphia, PA—Morning

EXHAUSTED, VANDER CAST A LONGING GLANCE AT HIS bed, its unmade sheets looking like a sanctuary of comfort and tranquility in the grim atmosphere. His body screamed for rest, for a few hours of escape from the mental and physical marathon Alexander had him running. But rest was a luxury he could not afford, not when the finish line seemed to recede with each step he took. As he studied his reflection in the dusty mirror, his sunken eyes echoed the haunted determination that lived within him.

Gazing at his reflection, Vander thought about the bloodied clothes, gloves, shoes, and items he had burned along with the junkie's car. When the police found the charred remains in that old scrap yard a few miles outside the city, there would be no evidence of what happened in Austin to discover. If, in fact, they cared to investigate the scene at all, which was highly unlikely.

It had been a full moon two nights ago, that had given Vander enough light to do the necessary cleanup to close the chapter on his quick visit to Austin. Two nights before, the cold had seeped into his bones, joining the icy resolve in his soul to see this thing through, no matter how dark the path ahead was.

Dark Variations

As he walked back to the dorm, in his clean clothes and fresh shoes, he could not help but replay the previous events. So much had changed in the past few days. Nothing was the same, he was not the same. There would be time enough to ponder this revelation another day, another time, but for now, he had to make an appearance at the school, then head home to ensure he met with the unwelcomed guests that even Alexander himself was not expecting.

Vander knew he would need to be at the top of his game with Peter O'Reily and the new agent assigned to the case. If memory served him, O'Reily was a sharp-witted man, he missed little in his observation and it was imperative to Vander's future that he handled the man with both utmost care and cunning.

Peter O'Reily was no fool, he and Agent Reese had nearly caught their Sculptor suspect and would have if he had not helped Alexander. Deep down, Vander respected O'Reily. He was a great agent, trustworthy, steadfast, someone a person could respect. It had troubled Vander to see how devastated O'Reily had been upon discovering Agent Reese. There was no doubt in Vander's mind that the man had loved his partner and had wanted more than the working relationship they had shared.

Early on, Vander had asked about the agent, because he had wanted to know what had happened to the man. Alexander had told him that he had retired from the agency, took a job as a college professor, and had moved on with his life. Mostly true, Vander imagined, but he also could not help but wonder what scars the gentleman must carry from the horrific way in which he lost his partner and lover.

How was it possible to wreak so much devastation by the sheer act of merely wanting to live? Vander could not help but wonder what life might have been like if someone other than a serial killer had been willing to help him. His thoughts were consumed by dark, mysterious visions of what could have been.

If Erin Reese could have found it in her to put aside her mission to go after the Sculptor to save him from Kgotso, from his parents, would she have been spared the horrible fate she was given? Would he have grown up in a world where he was an agent, a cop, or something other than what he had become?

Casting one last look at his refined reflection, Vander dusted off his jacket. None of that mattered now. All the other possibilities had died

Chapter 63 — Act Normal

with Agent Reese. This was the world in which he had been cast. This was his reality, as dark and foreboding as it was.

As always, Vander would find his way through this nightmarish labyrinth and survive, on his own, because there was no one else on whom he could rely.

CHAPTER 64

CURIOUS

PETER

Philadelphia, PA—Afternoon

It had been a short drive from the airport to Alexander Dayton's townhome, where Peter O'Reily and Agent Robinson sat watching the residence. There had been no activity since they had arrived thirty minutes earlier. They were prepared to get out of the vehicle and go knock on the door when they spotted a stylish young man.

As Peter watched him approach, he could not shake the feeling that he knew the young man. Head held high, his manner almost graceful, the young man with jet-black hair and piercing blue eyes ascended the stairs, opened the door, and entered the residence.

"No, it couldn't be?" Peter said, more to himself than to the agent sitting next to him. He felt a chill run down his spine as he watched the young man disappear into the townhome.

Taken aback, Robinson asked O'Reily, who looked like he had seen a ghost, "Couldn't be what?"

Peter slumped back in his seat. "The boy from Africa."

Confused, Robinson held up a hand and stared at him. "Ummm, you're going to have to be more specific."

Shaken, Peter could not tear his eyes away from the door in which the young man had entered. "Sorry, it's just, it can't be."

Chapter 64 — Curious

"Can't be what O'Reily?" Losing her patience, Robinson pressed, "If you know something, spit it out already."

Taking a deep breath, Peter turned to her. "Seventeen years ago, while Agent Reese and I were working the case in Africa, there was a young boy, around seven or so, who kept popping up at the oddest times."

"Okay," Robinson said, still confused but trying to follow Peter's line of thought.

"We first encountered him in a junkyard, where one of the bodies was found."

Shocked, Robinson interrupted him, "What, the kid was at one of the Sculptor murder scenes?"

"No, no, this murder was unrelated," Peter continued. "There had been an American woman murdered and dumped in the slums. The boy accidentally stumbled upon the body while fighting with a group of hooligans."

Robinson asked, "So, what does that have to do with us, with the here and now?"

Brows furrowed, Peter's gaze returned to the front of the townhome. "I believe that young man who just walked into Alexander Dayton's townhome is one and the same." Troubled, Peter continued, "And if so, that would lead to more questions in our case." The eerie feeling that hung in the air only intensified, as if a dark presence was looming over them. Peter's determination to solve the case had grown stronger, fueled by the unsettling mystery surrounding it.

Wanting Agent Robinson to understand, O'Reily pressed on, "The body in the slums was not my only encounter with the boy. Agent Reese and I also ran into him with Dayton a few days later at the precinct in Cape Town. He found his way into Agent Reese's hotel room, where he had told my partner that he was seeking sanctuary from his abusive father... then one last time at the crime scene where Agent Reese's body had been discovered."

Shocked, Agent Robinson bolted up in her seat next to O'Reily. "What?!"

Peter could tell she did not believe what she was hearing. The horrifying details of the case were slowly unraveling before her, piece by piece, and her mind was racing ahead, trying to absorb the information he was giving her.

"At the time, as you might imagine, I was so horrified at the death of my partner I did not stop to wonder why the boy was there," Peter offered.

Calmly, Robinson asked, "But later, once you had time to think?"

Peter's hands, weathered and worn from years of relentless pursuit, told a story all their own. The lines etched into his skin, like secret codes waiting to be deciphered, bore testament to his ceaseless determination. The shadows danced across his features as he lowered his gaze, his eyes reflecting a resolve that was as haunting as the mysteries he sought to unravel. "In this grim and unyielding journey," he began, "I started asking questions, began to put the pieces of the puzzle together."

Lost in thought, Peter continued, "The timeline is a little fuzzy to everyone I questioned. But, as far as I can tell, close to the time my partner was killed, Vander's father, having apparently murdered his mother, was shot, and killed by the responding police. The child fled the scene and went looking for Alexander. Upon arrival at the dig site, the boy heard gunshots and called the police. The police responded and found Dayton and the boy outside the kill room where Erin and the body of the Sculptor whom Alexander Dayton supposedly killed after finding him carving up Agent Reese."

Trying to take in the swarm of information, Agent Robinson shook her head. "Okay, that is beyond weird." Robinson pointed up at the townhome. "But what makes you think that guy is the boy from Africa? He could just be an associate of Dayton's."

As she stared skeptically at him, Peter O'Reily felt a sense of unease settle over him. "I always remembered the child had the most vivid blue eyes against that dark skin and jet-black hair. That man who just walked into that townhome had the same striking features."

"And just happens to be in America with Dayton?" Robinson scoffed.

"From the information I gathered seventeen years ago," Peter continued. "I learned that Mr. Dayton legally adopted the newly orphaned boy, brought him to America, had him tutored privately, then enrolled him in the finest schools to further his education."

The details sent shivers down his spine and only added to the already haunting atmosphere surrounding Mr. Dayton.

Confused, Peter watched as Agent Robinson began working things out. "But why would a billionaire, philanthropist adopt some random kid in Africa?" she asked.

Chapter 64   Curious

Peter gave her a knowing smile. "That, Agent Robinson, is an answer I would very much like to discover." Reaching for the handle, Peter nodded toward the townhome. "Shall we?"

Eager to get to the bottom of the case, Robinson opened her car door. "Absolutely!"

As they made their way to the mysterious townhome, Peter's mind was filled with a sense of unease and foreboding. The dark clouds overhead seemed to reflect his own troubled thoughts as he thought about the strange circumstances surrounding the case and the troubling journey they still must navigate to solve it.

MAY 9TH—2 DAYS

CHAPTER 65

ALL ARRANGED

ALEXANDER

Philadelphia, PA—Day

"Tone light, Alexander spoke into the phone. "Indeed, the pleasure is mine," murmured Alexander, his voice echoing through the quiet townhome. The arrival of the Amorphophallus titanium, with its morbid allure and deathly aroma, was the final piece of the puzzle he had been putting together for the past year. The exhibit, now a surreal stage for the cadaverous bloom, was a testament to his insatiable fascination with the peculiar and the macabre. Alexander couldn't help but revel in the anticipation of the corpse flower's imminent, grotesque blooming, a chilling spectacle that would soon engulf the museum with an atmosphere of spectral beauty. "Then I shall meet you at dawn of the fourteenth to finalize the premiere."

Alexander hung up the phone, a bright smile illuminating his hardened features. The anticipation was palpable, nearly a tangible entity in the room. The upcoming exhibit promised an allure of mystery and intrigue that was uncommon even for his standards. A sense of satisfaction washed over him, however fleeting it was. There was, after all, a missing piece of the puzzle yet to be secured. His brows furrowed, a crease of worry etched into his otherwise confident façade. Between dealing with the authorities and coordinating the transportation of the rare flower, his attention had been divided. A sudden realization hit him—Vander.

Chapter 65 All Arranged

Always considerate, Vander had called him the night before upon his return to the States and said that he would be staying at the school for the evening due to his need to complete a rather tedious term paper. Which made sense, since Vander had insisted upon going to Cape Town before he completed all the necessary assignments before the end of his final semester.

However, it was unusual for his young ward not to stop by in the morning, especially considering his graduation party was that evening. Looking down at his calendar, Alexander mused. Perhaps he should not be surprised. It was, after all, his fault that Vander was preoccupied. He had set things in motion the moment he had made his decision to end his young ward's life.

That's why, when Vander had asked him for his graduation gift of returning to Africa, Alexander had known the true reason Vander felt as if he had to go immediately and not wait until after graduation. Because somehow, with the extraordinary gifts that Vander refused to share with him fully, the young man had discerned not only his dark intentions, but also the timing of them.

This knowledge had led to many of Alexander's moves. For, just as he would hope to secure victory in the complex game of chess, he had to navigate the intricate labyrinth of strategy and foresight. Foresight, being forever in Vander's favor. Therefore, Alexander was forced to begin with controlling the center, an essential tactic that allowed for greater mobility of the pieces. It was akin to securing the primary exhibit in a gallery. Chess demanded the development of minor pieces—knights and bishops. For Vander, those pieces were his classmates and girlfriend. Make Vander think they were threatened, and that created one distraction.

Then you turn your focus on the more powerful rooks and queen. Those took the shape of Vander's most hated enemy, Kgotso and the ghosts, memories of his parents back in Africa. Those pieces aided Alexander by helping him prioritize the minor leads before landing the major ones. Always be alert to your opponent's threats, just as Alexander must vigilantly anticipate hurdles in securing his final display piece. Lastly, Alexander knew to protect the king at all costs, for the game's conclusion hinged on that one piece's survival.

To protect himself, to win at this game with such a worthy advisory, Alexander had risked everything. He had painstakingly sought out the artist, yes. But not only her. Alexander had purposely killed in that city. Because after months of research, and following dozens of leads, Alexander had learned that there was a very gifted psychic in her own right, Alayna Sage. He had sent a very dear friend to test her skills to determine if she would pose a threat to Vander.

Of course, it had been a very big gamble. After finding out about the mysterious shop owner, Alexander had given her name to Vivian Richards, a logical, no-nonsense widow, who was grieving the loss of her dear husband. Vivian would not simply hear what she wanted to hear, for she was no fool. After her first visit, Vivian had called Alexander to tell him how incredible her session with Alayna had been. After that, there were many more to follow, each revealing more truths that gave credit to the psychic's gift of mediation.

From there, Alexander began his search for the Sculptor's next victim. Once selected, Alexander made sure the young woman he was about to kill knew that her only hope for revenge against him was Alayna Sage and told the soon-to-be spirit where to find her. From all his research into the occult, he knew that the artist might choose to simply move on and not stay behind to settle the score. But knowing human nature the way he did, he felt sure the woman would reach out to Alayna and set her on his trail.

Alexander had also set up the drug-deal-gone wrong in front of Alayna's shop. Ensuring that she would meet and be rescued by the officers. He had hoped it would give Alayna a simple contact, should she need it. Alexander could have never imagined that she and the young, driven detective would become intimate. Fate had indeed favored him.

Once the two lovers started investigating, it would only be a matter of time before Interpol called. Alexander knew there was no possible way to connect him to the Sculptor's murders, save for his treasured collection, and only he knew where and in what form it was. However, Vander would not have been so sure. The young man would see the Sculptor's new murder as a threat not only to Alexander, his mentor, but also to himself and the future he had built.

Vander no doubt had exhausted himself exacting revenge on Kgotso, making sure to kill the man, while he still could. Then chasing down the many threats coming against him. Thus, leaving him vulnerable to the final move Alexander had in store.

Though Alexander would hate to lose Vander, he also could not stop the deep-rooted desire to make him his final masterpiece. With that final

Chapter 65 — All Arranged

act, Vander would be a part of him forever, would be immortalized in a way that would preserve him for all time.

"Sir?" Alexander turned at the sound of his name. Philip waited, ready to begin the evenings preparation. "Would you care to give final approval for tonight's meal?"

"I would be happy to." Alexander smiled as he followed Philip toward the kitchen.

"Mr. Dayton, before I forget," Philip said. "Vander requested that we make preparations for three additional guests, does that meet with your approval?"

"Yes, yes, of course. The more the merrier," Alexander assured Philip. "Now, let me see what you have prepared." Alexander was intrigued with this new development; he could not wait to see whom Vander had decided to bring to his party. Mood light, Alexander decided to enjoy the night and let the next day take care of itself.

CHAPTER 66

WHATEVER IT TAKES

PETER

Philadelphia, PA—Night

Chantal had circled the neighborhood for the past twenty minutes, trying to find a parking space before she scored a spot two blocks shy of their destination. Chantal put the car in park, killed the engine and looked at Peter. "You don't think it was a little weird that Alexander's ward invited us to dinner?"

Peter knew full well that it was, but he did not care. "Yes, but does it matter?" Peter knew that Chantal was as eager to get to Alexander Dayton as he was, especially after what had happened to her friend and colleague back in Austin. "Either Alexander Dayton is responsible for these murders, or someone close to him is… Either way, we need a way into that townhome and a chance to question people without having a restraining order placed upon us."

With a smirk, Chantal said, "Very well. I can see why accepting the invitation to a graduation party from a kid you met twenty years ago is a viable option?"

O'Reily corrected her, "It was a little over seventeen, and yes, this will get us into the property without the need for a search warrant." Peter thought back to the day he met Vander all those years ago, his partner Erin had taken to the boy instantly, but he had found him a bit odd and strangely aggressive for a seven-year-old, but he supposed it made sense considering how he had been raised.

Agent Robinson laughed. "Sure, if Alexander doesn't have us thrown out before we can even sit down."

Face grim, Peter reached for the door handle. "Unlikely, it would not be gentlemanly of him to turn away an invited guest." Peter got out of the car. If there was one thing Peter knew for certain about Alexander, it was that he stood on the appearance of propriety. If his young charge had invited them to his dinner, Alexander would be sure to play the gracious host even if the guests he entertained were unwanted.

Feeling the warm May air, Peter regretted wearing his heavy suit. He had forgotten that May in the States was far warmer than back in England.

"Mr. Dayton stands on formality?" Chantal asked.

"Always," Peter affirmed. "While in Africa, even in the direst of circumstances, he carried himself most respectably."

Shutting the car door, Chantal looked around to make sure there were no parking meters needing to be fed. It was after hours, so they were good until 7:00 a.m. "So you actually spoke to him there, in Africa, during your Sculptor investigation?"

Pain etched on his face. Peter started down the street toward the townhome. "Yes, my partner Erin Reese and I both spoke to him on two separate occasions." Peter thought back to how calm and controlled the man had been while looking at the dead body of his young grad student. *What was her name? Ah, yes, Carol.* At the time, Peter had thought his collected demeanor was nothing more than habit and mature control. Now he was not so sure.

Hurrying to catch up to him, Chantal continued, "Back then, you had no suspicions of Dayton?"

Peter stopped, his haunted eyes fixing on hers. "No, I did not, but my partner Erin Reese did. At the time, it seemed ludicrous, unimaginable, but she was certain he had been involved somehow. So much so that she began investigating him on her own."

Undeterred by Peter's feelings, Chantal summarized, "Then Reese was supposedly killed by Dayton's engineer and Alexander just happened to show up too late to save her?"

"Pretty much."

Puzzled, Chantal continued, "Sounds amazingly convenient."

Knowing Agent Robinson would not stop until she understood the whole story, Peter once again began the trek to the townhome as he began filling in the blanks. "Truth of the matter, I was in love with Agent Reese. I had been for some time. As you might imagine, losing her, in that horrific way, not only distorted my perception of things and sent my world reeling, but due to my personal involvement with her, I was removed from the case."

"I see," Chantal exclaimed. Her tone unsatisfied.

"After the initial shock wore off, I did begin to reason things out." Peter tugged at his tie, which seemed to be choking off what little air he was able to breathe in. "Started examining the pieces to the well-organized puzzle that seemed to seamlessly complete the case which we had been so driven to solve."

"And?" Chantal asked as they stopped at the bottom of the stairs.

"I found it all too bloody perfect." Peter motioned for Chantal to start up the stairs ahead of him. "On my own, I began an investigation into Dayton, hounded him for weeks, and even attempted to speak to Vander at his private school."

Making her way up the stairs, Chantal turned back to him. "You did?"

Unapologetic, Peter stated, "Yes, but unfortunately I was not granted permission and for my efforts, I was put on the first of many leaves."

Horrified, Chantal's eyes widened. "They didn't let you investigate the lead?"

"Money, power, and influence blind the very best of us, I'm afraid." Sadly, Peter studied his shoes. "I fought hard to reopen the investigation. For my efforts, I was discredited as an agent, sacked and as a farewell gift from my agency, served restraining orders, barring me from any future access to Mr. Dayton and his young ward."

Chantal smiled. "Until tonight?"

Looking up, Peter returned her smile. "Precisely."

MAY 9TH—2 DAYS

CHAPTER 67

SURPRISE!

ALEXANDER & VANDER

Philadelphia, PA—Night

SATISFIED, ALEXANDER SURVEYED THE DINING SETTING that radiated elegance and sophistication. The grand dining table, meticulously crafted from rich, dark mahogany, stretched across the room, set to accommodate twelve esteemed guests. Adorned with fine china, the table gleamed with silver cutlery, and hand-blown crystal stemware that caught the soft light from the chandeliers overhead. Plush, high-backed chairs, upholstered in velvet, added a touch of opulence that would invite guests to linger over their meal.

Large, floor-to-ceiling windows unveiled a mesmerizing panorama of the city's twinkling skyline, adding an atmospheric layer to the exquisite setting, which would leave guests in awed contemplation. Turning to Philip and the other members of his staff, Alexander said in praise, "You have outdone yourself, Philip! The room is exquisite."

"Indeed, it is," Vander agreed, his low timbre sounded behind them.

Taking note of Vander, Alexander beamed. "The prodigal son has returned at last." Alexander could not have been prouder of his young ward.

Strolling into the room as if he had not a care in the world, Vander appeared to be a force to be reckoned with, his towering six-foot-two-inch frame eloquent of stature and power. His handsome features, chiseled and symmetrical, a testament to the aesthetic standards of the finest of sculptures, his eyes, an enigmatic mix of blue sky and steel. Complementing his physique was the expensive custom suit that Alexander had tailored for him, fit to perfection. Vander had become the embodiment of sophistication and refinement.

With a twinkle in his eye, Vander turned to Alexander, his face half-concealed by the dim light of the room. "My apologies," he murmured, his voice a low undercurrent in the soft hum of the gathering crowd. "Preparations for graduation proved far more complicated and time-consuming than I had anticipated." His words hung in the air, a veiled confession of delays and surprises wrapped in the mundane excuse.

Alexander, ever observant, had not missed the subtext to Vander's explanation. He met Vander's gaze with a steady one of his own, the slight quirk of his lips revealing his understanding. "Well," he replied, his tone light yet carrying an edge of seriousness, "you're here now, and it's my intention that you enjoy every second of your special night." The room seemed to hold its breath, the cadence of their conversation casting an atmospheric cloak over their exchange, without a hint of detection from the staff.

The doorbell sounded, cutting through the tension like a finely honed blade. It was as if the universe itself had declared a ceasefire to the subtle battle of wits between Vander and Alexander. Alexander, with a jovial clap of his hands, announced, "Ah, our first guest has arrived. Thomas, would you do us the honor?" Thomas, the epitome of grace and age in his immaculate uniform, bowed and stepped out of the room to attend to the newcomer.

Vander, seizing the momentary reprieve, shot Alexander a curt nod, a glint of mischief in his eyes. "I trust you did not mind me inviting a few additional guests?" Vander's voice, filled with a charm that could disarm the wariest, hung in the air.

Alexander, always the gentleman, was gracious in his response. "Of course not, my dear boy. This is your graduation party, after all. You are free to invite as many friends and acquaintances as you'd like." His words were diplomatic, but his tone held a touch of curiosity.

Just then, Thomas returned with Vivian Richards, her arrival announced with a flourish. Vander didn't miss a beat, keeping his eyes fixed on Alexander, gauging his reaction to the sudden appearance of his old friend. The room held its breath, the conversational hum quieting

Chapter 67 — Surprise!

down a notch. "Mrs. Vivian Richards," Thomas announced with an air of finality.

"Indeed, Vivian," Vander chimed in. "We literally bumped into each other on the sidewalk. Imagine that!" He added a hearty laugh for good measure. Alexander, who was usually so composed, seemed momentarily thrown off by the presence of Vivian in a city so far from her usual stomping grounds. Vander reveled in the unexpected joy of having the upper hand, even if it was just for that fleeting moment.

Knowing Alexander as well as he did, Vander could read the waves of surprise cascading over his usually composed façade.

A brief flicker of anger surfaced, quickly smothered by a masterful display of surprised charm. "Vivian?" Alexander held out his hands, his tone mingling disbelief and delight. "What on earth are you doing in Philadelphia?" He pressed a gentle kiss to Vivian's cheeks, her soft laughter ringing out at his genuine surprise.

Vivian, basking in the success of her surprise, tilted her head and shared her story. "It was the oddest thing, actually. I bumped into Vander on the street, right after one of my sessions with Alayna." Her eyes twinkled with mischief, setting the stage for the unexpected tale she was about to unfold.

Vander stood by as Vivian regaled Alexander with the remainder of her tale of their impromptu meeting in Austin, Texas.

"After wrapping up his affairs for the day, Vander, the perfect gentleman that he is, took me and Philip out for a delightful lunch," Vivian recalled, casting a warm glance in Vander's direction. "You should be proud, Alexander. Your young ward is a treasure. As we were reminiscing over our meals, Vander let slip about the graduation party you're throwing him tonight. He thought I might provide you with some welcome company among the sea of his young friends. His invitation was so sincere and well-intentioned, how could I resist?"

Taken aback, Alexander jumped over the part where Vander and Vivian had accidentally met and jumped to the part about his chef. "Philip was there?" Alexander turned to Philip.

Smile brightly, Vivian answered, "Yes, and he was charming as well. Alexander, you're very fortunate to have had someone like him all these years. I do hope you take as good of care of him as he does you. Otherwise, I just might steal him away."

Slightly offended, Philp grumbled, "Yes, Sir, while you were away in Virginia, Vander asked that I accompany him to do a cake tasting in the area. He had heard of this so-called renowned baker from one of his classmates at the university. Though I had assured Vander I could make his graduation cake myself, the young man insisted."

"I see," Alexander said. Vander could tell his mentor's mind was racing to catch up.

With a hint of disgust, Philip motioned to a far table where a fancy, sophisticated, three-tiered cake sat. "I had to return to Austin two days ago to ensure its safe delivery." Philp gave Vander an irritated glance. "Thus, returning on the red eye last night in order to begin preparations for tonight's festivities."

Patting Philip on the shoulder, Vander beamed. "And your efforts are greatly appreciated, Philip. I could not be happier with the cake or with the incredible dinner you have prepared."

Recovering, Alexander tucked Vivian's arm into his and led her to the sitting room. "Well, my dear, I am thrilled you are here." Alexander looked at Vander, his eyebrow raised. "Thank you for thinking of me, Vander. I must say, it looks like you have thought of everything."

"I most certainly try," Vander said as the doorbell chimed once more. "Thomas, let me get that." Vander hurried off. He wanted to greet his friends personally. One to be polite, two, to ensure that they had come in a couple of larger groups for their own safety as they ventured home later.

The threat of Alexander poisoning his friends had diminished tenfold upon Vivian's arrival. Still, Alexander might be able to convince himself that killing his lifelong friend, Vivian, was worth the reward of getting to Vander, especially considering her age, but he would not dare attempt it with the last two surprise guests that were soon to arrive.

Unlike Alexander, Vander would not underestimate his opponent. Alexander was brilliant. Vander had watched the man play the game for over seventeen years and no one had even come close to seeing the darkness behind those seemingly kind blue eyes.

The bell rang again. Vander reached out and pulled it open, to the delight of Christian, David, Jonathan, and Marco. Vander was happy to see that his friends could indeed follow instructions, especially considering their lives depended on it.

CHAPTER 68

DINNER INTERROGATION

PETER

Philadelphia, PA—Night

THE ELEGANT FIVE-COURSE MEAL BEGAN WITH A DELICATE amuse-bouche, a truffle-infused mushroom tartlet, sending a symphony of earthy notes to the tastebuds.

Before being seated, Vander had greeted them at the door with the same happy demeanor as he had done so before when they had met earlier. To Peter, the young man had seemed utterly delighted to have them as guests to his graduation dinner. However, from Mr. Dayton's expression, he did not feel the same way about their sudden appearance.

Still, despite Vander's friendly façade and apparent joy at having them as guests, Peter could not shake the sense of unease that settled in the pit of his stomach. There was something off about this dinner invitation and he was hard-pressed to discover what that something was.

Peter and Agent Robinson had allowed the cheerful group of college students to dominate most of the conversation through the appetizer and the fresh and vibrant citrus-kissed arugula salad. They had all seemed to enjoy its crisp leaves contrasting with the tartness of grapefruit segments until Agent Robinson lost her patience and asked the burning question, "So, Mr. Dayton, did you enjoy your trip to Austin?"

All eyes turned to Alexander, who did not miss a beat when he replied. "I did. It was quite lovely. Is that where you're from Agent, what was it? Robinson?"

Playing with her wineglass, Agent Robinson cast Peter a knowing look. "No, I'm from the Washington, DC area."

"Really?" Alexander exclaimed. "That's marvelous, so many extraordinary museums and exhibits in your area."

"I wouldn't know. I'm not really into that kind of thing," Chantal Robinson said, obviously trying to goad Alexander. The air around them grew thick with tension, as Chantal's words hung heavy in the suddenly darker atmosphere.

Alexander remained stoic; his gaze fixed on her with an unflinching determination. "Pity, there is much to be enjoyed with the arts."

Trying to salvage the conversation, Peter pipped in, "Is that why you were in Texas, seeing the latest exhibits?" Peter could feel the tension in the room.

Vander's young guests were all looking at one another, not comprehending the direction the conversation had taken as Philip brought out the intermission of the meal, the sorbet palate cleanser, a refreshing lemon basil sorbet that tingled the tongue and prepared the palette for the main course.

Peter knew there was more to this story than just a simple business trip. His curiosity and determination to uncover the truth made him continue the conversation, despite the eerie atmosphere that seemed to surround them.

To his surprise, it was Philip who answered the question. "Mr. Dayton went to Austin to offer his assistance to the museum by agreeing to be one of its benefactors."

Taking in his and Robinson's puzzled looks, Vander pipped in, "Many people don't know this, but, along with being a charitable philanthropist, Alexander is also a generous contributor and admirer of the arts."

Proud, Philip, head held high, placed a perfectly seared medium-rare filet mignon, its rich juices mingling with a glossy, deep-red wine reduction down before Alexander. The sound of the cutlery against the china plate echoed in the large dining room.

Smiling brightly, Vander motioned to Philip. "And both he and Thomas have served alongside Alexander, wherever his journeys have gone, for what Philip, the past twenty years now?"

Chapter 68   Dinner Interrogation

"Twenty-five, Sir, give or take a month or so," Philip answered as he set the last plate before Peter.

Clapping his hands together, Marco laughed. "If Philip was with him in Africa, he should have told him to leave your ass there... would have saved him a hell of a lot of trouble." The room broke out with nervous laughter. The tension, at least for the moment, dissipated.

The conversation returned to more mundane topics, such as what each of the students was looking forward to after graduation: trips with their families, a break from their studies, time away from school, and what new possibilities awaited the graduates.

Finally, it was time for the dessert. The exquisite graduation cake, custom-made to perfection, emanated with an air of sophistication and festivity. Each layer was a testament to skillful craftsmanship, meticulously sculpted from a fine blend of premium flour, rich in its velvety texture. A decadent filling of velvety chocolate ganache punctuated with flecks of fresh, vibrant berries provided a surprising burst of flavor.

Peter took note of a faint aroma of vanilla and chocolate that tantalized his senses. It was topped off with a smooth fondant that had a delicate shade of ivory, etched with intricate gold accents that mirrored the triumph of the graduate.

The topmost layer was graced with a handcrafted edible diploma, a sugar-spun cap, and golden laurels, symbolizing academic success. A success that he hoped extended to him and Agent Robinson when they shared their information with the police back in Austin. Not only did they discover that Alexander had been in Austin at the time of the artist's death, but that Philip, his right-hand man, had also been in Austin at the time of Brayden's family's murders.

This was more than a leap, knowing that Alexander, Philip, or more likely than not, both men had been near all of the Sculptor's crime scenes for the past twenty years, was more than enough probable cause to reopen this investigation.

MAY 10TH—1 DAY

CHAPTER 69

PRICELESS

ALEXANDER

Philadelphia, PA—Morning

Alexander allowed Thomas to open the door to their Mercedes-Benz S-Class and slipped into the backseat. Vander refused to wait, insisting instead on getting into the car without waiting for the driver to assist him. "I appreciate you choosing to attend the opening of the exhibit with me, Vander. Though, I would imagine you might enjoy being with your friends more, considering your graduation is tomorrow."

His smile sad, Vander met his gaze. "There is no place I'd rather be."

The driver settled into the seat before them. "Sir, traffic is light. We should be at the museum by 9:00 a.m. as planned."

"Thank you, Thomas," Alexander said, then pushed the button to the privacy glass and watched as it went up to ensure their privacy. With a smile, Alexander met Vander's intense blue gaze. "I want to commend you on a game well played, my boy."

Alexander knew Vander had reason to doubt his motives, his every word and action. He watched as Vander's eyes, once bright with youthful exuberance, were now clouded with a palpable sense of trepidation. "Are you saying the game has ended?" he asked.

As the car moved through the near-abandoned streets, Alexander couldn't help but feel the weight of the disquieting silence, punctuated

Chapter 69   Priceless

only by the occasional moan of the wind. The day was supposed to be a day of celebration, a testament to his tireless work. The museum doors should have opened to a throng of eager visitors, their anticipation palpable in the air. They would have gazed in wonder at the grandeur of the Amorphophallus titanium, and stood in awe of Vander, Alexander's most prized achievement, forever frozen in time, carefully crafted, and displayed proudly next to it. But the day had been robbed of its light, and Alexander of his glory.

"Indeed, I am. You have won the game and have played it with incredible skill and stealth," Alexander offered Vander his highest praise.

Vander had bested him at the game he had once considered his personal domain, a realm where he reigned unchallenged for decades.

The city's silhouette approached as their car sliced through the traffic amidst rays of streaming sunlight.

The loss was a cold, hard stone in Alexander's gut, yet coated with a layer of sweet pride. His greatest prize, his most satisfying victory, had slipped through his fingers. Yet, in its place, there was something else—a strange, proud satisfaction. Vander, his protégé, had metamorphosed into a formidable challenger, his transformation a testament to Alexander's tutelage, making this defeat somehow a victory of its own.

It was clear to Alexander that Vander, wanting to believe him, was still afraid to let down his guard. Even then, Vander watched him like a weary antelope with its eyes fixed on an advancing predator.

Alexander thought that Vander would be elated, wearing a victorious smirk. Contrarily, Vander's countenance was shrouded in a deep melancholy, his eyes distant, reflecting a universe of private torment. Alexander's voice, low but insistent, cut through the dense silence like a disembodied spirit. "Vander, did you hear me? The game is over. You have won."

The desolation that clung to Vander seemed as immovable as a shadow on a moonless night. "Yes, I have won, but at what cost?" Vander looked out the window and refused to look at him. "I thought you cared about me. I believed us to be friends all these years. I knew you could not love me in the way that I had hoped, but at the very least, had hoped you would not seek to kill or destroy me."

Alexander knew that Vander craved an admission of guilt, a verbal acknowledgment of remorse that was simply non-existent in his heart. It was a ludicrous notion, a laughable demand, teetering on the precipice of absurdity.

Alexander was devoid of such sentiments. Vander knew that and knew it was not out of some inherent cruelty, but rather, an innate inability to comprehend their purpose. "You're upset with me, but I don't understand why?"

With the warmth of the day seeping into the car, the atmosphere hung heavy with unspoken revelations. Vander's laugh, bitter and pained, echoed in the confined space, a ghostly lament torn from the depths of his tormented soul. "I know," he rasped, his voice a barely audible whisper, "and that is the misery of it." The chilling admission lingered ominously.

Not for the first time in the past few days, an icy tingle flowed through Alexander, as though the chill touch of death had grazed his heart.

This wasn't the first onset of the bizarre sensation; rather, it was an unwelcome encore. The irregular rhythm of his heartbeat was as disconcerting as it was unexpected. The medical report from a mere two months prior made him question the current pain and unease in which he found himself. The report was a testament to his health and vitality, which was in stark contrast to the reality he was currently experiencing.

Taking note of his pained expression, Vander reached over and put a hand over his. "Are you all right?" Vander's expression had gone from anger to despair and now had turned to concern. "Alexander?"

Returning to its usual rhythm, Alexander felt his heart grow steady once more. "Yes, yes. I'm fine. No need to worry."

With the sun shining just outside their car window, Alexander knew their time together was growing short, for he knew that his ward would soon be leaving home to make his own mark on the world after graduation. Alexander refused to quarrel or spend what time they had left downtrodden. "Today is a beautiful day, Vander. Let's not waste it reminiscing over the past."

Putting on the smile that Alexander knew so well, Vander said, "Agreed."

Later, Alexander and Vander greeted the arriving guests alongside the museum's curator. Thanking each of them for coming to this once-in-a-lifetime event.

As the clock struck noon, the corporeal transformation commenced. A dark energy seemed to pulsate from the corpse flower, the silent harbinger of life and death. Its monstrous bud, tightly wrapped in its own mystery, began to unfurl.

Chapter 69   Priceless

Slowly, the unspeakable beauty of its maroon interior was revealed, an eerie spectacle that held the onlookers spellbound. The bloom was a sanguine chalice, an enormous goblet of nature's darkest secrets. An alien, fetid stench filled the air, the scent of decay and rebirth intertwined. The corpse flower was blooming, an event as rare and as enigmatic as the flower itself.

With Vander by his side, Alexander looked at him for a moment, remembering the once small and frightened boy who now stood beside him as the proud, intellectual, and resourceful man he had become. Though Vander would not be the one forever immortalized before the gathered crowd as he planned, Alexander knew his protégé would forever be etched in his memory.

Sadness washed over Vander's features as they both listened to the oohs, aahs, and soft murmurs of astonishment from the crowd as everyone gazed at the mesmerizing display.

Content, Alexander took a step closer to Vander. "I'm glad you are here with me today." Alexander beamed.

Vander offered Alexander a pained smile. "As am I, Alexander. As am I."

MAY 11TH—0 DAYS

CHAPTER 70

GRADUATION

VANDER

Philadelphia, PA—Day

FACE TURNED TO THE MID-DAY SUN, **V**ANDER SQUINTED his eyes as he looked up at the bright light that shone over the stately campus with an air imbued with a sense of anticipation. Wanting to take it all in, he closed his eyes and listened to the staccato heels clicking and polished dress shoes reverberating up and down the cobblestone walkways.

Vander stood in a sea of students who, like him, were adorned in the traditional graduation regalia. Graduation gowns rustled amongst them. It was a harmonious symphony that played in the gentle breeze, while the students' tassels danced around their caps and fluttered in the wind.

Whether it was joy, happiness, or relief in knowing he was still there, alive, free to enjoy the moment, Vander was not sure. More than likely, it was an equal measure of all those things and more. Smiling, Vander took in the scent of freshly cut grass and blooming flowers that filled the air.

In the distance, the resonant peal of the university bell tolled, signaling the commencement of the graduation ceremony. As the first strains of the university's song filled the air, the atmosphere became palpable. There was a blend of joy, nostalgia, and hope for futures yet to be lived.

Taking his place in line, Vander moved along the path with his classmates. As they made their way to the stadium, his eyes began to scan the large crowd that flanked either side of the field.

Chapter 70   Graduation

Parents, grandparents, and well-wishers rose to their feet as they stepped onto the field. Some clutched bouquets of vibrant roses and carnations; their bright colors mirrored amongst the proud smiles of those happy to attend the celebration. Others applauded and shouted, their laughter adding to the soft murmurs that enveloped the stadium.

As much as he wanted to, Vander could not stop himself from looking for Alexander. No matter what had happened, no matter what was to come, he desired nothing more in that moment than to spot him standing amongst the others in attendance. To share this moment of triumph with the man responsible for giving him the life that he could have only dreamed of if he had not saved him.

Silver chairs waited for the graduates, arranged meticulously into neat rows. The stage at the end of the aisle was decked out in the vibrant college colors as everyone waited anxiously for the procession to end and the graduation ceremony to begin.

For Vander, this was not merely a college graduation; it was a rite of passage, a pivotal transition from a precarious life to one of endless possibilities.

Before taking his seat, Vander scanned the bright faces of the families, friends, and acquaintances once more, hoping to catch a glimpse of his mentor. Frozen, Vander stood before his chair, his eyes fixed on Alexander.

Clad in an expensive summer suit, Alexander stood, his cane tucked under his arm, seemingly immune to the heat as he held out his hands and applauded him. The suit, tailored from the finest Italian linen, was a shade of navy so deep it was almost black. Yet, it stood out against his drab surroundings like a single star in a stormy night sky. In true Alexander style, the suit had been designed with meticulous attention to detail.

A surge of unexpected joy coursed through Vander as his and Alexander's eyes met. Vander offered Alexander a curt nod and a bright smile as he turned and took his seat and listened as, one by one, his classmates' names were called.

Then it was his turn. His name echoed across the stadium as he heard the jubilant cheers of his classmates and a lone shout from Alexander. "Well done, Vander!"

As Vander ascended the steps, he took note of each footfall that seemed to take him farther and farther away from his burdensome past. Within what seemed like seconds, he had his diploma clutched in his fist, a symbol of his academic accomplishment and the manifestation of his relentless determination.

However, as Vander began his descent down the stairs, he felt his joy fade like the palpable golden light. Soon the ceremony would be over, and the farewells would begin.

From a distance, Vander heard the dean conclude the ceremony. Wild cheers sounded all around him, but Vander's response was muted as hundreds of tossed graduation caps and tassels rained down upon him.

The cheers and accolades that earlier sparked his pride now echoed hollowly in his skull. The joy of the day had been replaced by a sorrow so profound, that it felt as though it would not rest until it had entirely consumed him.

Shaking him out of his dark mood, Jonathan, David, and Marco came rushing up to him.

Oblivious to Vander's musings, Marco grabbed his cap and tossed it into the air. "What's the matter with you? The hard part is done, my friend... Now it's time to party!"

Ruffling his hair, Jonathan teased, "Yeah, and you're buying the first round."

David punched Vander in the shoulder. "If you don't stop acting like you just got invited to your own funeral, you're going to be buying all the rounds. Now come on."

Forcing a smile, Vander held up his hands as the three of them began to drag him toward David's waiting car. "Fine, all right, but I have to do something first."

"If you're looking for Christina, she is already on her way to the bar with Stephanie," Marco growled.

Looking back at the stands, Vander spotted Alexander standing there with his cane in hand, patiently waiting. "I've got to see Alexander first."

The three men followed Vander's gaze and reluctantly patted him on the head and shoulder.

"Fine, but hurry up or we're leaving without you," Marco said as he gave him a quick slap on the butt.

Hesitantly, Vander made his way over to the stands. It was as if the world had faded away and left the two of them alone in it. Vander stood on the field, looking up at his mentor. There was so much he wanted to say, so much left undone between them. "Alexander, I cannot thank you enough for all that you've—"

Chapter 70 — Graduation

Head held high, Alexander smiled as he looked down at him. "Dear boy, you have enriched my life as much as I have yours, I imagine. My life has been far more interesting with you in it, I dare say."

Hanging outside the car window, Marco shouted, "Come on, let's go get drunk already!" David wrestled him back inside the car.

Laughing, Alexander nodded toward the waiting vehicle. "Go on. You have earned a night of celebration with your friends."

Reluctantly, Vander's eyes went from his friends, then back to Alexander. "I don't have to go with them. We could go out and celebrate... just the two of us."

"Nonsense. This is your day to celebrate all that you've accomplished, Vander. This moment is to be shared with your classmates and those starting this new journey along with you."

Torn, Vander looked back at his friends. "Are you sure?"

"Absolutely." Taking out a handkerchief, Alexander patted at the tiny beads of sweat that suddenly appeared on his brow. "Besides, I'm feeling a little under the weather and feel a quiet evening at home would suit me better."

Guilt washed over Vander. "How about I see you home first?"

"No need. I have a driver waiting for me." Alexander tipped his hat to Vander and gave a soft chuckle as he turned and started walking away. "Now go before you end up walking to your and your friends' party."

As Vander watched his mentor make his way to the parking lot, he felt as if the world had suddenly turned to sorrow. It was as if the graduation ceremony, which had been a celebration of his accomplishments, now felt like a death knell of the future he had so meticulously planned.

CHAPTER 71

FINISSAGE

VANDER

Philadelphia, PA—Night

It was late when Vander finally bid farewell to Zane, Wanda, and Marco. The echoes of their laughter and the shared stories of college antics still hung in the air. The road home, now silent and empty, felt too still, too quiet.

The graduation had been a day of celebration, a culmination of hard work and enduring friendships. Yet, as Vander walked home alone in the moonlight, a sense of melancholy set in. There was an unmistakable tinge of regret, a longing for the days now relegated to memory.

When he had kissed Christina goodbye at the bar before she had left to catch her plane, Vander had already felt the invisible threads of their intertwined energy beginning to fray.

They each knew their relationship was over, but both refused to voice the words. Perhaps it was better she had left that way. Because, despite the emptiness, Vander found a strange comfort in the solitude. It was a tangible testament to their shared memories, a silent witness to their story that ended too soon.

Vander stopped before the townhome he and Alexander shared. There were a few golden lights still on. One of them, Vander knew, was Alexander's—a beacon that had once signaled warmth and security for him.

Chapter 71   Finissage

Yearning washed over him in waves as he wished he could rewind time, go back to the days of his youth when he was certain of Alexander's parental affection. Those were the days when he idolized him, when the world was simple, and love was unconditional. But now, all that seemed like a mirage, a fleeting dream dissolving into a stark reality. How could so much change in the span of just two weeks?

Vander hesitated for a moment, then started up the steps to the townhome, each footfall resonating with a melancholy echo that matched the rhythm of his heavy heart. With each ascending step, the weight of unspoken words and unresolved issues pressed harder against his chest.

He paused at the door, hand hovering over the doorknob, an invisible threshold standing between him and the conversation he both dreaded and desperately needed. He knew he had to face Alexander, to traverse the chasm of misunderstandings and horrible deeds done by both.

Vander slipped in, the familiar creak of the door echoing through the quiet foyer. In the dim light, he spotted Thomas, the loyal driver and doorman, slumped in a chair near the doorway, the rhythmic rise and fall of his chest revealing his deep slumber.

Alexander, Vander presumed, had issued Thomas with strict instructions to remain vigilant throughout the night, anticipating Vander's potential need for a ride home after an evening of indulgence.

Unwilling to let Thomas spend the rest of the night in such discomfort, Vander decided to rouse him. Mustering more force than usual, he slammed the door, the resulting bang echoing around them. Thomas jerked awake, his bewildered eyes meeting Vander's apologetic gaze. "So sorry, Thomas," Vander offered, a hint of apology in his voice. "You didn't have to wait up. Please, go to bed and feel free to sleep in."

It took a moment for Thomas to gather his bearings, his drowsy eyes struggling to focus. He nodded, attempting to put on a brave front as if he hadn't been caught sleeping on the job. "Thank you, Sir. I believe I will." And with that, he headed off to rest, leaving Vander alone with his thoughts in the quiet foyer.

Vander looked up the stairs, closed his eyes, and drew in a shaky breath. The familiar creaking sound echoed through the empty hallway, each step an echo of the countless times he had ascended before.

With a face grim, Vander started up the stairs. Every corner, every scuff on the wood, a reminder of a shared past now lost. He paused by Alexander's door, the faint light creeping out from the cracks at the base a stark contrast to the enveloping gloom. Alexander was not in there. Vander knew it in his heart.

Head held high, Vander walked past Alexander's room, his every step a testament to the strength it took to keep moving forward. He stepped into his quarters, a silent sanctuary farther down the hallway.

Vander entered his room, but did not turn on the light. He didn't need to. He knew every inch of this room, every shadow, every silent testament to a life lived and lost. Instead, Vander went to his window, the world outside a silent observer of his solitude. He opened the blinds, allowing the light from the faint moon and the distant streetlight below to cast a soft glow, illuminating his room.

Vander stood still, waiting. A few moments later, a shadow detached itself from the surrounding darkness, edging into the scant light that pooled around Vander. Even without turning, Vander could sense the spectral presence beside him.

There was no need to visually confirm his gut feeling; he knew Alexander's ghost was there. Alexander, always the picture of elegance, materialized in his finest suit, his ethereal voice thick with pride as he commended, "Well done, Vander. Well done."

Vander's eyes tightened, striving to stem the threat of tears that welled up. A sob hitched in his throat. "I'm so sorry Alexander," he murmured, his voice choked with raw emotion. How was it that he could still feel, still grieve after all the horrible things he had done?

As the ethereal figure of Alexander shimmered before him, Vander felt a pang of melancholy. He remembered the countless times his mentor had reached out to him, providing comfort and guidance with a mere touch. "No need to feel bad, Vander. Dear boy, we both understood that there could be only one victor in this game."

As the light danced through Alexander's spectral hand that rested upon his shoulder, Vander was reminded of their new reality. "There is no need for regret," Alexander said.

Yet, as Vander stood before his mentor, his victory felt hollow. Alexander was no longer of his world, unable to touch, to speak to him, in the way he had done for so long.

Vander was alone. He had surpassed Alexander's expectations, exceeded the potential his mentor had seen in him. But the pride in his mentor's spectral eyes could not chase away the bitter truth.

Chapter 71   Finissage

Angry, Vander looked at Alexander's spirit, his eyes a blazing mirror of the turmoil within. "It did not have to be this way. You did not have to try to destroy me, thus destroying yourself!" he seethed, each word laced with a bitter cocktail of fury and regret. "Why couldn't you just be…"

Alexander held Vander's heated gaze. "Vander, remember that day at the zoo, the one after you had struck your teacher?" Alexander saw that he understood the time he was referring to. "I told you then, a lion is a lion. A deer was a deer. A chameleon was a chameleon.

No matter their habitat, the animal remains the same. I may have lived in fine houses, traveled abroad, and appreciated the fine arts. But, at my core, I was a killer, a killer, who possessed an insatiable compulsion to preserve the things he cherished. And of all the treasures, all the beauty I've witnessed, it was you, Vander, who held my highest admiration."

In Vander's heart, he knew that this was the highest form of love Alexander was capable of. It was a twisted affection that bore a destructive power, leaving a trail of ruin in its wake. And for this, a strange gratitude welled up within Vander, though it was shrouded in a deep sense of loss, as if his soul had been hollowed out.

Alexander, in his sick pursuit, had forfeited both their lives, pushing Vander to the brink; forcing him into unspeakable acts just to survive. The echo of these actions reverberated through Vander's existence, a remorseful refrain that underscored the tragic dance of their intertwined fates.

Nightshade called. The sound echoed through the quiet night; a mournful melody woven with memories of times past. Alexander tilted his head, his eyes reflecting a world Vander could barely grasp.

Its lingering notes danced in the chill air, a rhythmic cadence that seemed to beat in time. Through the frosted window, the burgeoning dawn painted the sky in hues of melancholy blues and purples, a somber backdrop to their inevitable parting.

As Alexander's soul felt the gentle tug of the ethereal realm, Vander found himself grappling with the sting of solitude. Soon, Alexander too would fade into the realm of the intangible, another cherished presence to join the procession of shadows that had abandoned him. Yet, in the deafening silence that followed the call of the Nightshade, Vander felt not anger, but a profound sadness steeped in regret.

There was little else to say for Vander. "Alexander, thank you for saving me all those years ago, for giving me the life I had but dared to dream of."

Like days past, Alexander gave Vander the brightest of smiles as he tipped his hat to him. "You are most welcome, my friend." Alexander began to fade.

"One more thing," Vander said. Alexander fought to hold on as his spirit shimmered. "When you see Nightshade, follow him to the light and cross over." Vander knew that whatever fate awaited his mentor on the other side could not possibly be as bad for his friend as being trapped in the muted gray, lifeless space bridging the two realms. "Don't hesitate, don't delay."

Torn, Vander watched as the light of dawn chased Alexander's soul from this realm. He knew his friend would heed his warning, knowing that Vander's instructions were to help him find his way on his new journey.

Running a hand down his face, Vander felt the cold absence of Alexander's presence. The rooms that once echoed with his laughter were now cloaked in an unbearable silence. Each corner, each object, was a stark reminder of his departed friend, intensifying the engulfing reality of the loss.

Vander pictured the coming chaos, the flashing lights, the hushed whispers. He steeled himself, preparing to orchestrate a send-off as grand as Alexander's life had been. Yet, in the quiet solitude of the pre-dawn, he allowed himself a moment of raw grief, a private farewell before the public spectacle.

Alexander might not have gotten to have his masterpiece of Vander's broken body and his beloved corpse flower at the heart of the museum. But Vander would give his old friend the grandest *finissage*. It would be a testament to Alexander's brilliant existence.

Vander would curate a farewell that mirrored the depth of Alexander's personality, a mixture of quirky humor, intellectual curiosity, and unwavering kindness. Leaving out the darkness that only he knew of. Vander would gather all those who had loved and been touched by Alexander for a final gathering not of mourning, but of celebration. Despite the heavy sadness tugging at his heart, Vander knew Alexander would have preferred laughter and shared stories to tears and consolation.

Then, once the celebrations of life had drawn to a quiet close, and the echoes of laughter and shared stories faded into the hushed whispers of the night, the task of settling Alexander's affairs would begin.

The legacy of Vander's new life would begin. Vander was done pretending he was normal, done lying to himself about love, friendship, and

Chapter 71　Finissage

what could be. He was a unique soul who could wander through the corridors of time, seeking solace in the space In-between. For Vander, fate was not a predetermined path. It was a choice, a crossroads... for him, destiny was an option.

THE END

BOOK THREE

MAKING MONSTERS

DARK EVOLUTION

Battered and broken, Ethan Williams struggles to raise his gifted young son Hunter after the brutal killings of his wife and daughter. Dealing with a son who is cursed with the same dark gifts that led to his wife's tragic death, Ethan battles against forces he does not understand as he tries to protect Hunter from those he views as a threat.

Torn, Ethan continues to shield Hunter from his brother-in-law Brayden, a tormented and obsessed detective who will do anything to catch the killer responsible for destroying his family, even if that involves exploiting Hunter and his supernatural gifts.

Offering Ethan hope in his despair, Tracey Evans, a caring school counselor, seeks to guide Hunter and Ethan back to a life of love, light, and redemption.

But Vander, the man responsible for their family's destruction, waits patiently in the shadows. For Vander believes his chance at redemption comes in the form of drawing Hunter into his dark world and becoming the mentor to the young man that he, himself, never had.

BOOK CLUB QUESTIONS

1. In the somber silence that envelops us, we seek to unravel the intricate tapestry of motivation that propels our characters forward on their damned paths. What sinister forces drive Vander Masozi, Alexander Dayton, and Braydon James to the brink of morality's abyss? Are their actions a mirror reflecting the grotesque face of necessity, or is there a deeper malice that festers within their souls?
2. In what ways did the author use abandonment to augment the sense of isolation and desperation felt by the main character?
3. How do you interpret the protagonist's journey of self-preservation? Is it purely instinctual or laced with elements of psychological manipulation?
4. At which points in the narrative did you feel the tension of impending revenge was most palpable, and how did it affect your reading experience?
5. Discuss how the author employs foreshadowing to build suspense throughout the novel. Can you pinpoint specific examples?
6. What are your thoughts on the multiple instances where the protagonist must confront their dark past? How does this deepen the theme of abandonment?
7. How did the author explore the psychological impact of betrayal between the characters? Were there any particular betrayals that affected you more than others?
8. Dark Variations weaves a complex web of characters. Whose secrets/stories were you most intrigued to uncover and did their revelations alter your reading experience?

9. If you could ask the author one question about the writing process of Dark Variations, or about any element within the book that perplexed you, what would it be?
10. The ending left many readers stunned. Without revealing spoilers, what clues did you pick up that hinted at this outcome, and how did they enhance the story's dark allure?
11. In the end, do you think the main character's path to revenge was justified? Why or why not, and what does that suggest about the nature of justice and retribution in the novel's dark world?

AUTHOR BIO

AJ **Parnell is an American author born in Depoe** Bay, Oregon. Parnell's novels tackle the darker side of the human psyche. Her various novels incorporate elements of thriller, fantasy, and horror with a touch of irony that traverse the dark corridors of the human experience.

Visit www.ajparnell.com for more!

Discover more at
4HorsemenPublications.com

10% off using HORSEMEN10